About the Contributors

A resident of Mobile, Alabama, **LINDA P. BAKER** has been writing most of her life but only recently came out of the closet with her work. "Into the Light" is her first professional sale; she dedicates it to her husband, Larry, and Margaret Weis.

NANCY VARIAN BERBERICK has written stories for several of the Tales collections, and *Stormblade* for the DRAGONLANCE® Heroes series. Apart from the DRAGONLANCE saga, she is the author of *The Jewels of Elvish*, *A Child of Elvish*, and *Shadow of the Seventh Moon*. ACE/Berkeley will publish her novel *The Panther's Hoard* in 1994.

A game designer for TSR, **JEFF GRUBB** has been a contributor/mastermind for a number of popular fantasy settings, including the DRAGONLANCE, FORGOTTEN REALMS®, SPELLJAMMER®, and AL-QADIM® worlds. He is currently finishing *Lord Toede*, his first solo novel, set in Krynn. He promises (threatens?) it will be a comedy.

DAN HARNDEN is a writer of many interests and a long-time resident of the Greater New York area. He is currently concentrating his efforts on works for the stage and screen.

RICHARD A. KNAAK lives in Illinois and has contributed to each of the Tales collections. He is the author of two novels in the DRAGONLANCE series, including *The New York Times* best-seller, *The Legend of Huma* and its sequel, *Kaz the Minotaur*. He has his own successful fantasy series published by Warner, which includes *The Crystal Dragon*. His most recent fantasy *King of the Grey* takes place in Chicago.

ROGER E. MOORE, ever a fan of tinker-gnome technology, acknowledges his debt to Jules Verne, Edgar Rice Burroughs, and all the horrible movies made about their novels. His tale is dedicated to Gail, who was there all along.

DOUGLAS NILES has been involved with the DRAGONLANCE® saga for many years, contributing novels, short stories, role-playing accessories, and a board game to the world of Krynn. He recently completed *Emperor of Ansalon* in the Villains series.

NICK O'DONOHOE is the author of several DRAGONLANCE stories. His novel about a fantasy veterinarian, *The Magic and the Healing*, is due from Berkeley Press in 1994. He once set fire to his own beard and does not advise anyone to drink anything that is flaming at the time.

JANET PACK is well known to GEN CON® Game Fair-goers for her portrayal of kender Tasselhoff Burrfoot and also for her singing and original music. She lives in Lake Geneva, Wisconsin, with her husband, Gary, and cats, Bastjun Amaranth and Canth Starshadow.

DONALD BAYNE STEWART PERRIN, Capt. (Ret'd), BSc, rmc, cfss. recently retired from the Canadian Army where he specialized in artillery computing. He is now working as a defense contractor in Ottawa, Canada, and is writing a science fantasy novel with Margaret Weis for N.A.L.

MICKEY ZUCKER REICHERT is a pediatrician and the author of nine national and international best-sellers, including the Renshai trilogy, the Bifrost Guardians series, and *The Legend of Nightfall*.

Author, poet, and screenwriter **KEVIN STEIN** has a degree in English and has studied in both England and America. *Brothers Majere*, his first novel, is part of the Preludes I trilogy. He has also written *The Fall of Magic* under the name D. J. Heinrich.

AMY STOUT has been a fantasy and science fiction editor for the past ten years. This is her second published story. She lives in New York with her husband and daughters.

MARGARET WEIS is, along with Tracy Hickman, the author of the first two DRAGONLANCE® trilogies, Chronicles and Legends, which have sold upward of 12 million copies, worldwide. This story first appeared in the 200th Issue of DRAGON® magazine.

MICHAEL WILLIAMS has written seven novels, four of which—*Weasel's Luck*, *Galen Beknighted*, *The Oath and the Measure*, and *Before the Mask*—are set in the world of Krynn. He has also contributed poetry and fiction to all of the DRAGONLANCE Tales anthologies.

TERI WILLIAMS is the co-author of *Before the Mask* and the short story "Mark of the Flame, Mark of the Word" in Tales II, Volume Two: *The Cataclysm*. She and husband Michael are currently at work on a book in the Villains series, for which she is learning falconry.

DragonLance® Saga

TALES I

The Magic of Krynn

Kender, Gully Dwarves, and Gnomes

Love and War

TALES II

The Reign of Istar

The Cataclysm

The War of the Lance

The Second Generation

Margaret Weis and Tracy Hickman

Now Available

Saga

The
Dragons
of Krynn

Edited by

Margaret Weis and Tracy Hickman

THE DRAGONS OF KRYNN

Copyright ©1994 TSR, Inc.
All Rights Reserved.

Cover art by Paul Jaquays. Interior art by Ned Dameron.

First Printing: March 1994
Printed in the United States of America.
Library of Congress Catalog Card Number: 93-61434

9 8 7 6 5 4 3 2 1

ISBN: 1-56076-830-4

TSR, Inc.   TSR Ltd.
P.O. Box 756   120 Church End, Cherry Hinton
Lake Geneva, WI 53147   Cambridge CB1 3LB
U.S.A.   United Kingdom

TABLE OF CONTENTS

1. Seven Hymns of the Dragon 1
   Michael Williams

2. The Final Touch...9
   Michael and Teri Williams

3. Night of Falling Stars..33
   Nancy Varian Berberick

4. Honor Is All..63
   Mickey Zucker Reichert

5. Easy Pickings..77
   Douglas Niles

6. A Dragon to the Core 93
   Roger E. Moore

7. Dragon Breath...147
   Nick O'Donohoe

8. Fool's Gold 178
   Jeff Grubb

9. Scourge of the Wicked Kendragon............................211
   Janet Pack

10. And Baby Makes Three...230
    Amy Stout

11. The First Dragonarmy Bridging Company 242
    Don Perrin

12. The Middle of Nowhere 267
    Dan Harnden

13. Kaz and the Dragon's Children 292
    Richard A. Knaak

14. Into the Light 326
    Linda P. Baker

15. The Best 364
    Margaret Weis

16. The Hunt 382
    Kevin Stein

Seven Hymns of the Dragon

Michael Williams

I. Approaches

In the burning house
    in a scattered country
you will see us rising
    the shadow of wings
crossing your sunlight
    obscuring the moon
as the red sky blossoms
    in fire and confusion.

Do not say you awaited
    the flight and the shadow
the first incandescence
    of your villages:
O do not say you expected
    this fire, this turning,
the breath of the coming year
    as it passes
above you and through you,
    bearing no promise
no memory of grief and effacement.

Do not tell your children
    that you understood
the explosion of air and light,
    the last implausible burning
after the wings
    had passed above you,
the red wind exploding
    like fire in dry thistle.
They must not remember us,
    so that when we return

1

our price is exacted
        from copper to diamond,
and above your country
        the thorn trees spread
over collapsing time
        as the past and the future
close into single flame.

II. DRAGONHOARD

In the heart of the lair
        lies the fortunate substance:
lost in the incandescence of sapphire,
        drowned in an attar of violets.
In the heart of the lair
        in forgotten cloisters of granite
down where a second darkness
        covers the light carnelian,
there in our midst, we imagine,
        lie the stones of redemption
where we have relinquished them
        to a light so brilliant
that after the days of sun
        and the stars' corona,
the memory marks the eye
        in its changed interior
where the color of light inverts
        yellow remembered as violet
green as the red of the blood unveiled
        as the blood we have spilled
over hearts and stones
        as the last of the light assembles
hard upon what we imagine
        here in the marshes,
on wing in the early
        and the blackening swamp
where the heart of the lair
        is fixed and holy
speaking forever of miracles
        because we remember it so.

III. The Language of Dragons

The language of dragons
is the sleep of magic.
Hard as agate
slick as quicksilver
cold barometer
of the brazen heart
and the destined wing.
Out of the country
twinned and murderous
in a spring of stars
let the word bind the body
to the wind of the senses
bind the invisible
nerve of the air
bind and loose
jess and unfetter
the blank and awaiting country
here in a season of hawks
and O may the word
upon word engender
past fear and sleep may it ride
limning the imagined
life of the planets
Gilean and Sirrion
book and flame
here at the Alchemist's Gate
where the sound of our singing
assembles, dissembles,
weaving a veil over nothing.

IV. Hymn of the Lair

The lair is the plan of the body,
the yearning of blood
in expectant country,
as over the desert
the lightning stalks
in the promise of promises.

The lair is a whisper of stars,
is the way we remember
the lapsed constellations,
forgetting the passage of years
as inclement time
shrinks to arrangements
of pearls in the dark
of our summoned caverns.

Let it never be said
that the country of dragons
is barren, is settled with specters,
now when the tangible
glitters around us,
the eggs hard as pearls,
the smell of acanthus,
the watery shift
of blue upon blue,
the arrangement of stars before us.

Now our heritage
rests in old vintages
    wine of the dark
    wine of the maple
    wine of the cane
        at the edge of the prospects,
    and all of our children
        harbored in stone,
        in a pure and invulnerable light.
O let them rise from that light
on a blue and immaculate wing,
let the violent sun
be their rising and falling,
and let them remember
past desert, past dark
past all definitions
of star and lightning,
let them remember
this place where the mind

bows down to the heart,
where the blood gives over
into the veins
of forgotten metals,
where the seed of the father
carries the pattern of stars,
where the last of the words is remember.

V. Paladine

He is the one we remember
the word for the children
the light of the blood
in its native season
the hard incandescence of rubies.

Alive in the heart
of the wheeling planets
he is sun and nebula
the tipped and generous cup
of the trining moons.

And O we remember
that somewhere in rumor, beyond
the cramped articulate country
where the visions of stars
open to breath and belief,

where faith is the evidence
and all constellations
converge on a still
and joyous center,
there in the reconciled bays,

in the last home of waters
the millennium of fire
where the earth perpetual
blossoms the trust of the air
in the sunlight of memory,

there where the vision
and heart reconcile
with the high mathematics
of judgment and logic,
he is there and beyond there

free of arrangement
of reason and passion
where the scent of rosemary
harbors his presence
and the light glints over the sun.

VI. The Journey

Blood of the sun
and the lone hawk turning
spiraling under me
gold upon gold
blood of the sun
through nine generations
of fire and cloud
until the mined vein
of heaven opens
and gold upon gold
is the country beneath me
gold upon gold its story.

I turn above clouds
above the tipped cups
of the moons' penury
where only the sun
is behind me, only the light
refracted through gold upon gold
as I dive through the eons
and the sunlight fractures
in the blood of my wings.

From immutable distance
the story of men
is a cry in the sun

the faint wing's rustle,
the song of the sky
is bright, indecipherable,
imagined in prayer,
in the breath of the mortals,
the long, effacing sigh
of the elf,
encoded in time
and the first of the season
always returning
under my wing.

The blood of the sun
in a steady light
glitters above
lamentations of earth
and the vein of heaven
opens in song,
the first of the hymns,
the hymn you will always
and always remember,
the first of the breath of the light.

VII. The Dreams of Dragons

House of the whirlpool
month of the drowned rose
We in the absence
    of light remember
        the turn of winter
        the chromatic dazzle of wings
here in the prison
    of sleep and forgetfulness
        amber of winter
    refracted country
the lady remembered
in the altered veins of the throat

Month of the rains
month of the secret water

Under the light
   the lapse of memory
      rises to sound
   to the lost blood calling
to the loud gate of knives
   and the world's entry
         parabola of the hawk
      as the sun descends.
O let the lady rise in fire
as the last sky burns to nothing.

The Final Touch

Michael and Teri Williams

Mort the gardener's broad hand rested lightly on the cottage door.

The old board warmed pleasantly under his creased palm, and Mort looked into the faded heart of the ancient tree that the door had once been. The green world held few secrets that Mort could not see through his fingers—this tree had fallen in the Cataclysm, and its memories had slowly faded from every growth ring but the last.

Mort closed his eyes and removed his hand. He recovered his smile by remembering why he'd come—it was L'Indasha's birthday. And just in time, for Robert caught sight of him through the window and swung open the heavy door.

"Mort! Welcome! Come in from the cold. Have something to drink. It's been too long again!" Robert boomed.

It was true.

He had not seen his friends since the middle of last year—neither the druidess nor her husband. Now the early snows had fallen in Taman Busuk, and the seasonal birds had deserted the high country as the first autumn of peace returned to the Khalkist Mountains.

A little snow had descended on L'Indasha as well, Mort thought, smiling wider. He looked past Robert to see her framed in firelight, frowning as she inspected a small, decorated bucket, the first slight frosting of silver in her auburn hair.

As the seasons and years passed, she was settling gradually into age. Someone else had taken over her long secret watch in the Khalkists, and L'Indasha's immortality had been transferred to her successor.

L'Indasha rose and hugged Mort as he spoke his birthday blessing. She smelled of sunlight and fresh herbs and falling water.

"Oh, Mort! It's good to see you!" she exclaimed. "I was just trying to figure out why my augury bucket formed no ice last night. It happens every so often, and somehow always on the coldest night of the year. Why, the water was still warm when I brought . . ."

Suddenly, fiercely, she hugged Mort again.

"But this is no night for complaint!" she said with a laugh. "My friend is here, and we've things to celebrate."

Robert brought Mort a cup of brandied coffee and said, "You're just in time for a tale. L'Indasha is about to tell me the story of the dragons. . . ."

"When the wars began and Nidus burned?" Mort asked, setting a small parcel safely at the far edge of the hearth.

"Much earlier. When the Dark Queen's minions first returned to the continent and pillaged the nests of their noble cousins," L'Indasha explained. "We know too well the story of the War of the Lance. But this is different, a smaller tale. A story to tell on a birthday."

She grinned, relishing her first birthday in thirty centuries.

The druidess began the story, and the gardener settled into the chair beside her, sipping his drink. He reached for the small decorative bucket and ran his hands over its burnished slats, his fingers finding places that seemed to have been chewed or gnawed at.

Mort's eyes widened slowly as he felt the magical grain of the wood. This was still a powerful augury vessel; its wood-hallowed memories were clear and breathtakingly alive. Touching it, he saw the very pictures of the words the druidess spoke, and more—for this bucket had not only been witness to the story she was telling, but its wood remembered things she did not know.

Mort began to see how. . . .

* * * * *

It was the time of dragons, and the first wings were passing over the red moon.

L'Indasha Yman crouched beneath the sagging branches of the blue-needled tree and watched the shadows over the snow-dimmed landscape as they weaved soundlessly in and out of the starlight, black between the sparse evergreens.

It took no druidical teaching, no augury or insight, to remind her to lie low, out of the piercing sight that could spot a rabbit or a vole from two thousand feet.

The villagers had told L'Indasha of the flights, of the mysterious wheeling shapes dark against the red moon, the silver moon. Of their spiraling path north into the impenetrable mountains.

They are bats, the villagers maintained. Enormous bats released by the wrongdoing of a thousand years. When the time comes, they will travel in daylight. Then they will swallow the sun.

L'Indasha did not correct them. The truth would raise even more panic, more discord.

For the evil dragons had come to the mountains of Krynn.

She had known about them for a month through her auguries—through the fractures of ice and the flight patterns of winter birds—and she knew as well, in that quiet faith beyond augury and knowing, that the good dragons would be coming as well, though their evil cousins might destroy the world in the delay.

She could have fled, sought shelter. But her strong, protective magic might shield the villagers from fire and plunder. So she had decided to follow the dragons as far as her legs and her bravery would go. Good as it was, gelomancy was an erratic oracle. She wanted to see what was going on with her own eyes.

The evidence was menacing and grim. There were ten of them, perhaps twelve—in the fiercely swirling snow it was hard to count. Dragons in such numbers were sure to be about momentous business.

"Hiddukel's legions," L'Indasha breathed. "The Dark Lady's minions."

She caught herself with a gasp.

Talking to herself again, when a voice might carry on the storm winds and the enemy wheeled above her in hopeless numbers! Silently, holding her breath, the druidess collected in her augury bucket and drew close against the fragrant bole of the tree.

One of the dragons, a squat young creature, pivoted and dove toward the aeterna grove, sniffing the air apprehensively, its black wings flickering obscenely in the bloody moonlight.

Slowly, mimicking the droop of snow-laden branches, L'Indasha spread the blue limbs like a veil in front of her and breathed a prayer to Paladine, to Branchala and Chislev, into the fragrant needles.

In unsteady flight, the young straggler brushed wings with a large blue dragon, the slap of scales cutting through the frosty air like the crack of falling timbers. The big blue shrieked and wheeled above the smaller monster, who sheered away in panic, breasting the top of the aeterna grove in a swift, fetid rush.

L'Indasha gasped. The creature stared right at her. . . .

And beyond her. Its eyes were terror-struck, blank.

With a gibbering cry, the young dragon flashed through the trees, scattering branches, needles, and snow. For a moment it reached out blindly to break a fall that never came, its talons groping, clutching ice and frozen earth.

Something dropped softly from its grasp.

The dragon turned, puzzled and disoriented, shook the snow from its leathery wings, and soared to catch up with its company. It dipped once more, then vaulted a tall outcropping of vallenwood, wobbling on a frantic, unsteady path to catch up with its comrades.

"By Paladine's purple hat!" L'Indasha whispered, staring at the snow-covered object the beast had left behind. "An egg! And unbroken!" She caught herself again, clapping her hand over her mouth, stood slowly as the snow tumbled from her shoulders, and watched the last of the dragons vanish into the swirling night, heedless of her words.

With a deep breath, L'Indasha stepped from behind the

aeterna, the green light spreading from her fingertips to illumine her path up the treacherous slope of the hill. She clutched the bare, frayed branches of an old juniper to steady herself for the last few feet of ascent. The ancient tree glowed at her first touch, and it seemed for a moment that it was renewed with vigor.

At her feet, illuminated by the shining branches, the egg lay dark against the glinting snow.

She wondered if the dragons were moving their lairs—far to the north—and why. . . .

But there was another question, more serious and immediate. What would she do with this egg?

Her first thought was to smash it, to destroy the thing inside that would become a screaming killer. But then a sort of ambiguous protection began to rise up in her. What if the egg were stolen? It could belong to the good ones. Long ago, longer than she could count the years or reckon the time, the druids before her had known what to do with lost creatures. *Do nothing,* they had told her. *There is a harmony in the losing and finding, and the great balances of nature tilt for no one creature. Do nothing. You cannot be delicate.*

"So be it," she whispered, but lifted the egg anyway, for somewhat of a scientific observation.

The thing was leathery, the size of a small melon. L'Indasha marveled at its heft, at the strange texture of its shiny, almost metallic surface. She turned the egg carefully, balancing it with some effort in the palm of her left hand, noting its lines and contours, color and texture. Already her first instinct was passing from thought; the egg was now a curiosity, something to learn about and then leave alone.

It was just part of the great impartial balance.

Her hands glowing softly to guide her vision, L'Indasha stared through the shimmering, translucent shell into the interior of the egg.

Transparent, blue-veined wings shrouded a reptilian face with two great black eyes. Tiny arms slowly moved in the milky fluid, and one claw reached suddenly toward her, a fervent grasp that startled L'Indasha back into the moment.

It was almost formed. In a short season, given shelter and attention, its enormous, skewed egg tooth would break the shell, and the dragon would burst forth and take wing.

And it was a bronze. The good dragons *had* come. This was one of theirs.

The druidess sighed.

* * * * *

In the heart of the egg, hovering in a glittering amniotic fluid, the bronze dragon stirred.

A green light played across the edge of the world before him, strong and steady. He reached for the light, turning slowly in the metallic waters, his thin wings hunched.

It was a human hand he saw, green and golden, radiant with a strange and warming light. He knew this hand was no part of the dream that had kept him a year in the shell—the dream of flying, of hot arid spaces, of spellcraft and fifty thousand years of dragon heritage.

No. This was something entirely new and warm at the edge of his egg. He saw the light pulse and shiver, felt a roaring heartbeat in the depths of the hand. It was an overwhelming music, a power he could not resist.

It had to be the promised change. The dream had told him how the edge of this metallic world would crack, would open. . . .

And beyond it would lie yet another world, with hot arid spaces, and gravity and the buoyancy of air. There would be a high and dissolving sun, which you kept at your back in the hunt, in battle. . . .

And this touch must be the herald. Green and glowing, it would bring him to the new world, and he yearned to be there, to reach for this kindness and courage. . . .

He leapt forward with love and longing. . . .

* * * * *

L'Indasha Yman *gently replaced the egg where it had fallen* and backed away from it, wrapping her green cloak tightly around her shoulders.

Do nothing, L'Indasha told herself, again and again and again as she recalled the black, watery eyes of the creature staring softly through the shell. You cannot be delicate.

Only once did she look back at the leathery egg lying desolate in the snow, blurred by the swirling wind and by her own sudden welling of tears. When she reached the safety of her cave, a mile from the outcropping of vallenwood, the slope, and the icy plain, she had collected herself and was calmly pondering the new ice in her oaken bucket, reading its crazing and clouds for auguries, for insights and omens.

Why would the black dragons . . . ?

And this creature, accustomed to the dry, hot wastelands, would perish at once in a winter such as this. . . .

Do nothing. Some mysteries are to unravel, and some mysteries must remain.

Snow slowly covered the bronze egg, but the tiny dragon lay still, warmed magically by L'Indasha's touch, fiercely growing toward a new dream.

* * * * *

In the Khalkist Mountains, *winter passed into spring doubt-fully and gradually. Huddled by the fire, L'Indasha could tell by the return of the snow eagle, by the later arrivals of robin and larkenvale, that this winter was nearly gone. When the druidess looked up to see Lunitari adrift at the peak of the heavens, passing in full phase through the constellation Gilean, she began to clear the cave of winter's refuse, to air her musty belongings and plant the first of this year's seeds.*

On the second day of planting, as she knelt above the spare, rocky earth, dropping the glittering black seeds and singing a gentle incantation, L'Indasha heard an odd noise in the aeterna thicket below. Cautiously, the druidess rose, brushing the gray dirt from the front of her dress.

Shielding her eyes from the noon sun, she stared down into a swirl of blue branches and needles.

Thrashing, discordantly babbling, something had caught itself in the evergreens. The blue branches broke and tossed, and the druidess could see something, brazen and flickering, in the middle of the copse.

A great bleat pulverized L'Indasha's ears.

Quickly breathing a spell of protection, the druidess stepped into a globe of green light and moved toward the entangled beast. For beast it was—that much she could discern from the bending of the foliage, from the furious language of the scattering birds as they flapped out of the aeterna and flew, panic-stricken, down the mountain slopes.

After another sharp cry, the creature burst forth from its snare, its rust-colored wings shaking away blue needles, dirt, and dew. Without hesitation, as though it had expected her to be there, it wheeled toward the sloping hillside and lumbered over to L'Indasha, its babbling grown even louder, more frenzied.

"No!" L'Indasha shrieked. It was a dragon, and though it was a very small one, the druidess suddenly felt her legs shake and the blind surge of fear stiffen the back of her neck. This was known to the druids as dragonawe, a nearly uncontrollable reaction to the sight of the creatures.

"No," she said, fighting for control and the power to run, and "no" again, as the creature rushed toward her, sidling crablike, stumbling over loose rocks and crashing into a young vallenwood, uprooting the tree in its break-neck charge. Her warding held just as the creature stopped short of her nose.

Well, nearly.

"No," the druidess declared a fourth time, stumbling backward, and at last the calm of her heart matched the calm of her words. She regarded the creature—or rather, the gigantic, crooked egg tooth at the end of its snout—with a cold, level stare, and lifted her hands to the first of the seven stations of Kiri-Jolith. The air crackled with heat, and the wind rose.

L'Indasha shifted her hands to the second station, as a distant cloud rushed in from the western sky, boiling and darkening as it gathered speed.

Then the dragon sneezed hugely, spraying her with phlegm and smoke.

Her concentration totally broken, L'Indasha was well into laughter as the poor creature staggered backward from the explosive force, stepped on its own tail, and somersaulted down the hillside into a white outcropping of rock, where it struck its head and lay still, forlorn little wisps of smoke rising from its nostrils.

The druidess wiped herself off and crept toward the dazed dragon. Slowly, she leaned over it and then stopped laughing altogether.

"Oh, no . . ."

She reached out and touched the glittering scales, took the edge of one between thumb and forefinger. Less than a year old.

"Oh, *no*."

How had he ever found her? she wondered.

Do nothing, they had said.

But she *had* done nothing. . . .

Suddenly, with a sort of addled brilliance, the enormous dark eyes opened and regarded her with delight.

"*Blort*," the dragon slobbered, a foolish, innocent smile spreading over two rows of razored teeth.

* * * * *

The druidess saw no choice in the matter. Left to its own resources, the creature would no doubt maul itself in the rugged, mountainous terrain. It might even become the first of its kind to be hunted down and eaten by wolves.

Never had a dragon seemed so helpless, so guileless—such a sorry excuse for dragonkind.

Do nothing. . . .

But she swore to herself that it would be just for a short season, just until that egg tooth dropped off. She could not harbor a pet who would fill half her cave by the time it

---

17

was fully grown. Just until high summer, she told herself, until he was nourished and less awkward, until the weather warmed and the abundance of game in the grasslands lured panther and wolf from the mountain fastness.

Then she would take the dragon south, guide him to a place where the plains spread below him, vast and featureless and inviting. She would bid him farewell, then, and point out the Straits of Schallsea, beyond which lay Abanasinia, where the long stretches of wasteland would be more to his liking, the vallenwoods sparse and enormous and nontangling. There he would find friendlier terrain, joined with the possibility that somehow his kind were gaining force in Krynn.

If he survived the season, his chances would blossom from bleak to slim, and perhaps he would live to adulthood, to the legendary ages of his fabled and ancient kinsmen. It would balance nature, she decided—give the creature the chance that accident and the evil dragons' mysterious greed had taken away.

It was her part, she decided. But the balancing day— when nature was righted and her work ended—was still a trying season away.

* * * * *

One month passed, and then another. No more evil dragons were seen on the sloping face of the Khalkist Mountains as spring approached and passed, and summer followed.

Standing at the mouth of her cavern, broom in hand, L'Indasha told herself that this at last would be the week. For the dragon was still with her, snoring on a bed of straw and dried leaves, inhaling her foodstores and exhaling smoke and, occasionally, a little flame. The beast followed her through the gardens like an enormous, persistent dog, so close on her heels that the spring crops of rhubarb and radishes had been flattened beyond recognition.

Oliver, she called him in the old tongue, after the green cast of his bronze scales. She smiled as she whispered the name. Oliver was smoke in the back of the cavern, a rumbling and belching, and a strange, reptilian devotion.

He would slip his head beneath her hand, urging her wordlessly to scratch behind his ears.

L'Indasha straightened sharply. She must be on guard against softness. Despite the warring voices in her own conscience, there was no keeping a creature who fractured the furniture and singed the dried herbs.

She smiled again, this time a bit wearily. "But I told myself these same things at midsummer," she acknowledged. "And now the moon has passed to the ninth month, and Oliver is still here. . . ."

As the druidess swept the leaves from the mouth of the cave, an odd clattering in the cavern's recesses startled her. Instantly she turned and moved steadily into the darkness, raising her left hand to provide faint light, her right hand still clutching the broom.

She relaxed as she saw Oliver's huge shadow dance, heard him squeal and mutter as he battered his wings against the walls of the cave, his thick tail thrashing wildly.

"Again?" she exclaimed, dropping the broom and rushing over to him.

"*Mrgry*," the dragon explained, shaking his head, pointing clumsily at his snout, which was obviously stuck in a small bucket.

With a sigh, L'Indasha set her foot to the dragon's chest, seized the oaken bucket, and with one powerful yank, removed her oracle with a *pop* from the creature's nose. Druidess and dragon tumbled to opposite sides of the cavern, where they slumped dazed and breathless against the cool walls.

"How many times must we do this, Oliver?" the druidess scolded, brushing the dust from her robes. "My bucket is all scratched up, and you've ruined the ice for augury again. Now it's a trip to the mountaintops for more . . ."

The dragon hung his head, and crept to the farthest corner of the chamber. He stared at her dolefully, black eyes glittering between his folded wings.

"*Gawgr*," he murmured, a wisp of smoke rising lazily from his right nostril. His egg tooth, which seemed to be a permanent feature, jutted absurdly from beneath his upper lip.

L'Indasha rolled her eyes. "Enough!" she commanded, masking a smile as a wave of her hand dispelled the darkness in the cavern chamber. "You're not being punished. Now come with me. The north side garden needs attention."

She heard the dragon follow, shuffling and grumbling behind her as she stepped from the mouth of the cave into the evening solitude. It dawned on her again that the time had passed in which she could safely send such a creature into the wild on his own.

Oliver was defenseless where a dragon should have bristled with armament. His wings were little more than large leathery ornaments: the one flight he had attempted had lodged him tightly in the lower branches of a vallenwood, where he had squawked and thrashed his tail until L'Indasha freed him with a mild druidic spell. He was strong but clumsy, more likely to shock himself with his lightning breath than to turn his formidable weapons against predator or foe.

As for sense of direction . . . she had found him on two occasions, hopelessly lost, his head half-swallowed by a large pillowcase he had been exploring.

His lumbering footsteps slowed behind her, then stopped altogether.

"*Froof?*"

The druidess wheeled around, expecting an accident, or more probably, a near-disaster. Oliver teetered absurdly on the edge of the enormous barrel in which L'Indasha kept dried apples and nuts, and munched merrily, his outsized bottom and tail twitching like a contented cat's.

"It has gone on too long," L'Indasha murmured, rushing toward the glutted, grumbling hindrance devouring her autumn stores. "It's unnatural. The balance *has* tilted."

Then, as the first moon rose bright and pale over the

Khalkist Mountains, the druidess resolved to do the only thing remaining to do. L'Indasha Yman resolved to teach the belching, stumbling thing in her custody . . .

How to be a dragon.

* * * * *

Oliver . . . was not a good student.

Daunted by his first, ill-starred venture into the air, the dragon avoided aeronautics altogether, preferring to crouch on a beetling ledge above the cavern, wings folded tightly over his head. With the vast rubble-strewn and level stretches of Taman Busuk spreading out below, L'Indasha would stand at the edge of the bluff, clutch the hem of her bulky robe, flap her covered arms in her best imitation of flight, then stare hopefully at Oliver.

"*Nyawmp!*" Oliver always rumbled, his egg tooth protruding stupidly. It was his denial sound, his refusal. She had heard it dozens of times before—when she had tried to teach him to hunt, to use the lightning and cloud of gas that were his breath weapons by nature, when she had tried, with increasing desperation, to housebreak him. . . .

"*Nyawmp!*" The high mountain winds swirled about her, the Nerakan forest showed red and golden below, and Castle Nidus could be seen small and dim in the northern distances. Twenty times she had brought him here, and twenty times he had refused to fly, to move, even to flap those recently enormous and always useless wings.

But today would be different. Her kindness overstretched, her patience unraveling, L'Indasha had sneaked up here the night before, while Oliver snored and whistled in the musty throat of the cave.

All was ready. She sprinkled the dried fruit along the lip of the overhang.

"Where pleas and threats fail . . ." the druidess whispered with a strange half-smile ". . . then pick and shovel avail."

Without a word to Oliver, L'Indasha descended the

rocky stairs to the mouth of the cave below.

The dragon stirred, made to follow. *"Nyawmp? Ah . . . Froof!"* The sight and smell of apples and apricots were irresistible.

He considered. Dried fruit was his favorite treat, surpassing bread, beer, and even rosemary tea. But the delicacies lay perilously close to the edge of the bluff.

Perhaps if he stretched . . .

Oliver took a tentative step toward the ledge, then another. He extended his neck, stretched out his tongue toward the nearest apricot, lying tantalizingly out of reach.

"Shirrot," he grumbled, and took another tiny step.

Now the art of sapping is a dwarf's art, the pastime of miners and engineers. A clever sapper may undermine a keep, a wall, even a parcel of land, so that when any heavy vehicle, weapon, or creature strays onto it, the structure collapses immediately. Students of the art claim that its uses are almost all military, and that sapping is useless to woodland peoples—to elves and centaurs, dryads and druids.

However, L'Indasha Yman was a most resourceful teacher. Virtually nothing was useless to her. And if it didn't work, well she would just make a good story out of it.

But it did work, and the cliff crumbled easily under Oliver's weight. He found himself sliding over the edge of the deep ravine and hurtling breakneck through the crisp mountain air. He flailed, shrieked, and clutched for the rock face. . . .

And then something desperate untangled his wings. A strangely familiar power surged through his upper body, something he had dreamed of in the long spring nights and forgotten until this moment, this dire time in the air. And then he was unsteadily aloft, spinning gently toward Taman Busuk, rubble from the fractured cliffside toppling by him, bouncing harmlessly off his strong back.

With a snort of delight, Oliver steadied, banked, and soared toward Mount Berkanth, gaining altitude and strength and confidence as he drew nearer and nearer the lofty mountain. The sunlight poured over his bronze wings, and he bellowed in happiness, the sound echoing through the sheer valleys of the Upper Khalkists.

Far below, at the mouth of the cavern, the druidess leaned against her shovel and laughed with the same abandon.

* * * * *

During the long winter, the egg-dream returned to Oliver. He stirred restlessly in the cave, his enormous tail wrenching and thrashing, until the druidess, plagued by many sleepless nights, gathered and placed a sizable mound of straw and dried leaves by the cave mouth, on sturdy rock and out of inclement winds. She led the grumbling dragon out, and as Oliver settled disconsolately in his new bed, L'Indasha turned to the fire, ignoring one last pathetic *blort* before the creature fell asleep and snored merrily, impervious to the snow and cold.

For now, he thinks I am cruel, she told herself. But I must keep patience, must stay the time. The seasons and nature will take care of the rest.

Besides, this cavern is too confined for his smell.

* * * * *

Oliver was lying on the pallet at the cave's mouth, lazing in the new year's sun, when he saw the invaders. His tail thrashed nervously, and alerted by the noise, the druidess hurried to the mouth of the cave.

A dozen shadowy figures ranged over the ice, a squadron heading north toward the ruins of Nidus.

For a month, L'Indasha had known they were coming. She had read, in the ice, the movement of some kind of army. And this army was unlike the goblin regiments or the swift, elusive bands of barbarians.

These were winged creatures. She had never before seen their like.

Loping, almost undulating with a sinister, reptilian grace, the creatures passed by the fringe of the forest and farther out onto the clear and desolate plain. Their leathery scales glinted a dull bronze, laced with a chalky verdigris. Their wings flapped slowly like scavengers perched on a carcass.

From her high vantage, safely downwind from the stalking monsters, L'Indasha caught the faint whiff of metal and blood on the icy air. At her side, Oliver stirred and rumbled.

"Easy, child," the druidess soothed.

"*Eessie,*" the dragon echoed, and was obediently still.

But he was not at all easy that night, and the druidess gazed with great concern at his restless, shadowy form at the broken bluff's edge. Oliver paced and stared toward the ruins of Nidus, the old castle framed in the rising red light of Lunitari.

What is he thinking? the druidess asked herself. What goes on in that opaque, inhuman mind?

She knew something was calling to him from out of the ruins, for as the wind rustled the dry straw on the bluff, Oliver rumbled and boded, his eyes fixed on something that moved among the distant, collapsed walls and towers.

When he slept at last he found the long dream of the dragon, listened to the strange, winged creatures, all of them sharing a common dream as their heritage, as their destiny.

The invaders were called the Bozak, Oliver learned. Their thoughts were a fever of confusion and rage. They remembered only that a strange magic had coursed through them in the egg, as they coiled and grew and awaited their birth.

Had time and nature taken its course, the Bozak would have become bronze dragons, like Oliver. These monsters had been Oliver's nestmates, changed from their natures and ruined forever by an old and evil design. Instead of being dragons, they were draconians, dwarfed in body and spirit, tracking over the wastes of Taman Busuk on a mission so dark that the thought of it was a black and swirling spot at the edge of the dream.

Oliver awoke the next morning, raised his head, and wailed sadly into the dying wind.

* * * * *

"From that moment," the druidess proclaimed, lifting her eyes from the firelight, "the dragon was no longer the docile, eager creature of the spring and high summer and fall. Something turned in him as the year turned, and it was high time the change had come. I was glad to see it, even though it had taken monsters to bring it on. I thought he would never leave."

Mort was silent, staring into the firelight, a secret smile playing across his face.

Robert nodded. "It happens in war. The boy who sees his face in the face of the enemy is a boy no longer, though it may take him many years and many battles to know it. He puts away childish things. And sooner or later, he welcomes adulthood."

L'Indasha smiled. "Odd you should say that, my peach. It was a battle of sorts that brought Oliver to full maturity. But first, I should tell you that . . ."

* * * * *

Oliver had begun to hunt. At first, it was small game: a rabbit he snatched from somewhere on the plains and carried gently back to the cavern. There, he would set the trembling creature on his straw pallet, stare at it for an hour, then fall asleep. The rabbit would seize the opportunity to escape.

Later, in the new spring, the dragon soared over the rocky plains, bringing back a holly bush, a crenel from ruined Nidus, a rickety hay wagon, and finally, his first kill—a small centicore that he must have pondered over for about a week, for the smell was so dreadful that the druidess threatened to sprout his tail with mushrooms unless he removed the carcass.

It was about this time when young Sir Dauntless Jeoffrey, Solamnic Knight of the Sword, rode across Taman Busuk in search of . . . well, it was never very *clear* what Sir Dauntless Jeoffrey was searching for. He was awfully far east of the High Clerist's Tower and alone in a land quite hostile to the Order.

Perhaps it was adventure he sought, and honor.

Perhaps he, too, followed some undefinable dream.

Whatever drove him forth or drew him onward, Sir Dauntless Jeoffrey passed through villages where Solamnic knighthood was held in contempt, where his fellow knights were considered smug, self-righteous, and meddlesome.

Sir Dauntless was the perfect showpiece of that Order, the knight they had dreamed of.

Keen of eye and deft of hand, the locals never saved a curse or a rotten turnip for later. By the time Dauntless reached Estwilde, his shield was spattered with mud, refuse, and with things too vile to describe. He was tired of Oath and Measure, and *very* tired of the intricate code of his Order that told him to return dignity for scorn and to raise no weapon against a weaker soul.

By the time he reached the Khalkist Mountains, he was positively spoiling for trouble.

At the edge of the Nerakan forest, he came across a pair of hunters—farm lads from north of Neraka who were terrified by his armor and his big glistening sword, who dropped their field-dressed deer and made for the cover of some trees.

Raised among the Solamnic nobility, amid posted lands and private deer parks, Sir Dauntless mistook the ragged men for poachers and inquired in a voice that miles of indignities had stripped of any courtesy, just what they planned to do with this deer.

"Eat it, we reckon," the lads responded. "And then wear some of it, too."

It was all Sir Dauntless Jeoffrey could do to restrain himself. Instead, his face aflame with anger and his voice quivering with outrage, he asked the two peasants who they *reckoned* owned these woods.

The men exchanged wary glances.

"That would be the druidess?" the older one offered, more question than answer in his voice.

The *druidess*?

The young knight gasped. Suddenly, his true quest blazed brightly before him.

Had not the Order instructed him about the ways of the wicked druids? *Tricksters and illusionists*, they had said. *Worshippers of tree and shrubbery.*

Stealers of babies.

He instantly envisioned himself charging regally toward a certain victory, toward great honor and repute.

After extracting directions to L'Indasha's cave, Sir Dauntless abruptly left the two puzzled hunters and their erstwhile dinner/wardrobe for more important game. He would capture this monstrous forest temptress and make his name in all of Solamnia. This was a challenge he had yearned for since his first disastrous hunt in the Hart's Forest. The younger knights had laughed at him then; the older ones ignored him.

But now, when he returned, bearing druidic trophies . . .

Sir Dauntless skirted the smooth path into the mountains, preferring a precarious, narrow route by which he fancied he would catch the druidess entirely by surprise. Instead, it led him above the cavern, to a ruined bluff someone, evidently, had labored to collapse.

Dwarven work, the young knight supposed, dismounting and stooping to inspect the scattered rubble along the ledge—some of which, to his great perplexity, turned out to be dried apricots.

Ah. Poison, of course, he thought. Set out especially for him. And there was no telling how ancient was this creature's stronghold, how many more illusions and snares she had scattered for him, he reasoned shrewdly.

He shuddered, frightened of his own imaginings. But shaking it off, he leapt into the saddle, hoping to find a pathway down to the druidess's cavern.

His horse, however, was of another mind. The animal,

digging its hooves into the gravel, refused to budge, and despite cajolery, threats, and curses, Sir Dauntless Jeoffrey soon realized that he would indeed travel the rest of the way alone.

The horse had stopped for its own reasons, but a very good one would have been because L'Indasha Yman was not in the cavern, having taken the sunlit afternoon to tend her daylilies some hundred yards away.

The dragon, however, was home.

Hungry as usual, Oliver had sneaked into the farthest recesses of the cave, where he had previously entangled himself in pillowcases and buckets. This time, however, he was plundering the last of the winter foodstores—the vegetables put away and preserved by L'Indasha's druidical arts. Quietly, guiltily, and with great gusto, he gobbled beans, raw cabbage, and parsnips. Shifting his huge backside toward the mouth of the chamber so that tail, wing, and scales blocked the sunlight, he foraged greedily in the dark, thinking that L'Indasha could not see him if he could not see her.

Stepping up to the cave, sword drawn, Sir Dauntless Jeoffrey spied something hulking and dark hiding in the furthermost recesses and making disgusting sounds. He surmised it was the druidess, eating children, no doubt. He took a deep breath, planted his feet solidly, and braced for the fight of his life.

At the sound of Dauntless's clanking armor, the dragon, a great many parsnips still wedged in his teeth, perceived that he had company, and that it was *not* L'Indasha. Desperately, not risking the sound of further chewing, he tried to fold his lips over the lumpy vegetables. He tucked his tail and crouched, trying to make himself look like nothing, nothing at all.

But Sir Dauntless Jeoffrey threw down the challenge.

"Infernal creature of cavernous darkness," he intoned, "I have ventured for months and for hundreds of miles to treat with thee. Release those small sweet prisoners you are surely devouring! I declare war on you and your kind! Show thyself, and die an honorable death!"

"Nyawmp!" answered Oliver, horrified and amazed that someone had known to come and rescue his ill-gotten parsnips. He quickly spat them back into the barrel.

"Come forward!" Dauntless commanded, raising his sword. "Face the light, monster!"

Oliver turned slowly, apprehensively, his eyes adjusting to the sunlight. The man was a blur that seemed to be made of metal and mud. The dragon caught a strong whiff of rotten turnips.

This must be something from the grave, something from among the ferocious undead. Oliver fought down a sudden surge of panic.

But isn't fire the enemy of the undead? he asked himself, shifting his ponderous weight and staring at the outline of his adversary, half lost in sunlight.

And isn't lightning the mother of fire? Oliver took a moment for a quick calculation. . . .

The bronze dragon is famous for its two breath weapons. One, of course, is the lightning—the jagged, irresistible fire of battle. There is also the breath gas that drives fear and loathing into any adversary who encounters it.

Oliver fully intended to use the *lightning*, so the green, fetid cloud that billowed from his nostrils surprised him, as did the plaintive *blort* that rose from somewhere just above his stomach and rushed up the long tunnel of his neck, exploding from his mouth in a miasma of half-digested cabbage, beans, and parsnips.

Sir Dauntless Jeoffrey staggered in his boots as the smell slapped him senseless. His sword slipped from his hand. "What in the name of Paladine—" he began, but the floor seemed to tilt and rise, his stomach roiled, and he fell to his knees at the cavern mouth, the green mist eddying around him like some deadly stew.

"What . . ." he breathed, but he had forgotten what he was asking, and he would remember nothing else for hours.

With a cry of triumph, Oliver lurched upward and toward the mouth of the cave, his head and dragon-consciousness now raised. The dream erupted with visions of flame and lightning, of the knight's leg in his ravening maw. He bounded toward his helpless opponent. . . .

And struck his snout soundly against a low-hanging row of stalactites.

His silly egg tooth broke off and clattered to the floor of the cave. The dragon reeled. For a moment Oliver thought he was airborne and flapped his wings foolishly, then the darkness overtook him, and he collapsed in a heap next to the gas-felled knight.

L'Indasha heard the boom, saw the green cloud, and ran from the garden to find the two facedown amid vegetables, shattered stalactites, Dauntless's last shred of dignity, and Oliver's egg tooth.

She celebrated the armistice by having a picnic alone, far, far away from them all.

*   *   *   *   *

It was a full day and night before the dragon came to, and the knight took a whole day longer. Throughout the week of mending and cleaning that followed, the adversaries eyed each other warily from opposite sides of the cave.

Sir Dauntless Jeoffrey left on the eighth day, the stink of rotten vegetables lodged in his nostrils forever. He could not believe that the druidess had not mired him in quicksand or transformed him into a box elder, that she had patched him and fed him and sent him on his way. . . .

That his armor was polished, his sword sharpened, and that his horse was glossy and fed and newly shod.

After the knight's departure, it was scarcely a week until Oliver took to the air and headed south toward the ice caps, where the druidess's augury had suggested that fleets of good dragons would eventually appear.

L'Indasha stood on the shortened bluff and watched the great creature vault clumsily into the sky. Steer by the book, she had told him—by the constellation Gilean, and follow red Chislev in her nightly cycle, and soon you will fly over Abanasinia, and Qualinost beyond it, which you will know by the towers.

Beyond the Plains of Dust, you will catch a coolness in the air. It will be faint, but you will know it, like the feel of a distant mountaintop on a summer day. And you will keep the rising sun at your heart's wing and fly for a night, and another night, and there will be ice then, and the ancient nests of your kind. . . .

And there will be dragons. I speak this in faith, Oliver.

She looked after him sadly, then smiled as he soared above her, and waved as he banked his wings and circled in a widening gyre. Soon he was lost to sight, and she returned to the cave, her thoughts on the summer, and the late plantings, and a strange, large emptiness she had not expected to feel.

* * * * *

Mort started as the bucket nearly slipped from his hand. The brandied coffee was cold now, and the fire was a faint orange glow amid the ashes of the hearth.

"It was good to be rid of him," the druidess said a little too emphatically, as she turned her face from the hearth. "He never came back."

"Is that so?" Mort asked very quietly, smiling as he gently replaced the magical bucket. "I brought you a gift, L'Indasha. In the bag by the hearth."

It was a plant, of course—a daylily he had bred from his own ancient stock on Paladine's hillside. He knew how the druidess loved the brief, abundant blooms.

L'Indasha smiled, admiring the leaves, the scapes, the pod-shaped buds. She marveled that it was not dormant, like the others in the deepening cold of autumn.

"I've handled it, L'Indasha," Mort explained, "so that for this year, it's the latest bloomer of all. Happy birthday."

His big gentle hand passed over a swelling bud, and immediately, as though it were touched by a month of sunlight, the small flower opened and blossomed, pale orchid petals, a purple eye, a green throat. . . .

And a skewed and jagged edge to the blossom, like . . .

"Like his tooth!" the druidess exclaimed. "Like his egg tooth!"

"Oliver Dragontooth, I'll call it," the gardener announced with a laugh. "Though it blooms out of season, it blooms nonetheless, and in the years to come, it will find its own cycle, its own balance in nature. It's a fitting final touch to the dragon's story."

It was time to go.

"Ah . . ." the druidess asked, "before you leave, would you mind setting my bucket just outside the door? I'll give it another chance to gather ice before I scrap it for firewood."

Mort smiled, knowing L'Indasha would do nothing of the kind. Fastening his cloak, he stepped into the darkness and softly closed the big oaken door behind him. It had been a marvelous evening.

Mort paused as he looked out into the mystic night sky and set the bucket on the cottage threshold. He chuckled at what his gardener's hands had discovered in the weathered whorl of that wood.

For the wood's secret, unknown to any but the most magical of hands, was that Oliver *had* come back. Again and again, season after season.

When the dragon dream is first broken by the touch of a hand on the egg, the creature is bound forever to that hand—not by curse or enchantment or even instinct, but by the softer, more willing bonds of love.

That was why no ice had formed in the bucket, even on the coldest nights of the year. The steam of dragon breath had warmed it as it lay in the frigid darkness. Oliver had returned, and with a silent grace, newborn from his survival in the wild, crept slowly to the threshold of L'Indasha's house, new snow covering his tracks, and gazed curiously into the familiar bucket.

"Forever auguring for *froof*," Mort muttered with a laugh, as he trudged down the snow-covered hillside.

Night of Falling Stars

Nancy Varian Berberick

EVERYONE SAID THAT IT WASN'T MY FAULT, what
happened when I was fifteen. No one said, "If Ryle had
only been faster . . . if he'd only been stronger . . . " No one
said that my father would be alive today if I'd seen the
boar in time, if I'd shouted louder—if I'd not been fear-
frozen and unable to draw bow and loose bolt in time. But
I knew the truth. I'd had a long way home to Raven that
hot summer's night, riding one horse and leading the
other, the little bay mare who carried my father's torn and
broken body. It had been a night of falling stars, bright bits
of light streaking across the black sky, showering the
darkness like tears fallen for the truth.

The boar had gored my father and mortally wounded
him, but it was my fear that killed him.

When I grew up, people named me Ryle Sworder
because, in the ten years since my father's death, I'd
honed my fighting skills as if they were teeth and claws,
and then I put them up for sale. Likely you'll say it's brag-
ging, but I'll tell you anyway: There were few better
swords for hire in this part of Krynn than mine. People
said, "Never worry that Ryle Sworder will run away
scared from robbers and freebooters. And he's not afraid
of goblins, either, nor of any beast in the forest."

That was so, as far as it went. I wasn't fearless, as folk
said. The terror that haunted me was this: That someone
would again die of my dread.

I chose my work in order to pit myself against the terror
and defeat it, like a boy afraid of ghosts and eager to go
whistling past every graveyard he can find, just to prove
that he isn't afraid at all. After a while, I began to believe
that I'd done a good job of forgetting the old dread. There
came a time when I didn't think I was whistling past
graveyards when they paid me to escort tender virgins

and their dear dowries through the forest to the wedding feast, or to shepherd wealthy old men down the river past lurking robbers to kin. After a while, I thought I was just doing an honest job of work. I didn't know that fear isn't laid to rest until it is forgiven.

When I wasn't hired out, I lived at the tavern in Raven, in the small chamber above the common room. In those days the village wasn't more or less than it is today—a crossroads jumble of wine shops, inns, taverns, and smithies gathered round the best ford across the Whiterush River where it winds through a narrow valley at the feet of the Kharolis Mountains. One summer I fell in love with golden Reatha, the ferryman's daughter. As I loved her, she loved me, but by winter she was telling me that there wasn't enough room in my heart for her and the ghostly past.

"Let it go," she said, sad and sorry. "Ryle, hunting accidents happen. Please let it go."

Talk like that stirred up the deep-buried dread, the old guilt. I had some stake in not wanting to rouse those, and so I argued with Reatha as if she were telling me to forget my father. She tried hard to make me understand what she meant. I tried harder not to hear her. We didn't stay together past midwinter, but we watched each other from a distance. My eyes could find her across a crowded street; hers could find me in the dark.

*   *   *   *   *

The tavern was called the Raven's Rose, named for the village and for the twining white and red roses that covered the wooden walls enclosing the tavern's garden. The rose bower sat behind the marching ranks of turnips and carrots and potatoes and beans and beets, and it belonged to Cynara Taverner, tended over all the years since she was a child. This was the kind of garden they tell about in songs, and you got to sit yourself down in the comfortable wooden chair, or on the stone bench against the rose-tapestried wall, only by invitation. I enjoyed that bower from time to time, for I had a good friend in Cynara. A widow, she would have married my father, the widower, if he'd survived the hunting trip with me. She'd been looking after me with a mother's eye since my own had died, and she kept on doing that after my father's death. She said, "Bad luck and boars can't change how I feel about you, child."

One day in early summer, I sat in the rose bower dozing to the sound of the flower-drunk bees, when the gate behind me opened, the bottom hinge squeaking as it always did. A dwarf strode into the garden and banged the gate shut behind him. He came and stood before me, in that head-back way that dwarves have even when you're sitting and they're standing and everyone's comfortably eye-to-eye.

The dwarf asked if I was Ryle Sworder, and I told him I was. He didn't do more than grunt to acknowledge the answer.

"Who wants to know?"

He told me that he was an old friend of Cynara's and that his name was Tarran Ironwood, then he went and sat on the bench by the wall. It was a lovely bench, crafted by a master stone-wright from whitest marble, a relief of twining roses worked on the sides and the legs. Most people stopped to admire it, even those who saw it often. Tarran Ironwood didn't give it a glance. He sat himself down and stared at me.

Studied, I studied back. His face was pale, his black beard trimmed and glossy. He was whip-thin and of good height for a dwarf, about heart-high to a middling tall human. He had the well-heeled air of Thorbardin about him, and he looked to be in his early middle years, which means he was about ninety or so years old. Thin as he was, he was hale enough, but he was missing his right arm. A brooch of gold and emeralds, shaped like a dragon winging, pinned up the empty sleeve.

"What do you want, Tarran Ironwood?"

"I came to see you."

A great shout of laughter thundered out from the tavern, a dozen voices raised up in hooting derision. Someone cried, "The dragon! Oh, aye, tell us all about it—and the story'll be told for the hundredth time this year!" And the storm of laughter rolled around the Rose again, splashing out into the garden.

The dwarf sat still on the stone bench among the roses, head cocked and listening.

"Have you never heard the tale, Tarran Ironwood?"

He nodded. "I've heard it. There's a copper dragon lives under the mountains, far away and down where even we of Thorbardin don't go. Claw, they call him."

A warm breeze stirred among the roses, rousing a heady scent you could almost see.

"That's the one," I said. "Though I've never heard the part about his name—or even that it's a him. Anyway, the rest of the story says it—*he*—sits on a treasure mound the size of the Rose, and they say the dragon's not the worst of what you can find down there."

"There, the story is wrong." Tarran touched one of the sculpted roses on the side of the bench, traced the shape of a marble petal with a finger, stroking the overlying softness of greeny-gold lichen. "Claw is the worst of what you can find under the mountain."

Tarran sat very still, and the afternoon light glittered on the gemmed brooch where his arm used to be. All that shining made it seem as if the small emerald dragon were alive and breathing there on his shoulder.

"You've seen that dragon," I said.

"I've seen him. Twenty years ago." Tarran sat still as stone, but for one finger tap-tapping on the stony rose. "Tomorrow I'm going back."

"Let me guess," I said. "You want to kill him, right?"

That was a joke, of course; everyone knows it takes a few armies to kill a dragon. But Tarran took the jest soberly, just as if I were serious.

"If I could kill the beast," he said, "I wouldn't. I want revenge, and a longer one than Claw's death would give me."

I stopped smiling. "And you've got this revenge all planned out?"

"I do. And maybe you think it'll be a cold revenge, coming this late, but it took me a long time to stop screaming in my sleep."

Screaming in terror, howling down the long night.

I looked away from him and his admission of fear as you look away from a deformity, pretending to the politeness that common sense says is kinder than staring at the maimed and making him feel self-conscious. What common sense says, and what the gesture really is, are two different things. In some deep place within, often as not folk see injury or deformity as illness, something that might be catching. So it was with me and any confession of dread.

But one-armed Tarran didn't seem to care if his fear was too ugly for me to see—it was his, and he owned it. He sat forward on the bench, his elbow on his knee, his dark eyes glinting.

"Ryle, Cynara says your sword is for hire. And the word around is that when you're hired, you stay hired, and you won't run off because you've killed me and robbed me—or because you haven't got the heart to see a thing through."

"Word's right," I said. "There's no future in either."

He took the dragon brooch from his empty right sleeve and tossed it to me. I caught it, and got lost in the brilliant green of the emerald wings, the wink of light in the ruby eyes.

"That's the least of what treasure is under the mountain, Ryle Sworder."

I tossed the dragon brooch back. The gold and emeralds and rubies shone like an arcing rainbow between us. His right shoulder twitched, as though his body couldn't forget what used to be true. He'd been right-handed before he met the dragon. But he recovered in time, and caught the brooch in his lone left hand.

"As you see," he said, smiling for the first time, and grimly. "I need a hand. If you come with me and help me get my revenge on the dragon, half of everything you and I can carry out is yours."

I decided quickly, as I always do.

"My sword's yours," I said. "And since you're Cynara's friend, I'll not haggle over the fee."

That was a joke, too, but Tarran had already smiled once

that day and didn't see the need to indulge again. He said we'd leave in the morning, and he didn't say anything else. After he left me, I sat alone for a long time, all the way into the dimming and beyond to twilight. Twice I heard Reatha's voice—once lilting in laughter, once couched in quiet confiding tones as she and a friend walked past the garden on the other side of the wall. I closed my eyes and imagined how she'd look dressed in treasure from the dragon's hoard, a golden chalice in hand, a diamond necklace spilling all down her breast like water running.

When the last of the light was fading, Cynara came into the garden to bring me a plate of supper, and she sat on the stone bench to watch me eat. After a time she said, "Has Tarran hired you?"

"Yes."

She heard that and stayed quiet for a while, a small woman on the white marble bench in the last light of the day. Her roses arched over her, trailed around her, and the scent of them was always the scent of her.

"Ryle, he's going to lay a ghost," she said, when night was almost fallen. "That's what the dragon really is to him."

I shrugged, and I said that if that's what Tarran was going to do, it was his business. Mine was to keep him safe along the way, help him as he wished, and come home a rich man.

"Aren't you afraid you might meet some ghost of your own, Ryle, there in the dark under the mountain?"

A chill touched me, a strange breath on a hot summer's night. But I smiled, as though she were joking, and I said, "I've never seen a ghost in my life, Cynara. I don't expect I'll start seeing 'em now."

I went and kissed her cheek—the skin as soft as a petal from one of her beloved roses—and wished her goodnight.

She took my hands in hers, and she wished me good luck.

* * * * *

In the morning, when Tarran and I went to take the ferry across the Whiterush, we found Reatha by the waterside fishing, her hair unbound and streaming gold, her skirts kilted up and tied out of her way. Rosy dawn light shone on her legs, and she kicked up a little spray like diamonds in her wake when she ran to fetch her father, the ferryman.

She watched me all the way across the river, and she knew I knew that. On the far bank I turned, and Reatha lifted her hand to wave.

"Friend of yours?" Tarran asked.

"Yes," I said tightly.

"Ah." He shook his head, understanding. "Too bad."

We didn't have much else to say to each other for the rest of the day.

* * * * *

Tarran sat watching the stars dazzling the summer night, the tiny lights swept together and shining their best in the absence of the preening moons, the red and the silver only lately set. We were two days out of Raven and camped just above the tree line near a high sloping rock face. Midway up the slope, dark against the stone, the entrance to the storied caverns gaped out into the night. We'd take that way in and down in the morning.

Cynara had sent us off with our packs filled with dried meat and fruit, and bundles of brands for torches. Inside the caves there'd be no forage and no light. Outside, we trusted my hunting skill for supper, and with the little bird-arrows I fetched us a brace of fat grouse. Tarran ate, watching the sky glitter, and when the eating was done, he left the stars to shine on their own and came close to the fire.

For a while he said nothing, and he sat looking at me across the fire as if he were trying to see deep in and down.

I took my sword and laid it across my knees, took a whetstone and honed the glittering blade. That deep-looking made me edgy, and I kept the steel between him and me, as though it could deflect his gaze.

He smiled—only faintly—as though he understood. Very softly, he said, "We were five who came here twenty years ago. Me and my brother, and three of our kin. In Thorbardin they say these caverns are filled with veins of silver and gold. But we didn't come here for that. In Thorbardin we curse the dragon and mourn the loss of the silver and gold, but we leave it be and delve in other places. Me and the others . . . we were young fools out to find legend's treasure."

The golden firelight glinted from the knives he had stowed about him—a couple of straight-bladed dirks, three wavy-edged daggers, and one jewel-hilted long knife. One-armed, he had no use for a bow, none for a broadsword, little for any axe that wasn't a throwing axe. One-armed, Tarran liked knives.

"There was treasure," he said. Now his voice wasn't soft, and it had a jagged edge to it. "It was so lovely that it made our wild dreams pale. And there was Claw. He's well named, like a talon, long and swift, and very keen. He's a copper, and he's old and swollen with greed. . . . "

His words trailed off into silent remembering, and he had such a shut-tight look on him that I wasn't sure he'd finish the story. Down in the woods an owl hooted; another answered.

"We found the treasure," Tarran said on a sigh. "And the dragon found us. Of course. I don't have a brother now, only the memory of him dying. Yarden was his name, and our friends were Rowson, Wulf, and Oran. They were the sons of Lunn Hammerfell, and they were kin of mine. I will avenge them all."

"How will you take revenge without killing the dragon?"

"Claw's a miser," he said. "In Thorbardin we say that a miser hoards to hide the one thing that is most dear to him. I know what the dragon loves. Take it from him, and he'll feel the hurt all the days of his life. That long will have to be long enough."

Flames leapt up from our fire, then fell, dragging the light away from Tarran's face. He tilted his head back a little, looking past me, up to where—darker than the dark—the way into the caverns gaped. I couldn't see his face; I couldn't read him, or guess what he was thinking. After a moment he looked back to me, and he nodded shortly.

"Good night," he said, and his voice had a haunted, hollow sound to it.

I sat up a long while, making my weapons fit. I bundled the bird arrows and replaced them in my quiver with steel-heads. In my hands weapons always felt like comfort—good steel to raise against foes and fear. So it was that night.

As I worked, I fell to thinking about Reatha, her gold-running hair, her sun-browned legs, the smooth calves rosy and plump in the morning light. With the Whiterush between us, she'd lifted a hand to wave me farewell. After all this time, there was still no one she looked to the way she looked to me.

My work soon done, I stretched out before the fire and fell at once to sleep. I wasn't restless, and I slept well. But once, toward dawn, I woke with a chill, and across the sky, in the dark west, I saw the bright plumage of a shooting star sketch a falling arc, like a silver arrow coming to ground.

I piled some wood on the low fire, warming myself and waiting for Tarran to wake. I should have seen a warning in the falling star, the reminder of a fear I wouldn't admit to, but I didn't. I had too much invested in the pretense that I'd long ago vanquished the old guilty dread that someday, once again, my cowardice would cause a death.

* * * * *

We left the outworld just before sunrise, when the rock face was cool to touch and dewy damp. We had some climbing to do to get to the entrance, and Tarran made me go first up the stony wall.

"You don't want a one-armed climber ahead of you. If I fall, I'll take you down with me. Go."

That made sense. I went scrambling up, finding good hand- and footholds. At the ledge I got a brand and set to with flint and striker. The flaring torch spilled light over the ledge, and by it I watched Tarran come up. Unlike me, he didn't use handholds for pulling; he used them only for balance. He put all his faith in the footholds. When he was within arm's reach, he accepted the hand I offered and let me hoist him onto the ledge. Thin as he was, he was an easy lift. Safely up, Tarran put his back to the rising sun and led me into the mountain, the landscape of his nightmares.

The light from without came trailing after us for longer than I'd thought it would, like a little pale dog at our heels, but soon it left us, and there was only the torchlight running on damp walls, the pale smoke drifting ahead of us to the call of some cavern breeze. We went along a narrow path, with the walls closing tighter each yard of the way, the ceiling dropping lower, until I had to stoop to pass where Tarran easily went. After a while walking, he held up a hand to halt.

"Listen!"

"To what?"

He stood perfectly still. Torchlight gleamed in his dark eyes as the pupils widened to take in the flickering fireglow. He turned his head a little, and his eyes—till then black—suddenly flashed reddish, like a wolf's in the night. Dwarves have eyes like that, shifting and changing to adjust to whatever light is found.

"There," he said. "Hear it?"

Now I heard breathing that wasn't Tarran's and wasn't mine.

"This is what the dragon sounds like sleeping," Tarran said. "Whether he's sleeping just now, I don't know. Things echo in here, and the echoes echo." He eyed me closely, head cocked. "You all right?"

"Of course I am," I said, a little coldly.

He raised an eyebrow, as at something strange. "No law says you can't be afraid, boy."

I told him I wasn't afraid of an echo, and he laughed, a short dry bark. "Right, then. We've got some walking to do."

I checked the set of the quiver on my hip, the heft of the sword at my side. My longbow, the weighty yew, lay unstrung in a holder across my back. Torch high, I followed

Tarran through the narrow passage. All the while and all the way, the sound of the dragon's breathing rose up from the floor under our feet, flowed down from the damp ceiling, seemed to roll off the very walls themselves.

I am here, I am here, I am here . . . whispered the echoes of the beast, the dragon deep down in his lair.

If I'd been wise enough to listen within, I'd have heard the deep-buried fear in me stirring awake.

I am here, I am here, I am here!

* * * * *

When we came out of the narrow shaft, Tarran halted again, and I held the torch up and out. Before us lay a new path, and we stood above a void so wide I couldn't guess where the other side must be. Tarran kicked a stone over the edge of the drop. We waited to hear it hit bottom, and we waited, and we waited.

"Come on," he said, when he was sure his point was made and taken.

The path wound down the side of the pit, spiraling around, and here the echo of the dragon's breathing had company. Voices whispered, like ghosts rustling up from the blackness.

Someone, long years ago, whispered a secret. Another voice moaned in dread's cold grasp, the sound like a chill finger on the back of my neck. A treasure-stalker spoke of hope and gold—and someone screamed, a hundred years ago, falling into the swallowing darkness.

In the next breath all the whispering ghosts, all the ancient echoes, fled to silence before a hollow, groaning roar. In the wavering torchlight, Tarran's face showed waxy and white above his black beard. He shuddered, and the gems on the dragon brooch glinted, little darts of light in the blackness.

"That's Claw," he said, peering up at me as though he were watching for sign of the fear I professed not to have.

Cold in the belly, I said that I reckoned it was Claw, and then I said that we'd best be moving on. He went forward carefully and slowly, and I followed after.

The path was wide enough for Tarran and me to walk side by side with a man's-length of room between us and the drop. We'd entered on a west-running path, but I soon lost any sense of our direction on the spiral way. The brand I'd lighted outside burned down to a stump, and I sparked a fresh one off the ember. When the third one was half burned, Tarran stopped and took the torch from me. He held it high and a little forward. Light spilled all down the rocky wall, like a firefall, a silent gold-shining river, and he stood like he was stone-carved.

Whispers from below rustled around us.

"What is it?" I asked.

He stepped back to let me see what lay ahead. At his feet was a break in the path, a gap almost twice as long as I am tall. I kicked at the slender ledge remaining; stones tumbled down into the chasm, pebbles clattering on the sides, the larger rocks silent in their fall.

"We'll go back and find another path," I said.

"There is no other path." He went down on his heels, peering into the darkness and so close to the edge it made my belly clench to see him. Ghosty echoes sighed about gold and silver, about treasure and wealth. *Keep on . . . hold on . . . we'll find . . . more than you've ever . . . worth a man's life to risk . . .* Now, or then, the dragon rumbled and moaned.

I lifted the torch as high as I could reach and saw that here, as all along our way, the wall was studded with small outcroppings. Most didn't look like good anchors, but one long knob looked as though it could easily bear weight.

"Are you afraid of heights, Tarran Ironwood?"

I said that in jest, and he laughed—not that short dry laughter, but a sudden gleeful amusement I'd not have thought him capable of.

"I'd like to meet the dwarf who is."

I took a stout coil of rope from my pack, tied a swift noose, and tossed it high. The noose slipped over the knob and lodged there securely. I tied a stirrup in the end of the rope and asked Tarran if he wanted to go first. He gave me the torch, wound the rope once around his hand, gripping, and shoved off, leaning a little out toward the chasm and letting his weight swing him back to the path.

Safe aground, Tarran sent the rope back to me, and I tossed the torch across the gap to him. When the light was steady again, I settled my pack, took my place, and kicked off. I was but a few beats of the heart hanging there at the top of the arc. Almost still over the dark and the void, I looked down, into the pit, into the black. That endless emptiness made me feel light in the belly, like I could soar if only I let go of the rope.

A shrieking, wrathful roar blasted up from the unseen deep.

Startled, I clenched. My hand slipped on the rope; the rough hemp burned the skin. I felt the sickening drop— then caught myself.

The echo of the dragon echoed, and Tarran cried out as the arc of my flight wobbled.

Ryle! . . . Ryle! . . . Ryle!

I couldn't feel my grip on the rope, and I seemed to feel the drag and pull of falling again as Tarran flung the torch away and reached out as far as he dared—farther than he should have—and caught hold of my pack, trying to correct the swing. Below, the torch was a little falling star, shooting down into the eternal blackness.

I hung, but whether over emptiness or the ledge, I didn't know.

"Let go the rope!" Tarran shouted. "Now!"

In leaping echo, the cavern pleaded, *Let go now! . . . Go now!*

Blindly, in utter darkness, I trusted. I let go of the rope and fell hard against the rock wall. Sick to my stomach, my knees gone suddenly watery, I stumbled, clutched at Tarran's shoulder.

"Stand still, boy! You'll spill us both over the edge!"

The terror that had been like ice in my belly now bled all through me, like a poison. I staggered when he moved back and away from me. Tarran grabbed my arm to hold me still, gripped so hard I knew there'd be bruises later.

"Stay right there," he said. "Stay right there. I'm going to light a torch."

Shaking, belly-sick, I clung to the stone while he got a brand from my pack. He struck his steel against the rock wall. A spark leapt and fell. Another. The third caught, and Tarran praised his dwarf god, his red Reorx, for the grace of light. He held the new torch high, and for the first time I saw some color come into his face, a flush of relief.

"You all right?"

Sweat ran cold on me, down my neck, down my ribs, like death's icy touch. I said, "Of course I am," and I was pretty sure I looked like I was.

Yet, like an accusation of the truth, the afterimage of the falling torch, the shooting star, lingered in my mind. Panicked, I'd come close to tumbling us both off the ledge. I might have caused Tarran's death. So it had been, once before, when— panicked—I could not draw the bow, loose the bolt, and kill the boar that was bearing down on my father.

Tarran put his hand on my arm, and I tensed under his grip.

"Easy now. You're back to the wall, and feet on the ground again."

But it wasn't height-fear that had me, not the fear of falling. It was worse, and he must have sensed it, for now I heard a new note in his voice. Beneath the reassurance I heard doubt, a thin qualm.

"Let's go," I said gruffly, taking the torch from him.

Narrow-eyed, he nodded and set out. I could feel it as you feel a storm coming—Tarran was wondering if he'd made a mistake to hire me. He said nothing to me about it, and I was cold and surly—asking no questions of him and permitting none from him. I was not minded to talk about the fear he suspected.

And there was this, to keep us both quiet: Tarran had been twenty years at learning not to scream in his sleep, twenty years waiting till he could tame his terror and take his revenge. He'd take the chance that he'd not gone wrong in hiring me. And I'd been ten years at the work of building an honestly earned reputation behind which to hide the one naked dread I must let no one see—that my fear would once again kill someone who trusted me. If I went back now, I'd go back shamed, a coward for old men to point at, for women to cluck over, and children to laugh at. A coward for Reatha to turn from in pity.

Tarran and I, we had to go on.

*   *   *   *   *

We left the spiral path after only a little while more of walking. We'd not come to the bottom of the chasm—Tarran said we'd not gone even a tenth of the distance down—but there was a fork in the winding road, and the left-hand way led us off the rounding path and into a tunnel, a small shaft. As we walked, me stooping again, the lesser echoes from the chasm faded and fell behind. Claw's breathing, his long ago groans and cries, followed. The sound of the beast was with us still as we stepped from the shaft onto a great wide plain of stone.

A stream of water in a stony-edged channel ran through that plain, an underground brook that seemed to spring from the rock itself and wander away into the dark.

"Where does it come from, Tarran?"

He shrugged. "There are layers and layers under the world. The water comes from under here, just like any sudden wellspring in the outworld."

Stalactites, like stony icicles, dripped down from the roof. Groves of stalagmites rose from the floor, some as high as trees. Just past the tunnel's mouth, in two places, pairs of each kind of formation joined, making floor-to-roof columns like a formal entrance. Tarran said that here would be a good place to stop and rest, and he told me we'd been underground for most of the day.

"Outside," he said, "the moons are rising."

I ached for the sight of that, and the sound of crickets, and the dazzle of stars on the black, black sky.

*   *   *   *   *

Tarran ate walking, pacing round the wide cavern, touching the walls, stroking a pile of stone, and always coming back to the three columns. We'd wedged a torch between some rocks and near the brook for the water's reflection, but even so it gave little light. I sat close to the brand, watching Tarran and seeing him as only a black shadow.

"I used to be a stone-wright," he said, his hand on a glistening column. He had a look about him as if he were touching a living thing. "I'd take a hammer and chisel to a reach like this and call any shape you wanted from it." Softly, almost tenderly, he whispered, "It isn't magic, but it used to feel like that."

He turned, moved abruptly away from what he could now only dream about.

"That's how I know Cynara," he said. "Not all the good stone is in Thorbardin. I used to come out of the cities from time to time, looking. She was a little girl when I first saw her, out behind the tavern and planting thorny rose bushes. It was I who made the bench in the garden, for her wedding gift." He stopped, smiling ruefully. "For her first wedding gift. There was another wedding planned, after she'd been a widow for a while. But her man died. Ach, you probably know more about that than me, being from Raven. Any case, Cynara's been a friend for a long time. How do you know her?"

I leaned away from the light, scooped up icy water and drank. I was a while swallowing, keeping the water in my mouth to warm. It was that cold, like snowmelt, and swallowed too fast that stuff can cramp the belly.

Finally, I said, "It was my father she was going to marry, that second time. He died in a hunting accident."

All around us the dragon-echo sighed, and if Tarran heard anything but the thin fact in my answer he gave no sign.

"I'm sorry," he said, awkward and caught unaware in the act of trespassing on another's pain.

"Me, too."

Tarran walked away from the stone. He sat down near the torch, and the light glinted on the hilts of his knives, darted from the ruby-eyed dragon brooch where his right arm used to be. He had a tentative look on him, as though he wasn't sure he should say something. But he said it, sure or not.

"Feeling better?" He glanced away, then back. "From before, I mean."

"I've got the solid ground under me again," I said flatly. "I feel fine."

His thin lips were a grim line, pressed tight, while he sat there thinking. In the stony channel, the icy water rippled over rocks, murmuring softly.

"You're not afraid of heights, Ryle, are you?"

"No more than you are." And that was the truth. I laughed, for show. "But I was afraid I wouldn't grow wings fast enough."

The torch spat embers. Tiny bits of light arced over the brook and fell into the breathing darkness. Tarran watched me intently, never blinking, his black eyes never moving.

"Ryle, listen."

The dragon breathed in echoes, like the sea lapping at the shore. Tarran reached and touched my chest. He had a dark and strange look on him now, like a man seeing visions—as though he could know everything in my heart just from touching me. I wanted to move away, but I kept still, afraid to seem afraid.

"They say you're fearless, Ryle Sworder. But surely they say wrong—no one is fearless. Listen to yourself, Ryle, and search for your worst fear, your most dire dread. Listen!"

He stood up, head cocked, eyes black as the chasm as the pupils widened, adjusting to the greater darkness.

"Claw feeds at night, in the forest where no one goes. If we're very lucky, and very careful, we won't see him. I'll get my revenge, and we'll get out of here with our pockets and packs filled with enough treasure to keep you like a king.

"But if our luck misses," Tarran said, "if we once come in sight of Claw, he'll know how to look at you and see your worst fear, the terror that cripples you. He'll use that fear, and he'll kill you with it just as if it were a sword to cut you apart."

The torch guttered, spat sparks into the darkness, arcing bits of light. Then the darkness fell; the stumpy little ember couldn't stand long against it.

"I was the first one Claw spotted," Tarran said, whispering. "The first one he came for. He hurt me, and he left me bleeding halfway between him and my friends."

His words were like heavy stones, one then another, and I felt the weight of them on my chest, like a barrow being built too soon over me.

"Claw used me for bait, and they took it. First Yarden . . . then the others. I couldn't do anything to stop it happening. Between the dragon and them . . . I was helpless."

Even in the dark people shouldn't talk about such dread. I said, "Stop, Tarran. I don't want to hear it."

I spoke roughly, as to a coward baring his worst craven deed. I had no right to speak like that, and I hated the silence my words caused. But I couldn't apologize, though I knew I should. His talk of worst fears was like one more crack in a weakening dam.

"It's all right to be afraid, Ryle. Here, you'd better be."

I closed my eyes, coldly quiet.

"All right, then. I'll say no more but this: if you don't know what your worst fear is, you'd better spend the night reckoning it out. You don't want Claw to be the one to show it to you."

I didn't answer him, nor did I speak again for the rest of the night. In the morning, Tarran asked if I'd slept well, and I told him that I had. He shook his head as you would over a stubborn fool. Once, when he thought I wasn't looking, he glanced back toward the tunnel that led to the chasm and the spiral path, the way back.

But he said nothing about not going forward. He'd come too far. So had I.

*　*　*　*　*

We went all the day through a series of chambers, caverns small and large, narrow and wide, and Tarran Ironwood remembered his path.

"I came in this way, and I went out this way." He smiled bitterly. "The last somewhat more slowly than the first."

He'd had his right arm on the way out; the bone had still hung to the shoulder. In two places the meat of the arm had been laid open, the muscles naked to his sight. He told me that, and he said that a man should never have to see what the inside of himself looks like. He'd bound the wound and done his best to keep it clean, but the arm already had the gangrenous stink about it by the time he got out and got found. He knew before anyone had to tell him that he'd be one-armed for the rest of his life.

I followed him closely, and he never took a wrong turn, never stopped for more than a moment to reckon a direction. I marked time passing by the count of the torches, and so I knew we'd walked a full day by the time we came to a low narrow tunnel like the one that led off the spiral road along the side of the chasm. This tunnel was much longer than that first, and as low. All the muscles in my back and shoulders were cramped with stooping by the time we came out of it and onto a wide ledge, like the gallery rounding a king's great hall.

The whole place stank of dragon, the dry, dusty reptile smell, the scent of endless age, and Tarran's breathing got rough and choppy, like he was trying not to gag. I looked up to the edge of light around the hole in the ceiling. The silver moon and the red sat together in a quarter of the sky, their light pouring down through the opening. By that shining I saw bones littering the stony gallery, the large rib cages of cattle and horses, the smaller bones of deer and elk. I saw a bear's skull, and what had to be the skeleton of a minotaur, the horned skull larger than that of any bull you'd ever hope to see. Old blood painted the ledge, rusty brown, dripping over the edge, streaking the walls of the beast-hall below. Here was where Claw brought his night kills. Here, on this wide ledge, was where the dragon dined. Below us—almost sixty feet down—lay the beast's lair, empty, as Tarran knew it would be. Claw was a night hunter. Above— so high I had to crane my neck to see—yawned the dragon's way out, and the dragon's way in.

"There's a way down," Tarran said, his voice hushed, hardly heard. He pointed to the left, and I raised the torch, saw gouges in the stone, like stairs.

"They're not as regular as stairs," the dwarf said. "Some are a longer step than others. But they'll do."

"Who built them?"

"Claw. The dragon's got a way of changing his breath and spit into acid when it suits him. You knew that, didn't you?"

I didn't before then. "Why'd he build steps in here?"

"You'll see."

He didn't say anything more, and now he was all pulled into himself, as he'd been when I first saw him in Cynara's rose bower. I strung my bow and slung it over my shoulder, then checked to see that the steel-heads were close to hand. I took my sword from the sheath. These were good weapons and strong, and they'd always been my comfort. Not this time, and all the hair rose, prickling on my arms and neck as I followed Tarran Iron-wood down into the dragon's lair.

* * * * *

I thought I saw the empty-eyed skulls scattered on the floor before Tarran did. Maybe that's so, but he knew they were there.

They were four, the bone-naked remains of dwarves by the size of them. The skulls weren't bleached white, for they'd not lain out in the sun and the wind and the rain. They were brown, old and shiny things with gaping jaws and staring eye sockets. One of the skulls was split right down the middle, and the three whole ones were cracked, the cracks like dark lace.

"Rowson," Tarran said, pointing to one of the three whole skulls. "And there's Wulf. Oran's over there."

He went and knelt beside the broken skull, the one that lay in two pieces away from all the others. I raised up the torch. Tarran knelt right in the middle of a dark stain on the floor, a wide sweeping streak of rusty brown. There he'd lain, bleeding and begging his kinsmen to flee. They hadn't done that. One by one they challenged the dragon for him, biting the bait every time, until they were all dead and Tarran lay alone in his gore, the broken bodies of his kin scattered around him. Their dying screams framed his nightmares for twenty years.

Tarran touched the broken skull, very gently, as if he were touching living flesh. Here was his brother, and the stain on the floor was the shadow of their blood.

"It was a hard way to kill them," Tarran said. He got to his feet, and he came to stand by me. "It was a cruel, hard way to do it."

He wasn't looking at the blood mark as he spoke, or at me. He was checking the release of every one of those knives of his, making sure each would come swiftly from its sheath when needed. He kept the jewel-hilted long knife to hand.

"Are you ready, Ryle?"

Dry-mouthed, I said that I was.

"Put the torch out."

I hesitated, wanting to cling to all the light I could.

"Do it."

I did, and when my vision settled, there was more light to see by than I'd reckoned could be so. The great opening in the ceiling channeled the starlight and moonlight downward in a slanting, milky column. And now, with the light evenly spread, I saw more than blood and the browned skulls of Tarran's luckless kinsmen. Now I saw the dragon's hoard rising like a mountain of moonlit rainbows under the ground.

"It's a fine hoard," Tarran said, his voice low. "Raw gems from the mountains of Karthay, golden torques from Istar, rings from Palanthas . . . chalices and plate from the towers of wizards, from the halls of knights, from the tables of the elf lords in Silvanost. There," he said, pointing to a sword. The blade was rust-pitted, age-dulled; the grip was a ruby, one solid stone shaped for a slender hand. "That belonged to an elven queen, and it's said that she forged it herself, so long ago that these days her people hardly remember her name. All this Claw has stolen to hide the single thing he holds dearest."

Whispering, like a worshiper, I said, "What could the beast hold dearer than this hoard?"

"I saw it," he said, answering me only glancingly. Now he sounded like a dreaming man. "When I was lying for bait, I saw what the beast guarded, what he always tried to hide with every turn, every spread of his wings."

We went wide around the bloodstain, wide around the skulls. Tarran was white in the moonlight, like a ghost walking. We went past piles of uncut topaz, and that was like walking past frozen fire. In the shadow of the mound, behind the hoard, we found another skull. It was a dragon's, and it paled every treasure Claw had in his hoard.

Long as me, and half as long again, this skull was—like the others—browned with age. Its fangs were gilded, its eye sockets dressed in silver and filled each with a ruby the size of my two fists together. Seven bony spines, the start of a crest that must have run down the length of the dragon's back, wore sheaths of silver and were hung with nets of slender gold strands from which diamonds and blue, blue sapphires dangled.

I touched one of those nets, and the jewels chimed gently against each other, a delicate tinkling.

"Tarran, what is this?"

He sighed, a whispered groan. "What the miser hoards to hide. Who would look past that mountain of trinkets to see this, aye?"

This skull, dressed in gold and silver and gems, was Claw's treasure. Tarran had seen that. When his kinsmen were dying, one by one murdered, Tarran had seen the shape of his revenge behind the shining mass of stolen treasure.

Now he moved a little, as if to reach to touch the skull. But he didn't reach, and he didn't touch. He let his hand fall, barely raised.

"This is why Claw built the steps in his lair," he said. "A gemsmith, or more than one, had to come in to do this work. It's dwarf-craft. Claw made a bargain with someone out of Thorbardin, a long time ago."

He lifted his long knife, eyeing it as though he'd never

seen it before now. He turned it this way and that, the jeweled hilt and blued steel glittering in the moons' light. Then, suddenly, he reversed his grip and made a shining hammer of the hilt. Groaning, aching right to his soul, he struck the dragon skull. Under this first of revenge's blows, a silver-sheathed spine fell from the bony crest and shattered at my feet. A golden net of sapphires rattled, slithered, and clattered to the floor. I reached for it, and Tarran turned on me, his eyes like dark fire.

"Not till I've powdered this damn skull!"

He broke another spine from the crest, and he shouted a curse, the cry a longed-for release from old, old pain. He pried a rubied eye from one of the sockets, and his cursing now sounded like the cries of a blood-lusty soldier sacking a foeman's hall.

This wasn't my vengeance; it wasn't for me to do this breaking. I stepped away, out into the moonlight, tight and tense and doing the job I was hired for—warding the vengeance-taking. Eyes on the great opening above, I walked past the hill of treasure, out into the middle of the lair. I stepped wide around the skulls of Tarran's kinsmen, wide around the old blood mark on the stony floor.

Tarran kicked a tooth from the dragon's skull. Now his cursing sounded like sobbing. I didn't turn to look at him. Revenge is a private thing, and if a man wants to sob over it, he should be able to do it in privacy.

I walked round the lair, pacing, watching the sky—and, not watching the floor, I tripped on something. I flinched back, thinking it was an ancient bony relic of some unfortunate death, and saw that it wasn't. In the shadows, I couldn't tell more than that, and I toed it out into the center of the lair, into the light of the two moons. It was a shard of an old, leathery eggshell. Once a she-dragon had lived in this lair. With a sudden chill, I turned to see Tarran kicking another tooth from the skull that a gemsmith out of Thorbardin had dressed like a queen in jewels and gold.

The wind outside moaned like grief. The sound shivered down my spine. Tarran never seemed to notice. He kicked another tooth out of the dragon skull, and the wind's moaning rose in pitch. The hair on the back of my neck and arms bristled.

"Tarran!"

A shadow, a wide pool of darkness, slid across the floor, and I saw the dragon, the beast framed in the opening. Broad black wings were just tucking in, his copper body gleamed, a long shining streak of red across the blackness, a bright star loose from the sky and running between the moons.

"Tarran!"

The lair filled with thick blood-reek—and the bone-crunch sound of two heavy bodies hitting the stone of the ledge, an elk and a cow. Supper. I grabbed Tarran's arm, yanked him away from the skull.

"Come on! This isn't worth dying for!"

His dark eyes wild, Tarran pulled away from me, but he was one-armed—and I had that arm in a tight grip. He couldn't help but go where I dragged him.

I didn't drag him far, only behind the jeweled skull. There, I went to my knees and pulled him down with me, so that we had Claw's precious heirloom between us and the beast. For good measure, I shifted my grip on Tarran and clamped a hand over his mouth and nose. He couldn't breathe behind my hand, and so he was forced to calm down. When I was sure he'd come all the way back from rage, I let him go. I pointed upward, then put a finger to my lips for silence. I could only hope that Claw's hearing wasn't so good that he'd catch the sound of my heart thundering.

We heard the beast eating, we heard the ripping of flesh, the crunching of bones. We heard the copper dragon lapping up steaming blood before it could all run off the ledge. I buried my face in my arms to hide from the reek, to keep from retching.

As Claw ate, groaning, a glutton over a feast, Tarran leaned close and by gestures let me know that the dragon would leave as soon as he'd fed, wanting water. I settled to wait, my hands shaking so hard I had to clasp them together, a fist against fear.

In a sudden silence, I heard the tapping of blood where

it dripped over the ledge and down to the floor of the lair. And then Claw rose up on massive hind legs, thundering pleasure, sated. Moonlight ran on blood-dripping fangs, and talons still clotted with gobbets of flesh. The light raced down the beast's crested neck, glinting from spine to spine, spinning down the copper scales. Claw stretched black wings, leathery and broad, then thrust them suddenly downward while leaping upward.

In the wake of his leaving, wind roiled the stench of his leftovers, blood and bone and the undigested contents of the creatures' stomachs.

Tarran and I scrambled out from behind the dragon skull and ran for the blood-wet stairs and the way out. We bolted past the heaped treasure as if it were no more worthy of a glance than the leavings of a gravel pit.

Claw must have seen something as he wheeled, turning, above the lair—the wink of starlight on my sword, the sudden shine of moonlight on Tarran's long knife, our shadows where none should be. The dragon screamed down on the opening to the lair, confusing the light.

Acid fell like rain, the dragon's deadly slaver hissing on stone. Things melted—golden rings and torques, a silver chalice, the rusty blade of the elf-queen's ruby sword. One single drop of acid hit my own sword. I only dropped it in time to save my hand. Claw screamed again, and I heard no dumb bestial roaring now, but one raging word.

Thief!

The sound of it rang through the cavern, echoing in the very bones of me as I fitted arrow to bowstring with clumsy, shaking hands. And then the dragon saw what we'd really been doing.

He howled, lunging at Tarran.

Desecrator!

All my carefully honed instincts took over. I was like a vessel for some cooler intent. I turned, drew, and let fly a steel-headed arrow. I missed the beast's eye by a hand's width, and the bolt caught up under a plate-scale. Howling curses, Tarran sent a dirk flying after my arrow, and that blade caught the beast in the unscaled place right under his left eye. Tarran shouted, "I'll blind you, you bastard!" and he threw another dirk just as I let loose another arrow.

But our target wasn't there. Thrusting down with leathery wings, Claw rose up to the opening in the ceiling.

The dragon was gone, and I hadn't clenched when most needed! I shouted gratitude to whatever god was listening.

"Too early for that," Tarran said. "He's just getting room for another dive. Come on!"

His warning was like a spur. Forgetting gratitude, and anything else that didn't have to do with survival, we ran for the stairs, scrambling around acid-hewn pits still hissing at the edges. But inside me, gleeful, a voice celebrated victory with laughter. I'd not clenched, nor frozen with fear!

The lair grew dark as the dragon came between us and the moons' light. The stairs were in reach.

Suddenly it wasn't *we* running—it was me scrabbling up the first few steps. Tarran slipped in blood, staggered, and fell as the beast came raging down again.

I turned on the stairs, arrow nocked to bow, and sent a steel-headed bolt right into the beast's gaping jaws. In the same instant, Tarran raised up on his knees—now his howling was for pain, his curses for helplessness—and let fly the jewel-hilted long knife and pierced the beast's tongue.

Claw bled, and he shrieked in fury and pain. He sheered away and thrust upward, out of the lair again. Tarran tried to get up, but he fell back. He'd broken an ankle.

"Go," he groaned. His face shone white in the moonlight; his eyes glittered dark as polished jet. Dread etched deep lines into the flesh of his face. "Now, Ryle. Go!"

I wouldn't, and I took a step toward him, down one bloody stair. Then I stopped, sweat running on me, cold as terror.

Something touched me. Not a hand on the shoulder, not a breeze wafting by, not anything like that. It was the dragon's thought, him perched on the lip of the opening in the roof of his lair and looking down like some enormous, brooding vulture.

Claw raised wings and beat up a wind so strong it flung me against the stone wall and held me there, a foul-smelling fist. The beast looked at me, a helpless thing, a useless thief come padding, a wretch on two legs. Him seeing me was like something cold and hard and sharp piercing the inside of me, where the heart is, and all the things I know and remember and hope and dread. In that moment, I stood more naked than the old brown bones scattered around the dragon's lair, and the beast hovered on the edge of the opening, moonlight darting from talons and teeth.

Aren't you going to help your friend, Ryle?

Tarran groaned. We knew it, both of us—he was bait again.

Are you afraid? Are you afraid you won't be fast enough? Or brave enough? Are you frozen there, Ryle Sworder?

My belly churned with the fear he accused me of; my hands shook so that the arrow I tried to nock rattled against the bow.

I'll give you the chance you didn't have the courage to take for your father. Claw laughed as he wove two nightmares into one. *Run for the dwarf, Ryle Sworder—I'll give you a count.*

"Ryle! Don't!" cried Tarran, cried the bait. "Don't!"

I tried to place the arrow again, and cut my hand on the steel head. Blood ran down my arm. I'd sent one arrow into the beast's mouth, another to wound him near the eye. He was hurt, but he was a long way from dying. This futile arrow of mine couldn't harm the beast.

With the voice of winter, Claw hissed: *The man's got no more courage than the boy, does he? The boar killed your father while you stood quaking, Ryle Sworder. Things don't seem much different all these years later.*

In Tarran's glittering eyes, in his hollow pallor, I saw sudden understanding and swift despair.

The dragon laughed, seeing into both hearts. *Tarran Ironwood! Old friend! Do you suppose he'll be calling this latest cowardice a 'hunting accident,' too?*

Tarran got to one knee, tried to get his good leg under him to rise. When he couldn't, he crawled, elbow and knee, elbow and knee again, an agonizing progress. He didn't get but a yard before he fell.

That dragon had the cold soul of a cat; he liked to play with prey. Laughing, he spread his wings, fanning the air. The stench of his feast filled the air with death-reek. Shadows skittered all over the lair and some magic—or guilty terror—changed every patch of darkness into the ghost of my father. And the bones littering the ledge were his, the blood staining the lair, even Tarran's panting groans as he tried to get to the stairs.

It was sweat or tears running on my face now. It felt like blood. It was going to happen again. As my father had died, so would Tarran die, killed by my fear. Or, as Tarran's kinsmen had, I would be killed taking the bait the dragon offered, the chance of saving Tarran's life.

You are helpless, Ryle. You have always been. Now Claw's voice was hollow, like a ghost's. *Helpless, useless, and it wouldn't have mattered if you had seen the boar in time. No puny arrow from your bow would have stopped it. Helpless!*

Utterly. Then, as now. And my puny arrows, the honed steel tips, wouldn't hurt Claw, but he could snatch Tarran up and dash him to death before ever I could reach him. There was no way to win this cruel game, as there had been no way to stop the boar fifteen years ago.

Fear drained away from me in one sudden rush. Shadows were shadows again, and no ghost was here to haunt me. Forgiveness is that achingly swift and final.

I turned to change my aim. Claw stopped laughing. In the silence I heard Tarran's labored breathing. I sighted down the sure, straight shaft, dead center on the dragon skull glittering in its jeweled garb. Swift, I caught the edge of the beast's unguarded thought.

Flame!

So had his mate been named, the copper she-dragon who'd shone like a blaze, like flash and glare and, in the light of the moons, like shimmering golden fire. And if my aim was true, my arrow would strike the brittle relic and turn it into a pile of gems and bone slivers. Claw and I both knew that.

"Tarran," I said, like a soldier snapping an order.

"Come here."

Elbow and knee, he crawled again, and it seemed like forever till he touched the first step with his hand. Claw rumbled. Fat drops of acid spilled down into the lair, hissing. But that was an empty threat, a useless gesture. If once that corroding slaver came so close as to splash near Tarran, I would loose my arrow. Claw knew that, and the knowledge was like an iron shackle on him as he watched Tarran make a painful way up, one blood-wet step at a time, bracing on one hand, dragging one leg, sweat running on him as if he were a man in a rainstorm.

When Tarran passed me on the stairs I couldn't watch him anymore, only hear him. A step at a time, I went up behind him. I never took my eyes off the dragon skull, and that wonder-dressed relic was like a lodestone locking my arrow's aim. Tarran got onto the ledge, the rounding gallery strewn with gore and bones and offal. He got into the shadow of the opening. His groaning sigh told me that he'd got as far as he could on his own.

Claw knew it, too, and he turned, his long neck snaking toward the gallery and the shadowed opening where Tarran lay.

The beast was just starting to laugh when I loosed my arrow, sent it whistling low through the lair. Moonlight winked on the steel head. The treasure-dressed skull, the relic of his beloved Flame, shattered like ice, shards flying everywhere.

Claw screamed as if he were dying, and I bent and lifted Tarran in my arms. He made no sound but one, a groaning like a man waking from nightmares. Or maybe that was me.

We were not hunted through the caverns, but the sound of Claw's grief, of Tarran's revenge, followed us all the way.

* * * * *

We came back to Raven at the end of the summer. It was no easy thing getting out of the caverns, and once out I wouldn't leave Tarran alone. I nursed him carefully, as if he were my kin. Once he said that he owed me a fee, for we'd not taken the smallest trinket from Claw's hoard. He said he'd make it good if I would wait till we got to Thorbardin, for he wasn't a poor man among those mountain folk. But I told him that I'd not be going to Thorbardin with him, though I admitted it would be a rare thing to see, the seven great cities under the mountain. I told him I'd tend him until he was well and able to make his way.

"Then I'm bound home," I said. "Back to Raven."

He smiled, that lean smile of his, and said he supposed he'd go with me to see his old friend Cynara. Later that day, he asked if I thought the ferryman's daughter would know me when we met again.

"Why not?" I asked, surprised into laughing.

"You're not the same boy who went out from there, Ryle. Take a look at yourself some time."

I did, in a still pool one morning while the mist was still rising, and I looked about the same as I always did. A little thinner in the face maybe, but about the same.

Still, Tarran was right about me not being the same as I used to be. When we came to the Whiterush, it was Reatha who brought the ferry across. She greeted Tarran gravely, but she lighted up to see me. Quietly, she asked if I was well. As quietly, I told her that I was. Smiling, golden at the end of the day, she knew the truth when she saw it, and she believed me.

We were married in the rose bower soon after. Tarran stood by me, and Cynara stood at Reatha's side. There was no jewel to be had for dressing my bride, only a thin gold band for her finger. And there was not a ghost in sight to stand between us.

Honor Is All

Mickey Zucker Reichert

A sheet of clouds reflected spring sunlight into a glaze over the salt barrens. The hooves of Mercanyin's bay gelding sank deep into the sand with each step, and the wheels of the wagon it drew seemed to catch on every straggling weed. Earlier, the lightweight borrowed cart had rolled over three times, but since the knight had transferred his armor and supplies to the wagon's bed for ballast the going had proven easier. Still, Mercanyin could not help but question his decision to lug the dragon's corpse back to the village the beast had terrorized, once he killed it.

Wind slashed the unprotected plain, whipping Mercanyin's overtunic and cape into a frenzied dance. The wind tore off his hood, spilling hair as coarse and dark as the horse's mane. He squinted, shielding hazel eyes from the blowing sand with one hand, using the other to support his lance in its rest. The wind hammered his ears, making them ache, but the pain only fueled his determination.

Many of the villagers claimed the dragon had never harmed man or woman, just stolen a few of the herdsmen's cows and sheep. A merchant blamed the beast for his brother-in-law's corpse found floating in the river, though the old cooper attributed the man's death to drowning in a drunken stupor. Few doubted the dragon had made a meal of the seamstress's missing child, though the woman herself was too traumatized to speak of the incident. Some said the dragon was as large as a dozen men; others claimed its shadow blotted the entire village and all its surrounding fields. Some said it spouted fire, and others that it left icicles on sun-warmed stones. One detail never varied: every person who had seen the monster described it as white as cream. And Mercanyin knew all white dragons were evil.

Evil. Mercanyin had needed to hear nothing more to send him charging recklessly toward battle. A year ago, when his younger brother attained the coveted rank of Lord Knight, honor and glory had become Mercanyin's obsession. No act of heroism seemed sufficiently grand, no number of good deeds enough to satisfy his craving. One way or another, he had pledged to become the most famous, the bravest knight in all Solamnia's history. He would scrupulously follow his oath and make his honor his life. Word of the dragon had drawn him to the village just as tales of assassins, shapechangers, and evil wizards had driven him to so many others. So many that he had forgotten their names and the countless disasters he had resolved or averted.

From the village, Mercanyin had seen the eastern foothills where witnesses claimed the dragon had its lair, but his first day's ride had seemed to bring him no nearer to them. On the second and third days, the foothills had appeared closer, but deceptively so. Now, as the fourth day dragged into afternoon, his horse finally reached the base of the first grassy hillock. The gelding lowered its head to graze, and Mercanyin jerked back on the reins. The bay snapped its head up, ears attentive, though it snorted its displeasure. Soon enough, it would have time to roam and eat in peace. First, Mercanyin needed to locate the dragon's den, preferably before the beast found him.

Unhitching the wagon, Mercanyin rode around the base of the hill-studded knoll. It was smaller than he had anticipated, an island in a vast plain of sand, nourished by a spring that wound toward the dark bulk of ocean hovering eternally on the horizon. A traveler, braver than most, had followed the dragon's roar to its lair near the center, nestled amid hillocks that protected it on every side from view and from weather. The man had even peered into the impenetrable darkness of front and back entrances, though there his courage had failed. Mercanyin appreciated the scouting. Spying like a common highwayman was beneath his dignity. Braver deeds fell to knights like him, the handling of perils from which lesser men cowered.

A bird trilled in a distant tree, its call echoing from one end of the knoll to the other. The happy song boded no danger, suggesting to Mercanyin that the dragon had either gone out or lay remotely tucked in its cave. The birdsong brought other memories, ones he had fiercely driven to the farthest corner of his thoughts and tried to smother beneath dangerous missions in the names of virtue, charity, and kindness. The face of his wife, Dameernya, appeared in his mind's eye: her sandy hair always tousled; the too-thin body; the large brown eyes full of love for all weak and helpless creatures. Though she was far from beautiful, her dedication to animals sick or injured had made him believe she could understand his own unwavering dedication to the order of knights and to the oath: My honor is my life. But it had all been a lie.

Mercanyin grimaced, intentionally blurring Dameernya's face beneath the image of every woman he had ever seen or met. He chased the memory back to its corner, but her last words to him still haunted. Dameernya's gentle voice vivid: "If your honor is truly your life, Mercanyin, then that's all you'll ever have."

All you'll ever have. Mercanyin dismounted, removing bridle, saddle, and lance methodically and placing them on the wagon. That's all I ever wanted. He tried to convince himself this thought was truth, but time had whittled the lie until it had become simpler to avoid thinking about it than to face brutal reality. Since that summer day nearly a year ago when his driving passion for honor had sent him packing his weapons and armor, leaving his wife and home without a backward glance, he had suffered from a different need that seemed equally unquenchable. Mercanyin could not identify the need. He knew only that it sent him roaming and fighting long after his childish quest for perfection had faded, looking always over the next mountain, the distraction of various combats seeming gods-sent though they never sated the hunger for what he sought but could not name.

The horse lowered its head to eat, and Mercanyin forced his thoughts back to the present. The animal would not stray with food and water so near and nothing but salt plains beyond. He focused on the dragon, glad to place all other thought back into the limbo where it could not judge him. He had a job to do, innocents to protect from evil, an honor to follow with a devotion few could understand. Those men content to toil at their petty jobs from day to day, while others fought their battles, could never know the hallowed dedication that led the Knights of Solamnia to follow the causes of right and goodness to— some would say—the extreme. Few had the courage to find such dedication inside themselves. And, like most things uncomprehended, the knights would always be worshiped, feared, and reviled. So Mercanyin believed, yet the familiar platitudes rang hollow.

For the knights, he had given up his one true love. He had abandoned his home and the animals Dameernya nurtured, giving them all the love she would have lavished on her children had she borne any. Home life and family had stolen too much of Mercanyin's attention, weakening his honor. Therefore, he had had no choice but to discard them.

Walking to the wagon, Mercanyin sorted out the pack containing armor, his spear, and his sword belt. His heart quickened with a combination of excitement and fear, as it always did before a worthy combat. He unlaced the pack, peeling back the leather to reveal the familiar armor of a Knight of the Crown. He laid out each steel and leather fitting into the best position for swift donning. Quickly, he doffed overtunic and cape, hefting breastplate over mail and padding. Each piece found its proper position in practiced movements, and he placed the gauntlets last, flexing his fingers to restore circulation. Spear and shield in hand, sword readied at his belt, he headed toward the center of the knoll. He would face the dragon boldly, glad to die for the honor he embraced.

A few strides carried him to a vast opening in the side of a hillock, gaping black against spring greenery, the front entrance precisely where the scouting traveler had said. Vines dipped across the opening, and fronds veiled it from the ground, but these were scant cover for the massive cavity, even discarding the telltale, trampled line of earth and shattered stems where the dragon must have touched down more than once. Footprints in the dirt stretched as long as Mercanyin's body, topped with claws the length of his forearm. His mind conjured an image of the creature in its entirety, and the perception of size momentarily froze him in place. He felt a cold wash of sweat beneath his armor and told himself it came of anticipation, not fear. The more tremendous the evil he destroyed, the larger the gain for the forces of good.

Drawing himself to his full height, Mercanyin shouted at the opening. "Dragon!" His voice echoed through the confines. He raised his shield and tensed, preparing to deflect or dodge the icy breath weapon.

Something swished and thumped inside the cave. Then silence returned.

Mercanyin cleared his throat. "Dragon!"

More movement followed from within, but no roar or wild scramble to indicate a coming attack.

"Dragon!"

This time, an answer emerged, the voice rock-steady but no louder than his own and also speaking the common tongue of mankind. "Go away!"

"Evil One, come forth and meet your destiny!" Mercanyin stood proud, honor a savage heat in his chest.

"My destiny is here," the beast replied, its voice tired. "Go away. I will not fight."

Mercanyin squinted, trying to catch a glimpse of the dragon in the darkness. Though he had never seen a dragon before, legend called the white ones haughty and solitary. His vision carved form from shadow. A gigantic, pale creature hovered well back from the mouth of the cave. Though blurry, the dragon's shape and size were unmistakable. If anything, it seemed larger than he expected.

"Your evil reign has ended," Mercanyin roared. "Come

out and fight, or die a cowering craven."

"I've done you no harm, nor any other, but I will kill in defense. Go away now, and no one will get hurt." Apparently, the dragon believed the conversation finished. Its whiteness shifted. Its horned head swung about amid a rattle of scales, and the tail lashed a semicircle through the gloom, its tip nearly clearing the cave mouth. It lumbered into the depths, soon lost to Mercanyin's sight.

Mercanyin lowered shield and spear, enraged by the dragon's refusal. He felt cheapened, as if the dragon did not find his pitiful goodness threat enough to attack. The uncertainty that had already begun to crack Mercanyin's faith now fueled his anger. He was seized by the sudden urge to charge into the cave, but common sense intervened.

Rushing the creature blindly in its own dark lair was certain death. He had little choice but to draw it out. The traveler had reported a hidden back entrance to the dragon's lair. It seemed likely the dragon would hide its hoarded treasures there. Mercanyin had little interest in baubles, but reclaiming some of its wealth might goad the loathsome beast into daylight and a battle.

Several hours of searching, tramping about in armor that seemed to grow heavier by the instant, only fueled Mercanyin's temper. By the time he found the natural slot that served as the dragon's back door, he had fallen often enough to permanently scratch his armor and stamp bruises on every limb. Stale sweat made his skin itch beneath the metal, and the white dragon seemed more evil for its reluctance.

Quietly, cautiously, Mercanyin slipped inside, prepared for a trap. The white dragon had played his emotions too well not to have met and vanquished warriors before. Perhaps it kept an entire collection of trophies—shields or skeletons won from knights who either believed the dragon's foolery, charged it in a heedless fit of rage, or exhausted themselves seeking a second entrance. He threaded through the wide passage that smelled of damp, moving deliberately to keep from clanging armor against stone, glad he kept its parts well oiled so they did not clink or creak. The shape of the cave would funnel the slightest sound into echoes, and he worried even for the soft rhythm of his breathing.

The cave widened. Mercanyin slipped around a corner and suddenly found himself in a naturally rounded cavern lined with sticks, fur, scraps of cloth, and white scales pulverized into a supple nest. His eyes adjusted to the darkness quickly, and his gaze flowed naturally to the brightest spot in the lair. A creature white as a hen's egg and large as a man curled in the center. He approached with silent anticipation, guarding each step to keep from crushing something that might shift or crack beneath his foot. He kept the spear clenched in one hand, the shield strapped to the other wrist.

Ironically, it was Mercanyin's caution that betrayed him. The more deliberate each step, the more debris seemed to appear beneath his feet and the more solidly he shifted his weight onto it. Shed scales, as bleached as old bone, crushed to powder beneath his boots. Then he inadvertently stomped on a branch, and it pivoted, sending a wave of rattles and snaps through the rubble. He froze.

A squawk sounded from deeper in the cave, followed by the leathery whisk and scrape of wingbeats. Mercanyin scarcely managed to couch his spear and raise his shield before the white dragon charged him. The beast whisked over the sleeping animal, head cocked back, claws splayed. Its blue eyes flickered red in a beam of sunlight winding through a crack in the wall. Its tongue streamed out, and it huffed out a blast of breath that swirled, cloudlike, through the intermittent light.

Mercanyin dodged, boot catching on the branch. He stumbled, fighting for balance he only half caught. He twisted as he fell, dislodging the spear. He tensed for the cold agony of the breath weapon, but the sensation he expected never came. Its effect went beyond cold, freezing every muscle into a tight spasm he fought to unlock. His shield skittered across stone.

The dragon's frenzied charge left it no chance for a sudden

stop. Momentum slammed the dragon into the fallen knight, bowling him over. The beast clung, massive claws raking Mercanyin's armor in a savage chaos of offense. One claw tore a gauntlet from his hand and the other gashed his cheek, the helmet all that saved his ear.

Pain mobilized Mercanyin, and he managed to tear free of the breath weapon that had paralyzed him beyond winter cold. He flailed for his sword, the effort more desperation than intent. His hand closed on the hilt, the tug that freed it opening his defenses. The dragon latched its jaws onto his left shoulder, teeth indenting armor, the pressure of its bite raw agony. Mercanyin swung in a pain-mad fury. The sword blade crashed harmlessly against scales.

The pain in Mercanyin's shoulder became anguish he could no longer bear. He reeled and lurched, panic threatening to usurp training. He clung to his honor, filling his mind with need. Good against evil. Right against wrong.

His honor rose to the challenge, lending the second wind he sought. He lunged for the spear, and his fingers thrashed against wood. He caught the shaft in his unprotected hand, the intensity of his grip driving splinters into his palm. The dragon's foot caught him a blow that dented his helmet and shocked pain through his head. Blinded by a flash of light that threatened to steal consciousness, he thrust for the beast's eye. Metal jarred through flesh. The dragon screamed, and the smaller creature behind it howled an echo. Mercanyin twisted. The spear shifted off bone, gliding deeper into what he could now see was the dragon's breast. Warm blood splattered Mercanyin, and he hoped it was not his own.

The beast reared with a cry more pained than angered. Its teeth fell away, and it flopped to the floor. Its limbs stiffened, tail lashing a rapid but undirected cadence. Then its blue eyes, softened by the glaze of hovering death, rolled to Mercanyin. "Do you grant your victims a last request?" it rasped, blood foaming from its mouth with every word.

Stunned by the appeal, Mercanyin gave no answer, just

fought to catch his own breath.

The dragon closed its eyes, finishing without awaiting a reply. "Please. Take care of my son. He's not what he seems." Great lungs heaving, it struggled to open one eye a crack. "And neither am I." The effort proved too much. The eye snapped closed, and blood washed from its jaws, coloring nose and teeth scarlet. All breathing ceased.

Mercanyin felt his own consciousness wavering. A swirl of pinpoint lights unfocused his vision, and a roar filled his head, growing louder. He dared not move, gripping the rock floor with fingers that felt thick and detached. Gradually, sight returned. The sound in his head diminished, then disappeared, leaving a silence interrupted only by regular grunts from deeper in the cave.

For now, Mercanyin ignored them, not wishing to face another dragon, no matter its size, so soon. He studied his dead enemy. The massive body sprawled on the stone floor, still and harmless in the gloom. Old wounds marred its hide, some unnaturally straight, obviously carved by sword or axe in combat. Others left the telltale, parallel gashes of claws or the raggedly edged ovals that indicated bites. One fleshy head horn ended in a tattered stump. Scars crisscrossed its snout.

Despite his hatred, Mercanyin knew a moment of pity for a creature his honor told him should never have existed for its evil. Despite its surely feigned reluctance, it had long known how to fight. He wondered if all dragons bore the marks of many combats. It seemed unlikely. Only the bravest of men would consider facing such a creature, and surely all but the most foolish predator would seek a less spirited meal. Mercanyin wondered why this particular dragon seemed the victim of so much violence. Its inherent evil did not seem enough for any but a dedicated knight; it had acted disinclined to do battle with him. A creature which spent much of its life causing strife would surely have seen a knight as a challenge, not an intruder to be ignored until he breached the lair and placed family in danger.

The end of the spear protruded from beneath the dragon. Mercanyin seized it, braced himself, and pulled. Broken, the weapon jolted free easier than he expected and sent him staggering backward. He caught his balance, vertigo buffeting him at the sudden movement. He held a blood-smeared, shattered shaft in his hands.

Mercanyin tossed the useless stick aside. It thunked hollowly against the cave wall, then rolled across the piled debris with a wooden clatter. The dragon's last words echoed through his head. All the legends and all his study told him that white dragons had no honor at all. From where, then, came the loyalty to its child that had made it fight when it would rather hide and goaded it to beg an enemy to raise its young? The need to question bothered Mercanyin more than the circumstances. Each of the evil creatures he had encountered would fling its own mother on the knight's sword if it might gain its own escape.

Mercanyin headed back toward the nest and the small white creature that must be the dragon's son. He did not feel bound by a promise to evil. Honor drove him to choose the moral path and to damn all consequence. Yet, the dragon's desperation seemed to echo through his heart; the words remained lodged in his mind. "Take care of my son." He owed an enemy nothing, yet he would examine this baby.

The hatchling huddled in the middle of the passageway. It resembled its parent closely in shape and color, although its immaturity was obvious. It lacked the adult's angularity, all edges rounded and pudgy. Though softer-featured than its elder, there was nothing attractive about the creature. Its long, hairless neck stretched from a body plated with white scales. Its beak splayed open, forked tongue protruding. Stubby wings beat backward at the sight of Mercanyin, and it opened its mouth wider, looking like some ancient, reptilian bird. From his years with Dameernya and her animals, Mercanyin suspected its motivations were similar. Too young to yet know friend from foe, it wanted to be fed.

Unsheathing his sword, Mercanyin stepped up beside

the hatchling. Its actions became more wild as he approached. Its bleats blended into a frenzy, and its mouth seemed to unhinge with anticipation. Huge blue eyes riveted on Mercanyin, full of an intelligence that seemed beyond its age, though not beyond its breed. *Human* eyes. Mercanyin freed his mind of the comparison. He faced a creature of ultimate evil. Though it was small now, he could not let it reach the size of its parent. Mercanyin raised his sword for the kill.

The hatchling's eyes followed the movement, but it did not cower or cringe. Clearly, it had no concept of death or danger, all-trusting like a human infant.

Since longer than a decade ago, when Mercanyin had internalized the knight's oath in a flash of what had seemed Paladine-inspired insight, he had never questioned. Now, a million uncertainties bombarded him at once. The feeling of something amiss that had hounded him since leaving Dameernya now ignited into a savage bonfire that finally allowed him to recognize doubt. *Doubt.* It consumed him, spreading from limb to mind to heart in an instant. Doubt assailed him in the form of a trail of clues he could not follow as well as an inner skepticism he dared not contemplate. Too many details of this dragon and its offspring did not fit into his neat and narrow view of a reality based on a single sentence and the three hundred volumes that defined it: My honor is my life. Mercanyin focused on the phrase, trying to use it to fuel a now-trite action that should not have required thought. But, instead of descending, the sword remained frozen in place. Slowly, Mercanyin lowered blade and arm.

Common sense told Mercanyin that this creature was evil. People, not magical creatures, were born innocent, sinless, without bent toward any form of behavior. Legends from sources he would never doubt told that every chromatic dragon was evil and every metallic good. Breeding, not environment, determined the nature of such creatures. Yet, the hatchling's eyes bespoke a different story: guileless, trusting, and ultimately needy.

Mercanyin sheathed his sword. It seemed like forever

since he had needed to consider his actions. Always, his honor rose to steer him toward the moral course, quelling any misgivings with an understanding of right. Now, for the first time, honor failed him. He felt utterly alone and as desperately needy as the hatchling. The hole inside him grew to a vast and lonely desolation. The answer finally came; it had eluded him before because his mind would not accept it. The thing that had made him incomplete, the nameless something he chased was the very thing he had tried to escape: *Dameernya*. His obsession for glory could not, by itself, carry him any longer. Certainly, there was room in his life for love.

Mercanyin sank to the ground, sitting, lost in thought. The dragon's hungry grunts became distant background to thoughts he had denied too long, hidden behind a code he had chosen never to question. *For all its evil, the dragon showed more honor than I. Even near death, its loyalty was to its blood first, while I abandoned my love.* Guilt swam down on Mercanyin, and the introspection opened him to other details. Many particulars about the dragon still did not fit. First, it was larger than his studies suggested it should be, nearly ten times rather than five times his height. Until now, he had passed this off as the exaggerated perception of an enemy, the same that made villagers describe a biting puppy as a wolf. But he did not usually fall prey to the delusions that gave credence to the puny accomplishments of small-minded men. The dragon was oversized.

Second, the dragon's reluctance to fight seemed out-of-place. Clearly, neither fear nor lack of ability accounted for this. Mercanyin would not delude himself. As in most battles against competent enemies, luck had played as large a hand as skill. He, not the dragon, could as easily lie dead on the cave floor.

The last incongruity placed the picture into full perspective. The breath weapon that had barely caught him and temporarily paralyzed him was the piece that jarred the most. At the time, he had expected a white dragon's icy breath, and his mind had clung to the image of freezing his muscles in place. Now, he could recall no sensation of coldness in the attack, and the exhalation had been more gaseous than conical and blasting. The answer came swiftly: Only silver dragons have a gas weapon that paralyzes.

Horror clutched Mercanyin's chest, and his heart seemed to stop beating, leaving him gasping for life and air. He leapt to his feet, heedless of the dizziness that washed down on him. His hands and feet went icy as his blood flowed to vital organs. He rushed to the adult dragon, drawing his knife as he ran.

It seemed like an eternity before he managed to pry a scale free with the knife, revealing a patch of skin as pink as a piglet's. He charged outside amid the yelping chorus of the baby dragon, holding the scale up to the evening light. It was white, pure white, without even a hint of metallic sheen.

The relief that flooded Mercanyin barely budged the grim certainty that he had murdered a creature of ultimate goodness, a dragon he should have sacrificed his own life to protect. His mind flashed again to the image of a piglet. Not all pigs were pink, only those that would become white as adults. Only those that were albino. Light sheened softly from the scale, though it seemed blinding in the wake of realization. Dameernya had nursed more than one red-eyed rabbit to health, the same unbreachable white as both of the dragons he had faced this day. Albino rodents had pink eyes. Others, like the pigs, the horse, and the human child he had seen, had blue eyes. Blue like the dragon's.

Remorse followed realization in a wild rush that nearly overturned reason. I killed one of the most powerful servants of goodness. A worse thought usurped the first. I nearly murdered a baby silver dragon as well. Tears of frustration burned his eyes, and guilt hammered mercilessly at his conscience. He did not rationalize or try to justify what he had done. Others would have fallen as easily to conclusions, but he was not others. The tatters of his honor told him to make amends, and he delved the means from his core.

I have to tend this baby. I have to raise it. Dameernya will know how. Mercanyin knew his wife had never before seen a dragon, but caring for animals of every kind came naturally to her.

"My honor is my life," Mercanyin whispered, yet the words seemed to have lost all their ability to charge him. The loss frightened him, and he felt wholly alone for the first time since his training as a knight. There was more to his life than being a Knight of Solamnia. There was Dameernya, if she had the grace to take back a husband so undeserving, and, now, the albino silver hatchling. He wondered if he could reconcile that to his honor, wondered even if he should. Too many, including those who followed the way of right most staunchly, lived by appearances alone.

The dying silver dragon had charged him with a responsibility he dared not trust to another. There were those who would use its presence in his house to defile the knights, who would see his association with a "white" dragon as proof that the Knights of Solamnia leagued with evil and should be loathed and rejected, even killed. There would be those among the knights themselves who would not believe or even stay to listen to his explanation. Surely, the dragon had suffered the same fate, despised by evil for its goodness and by those of good for appearances only.

Mercanyin headed back inside, his mind already churning over the many possible ways to transport the baby dragon to the wagon he had brought for its parent's corpse. Now, for the first time since his obsession with honor and fame had made a fool of him, the idea of displaying his prize and prowess made him blush, his glory becoming a shame as well as a regret. He had chosen a difficult course, yet one that was barely sufficient for atonement. In the end, he hoped, it would redefine rather than destroy his honor.

Mercanyin removed gauntlet and helmet, then headed back into the dragon's cave.

Easy Pickings

Douglas Niles

"CAUGHT 'EM WIT' THE RIVER BEHIND 'EM—MORE better for killin'," Chaltiford growled, excitement pounding within his barrel-sized chest.

"Stupid place to ride," agreed Delmarkiam Slashmaster, Chaltiford's tribal chief.

The two ogres stood on a grassy embankment overlooking a river valley. A file of armored riders—Knights of Solamnia—patrolled the near bank, moving steadily downstream. With the vast army of Huma and his dragons rumored to be far to the north, this detachment—better than three score knights—certainly faced terrible danger.

Though all the war chiefs had advanced to the lip of the promontory, as yet they had not been observed. Chaltiford's kinsmen, six dozen strong, hunkered down out of sight, as did the other numerous companies of the hulking, brutish humanoids. As the chieftain of a small tribe, Delmarkiam commanded a band of his village mates and cousins.

"They'll git too far away," Chaltiford warned.

Indeed, Chaltiford's company needed to strike fast—else the human riders would soon slip out of range.

"Charge!" bellowed Delmarkiam, never one for long command conferences.

Twenty chiefs shared approximately the same thought process, and a long, rippling bellow rumbled from the heights alongside the river. Now the knights looked up, immediately wheeling their heavy chargers toward the threat. Chaltiford imagined their fear as a thousand ogres pounded toward them, and the thought pierced him with a chill of pleasure.

The dozen clans of ogres, all united under the banner of the Dark Queen, pressed forward. For brief minutes—the

77

time it took to charge a half mile—Chalt relished one of the most glorious episodes in his long and violent life. The hulking brutes, charging line abreast, made the very ground rumble beneath their awesome onslaught!

Before them, the small company of heavily armored knights wheeled their horses in a tight circle, but they were not able to protect their flanks. And the river behind them, too deep to ford, effectively blocked their retreat.

A great stallion reared before Chaltiford, and he smashed at it with his club, breaking the steed's leg. The rider's sword slashed downward, biting the ogre's wrist, but Delmarkiam Slashmaster thrust his stone-tipped blade between Chaltiford and the knight.

The human grunted, wounded in the belly, and Chaltiford's club rose again, sweeping the luckless fellow from his horse. Eight or ten ogres crowded near to eagerly administer the final blows, while Delmarkiam slit the horse's throat as an afterthought.

Raising his bloody club, Chaltiford howled in triumph. His chieftain at his side, the ogre lieutenant lumbered deeper into the fray, pursuing his next victim.

But the knights resisted with surprising discipline and impressive ferocity. After the first clash they drew their horses tightly together. The ogres tried valiantly, but could not press close enough to drag the insolent humans from their saddles.

The knights made a series of gutsy countercharges, keeping their brutish opponents off balance. Chaltiford admired their bravery even as he lusted for their blood, but his club remained unwetted by further bloodletting. Howling in frustration, he hurled himself against the wall of bucking horses, falling back with bruises from many an iron-shod hoof.

Eventually, numbers prevailed, and the brutish ogres fully encircled the small band of riders. Axes and hammers rang against swords and shields, and the field resounded with the clash and chaos of a fine battle. Cries of men, ogres, and horses mingled in a cacophony of pain and rage.

Still, less than half of the humans had been knocked from their saddles when Chaltiford's eyes swept skyward, compelled by some gut premonition.

Sleek metal death swooped toward him. The dragons of Huma had come, and now they dove from the heavens in gleaming savagery, golds and silvers, brasses and bronzes, all bearing riders—and many of the riders wielding the deadly lances that had so decisively turned the tide of the war.

The entire force of ogres quailed before the sight of the mature serpents. Many of the huge humanoids fell to the ground, groveling pathetically, too terrified even to try to fight the great wyrms.

The mounted knights found new life and lunged forward in an unexpected charge. Chaltiford raised his club, barely knocking aside a blow that would have split his face. Delmarkiam stabbed at a charging horse, but sliced at thin air. In an instant, it seemed, the knights had erupted through the ring of ogres.

The full fury of the dragons was vented on the fleeing ogres. Chaltiford's lair mates bled to the cut of talon and fang, or died in agony beneath scalding fireballs of dragon breath and the spittle of caustic acid. For frantic minutes Chaltiford's own life became a terrifying collage of near-fatal encounters with death.

He saw Delmarkiam borne to earth, crushed by powerful claws. The dying ogre cried out to his friend, but Chalt scrambled away, terrified by the nearness of the dragons.

Other wyrms soared past, blotting out the sun. Chaltiford dove to the moist earth and buried his face in the mud, quivering in horror as ogres to his right and left were rent by the claws of a huge gold dragon. Snapping jaws tore away most of one of his ears as he desperately crawled away.

The ogre dove for some bushes, feeling the searing explosion of a dragon's breath blossoming over his head—just high enough to spare his life, though crackling blisters rose on his back, and the long pigtail on the rear of his scalp was singed to ashes.

Clear of the immediate battle, Chaltiford rose to his feet and lumbered for the shelter of a nearby forest. Even then he was not completely safe, however, as an intrepid knight galloped after him on his great, barded charger. The ogre barely reached the entwined branches in time, plunging through a thicket of thorns with the knight's lance prodding him in the heel. Prickly branches tore Chaltiford's burned, bruised flesh, but his pain only drove him to greater panic and more desperate flight.

Only after hours of gasping, terrified running did he dare to slow his pace to a stumbling walk. As he blindly plodded along, his storm of emotions obscured any immediate sense of fatigue.

Chaltiford was wounded, angry, defeated, humbled, frustrated . . . a bleak and depressing litany. Yet he could not forget that, most of all, he was *alive!*

"A hundred curses on the Knights of Solamnia!" he snarled aloud, half expecting the trees on either side of the trail to cower in terror at the fierceness of his voice. After all, there had been a time here in the Kharolis Mountains when the bark of an ogre was a feared and respected sound! Of course, that had been in the time before the knights, and the dragons of metal, and the accursed lances, Chaltiford reflected ruefully.

Why did they have to fight an enemy so brutally capable? He groused that complaint over and over, telling himself that the Dark Queen's war had become a gigantic waste of time and blood. Ogres against knights and dragons? Too many ogres were getting killed.

What he needed were some easy pickings, Chaltiford decided. He was a big, strong ogre—he should be able to find something small and weak, like in the old days, and bash it pretty good. From now on, *that's* what he'd make sure to do. Chaltiford was done with wars and campaigns and battles against fire-breathing, flying serpents!

He maintained his trudging march for many days. His course took him deep into the Kharolis Mountains—not for any particular reason, but because his fear-crazed instincts told him that the rugged heights offered him some refuge from the hateful humans and their wretched allies, the dragons of metal.

Of course, in mountains the threat of dwarves was always present. Chaltiford knew dwarves, had killed many of the scrappy, bearded warriors, and he loathed them nearly as much as he did the Solamnics. But he knew that Thorbardin lay far to the south, and dwarves in this range were pretty scarce. For the time being, Chaltiford would have to take his chances against the possibility of dwarves over the certainty of the dragons and knights who ruled the plains of Solamnia.

He was trekking wearily through a rocky, barren vale when the ogre chieftain saw something that stopped him in his tracks. At first he feared that all his evasions had been for naught. Sunlight, slanting low over the western ridge, reflected over a gleaming surface before him—a skin of rippling scales, each as bright as a polished coin of purest gold.

Dragon! The big, serpentine body sprawled on a mountainside no more than a half mile away. The wyrm lay at the base of a sheer precipice, and for the moment at least had not noticed Chaltiford's presence.

The ogre's knees went rubbery, and he slumped to the ground with a low moan. Eyes wide, he gaped at the immense golden serpent that he hated and feared more than anything else. The creature lay, apparently sunning itself, on a rough and steeply sloping ridgetop of boulders. The cliff beyond the dragon extended upward for thousands of feet, culminating in one of the highest peaks in this part of the Kharolis Range.

Had the dragon spotted Chaltiford? The ogre wasn't sure—though the dragon had not moved. Then Chaltiford realized something, as the dragonfear slowly dissipated. There was nothing in this dragon's manner, Chaltiford told himself with growing cockiness, even to suggest that it was *alive!*

The ogre's drooping lids descended over his wicked, piglike eyes as a look of crafty appraisal replaced the stark terror that had distorted his face moments earlier. Climbing to his feet, Chaltiford scuttled to a nearby boulder. The stone jutted upward from the ground, high enough to screen him from the recumbent dragon. Peering around the rock, he studied the motionless creature.

Sure enough, Chaltiford spotted a gaping tear in the creature's neck, and its wing lay sprawled beside it in an awkward fashion, wrenched from its proper alignment.

Shrewdly, the ogre studied his ancient enemy. Chaltiford shuddered with revulsion even as he gloated over this dragon's predicament. The creature must have been truly awesome when it was alive, for its body was uncommonly huge. How much treasure might a wyrm like that acquire during a lifetime? Surely, an unimaginable amount!

As the thought entered his mind, another followed in unusually rapid sequence. Whatever treasure this dragon had amassed had to be presently unguarded!

Of course, the creature could have ended up here after flying from a virtually unlimited distance. But from the severity of its wounds, Chaltiford guessed that the dragon had not traveled very far in its weakened state. No, the golden serpent had been right in this vicinity, he suspected, when grim fate claimed it.

Trembling, Chalt crept closer. Even dead, the monster remained massive, awe-inspiring, and horrific. It was all the ogre could do to force his wobbling legs forward. Yet as he continued his cautious approach, and no sign of movement rippled those golden scales, Chaltiford began to master his fear.

By the time he had reached the massive corpse, the ogre was practically swaggering, puffing his chest outward and balancing his club on his shoulder at a jaunty angle. He stepped right up to a massive, lifeless limb, and even thought about delivering a scornful kick. Chaltiford contented himself by spitting in the dragon's direction.

The ogre's bloodshot eyes glittered as he inspected the corpse of his race's dread enemy. He saw that one of the dragon's wings was crumpled and scarred, as if it had suffered a grievous wound a long time ago. Chaltiford reasoned that, even after that wound had healed, the dragon had been unable to fly.

Other wounds were far fresher, and these the ogre deduced to be the mortal ones. Though no master of logic, Chaltiford had seen enough mangled flesh and dead or dying bodies to understand the general nature of fatal injury. A long gash tore the dragon's neck, and the ogre knew this to be the deathblow. Yet the golden wyrm had not succumbed to a weapon, for not even a dragonlance would inflict a wound so deep and wide.

Instinctively the ogre's eyes tilted, examining the steep face of rock stretching skyward to a high, snow-swept summit. Halfway up the cliff he saw a protuberance of rock. Dull brownish stains intermixed with a few flecks of golden scales marred the surface of that outcrop and confirmed Chaltiford's hunch: The weakened dragon had toppled, breaking its neck in the plunge.

Why was the dragon alone, here, when so many of its kin waged war over the plains? Of course, with its impaired wing the serpent would have been little use in the great flying formations—but then, why had it tried to ascend such a lofty and steep-sided peak? Ideas tugged at Chaltiford's avaricious mind.

A clattering of stones caught the ogre's ear. Whirling, the brute raised his club and squinted along the mountainside. Several pebbles rolled out from beneath the dead serpent's tail.

Chaltiford crept forward, club raised. He stooped to investigate, peering into a shadowy niche where the dragon's tail slumped over a pair of rocks.

Two golden eyes blinked fearlessly back at him. The dragon he saw was a miniature of its mother, though at barely two feet long it held none of the fearsome majesty of the adult wyrm. Too, its wings were tiny and not yet usable. The little creature took a step forward. When the tiny head emerged from the shadows, Chaltiford brought his club down in a sharp strike, smashing the serpentine skull with a single blow.

Then he froze, excitement tingling through his veins.

Why would this dragon's hatchling be around? The answer was obvious—somewhere nearby was the dragon's lair!

He saw gouges near the top of the cliff—surely the dragon's claws had made them, scratching desperately as it lost its balance and fell. With fierce glee, he made out, above the talon marks, the shadowy outline of a cave's mouth.

He had found the dragon's lair.

Trembling with joy, Chaltiford appraised the towering mountain. To the right and left of him were more gradual shoulders of rock. These, too, were steep, but the ogre— no stranger to mountainous terrain—knew that he could climb either side. Obviously, the flightless hatchling had made the easy descent.

The certainty that above him waited the dragon's lair proved a powerful intoxication. A mighty serpent such as this must assuredly have been guarding a veritable hoard of treasure!

The day's sunlight was already fading, so the ogre forced himself to rest for the night, intending to begin the climb with the dawn. Curling up between a pair of jutting rocks—not too close to the dragon's lifeless form—Chaltiford fell into a deep, restful sleep. His slumber was broken by pleasant dreams, in which he was surrounded by mountains of gold, which shimmered like a hundred brilliant suns.

When he awakened, he wasted no time. He bounced to his feet, hoisted his club, started toward one of the mountain's steep, curving shoulders, and began plodding up the rock-strewn base.

Steadily he climbed. Behind him lay a vast panorama of mountains, ridges, and valleys. Yet the ogre's eyes did not turn from the rocks in front of him, and he moved continually upward, toward that black hole on the mountain's peak.

The going was rough, and in places Chaltiford was forced to sling his club through his belt so that he could use both hands to assist his climb. Nevertheless, he had climbed many such challenging slopes—and never with such a compelling inducement.

The lure of treasure grew vivid in the ogre's mind. The images of his dream, shimmering mountains of gold, fevered his imagination. Riches! Chaltiford knew he was on the verge of great wealth. When he returned to his village, the ogres would chant his name, telling the tale of his triumphant accomplishment. He would have his pick of the females, he knew, and even the swaggering young males would stare dumbly in awe at the wondrous wealth of Chaltiford!

Ogres loved gold without reason. In this, though in few other ways, they were much like dwarves. Gold seduced them, more than anything else. Just the nearness of the precious metal caused them to salivate. To possess gold overshadowed all other possible rewards.

The ogres of Chaltiford's village had been suffering from near-starvation when the Dark Queen's scouts had come to recruit them for war. Yet, when offered their choice of payment, none of the humanoids had asked for food. Instead, each had desired gold. The human commanders had engaged their services for paltry nuggets. Now those tidbits would be mere baubles compared to the treasure that was about to become Chaltiford's—and his alone!

How much gold would he find in the great dragon's hoard? Would there be piles of coins or trunks of nuggets? Perhaps—the very thought took his breath away—he would find a stack of gleaming ingots, each weighing as much as a kender!

Of course, there would doubtless be gems and silver and other ornaments, and these, too, Chaltiford intended to claim. Silver would provide gifts for the wenches back home, while the other trinkets might prove useful for barter on the road. But the thought of these paled beside the gold that drew him upward.

His mind thus occupied, Chaltiford took little note of the passing of the day. When he finally paused to reflect on his progress, he realized he had almost reached the top of the mountain—and that the sun had already dropped far into the western sky.

From the crest of the ridge, the ogre saw the dragon's lair—with its wide, shadowy mouth. Excitedly, the ogre started to inch toward it along a flat shelf of rock. With his long arms, he reached to grasp a tight crack in the rock wall as a handhold. Shuffling his feet sideways, he edged closer to the lair. The ledge was not very wide, and in some places Chaltiford's heels hung suspended over a many-thousand-foot drop.

Each step was made with painstaking care, and each move necessitated a firm handhold. In this slow fashion, Chaltiford made remarkably good time, and within an hour the shadowy, arched entrance of the cave was within reach—just slightly overhead.

Now he strained to lift the bulk of his massive body upward. His rough-toed boots clawed at the rock, scrambling for lift, and a haze of red floated across his eyes as he grunted and gasped. With one mighty push, Chaltiford rolled up and forward and—despite the proximity of the lair—panted for several minutes before he felt ready to stand and begin plundering.

Rising to his feet, he peered into the shadow-darkened cave. Behind him, the full glory of the Kharolis range spilled into the distance, yet his attention remained riveted on the immediate goal of the lair.

For the first time a glimmer of fear tugged at him. He unslung the club from his belt, and the easy heft of the weapon considerably bolstered his courage. The smooth cavern floor beckoned him inward, and he carefully stepped under the arched roof.

Quickly his eyes adjusted to the darkness. His feet crunched over brittle rocks, and he looked down to see well-chewed shards of bone covering the floor. Several skulls—of deer, mountain sheep, and elk—lay scattered about. The rest of the bones had been broken and splintered by something eager to get at the rich marrow inside.

Another few steps brought Chaltiford within sight of a huge bundle of twigs and hide. It resembled a bird's nest, though it could easily have held the ogre and a pair of his kinsmen. Looking within, he saw shards of eggshells.

The nest proved beyond a doubt that this was the dragon's lair. Somewhere within—probably in the farthest recess of the cave—Chaltiford would find the serpent's riches. The thought sent tingles of pleasure rippling through his body, bringing goosebumps across the surface of his pale, bristle-stubbled skin.

Crushing shell fragments beneath his boots, Chaltiford stomped through the nest and probed deeper into the cave. The winding passageway continued inward, branching into numerous large chambers. Some of the corridors must have been uncomfortably narrow for the huge serpent, Chaltiford mused to himself.

The ogre advanced cautiously through several of these chambers, swinging his club this way and that. His eyes, shining with avarice, strained to penetrate the gloom.

He heard a scuttling, rodentlike sound. Whirling, he saw nothing but shadows and motionless rock. *There!* Something raced through the air with frightening speed, and Chaltiford yelped in surprise. Instinctively the ogre threw himself to the floor, only then realizing that he had been startled by bats. Hundreds of the tiny creatures winged overhead, flying out from the depths of the cave. In a few seconds, the plague of bats had passed.

The ogre snorted contemptuously, dusting himself off as he rose to his feet. Again he hefted the club, feeling the reassuring weight of its grip.

The next chamber in the cavern network proved unexpectedly large. A high ceiling, studded with iciclelike spires of dangling stone, arched well over his head. Pools of still, clear water dotted the floor. Beside these he found many fish skeletons, picked clean of meat.

Moving through this large cave, Chaltiford thought once more that he heard something moving behind him, but he saw nothing. Transferring his club to his left hand, the ogre found a good-sized chunk of rock and hoisted it in his right fist. Still walking, he swiveled his blunt neck to the right and left, daring the darkness to show any sign of movement.

The cave was silent as he crossed to the far end. A narrow arch led to a winding corridor, and he followed this for a dozen paces before the walls opened to each side, and he once more found himself in a large, subterranean chamber. Unlike the previous rooms, however, this portion of the cavern had no smooth floor.

Instead, the stone before the ogre's feet tumbled steeply away. Chaltiford could barely make out the rough, rocky bottom of a pit, some twenty or thirty feet below. The depression filled most of this cavern, though narrow, crumbling shelves of rock extended around the sides. Beyond the pit, the brutish humanoid saw the darkened archway leading to yet another underground chamber.

Something glimmered within that room, and Chaltiford's heart pounded. His palms grew slick with sweat as he squinted, straining desperately to penetrate the gloom. His eyes slowly confirmed what his mind had dared to hope.

The ogre's jaw dropped in amazement. Here was gold—a small mountain of it, just as he had pictured so vividly in his imagination! Even the shadows could not conceal the luster of the smooth coins.

Other colors glittered and teased him. He saw the lustrous green that could only mean emeralds, and many a crimson speck signified rubies. Larger objects of green and black he suspected were jade, while garnets, agates, and turquoise all added their multihued brilliance to the heaping mound of treasure.

Chaltiford licked his lips, unaware that drool had begun to trickle down his many-folded chin. Only a supreme effort of his dim brain stopped him from flinging himself across the pit in a desperate effort to leap to the other side.

He forced himself to look for a path around the obstacle. Either of the rubble-strewn ledges, he decided, offered a potential way. So, with a shrug of his stooped shoulders, Chaltiford headed toward the right. Peering into the pit, he noted that though its depth varied, it did not threaten a fatal fall. The bottom was strewn with irregular rocks, however, which would make for a very uncomfortable landing, so the ogre took great pains to make sure that he didn't miss a step.

Fortunately, there was room for him to walk without clinging to the wall with both hands, so he kept his club ready, swinging it with his left hand as he eased forward simply because the heft and feel of it reassured him and increased his confidence.

Not that he had anything to worry about, he reminded himself.

He heard scampering steps behind him and twisted around so that his back was against the wall. He was startled to see another minuscule dragon, leaping along the ledge just a few feet behind him. The head was no larger than a snake's, supported by a supple, curving neck. The creature's forefeet were tipped with sharp claws, and despite its tiny size it regarded the hulking humanoid without any obvious trace of fear.

Chaltiford's club smashed downward, splintering stones and scattering gravel, but the little dragon darted spryly backward before the blow struck.

The hatchling was darn fast for such a tiny creature, the ogre admitted to himself. If that had been a rat or squirrel—creatures of comparable size—the blow would have certainly splattered it all over the ledge. Yet the dragon had seemed to disappear even as the club started its downward plunge!

The important thing was that it had gone, Chaltiford told himself. It couldn't have hurt him very much, but the last thing he wanted was a pesky wyrmling nipping at his heels while he made this treacherous crossing.

Another step of his heavy boot knocked loose stones free from the ledge, and Chaltiford realized that the traverse was a little more challenging than he had first suspected. The ledge narrowed, and he was forced to turn his face to the cavern wall as he balanced on his toes for support. The rock surface was pitted and scarred with numerous cracks and holes, so at least he found plenty of handholds. He still clutched the heavy club in his left fist.

Irritatingly, the little dragon had appeared once again, scampering behind him on the ledge. It stood, a miniature image of its mother, staring upward at the ogre from about ten feet away. Tiny wings unfurled, flapping awkwardly, though—like its sibling down by the mother's corpse—Chaltiford knew the creature was still too young to fly. A tiny, forked tongue slipped between needle sharp teeth, and the creature's eyes glowed with a strange urgency.

There was enough menace in those little fangs for the humanoid to consider turning back and chasing the creature off the ledge—or preferably killing it—before he continued on to claim the treasure.

But the nearness of that gilded mound proved too strong a lure. With a sharp kick, the ogre sent the wyrmling scrambling away. Only then did Chaltiford continue his cautious traverse of the ledge. Loose stones tumbled away with each step, and the ogre concentrated on maintaining a tight grip with his free hand while he carefully examined the footing below.

More noises scratched the ledge behind him. Cursing, the huge humanoid wished he had left the club in his right hand—the hatchling was close by, but the ogre's precarious balance made it difficult for him to transfer the weapon. Even so, with his toes wedged firmly against the ledge, Chaltiford reached around behind himself to pass the club to his other hand. Now he raised the knobby stick, waiting for the little dragon to move just a tad closer.

Yet the creature hung back, regarding him with those penetrating eyes. Again the ogre almost started after it, but he knew by now that the wyrmling could flee far faster than the humanoid could pursue. Instead, Chaltiford turned back toward his goal, relieved at least that he was about halfway around the pit.

Once again he heard that familiar clattering of claws on stone—but this time the sound originated in front of him. On the ledge in his path another little dragon sat patiently, well out of striking range. And even if the serpent had been closer to him, Chaltiford snorted angrily, once again he held the accursed club in the wrong hand!

Of course, this hatchling wasn't about to stop him either! Grimly, the ogre continued on, kicking the ledge clear of loose rubble. His face was pressed close to the stone wall, and out of the corner of his eye he saw that the first wyrmling had again followed him onto the ledge.

Cursing, Chaltiford made out the outlines of several more little dragons, cautiously emerging from the darkness behind their bold sibling. When he twisted his face back to the left, he saw that more of the hatchlings had joined the one that blocked his forward path.

There was no doubt in the ogre's mind as to his course of action—he *had* to go forward. That treasure still beckoned, and he was not about to be deprived of his rightful reward. The insignificant lizards regarded him with huge, fascinated eyes, but made no move to retreat as he drew closer. Waving his club at the serpents to his rear, he again propped himself on his toes and reached his hands around his back to transfer the weapon to his other side.

It was then that he noticed the tiny dragon crouched in the shadows of a crevice right before his face.

Chaltiford blinked, crossing his eyes to focus on the serpent barely a foot from his nose. Tiny jaws gaped, showing an array of truly large teeth.

The wyrmling's eyes flashed wickedly as it gulped a huge breath. Golden scales bulged outward on the swelling chest, and then a small puff of flame belched from the serpent's widespread mouth. Fire seared Chaltiford's face, burning away his eyebrows and sizzling the skin of his bulbous nose.

With a bellow of pain, Chaltiford lunged away from the dragon—and away from the ledge upon which he stood. Tumbling backward, he flailed through the air until he crashed onto a pile of jagged boulders that comprised the floor of the pit. Bones snapped in his legs and shoulders, while his club clattered to the ground some distance away.

And again he heard that sound—the clicking of tiny

claws against the stone. Even blinded by fire, the ogre could easily locate the dragons by the clicking sounds. The hatchlings were creeping closer, climbing down the walls of the pit with no apparent difficulty.

Agony tore at Chaltiford's body, but he could do little more than groan. None of his limbs responded to the desperate commands from his mind. Though he strained to see, his eyes refused to function.

Instead, he listened in horror as the serpents advanced. They came from all around him, a hideous parody of the golden coins that had surrounded him in his dream.

Now he understood that peculiar urgency he had sensed in the hatchlings' eyes. The dragons' expression was only natural, he realized as he gritted his teeth in pain. After all, their mother was dead, and they had been left alone in the lair for a long time. The explanation was a simple one:

They were hungry.

A Dragon to the Core

Roger E. Moore

The third eviction notice arrived in the morning's post during a late spring thundershower. The landlady knew about gnomes and their mechanical devices firsthand (she had been caught in an Entrance and Egress Facilitation Device once), and so chose to contact her diminutive tenant from afar.

The rain-soaked postman, too, knew about gnomes firsthand. He had learned long ago not to put his hand inside the traplike opening of the steel Missive Receptacle outside the gnome's office. Now he approached with considerable caution. Holding the letter by a corner and taking care not to stand directly in front, he gently put the letter into the box without touching any part of the metal. He then flipped the letter in and jerked his hand back. The lid snapped shut with a loud clang. The postman sighed with relief and went on his way, fingers intact.

Gilbenstock, the person to whom the letter was addressed, was busy at his desk when the mail arrived. He took no notice as a large machine mounted to the wall by the front door—the Reactive Interceptor of Posted Parcels and Envelopes (Redesigned)—chugged loudly to life. The letter avoided being cut into confetti by the letter-opening blades (the fate of the first eviction notice) or being caught in the rollers of the letter conveyor and becoming so smudged with oil that it looked like an overused grease rag (the fate of the second). It was gently plucked from the belt by a mechanical arm, which crumpled the letter into a peach-sized wad and placed it on the gnome's desk.

Gilbenstock spent another fifteen minutes putting the final touches to his latest set of plans for a gigantic rock-boring machine, this one capable of drilling a perfectly triangular hole through a mountain, assuming anyone ever had a need for such a thing. "You never know where the next trend will be in tunnel boring" was one of Gilbenstock's favorite phrases, along with "That should do it," or "I put the rent money in the mail just yesterday," or "We'll have to watch for collateral damage when I turn it on, of course."

"That should do it," he said with an air of satisfaction, putting down his pen. He automatically reached for the wad of paper on his notepaper-covered desk, unwadding it without once taking his eyes off his finished sketches. Beaming with excitement, he glanced over the eviction notice, set it on a two-foot stack of papers in a box labeled "To Do," and got down from his stool. Stretching, he straightened his rumpled work clothes and wandered off into the kitchen, the door banging shut behind him.

"No broccoli," he growled after a brief search of the shelves. "I was positive I told Squib to pick up some at the market yesterday." He went back to the door and looked into the office room. "Squib! Squiiiiib!"

A rustling noise came from behind one of the many stacks of notepaper around the office. Moments later, a shabby dwarf only half a foot taller than the three-foot seven-inch gnome crawled from behind the stack and got unsteadily to his feet. Brown hair askew and beard sticking out in all directions as if it had been hit by lightning, the gully dwarf gave the gnome a cross-eyed salute as he sucked in his lips over crooked teeth.

"Ah, there you are," Gilbenstock said, going back into the kitchen. "Excellent. I've been searching for some broccoli for lunch. I've just finished a new set of plans that are certain to improve our financially challenged condition of late, and I should mail them out to potential . . ."

Hungry himself, the gully dwarf wandered over to the kitchen and was almost knocked to the ground as the gnome flung the door open and ran out, eyes as big as saucers.

Gilbenstock ran to the "To Do" stack and snatched the wrinkled eviction notice from the top. He held it up to the desk lantern as he read it a second time.

"Great Reorx!" he shrieked. "I put the rent in the mail just yesterday or maybe it was before then by a week or two, but still I can't believe she would throw me out of my office! *Three months* she says the rent is overdue! That's impossible, because now I remember that I filled out the bank note and stuck it in an envelope and handed it right to you, Squib, and the note covered our rent for the next three . . ."

Gilbenstock's voice failed him as he saw faithful Squib's face light up. The gully dwarf reached into a back pocket of his pants and pulled out a wad of stained, crumpled paper. With a broad grin, he held it aloft and handed it to the gnome.

Gilbenstock felt a need to sit down. He pulled up a stool, took a seat, and unfolded the paper. After looking it over, he closed his eyes. The paper fell to the floor.

"You were supposed to mail this," he said, without looking up at Squib. "I've spent all the rest of our money on food and had to borrow even more to pay the rent on the workshop so our bank account is empty because I was expecting another geological survey job right about now but now we're being evicted and I was going to make broccoli but maybe we can get something for dinner out of the garbage somewhere if I don't throw up first."

The gnome sighed deeply, then stood erect to his full though minuscule height. He absently brushed at his white beard and straightened his green vest. "We shall still persevere, patient Squib," he continued, though Squib was no longer there. "I've lived among humans for most of my life, and there have been financially challenging times before, and we shall yet see this one through, too. A righteous dragon has courage, and it knows what it must do and does it, so we must be like dragons inside, strong and brave and resolute. Just like dragons, Squib."

But for an instant, Gilbenstock's spirits flagged. Failure likely meant he would have to leave mighty Palanthas, jewel of all Ansalon, and return to the gnomish homeland of Mount Nevermind. The need for geological surveys was certainly greater at Mount Nevermind, built as it was into a dormant volcano, but getting paid for jobs was impossible. The Grand Bank of Nevermind had switched to a new accounting system after the War of the Lance and now the finances of hundreds of businesses and guilds were hopelessly fouled. Gilbenstock had left twelve years ago to try his luck in Palanthas.

It had been hard going here. Twelve years spent at odd jobs and menial labor in an unfriendly city, scraping together the money and materials to build his business and assemble the parts needed to build the Iron Dragon, his great mining machine and the core of his life. Twelve years spent learning the peculiar ways of humans, to the point where Gilbenstock was shocked to find he sometimes even thought and spoke in short sentences like them. The best part of those years were the moments he'd spent working on the Iron Dragon, fitting every nut and bolt into place in the warehouse he'd rented a few blocks away.

Gilbenstock grimaced, unconsciously rubbing his large nose. He did not want to leave Palanthas. He had grown fond of the great city, thick with wonder and magic, filled with aching beauty and wretched squalor. He had been glad to leave the noisy confinement of Mount Nevermind to see the "real world."

Gilbenstock wasn't like other gnomes. He understood humans sometimes, for one thing. More remarkably, his inventions worked more often than not. One even had marketable qualities—his Semi-Hermetic Receptacle Eradicating Debris by Dilution, Excitation, and Rotation. But it still needed work to avoid turning soiled laundry into strips of ripped cloth.

He had a good life here. He had his business. He had the Iron Dragon. He had trusty Squib, his only friend and the only person he trusted to pilot the Iron Dragon. Even if the gully dwarf couldn't speak a word, Squib was a genius at operating mechanical things.

But there was little else of cheer. He and Squib would starve in the warehouse with only motor oil and machine parts for food. No, correct that—only he would starve. Squib habitually ate out of the garbage behind produce and butchery shops; Gilbenstock was too proud and had too weak a stomach to even think of that. The gnome stared at his shoes in abject depression. No new plans came to mind.

Perhaps there was some nutritive value in motor oil.

There was a sudden, strong knock at the door. The gnome jumped, then yelled for Squib. The gully dwarf had disappeared again. Muttering to himself, Gilbenstock crossed the threshold and threw open the door.

Three men stood outside in the pouring rain, oblivious to the streams of water that ran down their faces. One was gangly and red-bearded, one was tall and black-haired, and one was thick-muscled and blond. For a reason he could not fathom, Gilbenstock had a momentary impression that all three were brothers.

"Good . . . sir," said the closest, the red-bearded man. He smiled as he spoke, but hesitated between words as if unfamiliar with the language. "Gilbenstock Mines and Minerals Survey for which we are looking." He waited for a response.

Gilbenstock blinked, his breath shallow. All three men were staring at him in a very peculiar way, but they did not appear to be armed or unfriendly.

"I'm Gilbenstock," he said finally, remembering to speak like a human.

At that, the three men smiled broadly, showing all their teeth.

"Gilbenstock, very good," said the red-bearded man. "Very good. A mine we wish a survey from you. You we wish hire."

Gilbenstock simply stared back at them. "You wish to hire me," he repeated. Then it hit him. "Oh!" he gasped. "Oh! Oh, yes!" Forgetting himself completely, the gnome slammed the door shut and ran back into his office, heading for his desk. He scattered papers madly, searching for his business files. Then he remembered the door and rushed back, flinging it wide open in a panic. The three men were still there, standing in the rain in their soaking clothes.

"By Reorx!" the gnome cried. "Come in! Come in at once!"

They entered, heedless of their wet condition, and Gilbenstock busied himself with clearing the papers from enough chairs to seat them all. Squib appeared from the food cupboard, his ratty brown beard filled with crumbs and half-chewed bits of dried fruit, and was immediately put to work bringing the rain-soaked customers warm cups of fresh goat's milk. The three men stared into their cups in silence, then carefully set them aside on nearby stacks of paper.

"You'll have to excuse the looks of the place," Gilbenstock said, unable to contain his excitement. "Business has been a bit slow, of course, what with the weather, but I've been keeping my hopes up that fine gentlemen like yourselves would need professional assistance with matters in geology, petrography, mineralogy, or even gemology, such as it may be, and I graduated first among my guild in mine engineering and geology, with a secondary degree in mechanics. . . ."

He slowed and stopped. Each of the three men was watching him in that peculiar way again. For a dreadful second, Gilbenstock thought that if he reached out and touched one of the men, the human would be hollow, like a papier-mâché mannikin. A shiver went up his spine. He suppressed the thought.

". . . but anyway, I'm just rattling on," he finished quickly. "What sort of professional assistance do you need?"

The three men looked at one another, then back at the gnome on the stool. This time, it was the big blond one who spoke. "A mine we need," he began, then corrected himself. "No, a mine we have. You we need a mine survey. Understand?" When Gilbenstock nodded, the man went on. "A mine we have was broken—"

"Collapsed," said the dark-haired man. "Fall down in mine."

"In mountains, near Palanthas," put in the red-bearded man.

"Yes, a mine we have was collapsed. You we need survey. The mine we must dig out. You we need dig out. Understand?"

"Yes, of course," said Gilbenstock. "You want me to survey your collapsed mine and see if it is safe, and perhaps see if it still contains any valuable ores or other resources. And you want me to dig it all out."

"Yes," said the blond man. "Slaves you have dig?"

"Workers," said the dark-haired man sharply. "Workers."

The blond man nodded quickly, flinging droplets from his long, wet hair. "Yes, workers."

How fortuitous, Gilbenstock thought. "It just so happens I have a *machine* that digs. I invented it. Faithful Squib here is the Onboard Starboard Command-Module Pilot. Squib will run the machine, and it will dig out your mine."

The men looked at each other and made peculiar open-handed gestures. "We hear tell machine," said the red-bearded man, turning back to the gnome. "Catapultlike?"

"No, no, no, not like a catapult at all. Not a siege machine. It's a digging machine, the Iron Dragon. I built it myself, with help from trusty Squib, of course."

"Dragon?" asked the red-bearded man and the blond man at the same time, with round-eyed looks of shock. "Dragon?"

Gilbenstock suddenly laughed, the tension broken. "Oh, my, no! It's not a *real* dragon. I quite apologize for the slip. It's a great machine, a steam-powered device that moves on wheels like a whooshwagon—oh, that's right, you probably haven't seen them unless you've been to Mount Nevermind, but that's quite all right, I wouldn't worry about it. We've had no *real* dragons around here—or none to speak of, anyway—since the War of the Lance, fifteen years ago, so things are quite safe here, more or less."

He hesitated, then plunged on. "You know, I don't mean to be rude, of course, but I have to ask—and it's only because of my great curiosity, you understand, I've been afflicted with it since I was just a little sprocket wrench—but I have the impression that you fellows aren't really from around here, from Palanthas. I was just thinking that you . . . have an interesting way of speaking, and I was quite taken with it—there's nothing wrong with that at all, you see—but I felt as if, well, you might be passing through here from somewhere else, maybe not very far away." He finished with a cough. "It wasn't very important, and we can get—"

"East," said the red-bearded man. "East we are of here, very far. Now, you hire we wish, make survey?"

"Of course," Gilbenstock said, embarrassed and glad to move on to another topic. A new subject came immediately to his mind. "Um, I hope you don't think me unusually forward for asking, but I would require a down payment, if possible—advance money, you understand."

The big blond man reached for a damp pouch on his belt and pulled it free. He tossed it to the gnome, who was somewhat disappointed. The bag was lighter than he'd expected. He'd counted on receiving steel coins. The pouch rattled faintly.

His nerves strained to their limits by the events of the morning, Gilbenstock pulled open the drawstrings. He peered inside, adjusting the bag so that the interior was illuminated by lantern light.

"Oh," he said in a small voice.

"Money we have no," said the blond man. "Diamonds, yes, but money we have no. Diamonds you take?"

There was a delay while Gilbenstock decided not to faint. "Of course," he squeaked. "Oh, of course."

All three men smiled, their teeth shining.

* * * * *

Two hours after the men had left, Gilbenstock splashed through the long, curved streets of Palanthas's Merchandizing District. His raincoat wasn't fastened in front, and he'd forgotten his boots, but he didn't care how wet he got. He ran as if he were weightless. He'd just paid off his landlady and the warehouse owner for the next year each, though the landlady had demanded double the normal rent as security against future nonpayment. Gilbenstock, now rich beyond his dreams, had locked away the remaining gems at a merchants' bank. He would be richer still once he was paid the final sum owed him after the mining operation was concluded. His financial troubles were forever gone.

The rain had let up for a while. Dark gray clouds shrouded the steep slopes of the Vingaard Mountains, which ringed the old city. Silent donkeys and horses, soaked and miserable, glanced up as the gnome hurried past. He could see the red roof of the warehouse now, and he pushed on, though he was out of breath and near exhaustion.

At the warehouse's great double doors, he slowed and stopped, puffing and leaning his head against the peeling paint. Catching his breath, he felt in his raincoat pockets for the padlock key, but didn't find it. He gasped, terrified that he had forgotten the key ring in his office or lost it on his mad run to pay off his debts. A moment later, he thrust a panicked hand into a pants pocket and touched the keys' cool metal, safe and sound.

Weak with relief, he reached up and carefully inserted one of the keys into the chain lock holding the doors closed. A twist of the wrist, and the lock released. Gilbenstock pushed open the door a crack and slipped inside.

The smell of oil and grease was thick in the cool air. Pale white light fell from a half dozen glowing metal globes suspended from the high ceiling on thin ropes. Gilbenstock had paid a young mage dearly for those continual-light spells, but it had been worth every steel. The lights safely illuminated his workshop at all hours of the day or night, allowing him to work until he dropped from hunger or sleep.

The result of his years of labor rose high above Gilbenstock, almost filling the great warehouse with its staggering bulk. The gnome sighed and looked up at his creation with tears of joy in his eyes.

The black monster slept soundly, unaware of him.

The Iron Dragon was as long as three wagon-teams and a third as wide. Beneath its six towering wheels, the paved stones had sunk a half foot into the earth under its stupendous mass. The main body was a great iron cylinder—a boiler laid on its side—from which a maze of pipes and valves sprang like gnarled black ivy. A pair of iron-covered cabins sat high on its back to either side, for its pilot and commander—Squib and Gilbenstock, respectively. At the bow of the cylinder was a massive block of gears and drive shafts from which projected a great set of three tapering, steel-gray rock drills, two below and one above, each as thick as a dragon's neck. The fanged drill ends hung in the air high over the gnome's head, gleaming dully in the magical light.

The machine was gargantuan, cold, and ugly beyond nightmares. To Gilbenstock, it was as beautiful as a lover's face. It had more power than a whole dragonarmy. And in just a matter of days, it would go on its first run.

"Thank you, Reorx, who guided my hand," whispered the gnome, suddenly humble in the presence of his own work. Then he took a deep breath, lifted his chin, and set off into the shop to give the machine a complete oiling and checkout.

The hours passed unnoticed. Covered with grime, Gilbenstock hummed to himself as he worked under the starboard central wheel chassis, checking the shock-absorbing coils. Aside from a couple of birds' nests and the usual leavings of rats and mice, the great machine had weathered well since he'd seen it last. He reached up to check the fit of a nut on a bolt.

A metallic noise rang to the floor by his right ear. Startled, Gilbenstock looked over and saw the bright steel key that he had used to enter the building. It lay on the paved floor astride a gap between two stones.

Just beyond the key, at the side of the wheel itself, were two tall black boots, muddy and wet. As he watched, one boot shifted slightly, flexing the toe.

"Time flies when you're having a good time, eh?" said a man's unfamiliar voice.

Gilbenstock let out his breath very slowly. He felt an unreasoning urge to crawl up into the machinery of the Iron Dragon and hide. With trembling fingers, he carefully picked up the key.

"You forgot it in the lock," drawled the voice above the boots.

Gilbenstock bit his lower lip. Could it be a meddlesome city guard? If so, that could be handled quickly: Gilbenstock certainly had the money, if it came to bribery.

The gnome collected himself. "Thank you," he called out, hastily finishing his check of the nut and bolt. "I shall be with you in just a moment, if you'll bear with me. I am just a bit busy here. A little maintenance goes a long way, you know."

The man stepped back as Gilbenstock grunted and pushed himself out from under the wheel chassis, avoiding the piston-driven bar that connected the three side wheels together. The gnome saw immediately that the man was not with the city guard.

He was tall, like all humans, with tightly curled black hair, a pockmarked face, and sallow skin. He wore no visible armor, only common clothes, and had no weapons—at least, none that Gilbenstock could see. His clothing was fairly dry except for his boots, and he wore a low gray cap that Gilbenstock had seen mostly used by visitors from the central part of Ansalon, around Estwilde.

Gilbenstock glanced behind the man and saw that the front doors had been pulled shut.

"Interesting," said the man, his gaze roaming over the iron leviathan beside the gnome. The man chewed something, probably a bit of flavored resin or gum, a candy that had grown popular in some places after the War of the Lance. "You build this yourself?"

Gilbenstock felt a glimmer of pride through his nervousness. "Why, yes, I did at that. Took me twelve years to get it all together, finding all the right parts and . . . and everything." He cleared his throat. "I confess I didn't expect to have company in my workshop this morning, Mister um . . ."

The man nodded, ignoring the cue. He continued to chew his resin and look the Iron Dragon over with a calculating eye. "You are a busy little guy, aren't you," he said.

Gilbenstock bristled. It had been a long time since someone had been so openly rude to him with remarks about his height. "I am," he said curtly. "Now, if you'll please let me get back to—"

"This thing safe to run, or does it blow up when you start it?" asked the man with a grin. "You never know with gnome things sometimes, do you? No offense."

It took a moment for Gilbenstock to find his tongue. "I'll have you know that this is no ordinary device," he said angrily. "I've included every necessary safety feature, and there's absolutely no danger of explosive boiler malfunction so long as the port commander keeps the pressure-release valves open while the vehicle is at rest and so long as the water levels are properly monitored. The heating elements require no fuel and are quite foolproof, since they are a little bit magical in origin, and I would dare say that riding a horse could be more dangerous, so it would be quite crude of someone to suggest despite past unfortunate incidents that simply because something is made by gnomes that it presents any real hazard to—"

"It's a steam-powered thing, right?" the man interrupted. He seemed amused. "Does it weed flower beds with those big drill bits on its nose? A steam-powered flower weeder?"

That was the last straw. Gilbenstock squared his shoulders. "I beg your pardon, but I've really had quite enough of this discussion and I'm going to have to ask that you please leave and let me get on with my work here as it is very important and I simply don't have the time to make chitchat—"

"You had some visitors this morning," the man said casually. "Three guys, wasn't it?"

"And what if I did?" Gilbenstock retorted.

The man didn't answer right away. Instead, he stepped closer to the Iron Dragon and rubbed a thumb over a black-painted pipe that ran along the top of the upper wheel housing. "They give you their names?"

"Unlike some people, they . . ." A nasty remark died on Gilbenstock's lips as he realized to his amazement that the three men had *not* given out their names, nor had Gilbenstock remembered to ask for them. "I won't say," the gnome finished. "What business could something like that possibly be of yours, anyway?"

"Well . . . let's say that, in a way, those three guys and I, we're in the same business. We're looking for things. Maybe I'm a little curious about what they're looking for. For personal reasons."

The man leaned against the wheel housing, then suddenly looked down at Gilbenstock in a way that was almost friendly. "You run a mining business, right?"

If I were bigger, the gnome thought, I'd punch him right in the nose and throw him out the door with one hand. His fists clenched helplessly. If I were only bigger. . . .

"Right?" prompted the man again, eyebrow raised.

"Yes," growled the gnome.

The man smiled. "They want you to dig something up for them?"

"That," Gilbenstock said slowly, "is between my customers and myself."

"Huh." The man's gaze lifted, and he stared into space at a secret thought. "Maybe." He thought for a moment more, then looked to the side at the silent bulk of the Iron Dragon. "You taking the job?"

"I said, that is between my customers and myself, and you are hardly better than a goblin in your manners."

The man stopped chewing his gum. His smile faded. He shook his head almost sadly as he exhaled through his nose and looked down at the gnome with cold, empty eyes.

Gilbenstock stopped breathing. His anger melted in the fear that he'd gone too far. He stepped back with a sudden awareness of his physical limitations.

A few long seconds passed. Quietly, the man reached for something under his overcoat. He pulled the object into view without hurry.

The cool overhead lights gleamed off the surface of a polished steel blade, an oversized hunter's knife with a single cutting edge and deep blood grooves, virtually a sword to Gilbenstock. Red runes decorated the steel. The gnome's stomach knotted in an instant. I've got to run, he thought wildly. I've got to get out of here. To his horror, he was paralyzed with fear, unable to do anything but stare.

The human lifted the hunting knife and began to scrape at the paint on the pipe of the Iron Dragon, rubbing the flakes away with his fingers. After scraping away an area about a foot long and a half-inch wide, he nodded as if satisfied with his inspection.

"Nice job," he said, letting his knife hand drop. The huge blade pointed down at Gilbenstock's feet. "Guess I'd better be going and let you get back to your work."

Gilbenstock said nothing, unable to take his gaze away from the knife.

The man smiled faintly and nodded, then turned and walked toward the double doors. He had almost reached them when he turned around. The knife was gone.

"Oh, you know, I was just thinking," the human said. "If your customers were to know about me, it might be a bad thing all around. I wouldn't mention this nice little chat of ours to them if I were you."

He waited just long enough to make sure the gnome had gotten the message, then pushed open the doors and left. As he did, he looked back at the gnome and winked. Then he was gone.

It took a while for Gilbenstock to realize that the sun was shining outside through the clouds. He heard the street traffic picking up, the sounds of hooves clopping and wagons rattling over the cobblestones. After a couple of minutes, he worked up the nerve to walk to the door and look up and down the street.

There was no sign of the human.

Gilbenstock pulled the door shut, dropped a heavy bolt into place, then pulled a chain across the double doors.

Passersby noticed there was no sound at all from the warehouse, which was usually quite noisy whenever the gnome was inside.

* * * * *

Trusty Squib was put in charge of making the *hors d'oeuvres* for the evening's meal, when the three men were to return to sign the contracts and clarify their mission for Gilbenstock. The gnome knew perfectly well that Squib's idea of edible fare did not match anyone's but another gully dwarf's, but he also trusted Squib to quickly get lost in Palanthas on his shopping spree, as he always did. This would give the gnome and his customers a few minutes of peace to discuss the mission. If Squib returned early, Gilbenstock could always generously allow the gully dwarf to eat his own cooking (by himself in the kitchen with the door closed, of course).

The three humans arrived at sunset. They hadn't bothered to comb their hair or straighten their outfits, but such niceties meant little to Gilbenstock, who welcomed them in and got them seated in short order.

"Yes," sighed Gilbenstock, "I must say it's been quite a day since you dropped in on me this morning, Mister um . . ."

The three men nodded in unison.

"Uh," mumbled Gilbenstock to the red-bearded man, who was nearest. "I'm dreadfully afraid that I've forgotten to ask your names."

Comprehension dawned in the man's face. "Harbis," he said. "Harbis my name is."

The other two men looked surprised, then responded as well.

"Klarmun," said the big blond.

"Skort," said the tall one.

Gilbenstock was flooded with relief. "My," he said, "I can't tell you how good it is to meet people who are polite enough to give you their names, unlike some people I know." He was on the verge of saying more when the memory of the hunting knife came back. "Would you like some goat's milk?" he said instead, seizing the pitcher and pouring out drinks. With a forced smile, he passed the mugs around.

Each man took his drink and set it, without a second look, beside his plate. "We you asked for speaking of about our mine, you hire for digging," began the big blond. He reached into his deerskin vest and pulled out a piece of folded parchment.

The muscular blond unfolded the paper carefully and smoothed it out in the flickering lantern light. The side facing up was blank except for some crude markings that seemed to have been made with a sharp charcoal stick. Gilbenstock looked at the paper in confusion until he recognized the northern Bay of Branchala, the city of Palanthas, and Old South Road, leading off into the mountains toward the Tower of the High Clerist and the lands of Solamnia.

Klarmun cleared his throat and pointed decisively at the paper. "Now we are here," he said as he indicated Palanthas, "and soon we are there." His finger slid to a point just east of the south road out of Palanthas. Gilbenstock guessed it to be ten miles out of town, and again felt relieved. The Iron Dragon could make that distance and back easily on a full tank of water.

"That's the location of your mine?" he asked.

All three men nodded. "From road here, you fly—" Klarmun coughed and began again. "You walk here, inside dry water flow."

"Dry creek," corrected the tall, dark-haired Skort. Klarmun nodded quickly.

Gilbenstock had rarely been outside Palanthas since his arrival all those years ago, so he was unfamiliar with the area the men indicated. The Iron Dragon, however, had a semi-flexible chassis and heavy shock absorbers. It might manage a drive up a creek bed. "Is the creek bed solid stone?" he asked. "Or is it muddy or gravel-filled?"

"Ah, stone," said Klarmun. "Very wide, easy walk."

"Excellent. That's where I'll have Squib take the Iron Dragon." Gilbenstock noticed the blank looks the men now gave him. "Oh, yes, good Squib is the pilot. I believe I mentioned that once. He will operate the Iron Dragon on its first run. He's actually quite a gifted sort with mechanical things, which I've noticed a great many people don't expect. In truth, he's helped me quite a bit with the Iron Dragon during its building, and I'd never have gotten so far without him. A savant, I believe is the word for it." Gilbenstock tactfully shortened the phrase *idiot savant*. "He's definitely a clever rogue and quite good-hearted, a real pleasure once you come to know him. He once found a way to . . . ah, that must be dinner. I'll be right back."

A low whistling sound of escaping steam had begun in the kitchen. Gilbenstock climbed down from his stool and hurried off, to reappear two minutes later (after a series of oaths and cries of pain) with several bowls full of various cooked vegetables. He set these on the table, one beside each customer, and blew on his burned fingers. The combination Food Steamer,

Masher, and Plate-Wiper was a bit on the blink.

"I do realize this is quite out of the ordinary for a contractor to supply a repast to those who hire him," he said
happily, "but this really has been an extraordinary day,
and I suppose I should be permitted to take a few liberties
with normal protocol. Ah, there we go, that's the lot of it.
We have some vegetable confetti there, with kelp substi-
tuted for the broccoli—the market was completely out of
it—and some Palanthas potatoes, twice cooked, and that
right over there by your elbow is savory squash, quite
fresh, and to wrap it up I've baked—although it is out of
season, I know—a Lord Amothus's Yule sour-cream walnut cake. It's a remarkable sort of cake, and this is the first
one I've been able to bake without setting the kitchen on
fire. I put extra walnuts in, I hope you don't mind. Squib
likes it that way."

The three men made no move to eat their food. The red-
bearded man, Harbis, swallowed and looked sick.

"Question," said Skort. He leaned forward, his hands
cupped over the bowl of savory squash as if shielding it
from him. "How soon the mine you dig out?"

"How soon?" Gilbenstock spooned mounds of vegetable confetti onto his plate. "Well, I inspected the Iron
Dragon this morning shortly after you left, and . . . um,
everything was fine there, so all I need to do is run a pipe
into the storm drains and top off the primary boiler, which
shouldn't take long at all given the runoff from the rain
this morning, then I'll need to give it a last systems check,
then I'll need to get permission from the city government
for moving an oversized vehicle through town—though
perhaps I could get away with it just this once, as the offi-
cials can be quite understanding sometimes but not
always so toward inventors, as I have learned in—"

"How soon?" repeated Skort patiently.

"The day after tomorrow," said Gilbenstock. He reached
for the potatoes but stopped short. "You can eat now," he
said, nodding at his guests' empty plates.

Harbis was sweating visibly. Klarmun toyed with a tiny
piece of fried potato. Skort never looked down at the

table. "Two days, good," Skort said with satisfaction. "At mine we three will be, waiting at noon. Walking good for us, we see you there." He paused, then went on. "Remember, you we ask not speak about mine or digging others. Secret our mine."

"Beg pardon?" Gilbenstock had finished serving himself and was preparing to eat the sour-cream walnut cake.

The three men looked at each other, then Klarmun gave it a try, gratefully putting aside his potato scrap. "You about this, our mine, not speak about. Not good, everyone know. Secret."

Gilbenstock nodded. "Yes, I recall you said that this morning just before . . . just before you left." He thought of the man with the big knife in his workshop. His face suddenly felt as if all the blood had left it. What was going on here?

"Diamonds we you gave, you our trust," Skort said. His eyes seemed to have grown larger. "If everyone our mine know, we have for us much trouble, yes, trouble. Our trust you and . . . your friend have. No trouble?"

There was a little silence. Gilbenstock felt light-headed with fear. "No trouble. None whatsoever."

"No trouble," Skort said again in approval. "If trouble, you we must—"

The front door banged open without warning. Cold night winds blew in. A squat, filthy figure carrying a bucket staggered inside.

"Squib!" cried the gnome.

The gully dwarf was covered with long, bleeding scratches from head to mud-covered feet. His normally ragged clothes were nearly shredded, and he smelled as if he'd been rolling in an alley latrine.

"Great Reorx, were you set upon?" Gilbenstock climbed down from his stool so quickly he nearly fell. He rushed to Squib. "Were you beaten?"

Squib rolled his eyes and shook his head, holding up the bucket. He first shaded his eyes with one hand, as if searching. Then he pointed, made a brief hissing sound with his free hand in the shape of a scratching claw, and pantomimed a scene of battle with a feline opponent. At the end, he held the bucket aloft again in triumph, his free hand now a fist waving over his head. He then offered the bucket to the men at the table.

Gilbenstock's eyes locked on the bucket and went wide with horror. The bucket was filled almost to the brim with dead mice.

Squib had brought back the *hors d'oeuvres*.

Gilbenstock was mortified. "Squib, by my twelve-times-great Grandfather Mulorbinello, no! We don't offer our . . . our guests . . ."

His voice trailed off. Harbis, face glowing in relief, took the bucket of mice from the gully dwarf. Grins broke out all around the table. Squib grabbed a chair and pulled it up to join the three men as Harbis quickly doled out mice to each of the others present. They accepted them with gusty sighs.

Gilbenstock grabbed his own plate from the table and made it to the kitchen in the nick of time. He hoped his customers would forgive his rudeness, though he now knew them to be barbarians wearing civilized clothing. Taking a seat on the floor, Gilbenstock made a stab at some of the sour-cream walnut cake, but he kept imagining it was full of mouse heads or tails. He glumly set his meal aside and poured himself a cup of water as he fought off nausea.

Not everyone, he reflected, is cut out to be a vegetarian.

* * * * *

The contracts were signed the following morning, when Gilbenstock was feeling well again. The meal had been a complete success from the humans' point of view—and from Squib's, as the gully dwarf got not only some of the mice but the entire sour-cream walnut cake as well.

The day passed quickly. Gilbenstock asked some of the city guards to take an extra walk past his shop to look for prowlers, and the generous donation he made to the city guards' treasury and widows' fund ensured that the guards took a friendly interest in chasing small children and vagrants from his doorway. The gnome felt much more secure and was able to tank up the Iron Dragon by lowering a hose into the drain in his shop, pumping out what water he needed from the storm sewers into the drilling machine's huge boiler.

After a long day spent in the final checkout of the machine, Gilbenstock brought Squib to the workshop for a test start of the Iron Dragon. The gnome and gully dwarf climbed to their respective cabins, and Gilbenstock, with his customary remark about "collateral damage," signaled for the Iron Dragon's boiler to be brought to one-quarter steam.

At first there was silence in the workshop. Over a space of ten minutes, however, a low rumble could be heard from the Iron Dragon's huge boiler. Gilbenstock felt the machine gather power and tremble slightly. Though Palanthas had strict laws about noisemaking after dark, the humans who couldn't stand the constant hammering had long ago moved away from this block, so Gilbenstock wasn't worried about civil trouble.

The rumbling grew until the walls of the warehouse shook under waves of sound so loud that the gnome believed he could see them. The wax earplugs and heavy-duty ear mufflers he kept tied over his head helped a great deal. Faithful Squib was calm and unaffected. He wore a combination of oversized goggles and earmuffs that made him look rather like a bug-eyed insect, with a thickly padded suit and heavy gloves to protect from steam blasts. Gilbenstock wore a similar outfit.

At one-quarter steam, the Iron Dragon gave all indications that it was actually coming to life. A small pipe burst near the port central wheel housing. Squib and Gilbenstock pulled levers, tugged cords, flipped switches, and turned knobs. The steam leak was shut off. Shortly after, oil sprayed from a loose joint just under the drill head mount, but Gilbenstock ignored it. The test start was all he could have hoped for.

Just as pleasing was the chance Gilbenstock had to see Squib display his unique genius with the controls of the magnificent vehicle. The mute gully dwarf couldn't count past two, like most of his kind, but he could disassemble any device and reassemble it flawlessly, a skill that had saved the gnome from disaster on this project a hundred times. Squib had passed all the piloting tests that Gilbenstock could devise. Without fail, he operated the Iron Dragon's array of complex dials, levers, buttons, gauges, warning whistles, timing bells, signal flags, and other devices that faced him in his little cabin. The gnome happily forgave Squib every offense—even last night's "*hors d'oeuvres.*"

Gilbenstock brought the boiler pressure down after a few minutes, seeing no need for further tests. Tomorrow at dawn, he'd bring it up to full pressure and engage the main drive. The Iron Dragon would roll off to meet his customers at the mine. It would be a historic moment. Perhaps, he reflected, the city would offer him some form of recognition for his achievement, such as a statue and a sack full of money. One never knew.

The machine was completely shut down by midnight, according to the shop's hourglass—the only glassware in the place that wasn't completely shattered by the noise. After final repairs, Gilbenstock motioned for Squib not to bother cleaning up, and they left by a small door in the back of the shop. Squib shortly thereafter disappeared to rummage through a garbage heap.

The gnome continued on alone, enjoying the night air and trying to get the loud ringing out of his ears. Perhaps a quarter of an hour went by before Gilbenstock could make out normal street noises. Curiously, all the dogs in the neighborhood were barking like mad. Many lamps were lit in the windows and rooms, and there seemed to be an extraordinary number of people out on the streets, arguing and pointing in the direction from which the gnome had just come. He shrugged, supposing the warm spring weather had brought everyone out, and began to hum a tune off-key.

He cut through an alley and eventually walked out onto a poorly lit street only two blocks from home. A rattling noise sounded behind him in the alley, like a fallen pebble. Glancing back, he saw nothing.

He looked ahead again just in time to run into a man's legs.

Badly startled, the gnome cried out in spite of himself. He backed away and looked up. "By my ancestor's aluminum-siding patent, I had quite a turn there! You must forgive—"

Recognizing the man's face, Gilbenstock instantly turned to run. A pitiless hand grabbed his upper right arm and shoved him back into the alley. Gilbenstock lost his balance and fell.

"Time flies when you're having a good time, eh?"

It took a few moments for the gnome to find his voice. Terror kept him from looking up. "I kept your secret," he gasped. "I swear that I did. If you can possibly see your way to making friends and letting me go, I would—aagh!"

The human's hands closed on the gnome's clothing and dragged Gilbenstock to his feet, shoving him against an alley wall. The gnome was too frightened to call for help. The man's hands slowly released their grip on the gnome's waterlogged clothing. Then he knelt down in front of Gilbenstock, his face and outline barely visible in the darkness. He began to gently brush off the gnome's clothing like a concerned old friend.

"Bad fall you took there," the man said gently. He finished his ministrations and gazed into the gnome's face. "I want to know if and when you're leaving town to help out your friends. And I hope you won't say it isn't any of my business."

Gilbenstock wanted so badly to fight back, to do anything to defend himself.

"I asked you a question," said the man.

"Tomorrow morning," the gnome whispered sullenly. "We leave just before dawn."

The man snorted in disgust. "I thought something was up when I heard your steam-powered flower weeder start up tonight. Great gods of Krynn, you could hear it all over the city. I wouldn't be surprised if the good townsfolk don't burn your little workshop down for all the sleep they've lost. You gnomes have dog crap for common sense. And you've got less than usual for taking up with those special pals of yours."

After a moment of thought, the man took a deep breath. "Well, little guy, I'll tell you what's going to happen. Before you get ready to leave town with your three big buddies, you're going to—"

"Zorlen," a voice said. It sounded like Klarmun.

Gilbenstock and the man immediately turned. In the dim light of a distant lamp, the gnome could see the silhouette of someone standing in the alley entrance—someone tall and thick-armed, with shoulder-length hair. The man froze.

Gilbenstock lunged forward. He threw his weight against the kneeling man before him, sending him sprawling backward. The gnome then fled down the alley the way he'd come, stumbling over cobblestones and trash in the blackness.

Behind him rang out curses, then metallic blows on stone, and more curses. The fight faded in the distance as he ran on and on.

An unknown time later, Gilbenstock staggered up to his front door and collapsed against it. His lungs were on fire, and he couldn't catch his breath. He tried to turn the doorknob. It was locked. He struggled with it, then released the knob as he felt in his pocket for the key ring.

The keys were gone.

After a fruitless search, Gilbenstock sat down on the doorstep and covered his face with his thick hands. He would have to go back and find his keys. He knew where they were now, remembering a metallic clatter when his assailant had pushed him against the wall. It had been the keys falling from his vest pocket.

Gilbenstock would rather have died than return to the alley, but his workshop key was on the key ring as well as his house key. If he waited until dawn, a child might carry them off.

"Be a dragon inside," he said to himself. He knew he was anything but a dragon. He could kid himself and believe he was brave and knew the right thing to do, but it meant nothing in the real world.

It was the very deepest part of night when he found the alley again. No sounds issued from it. All lamp lights had been extinguished; the darkness was almost complete. He was forced to feel his way along the alley wall.

Like all gnomes, Gilbenstock had infrared-sensitive vision that let him see heat sources in darkness, but he saw nothing warm in the entrance to the alley. He kept his face to the wall, his fingers straying into stinking, unidentified filth and debris as he slid his hands over the cobblestones.

The search for the keys went on for ages. Gilbenstock lost all sense of time. Haven't I suffered enough? he asked himself. His hands and clothing were covered in foul garbage. He could smell animal dung and rotting fruit and mold and, soon, blood—lots of blood. Don't let me find a body, he prayed. Let me find my keys and I'll go. Let me find my keys. Let me find—

His fingers touched something metal. Slowly he felt down with his whole hand. His fist closed on his lost keys.

In all his life, Gilbenstock had never believed it was possible to feel as relieved and light as he felt then. Reorx had been watching out for him, after all.

The gnome sighed and stepped away from the wall. He promptly stumbled over something in the alley behind him, falling against a large object that was soft and wet. Gilbenstock cried out in fright. He could almost taste the sharp odor of fresh blood.

A man-sized body lay on the alley's stones. It wasn't moving. It was also cooler than a live body would be.

Klarmun or the assailant? was the first question that came to Gilbenstock once his thoughts were coherent again. It was a minute before he could work up the courage to find out. He looked around, saw and heard no one coming, then inched over to the dead man's head. Slowly, the gnome put out a hand and touched the man's hair.

The hair was thick and wiry, set in tight curls. It was sticky with drying blood. Zorlen, Klarmun had called him. Zorlen was dead.

Gilbenstock released the man's hair and stepped back.

The head rolled freely away from the body and bumped against the gnome's foot, leaving a trail of blood behind it.

Gilbenstock went rigid with terror and made a choking noise. He took another step back, then fainted.

* * * * *

Something warm was pressed into his hands. Gilbenstock took it without thinking, dully aware of the smell of meaty broth. Someone then pushed his hands toward his mouth, spilling a bit of hot liquid from the cup he held. He began to drink. The broth stung his fingers and mouth, but he drank without flinching. Before long, Gilbenstock lowered the empty cup and pulled the blanket around his shoulders a little tighter.

To his surprise, he found that he was in his own bed. Someone pushed his feet onto the bed and tucked him under the covers. How nice, he thought. Within moments, the gnome was sound asleep.

A gnarled, dirty hand patted the snoring lump under the blankets and picked up the cup from the floor. Squib drained the last few drops of broth, then hefted Gilbenstock's filthy clothing and headed for the sometimes-functional, twelve-foot-long Eradication Receptacle in the back of the office. He had no idea what the gnome had been doing in the alley so late at night in such a horrible predicament, but it was obvious that it was long past time for his boss to go home. It had been a lucky thing for the gnome that brave Squib had chased his rodent quarry right into the alley where the fight had occurred. Otherwise . . . Squib shuddered to even imagine what might have happened. Something bad for sure, like what happened to that other guy, Mister No-head. Squib had been so shocked that he'd even let the rat get away.

On the way back from the Eradicator, which thumped cheerily as it mangled the clothing, the gully dwarf stopped in the kitchen and got himself another cup of broth. He drank a sip and sighed with satisfaction. Of all the things he knew how to cook, cream of rat soup was easily the best thing of all. He hoped his boss appreciated that.

* * * * *

The morning sky was bright over the mountains ringing Palanthas. Farmers drove their carts through the streets, bringing produce for the markets. Gulls shrieked and crows cawed angrily by the bay waterfront.

Gnarled hands opened a pair of wooden shutters to the dawn, then roughly shook the blanketed lump in the nearby bed. The gnome awoke with a gasp and accidentally kicked over a chair by his bedside. A five-foot stack of papers on the chair tilted and fell, burying the gnome beneath its whirling white pages.

"*Aaaaaggggghhhhh!*" Gilbenstock shrieked, convinced he was being attacked again. He flailed about, hurling reams of old notes from his bed as Squib wisely retreated and hid under a table.

When he had calmed down and correctly assessed the situation, Gilbenstock fell back among his covers, trying to slow his heartbeat. The previous night's events seemed more distant now, though hardly less frightening.

Cautiously, Squib crawled from under the bed and tapped Gilbenstock on the arm, pointing to the window and the light streaming through it. Gilbenstock stared, then looked back at Squib in confusion. And comprehension.

"Oh, great gods of Krynn!" In renewed panic, Gilbenstock struggled to get untangled from his blankets. "We must get to the workshop! We're scheduled to meet our clients at the mine at noon!"

The next few minutes were a blur. It was while he was hastily pulling on a clean pair of pants that Gilbenstock realized that his client Klarmun, whom he'd be meeting shortly, was a killer. The thought caused him to tear a hole in his breeches by jamming his foot into a trouser leg too hard. He dropped the pants and frantically hunted for yet another pair. Then again, he reflected, Klarmun had only come to his rescue, so perhaps a certain amount of bloodletting was to be forgiven. Maybe. The very idea still made the gnome blanch. He skipped breakfast (the Flagrationary Larder Appliance Maintaining Equipotential Radiance had burned all the waffles), and he and Squib—the latter clutching a warm cup of some sort of meaty broth—hurried off into the street.

To Gilbenstock's astonishment, large sheets of paper were nailed to the front doors of the warehouse. He squinted up at the writing.

" 'Warning,' " he read aloud. " 'On this day, the city guard of Palanthas has determined that the mechanical device kept within this facility must not be operated within these city limits, by order of Sergeant Liam Jeraws, until such time as its excessive noise, which so violently disturbed the public on the previous evening, can be permanently—' What rubbish is this?" Gilbenstock snorted as he led the way around to the back entrance. "To think of all the bribes I paid him, and now this! That's utterly disgraceful. No one has any respect for money these days."

Squib belched in sympathy. Wiping his mouth and beard on his sleeve, he followed his boss into the warehouse.

It took but a few minutes to don the protective clothing, gloves, tool belts, earplugs, goggles, and earmuffs. It took another few minutes to take them all off again when both gnome and gully dwarf discovered they had to visit the latrine before the trip ("Too much excitement," muttered Gilbenstock). Once again fully outfitted, they got on with a last check of the supply boxes, which contained food, tools, extra clothing, and yards of clean bandages—just in case.

Within ten minutes, the rumbling boiler was up to one-quarter power. A shrill whistle went off at half power, triggering a chorus of alarm bells around the two great driver pistons. The monstrous locomotive growled and shook as if an earthquake boiled within it.

All evil memories of the past night vanished. The gnome felt taller than he really was, even taller than a human. His blood rushed and pounded in his veins in time with the shock waves of sound that filled the warehouse. Dust fell from the ceiling.

Gilbenstock looked out of the window to his right for Squib's cabin, just as the gully dwarf looked over and caught his gaze. The gully dwarf grinned from ear to ear-muffed ear, his crossed eyes barely visible behind his thick goggles. The moment was at hand.

"Forward, into destiny!" cried Gilbenstock, but his voice was lost in the chaos as he pointed at the doors.

Squib nodded happily, though completely unable to hear a thing, and pulled down hard on the throttle. The Iron Dragon opened up to full power as Squib engaged the main drive.

A thought occurred to the gnome.

"First, let's open the front doors," Gilbenstock added a moment later. "We'll have to watch for collateral—oops!"

He was too late. Hammer blows of sound crashed into his bones. Turbines and pistons screamed. The Iron Dragon gave a tortured metallic shriek that went up to the roof and sky, the blast shattering the hourglass at the shop's rear. With a banging of gears, the great machine lurched forward.

Gilbenstock watched with a mixture of astonishment, horror, and wild pride as the giant rock drills punched through the locked wooden doors of the warehouse. Moments later, the Iron Dragon crashed through the whole wall with ease. The black monster surged forward through the gaping hole and rolled directly onto the street—surprisingly free of pedestrians in the immediate area. The machine's wheels crushed flat an abandoned melon cart. Squib's knowing hands flew over the controls, and the Iron Dragon smoothly pivoted on its starboard wheels to make a right turn down the street, which was rapidly emptying of all traffic. The people seemed quite excited as they fled.

As well they should be, the gnome thought proudly.

In his wildest dreams, Gilbenstock had never imagined riding his Iron Dragon would be like this. The iron floor thumped as if pounded by a giant, beating the soles of his feet mercilessly. He barely managed to keep upright by grasping levers and pipes with all his strength. Most of the glass-covered dials soon broke, and several dials stopped functioning entirely, but the Iron Dragon still appeared to be in good running order.

And the *sound!* The very air vibrated like waves on the shore during a great storm. Houses seemed to shiver in fear and awe of Gilbenstock's invention. Surely the city populace would welcome him back as a hero when he returned from his first mission! Surely hundreds would then fill his geological survey shop with new mines to dig, new fortunes to make, and rivers of praise for his genius!

The Iron Dragon drove down the street toward the intersection with the tree-lined Old South Road. Gilbenstock glanced behind but couldn't see much through the hurricane of dust and steam that followed them. He could tell, however, that the street was suffering considerable damage from their passage. He grimaced at the thought of spending another diamond or two for road repairs, but it would be worth the good public relations.

There were other problems, too. Two abandoned wagons were smashed to pieces beneath the machine's cottage-sized wheels, and a stray board from one briefly jammed the port driver bar. Lurching to the left, the Iron Dragon struck and splintered a half dozen old trees lining the boulevard before the board was dislodged and Squib brought the machine back under control.

Pivoting at the intersection with Old South Road, the Iron Dragon came about to make the final leg of its journey out of town. As it did, Gilbenstock found himself confronted by a nervous crowd of mace-wielding city guards, accompanied by a man and a woman wearing the red robes used by some of the city's mages. The posse was only a hundred feet away.

"Uh-oh," muttered the gnome, his voice lost in the racket. He reached up and pulled a cord to activate a warning whistle prior to his slowing down the machine. The guards doubled over in agony as the whistle screamed. Throwing down their weapons, mouths open wide and hands clasped to their ears, the humans fled for their lives. Those in red robes ran fastest of all. Gilbenstock decided there was no need to stop now, and so continued on.

The last buildings on the edge of town were now going

past the windows. The front end of the Iron Dragon rose steadily, climbing the Old South Road at the southeastern end of the Merchandising District. They were at the foot of the mountains. From here, the road curved back and forth like a drunkard's walk for several miles after leaving the city, but it wouldn't take but a few hours to reach the mine if the steam stayed high.

The Iron Dragon struck something in the road—a bronze statue on a low stone pedestal—and bounced particularly high before it crushed the figure and its stone base flat. As the gnome was tossed into the air, he caught a glimpse through the forward window of something ahead in the road, directly in the path of the juggernaut.

A man wearing black robes.

Gilbenstock got up on tiptoes and took a second look.

It actually appeared to be an elf in black robes. He stood calmly, not a hundred and fifty feet ahead, his arms crossed over his chest in careless fashion as he watched the oncoming machine. Gilbenstock could see the elf's liquid black eyes perfectly. They were focused on him.

His blood ran cold.

Even the most humble of gnome tinkers in Palanthas knew of Dalamar, head of the Order of Black Robes, one of the mightiest wizards alive. Gilbenstock vaguely recalled hearing that Dalamar had undead sorcerers for servants. Unspeakable monsters were at his beck and call. Other rumors about Dalamar had given Gilbenstock unpleasant dreams in the past. To see the dark elf actually looking at him was worse by far than any nightmare. The gnome tried to sound the warning whistle, but the cord had flipped up out of reach. Gilbenstock looked to the right and saw that faithful Squib appeared to be wrestling with a stuck valve and was not paying the slightest attention to the road ahead or its lone obstacle.

Greetings, Gilbenstockelburlindiosophamistilaliniar, said a cool, dark voice in the gnome's head. Gilbenstock had not heard the longer short form of his name in many years. It terrified him to hear it spoken now in his mind, as if by a ghost. His thoughts jammed up like a gearbox with a log stuck in it.

Forgive me for using direct mental contact with you, but normal speech is quite impossible, said the voice. *I was awakened last night by the racket of your machine, and only a quarter hour ago was interrupted in my studies by the same. Now I find that in addition to troubling me, your device has driven away all street traffic for blocks, reduced the population of this city to anarchy, and damaged this district at a cost of many thousand steels. It would not trouble me in the slightest to hurl both you and your miserable device into the bay, and I am greatly tempted to do so now.*

All the strength went out of the gnome's knees. He gripped the window ledge to keep from falling. He steeled himself for what would come next.

A smile flitted across the face of the dark elf, now only fifty feet ahead. *On the other hand, you have unintentionally amused and pleased me,* the voice said. *I greatly disliked Elistan's statue, which you've reduced to scrap. Elistan was as great a do-gooder and fool as I have ever known, and his statue was a drink of bile. Besides, it was a terrible likeness. We'll call it even. You may leave this city unharmed.*

The dark elf then turned into mist and faded from view. Just three seconds later, the Iron Dragon drove directly over the spot in the road where the elf had been standing, continuing its thundering drive into the mountains. After a long, breathless moment during which Gilbenstock expected Dalamar to reappear and carry out his threat anyway, the gnome closed his eyes and opened his mouth to say a prayer of thanks to Reorx.

I would encourage you to take your time about coming back, however, the voice added abruptly. *And you'd best come on foot, if you come at all.*

No more was said.

Aside from running over a wagonload of fruit and a deaf opossum, the Iron Dragon and its crew left the once tranquil city without further incident.

* * * * *

After frantic hand signals from Gilbenstock, Squib was able to bring the gargantuan device to a halt about sixteen miles outside of town, deep in the Vingaard Mountains. Blasts of steam sprayed from the locomotive's pipes and valves, the thunder echoing across the valleys and cliffs. Gilbenstock found that he was so affected by the bone-jarring ride that he was temporarily unable to walk or pick up things with his fingers. He reached the ground after falling halfway down the ladder and was removing sharp rock fragments from his palms when Squib joined him.

The gnome took off his ear protection and tried to speak, but he couldn't even hear himself over the endless ringing in his ears. He gestured helplessly, then caught Squib by the arm and dragged him to the port side of the idling machine. He pointed to the dry creek bed that ran across the road ahead, traveling perpendicular to their direction of travel. After a few more gestures, Squib caught on to the idea that they were to drive up the creek bed and, with shaky limbs, both of them remounted the vehicle. New blasts of noise rang throughout the peaks. The Iron Dragon slowly spun on its port wheels, rocks flying, and set out over the rough ground.

Traveling was now far worse than before. The Old South Road was hardly in the best of condition in this area, but the rocky ground was awful and forced the gully dwarf to drive at a fraction of their previous speed. Gilbenstock was regularly slammed from side to side in his cabin, the boxes and crates bouncing around him, and he banged his head painfully on nearby pipes and gauges more often than was exactly pleasant. More than once he was nearly thrown from the cabin through a side window.

After what seemed like a thousand years of this punishment, Gilbenstock dazedly noted that the Iron Dragon was coming to a halt. The machine rocked on its wheels slightly, then settled down with another chorus of steam blasts and metallic clanks and bangs.

I am not only deaf, he thought as he lay on the floor of his cabin, his short arms wrapped around a pipe, but I have also had every bone in my body broken to pieces. I will have to buy a new body, which means another diamond gone, but it will be worth it. I shall ask around for a taller body if possible.

Squib, grinning and hardly the worse for the wear, was able to bring Gilbenstock down the ladder and revive him with a drink of meaty broth from a sealed container. Gilbenstock soon pushed the cup away. Who knew what the gully dwarf had made the soup with?

Gilbenstock quickly saw that Squib had stopped the machine because there was simply nowhere else to go. The broad, trail-like creek had once flowed from what looked like a cavern in the side of the mountain. The cavern had long ago collapsed, and the creek had probably died with it. While Squib gave the Iron Dragon a brief checkover, Gilbenstock stripped off his earmuffs, goggles, and gloves, then set off on rubbery legs to examine the area.

The cavern was not truly a cavern at all, instead being the dwarven-made entrance to what was probably an old mine—an iron mine, judging by the reddish chunks of hematite that littered the ground. Gilbenstock blinked as he ran his hands over the fitted stonework that framed the buried entrance. There was a good chance that the very dwarves who had built Palanthas in ages past had also dug this mine. Gilbenstock guessed that the mine had seen no workers for . . .

"Hundreds of years," Gilbenstock sighed. He found his hearing had come back, though the ringing had yet to leave.

"Ten centuries," said a familiar voice behind him.

Clutching his heart, Gilbenstock gasped and spun around.

Harbis and Skort stood only a dozen feet away. Neither man was smiling. They were dusty but seemed comfortable in the heat.

"Merciful gods, you gave me quite a turn." Gilbenstock laughed and tweaked a pinky in his right ear. "My hearing's just a little off, but it should be back in shape soon enough. Is this the mine about which you were speaking earlier?"

"It is," said Skort. His gaze flicked to the entrance, then back to the gnome. "Forgive us for startling you, but we'd earlier retreated some distance around the side of the mountain to avoid being deafened by your . . . remarkable

Iron Dragon."

"Ah, no problem at all," Gilbenstock replied grandly. Something struck the gnome as different, but he couldn't quite place it. "Well, we have about five more hours until sundown, so if you wish us to start drilling we can get on with it in just a few more minutes after my assistant clears the Iron Dragon for operation. We had quite a rough ride up here, I must—"

He stopped in midspeech. He felt an unreasoning moment of fear, then swallowed and looked up at Skort. "I must say, you've really caught on with the language since I last saw you. You should be commended on your ability. You've managed to pick up the tongue far more quickly than most people do. I don't mean that as a slur against humans, you understand, but it does seem perhaps a bit unusual."

"I apologize for the deception, but we wished to appear as something other than we are," Skort said dryly. "My barbaric role serves me well; sometimes it pays to appear unsophisticated. My associates are not as skilled in your language as I, so their roles were more genuine. And, yes, the sooner you start drilling, the better. We are very eager to get our business underway again."

"Of course," Gilbenstock agreed uncertainly, unable to think of anything more to say. He turned to look at the mine entrance but instead saw Harbis, hands on hips, blocking his view. Rather, Harbis *seemed* to have both hands on his hips, but one hand was actually resting on the pommel of a long dagger that was strapped to his right thigh.

"Oh," Gilbenstock said, and looked back at Skort with frightened eyes.

"Just start digging, please," Skort said. "You have been well paid for your work, and we greatly wish to see the results."

"Um, results, of course," the gnome echoed. "Of course." He looked one last time at Harbis's dagger, then headed back toward the Iron Dragon, fighting the urge to run away.

Before he reached the Iron Dragon, however, he stopped

once on impulse and looked back. Even as he spoke, Gilbenstock knew he was risking trouble. He couldn't help himself. He had to know. "Forgive me," he called, "but I don't see our friend Klarmun here. I hope you don't mind my asking after him."

Skort and Harbis stared at the gnome for a few seconds. Three inches of Harbis's dagger blade appeared from its sheath.

"Klarmun was detained by an old acquaintance in town," Skort said without expression. "Carry on."

Harbis's blade slowly disappeared, though his knotted hand did not relax its grip on the hilt.

Gilbenstock nodded again, then went on to the Iron Dragon. He cursed himself as he did. For the love of money, he had sold his services to agents of darkness, and they now expected their due. They were not crude barbarians at all, but shrewd actors playing out their parts, secretly fortune hunters or thieves. They obviously thought the mine held buried treasure of some sort, and they'd kill for that treasure. Gilbenstock had been played for a fool. He was alive only because he was useful—and because no one suspected him of treachery.

The excitement the gnome had felt earlier on the drive out of Palanthas was gone. Now he shivered, anticipating the sharp pain of a knife thrust in his back, and wondering how long he had to live.

Skort had implied that Zorlen was known to them, an "old acquaintance." An old enemy, more likely. Did the three suspect that Gilbenstock had told Zorlen about their plans? What would they do if they thought he had?

His mind overrun with troubling questions, the gnome was barely able to keep his thoughts on his work as he checked back with his assistant. Worthy Squib pointed out a few areas of particular damage done to the Iron Dragon on its hours-long drive, but the machine as a whole had held up well. There was no reason it couldn't tackle the drilling right away.

With a heavy sigh, Gilbenstock waved to the two men and warned them that the drilling would soon commence.

When he spelled out the dangers of the noise and flying rocks ("The collateral damage should be extraordinary"), the two men nodded, then set off down the creek bed to be out of harm's way.

Gilbenstock distractedly patted Squib on the back, then started back up the iron ladder to his cabin. Once there, he carefully barred his door and raised several small shields in the windows to protect him from rock shards. He then peeked out the starboard window to see how Squib was doing.

One of the large supply boxes behind Gilbenstock shifted and creaked. Its lid came open. Startled, Gilbenstock spun around. A dirty figure arose from inside the box, holding the lid open with one arm. The man's curly black hair was damp with sweat. Old blood streaked his face.

"Time flies when you're having a good time, eh?" said the man in a soft, weary voice.

Gilbenstock couldn't think of anything to say. He was numb with terror—and astonishment.

The man—Zorlen—shook his head as if to clear it. "It's me, little friend," he said. "Don't bother to answer; I can barely hear a thing anyway from the racket your flower weeder put out. I just had to tag along on your little trip into the mountains. You had lots of things in this crate, but I figured you wouldn't miss them, so I took them out and put myself in last night after our meeting in the alley. It took a while to do it. Our friend turned out to be better with a blade than I'd allowed."

The man grimaced, then brought his other arm out of the crate and into view. In a bandaged hand, he clutched the huge, bloodstained hunting knife.

Gilbenstock found his tongue. "You were d-d-dead," he managed to gibber. "You had no h-h-h . . ."

Zorlen gave a faint laugh, quickly gone. "I looked mighty dead, didn't I? I thought so, too. The corpse looked just like me. They all do that, you know. Death changes all Sivak draconians, whether they kill or are killed themselves. I had to make sure he was as dead as he could get, before . . ." Zorlen raised the tip of his large knife and flicked it gently past his throat. "Best cure for headaches there ever was."

"Draconians," the gnome repeated dazedly.

Zorlen rubbed his ears. "Draconians. I knew the three of them were on to something. Followed the scaly bastards from Kalaman, east of here. They stole some papers from an old mage, a friend of mine, after they tore him to ribbons. They knew what they were after and where they wanted to go. The Dark Queen must have tipped them off. They took only the papers written down by the dwarves at Palanthas, about their mines. My friend collected old stories like that. Then they killed some peasants, took their clothes and identities."

Zorlen had to shout to be heard over the rising steam noises from outside. "The dwarves found something, years ago during the Age of Might, down in this mine. After they found it, the dwarves sealed off the shaft and never went back to it. Your three buddies discovered their secret. Now they want it for themselves, and you've been recruited to help them get it."

"Wait!" Gilbenstock protested. "They're no friends of mine—they're customers! I never met them until two days ago! They hired me! I don't know what they want, either!"

Zorlen sighed and nodded. In the background, the great engine began to rumble very loudly. "I thought that might be the case, but I wasn't sure. At first I thought you might even be one of them, but I decided you weren't. You did too many stupid things, acted too much like a real gnome."

Gilbenstock was unsure if he should be relieved or mortally insulted. "How could you mistake me for one of them?"

"Never hurts to be paranoid." Zorlen gave a rueful smile. "If Sivak draconians kill someone, they can take his shape for a time, whether gnome or ogre. I'm afraid I was a little rough with you, not knowing if you were one of them or just a lackey. I owe you an apology. What we need to do now, however, is—"

Zorlen stood up, leaning back against the box lid. As he did, the hissing noises from outside suddenly changed into roaring thunder. The Iron Dragon lurched forward. Gilbenstock fell on his side. Zorlen, who was off balance, pitched headlong into the rear wall, slamming his curly head into the thick black iron. He fell flat out of the crate like a rag doll. His long knife clattered across the floor.

"Zorlen!" Gilbenstock tried desperately to restore the man, to no avail. He was out cold. Gilbenstock hastily grabbed for his earmuffs and goggles, putting them on after inserting wax into his ears. The great device rolled forward, foot by foot, levered into position by Squib's expertise. What if the draconians looked inside and saw Zorlen? Skort and Harbis might become dangerously perturbed. Doing the only thing he could think of, the gnome upended the empty crate and covered Zorlen's unconscious form with it.

Gilbenstock gingerly picked up the bloodstained knife by its handle and, after some thought, placed it under the box next to Zorlen. The human sounded as if he were telling the truth. After all, he hadn't harmed the gnome when he had the opportunity. He deserved a chance to avenge his dead mage friend, though Gilbenstock hoped the large human wouldn't wake up until the job was done and he was safely back in Palanthas.

A new noise began from deep inside the Iron Dragon—a slow, regular vibration with a rising hum. Gilbenstock peered out a front window and saw the three enormous drills spinning, gaining speed by the second. Dust on the floor rose in a cloud under the increasing tempo of the vibration.

The Iron Dragon drove forward, jerked as the drills made contact with the old rockslide. Gilbenstock clutched his goggles. A thick cloud of dust and rock fragments sprayed into his cabin through all the windows. He buried his mouth in his protective coat and wished he'd thought to design an armored scarf. Not that it would matter, since he was trapped in his own drilling device with a mad avenger while outside waited humans who were probably bloodthirsty, shapechanging draconians.

Gilbenstock hunkered down. The spray of debris and dust grew worse, blocking out the light and air. But he had to admit proudly that, no matter how bad things were now, the Iron Dragon was working perfectly.

* * * * *

When the drills finally shut down, it was too dark to read the surviving gauges and dials. Three feet of rock dust filled the cabin. Gilbenstock opened the rear door to shovel it out, then realized why it was dark—because the Iron Dragon had broken through the entrance and was approximately one hundred feet underground.

He carefully pulled off his earmuffs and pulled out the wax. Lighting an oil lantern, he found a brush on a wall tool rack and was dusting off the machinery when he remembered Zorlen. He carefully checked on the man, saw that he was still unconscious, then dusted around the overturned crate and quietly left the cabin by way of the ladder.

Faithful Squib was already on the ground, inspecting the machine. In the faint light, his broad smile was as welcome as the sun on a stormy day. The gnome and gully dwarf hugged each other in congratulations, then proceeded to check out the Iron Dragon.

"I trust all is well," said Skort moments later, as he and Harbis walked across the crushed rock toward the drilling machine.

Gilbenstock jumped; he had almost forgotten his two threatening clients. "Excellent," he said quickly. "Everything is going smoothly indeed, no permanent damage or problems, at least beyond the usual sort of scarring, denting—"

"Good," interrupted Skort. "Kindly wait here." He motioned to stony-faced Harbis, and the two men stepped over the Iron Dragon's huge wheel ruts and walked ahead into the broad tunnel of the mine.

Without lights.

"I suppose I should get the lantern from the cabin for them," muttered Gilbenstock as he watched them go. "They might put in another diamond or two for . . ." His voice trailed off. The two men had vanished into the darkness ahead without slowing down.

For a few moments, he merely stared. "How peculiar," he said faintly, stepping forward and squinting. Only the faint sound of footsteps on rock marked their passing, and even that was fading away against the hiss of steam from the great machine.

In the space of perhaps twenty seconds, the forces of wisdom and daring warred within Gilbenstock's mind. It was curiosity—which has killed more gnomes than cats—that won out.

"Good Squib," he whispered to his friend, who was again picking his nose. "Please wait for me here, by the machine. Don't follow me, only wait." He hesitated, then added, "If those two men come back without me, you must climb aboard the Iron Dragon, lock yourself into your cabin, and drive back to Palanthas. Stop at the city limits and leave the machine there. Don't stop for anyone else. Um, except anyone in black robes."

Squib's brow furrowed as he tried to remember all of the instructions. With a pat on Squib's back, Gilbenstock undid his steam armor, took off his steel-toed boots and tool belt, and set off into the tunnel ahead in his stocking feet. He gritted his teeth from stepping on rock shards, but once past the Iron Dragon, the packed-earth mine floor was fairly smooth and level.

I'm going to be killed, he thought. Those draconians—if that's what they are—will hear me, then they'll cut me up like a sour-cream walnut cake. Not even the Mount Nevermind Guild of Anatomy, Physiology, and Meat-Packing will recognize me. I must be insane. I am insane. I should stop right here and go back to Mount Nevermind and take up hydrodynamics like everyone else in my family, with the exception of Great-times-twelve Grandfather Mulorbinello, who went into aluminum siding and got rich.

Gilbenstock saw light up ahead—cold, pale light, like the sun on a hazy winter morn. He slowed his hurried tiptoeing, feeling the mine floor start to angle down slightly and become rougher.

The gnome spotted something in the pathway as he moved along, and he slowed to pick it up. It was a boot.

Beyond it was another, then several articles of strewn clothing and two other boots. He couldn't tell if they had belonged to Skort and Harbis, but the items were still warm. They also smelled funny. Gilbenstock hesitated, then pressed a shirt to his overlarge nose and sniffed deeply. Frowning, he pulled the shirt away from his face. Lizard came to mind.

A noise came from downslope. Gilbenstock crouched, then tiptoed forward again, dropping the shirt. He could hear someone calling—Harbis. Finding a little bit of cover among some rocks, the gnome made for it and hid there.

At first he thought that Harbis was calling for "cat litter," but in another moment he heard Skort call in a clearer voice, "Bloodglitter!" The call echoed for several seconds. Gilbenstock carefully peeked around the side of a small boulder and saw both Skort and Harbis, with hardly a stitch of clothing on, standing at the point where the tunnel leveled out and opened into a vast cavern hall. On either side of the two men were large glowing globes, apparently of glass, mounted on stone pedestals. From his position slightly above and some distance behind the level of the men's heads, Gilbenstock could not see far into the chamber.

"Bloodglitter!" called Skort again, then lowered his cupped hands from his mouth. "I wonder if he died."

"Our queen no let that happen," Harbis said. He stroked his beard thoughtfully. "Maybe the drilling he heard."

"Shhh." Skort raised a hand. Gilbenstock strained his ears, and soon heard a slow, distant thumping sound. He swallowed, trying not to breathe.

"He's huge!" Harbis gasped. "Too big. Before here he gets, we—" He abruptly stepped back.

"Gods damn," said Skort. His mouth fell open wide. "Gods damn."

There was a low, rhythmic sound like air rushing in and out of a great bellows. With the sound came the deep thumping noise, the beats spaced several seconds apart.

A new voice echoed from across the huge room. It was a low roll of thunder, yet strangely like a whisper. "Who calls for me?" said the voice slowly. "Who knows my name?"

Skort took a quick breath. "We call for you, Bloodglitter!" he shouted. He smacked Harbis on the arm. "Change now!" he hissed.

Harbis nodded, but Skort was already changing. The human's face stretched out, elongating into a muzzle. His neck disappeared. His arms grew thicker; his feet enlarged. Huge toes branched out into claws, and strange projections grew out of his shoulder blades. A tail appeared from the base of his spine and grew thick, reaching down to the floor.

The projections from his back turned into large silver wings. His face was reptilian. And his skin changed in the pale, cold light from bronze to white, then to a gleaming silver. Harbis changed into the same shape, only a few seconds behind.

Gilbenstock had lived through the War of the Lance almost without noticing it, buried in his geological and mechanical studies at Mount Nevermind. However, he had overheard a lot of talk about the war, so he knew about the reptilian draconians. He knew that draconians were born of corrupted dragon eggs, came in metallic colors, and blew up or turned to stone or acid when they died, as reported by the survivors of Mount Nevermind's Subcommittee for the Vivisection of Dangerous but Potentially Fascinating Specimens of Local Fauna. He'd also heard stories that certain draconians were able to take on the shapes of beings that they killed. Zorlen had been right.

"We call for you, Bloodglitter," rasped the great Sivak draconian who had once been Skort. "We read of your entrapment in the ancient scrolls of the dwarves, and we came to search for you."

"You have found me," returned the thunder during a pause in the deep, rhythmic bellows-sound. A loud thump sounded; a shadow fell over the two draconians. A huge, scaled foot struck the rocky floor only ten feet from Skort and Harbis, a foot so large that it dwarfed both beings. Gilbenstock could clearly see the bright red reptilian scales.

A dragon! Bloodglitter was a real, live, fire-breathing, gnome-chomping dragon!

"I do not recognize you two," said the dragon cautiously. "How do you know me?"

"We are servants of our queen, and we are honored to greet you, Great One," said Skort reverently. "The legends of the dwarves gave your name and your lair, but we had not expected to find one as great in size as you. We wish to set you free. After that, we will serve you in any way possible."

The bellows-sound grew very loud—then stopped altogether. After a pause, there came a roar so horrendous that the gnome clapped his hands to his ears. Dust danced on the ground before him. It was a wave of sound like the Iron Dragon's, only from a living throat. It went on for what seemed like an hour.

Abruptly, the great roar died away, and the dragon spoke again. "You dare so mock me?" it asked in a voice that seemed both saccharin and venomous. Each word vibrated Gilbenstock's bones. "When I was awakened and trapped here by the dwarves of Palanthas, it was the second time I had been imprisoned in this great stone cell. First were the elves, the three wizards who commanded the earth to swallow up my brethren. In the eternal halls of silence here I slept, racked with dreams of vengeance, yet denied even the chance to move a claw.

"Then I heard a tapping, a clanging, the knocking of dwarven tools. Unknowing, they drove tunnels past me, above me, below me. Then one found me, exposing my flank. They mistook me for dead, a petrified relic from an ancient age, and labored like ants to free me and let me stand as the centerpiece to a great hall they carved from the rock around me. I ached to move, even to blink my eyes, yet I betrayed not a motion until the day when they had finished their work. As they gazed upon me, I brought myself out of my long, miserable sleep, and I fell upon them like the mountain itself."

The slow rumble of the dragon's breathing resumed for perhaps a minute before the creature continued. "Sweet it was to taste blood in my jaws, but short the sweetness lasted. Many escaped, sealing the cavern behind them and leaving me among their artifacts—their magical lights, their carved staircases, their piles of tools and bones. I could move, but not fly. I could see, but saw no horizon. I could speak, but no one heard. I investigated every part of this ruin for a means of escape. It was useless. The bones of my captors have decayed and vanished. How long have I been kept from the mortal world?"

The two silver draconians looked at one another, then looked up again. "Your Greatness, the war of which you spoke first, against the elves, was over three thousand years ago. The dwarves found you a thousand years ago, as best we can tell."

The heavy breathing ended with a loud snort. A drop of yellow liquid fell from above and splashed five feet from the clawed toes of the two draconians. The liquid flamed briefly as the rock floor sizzled.

"Takhisis has forgotten me, then," said the dragon. "But I have not forgotten her. I have fed on magic and stone, bones and dust, gems and blood. I have slumbered here through the ages, awaiting a chance to soar the winds of the world. I have waited too long to breathe vengeance on the green lands above. I can wait no more. You must free me. I care not how."

"We can do it!" shouted Skort abruptly, like an eager pupil. His eyes gleamed white with excitement. "We found a mad gnome and a degenerate dwarf who have built a mining device. We tricked them into coming here. They were able to drill through the debris at the entrance to the mine. The device waits for us at the tunnel's mouth. We will force them to widen the tunnels so you may pass through. You will be free within a matter of days!"

"A mining machine? This is so? Was that the cause of the rumbling and noise earlier? Takhisis must have guided you from the Abyss itself, then. Let us not delay."

The two draconians quickly stepped back.

"Wait!" the dragon commanded. Another drop of amber liquid fell from above and spattered on the rocks at the tunnel mouth. "Blood," said the dragon, and there was something different now in its tone. "I smell a live thing with warm blood. It has sparked my hunger. Who have you brought with you?"

The draconians looked back up the tunnel, frowning in confusion. "There is no other being here but us, Great One," said Skort.

"Fool!" said the dragon sharply. Another burning drop of amber fell from its open jaws to the blackened stone. "I have been without food for ten centuries. I know what is here and what is not."

Eyes narrowed, Skort looked up the tunnel. "Go back and see if someone followed you," he said to Harbis. After a moment's hesitation, the draconian obeyed, peering behind the small boulders and old debris that littered the way.

"Free at last," said the low thunder behind him. "Free at last. Bright will be the fires when I reach the cities of elves and dwarves. Bright the forests and fields as they burn beneath me. Too long have I waited and dreamed. Too long have my enemies known peace. I must be free!"

* * * * *

Gilbenstock raced back through the darkness toward the Iron Dragon. He was completely out of breath. He gasped as he stepped on sharp rocks in his stockinged feet and tripped on the bumpy ground, but he moved as quickly as he could. There was no time even to berate himself for having fallen so deeply into this trap. There was time only to flee.

Such was his hurry that he rounded a corner and ran straight into someone feeling his way slowly down the tunnel toward the gnome. With grunts of pain and surprise, gnome and human fell over in a heap.

Panicked, Gilbenstock tried to bolt past. A hand snagged the gnome's pants with one strong hand and jerked him back. Another hand reached out and caught Gilbenstock's beard. "Don't kill me!" the gnome cried out.

"Damn you, shut up!" Zorlen hissed, releasing his grip. "Do you want the bastards to hear us?"

"Dragon!" gasped Gilbenstock, his heart pounding.

"Dragon . . . back there . . . huge red one . . . draconians . . ."

"A dragon?" whispered Zorlen. "Tell me what you saw!"

Between ragged breaths of air and constant coughing, the gnome poured out the tale of what he had seen and heard. The human's face went slack; his hands released their grip on the gnome.

"With all the gods as my witnesses," Zorlen said at last. "I'd never imagined there'd be a dragon down here. My wizard buddy knew some stories about a monster encountered by the dwarves centuries ago in these mines. The draconians must have figured it out. *Damn!*"

Puffing less now, Gilbenstock looked the man over. The gnome's heat vision revealed that Zorlen was bleeding from a scalp wound, probably caused by his fall inside the cabin of the Iron Dragon. Zorlen's hand shook as he touched his head. He didn't look at all like the threatening figure he had once been. He looked like a battered, desperate human who had run out of luck.

"Just who are you?" Gilbenstock asked shakily. "I don't like being pushed around by someone I don't know, although it seems to have been the pastime of a great many people lately. Not that I'm bitter."

Zorlen looked in the gnome's general direction, smiled slightly. Gilbenstock realized that the human couldn't see him in the darkness. The man couldn't see anything.

"Name's Zorlen," he said at last. "Zorlen Margauff. I'm a mercenary, sort of a nosy odd-jobs man for rich folks in Kalaman. I was helping a friend, the wizard I told you about, who got a bad divination from his crystal ball. I left him for a couple hours and got back to find him cut up as though he'd been run through a butcher's meat grinder. I got a few divinations myself and picked up the trail of the killers. I've been hunting them for weeks just to see what they're up to. Never dreamed it would be this."

Zorlen exhaled deeply and made a gesture with his hands. "Sorry about roughing you up. It was in the line of duty, sort of. I really thought you were a draconian, too, the way you all buddied up there at the start. But, like I said, you were—"

He hesitated, sensing the gnome's sudden tension. "Eh, forget it. Draconians are good actors, but not that good. I was wrong."

Gilbenstock glanced back down the tunnel, but he couldn't see around the corner. "I suppose I shall have to be satisfied with that for an apology," he said quietly. "Our priority now is to get out of here as quickly as possible with our limbs and internal organs still intact."

"The Abyss it is," said Zorlen, pulling an object from his belt. It was the long knife. Zorlen reached down with his other hand and produced another long object from a boot, a heavy wrench, probably borrowed from one of the Iron Dragon's many tool boxes. "We've got two draconians to kill first. Then we're going to find a way to seal up this mine again."

"You've been eating too much cooked meat!" gasped Gilbenstock. "Forget the draconians! We've got to get out of here before they—"

Around the corner, a pebble rattled across the floor.

Man and gnome turned to look, words frozen on their lips.

A huge winged shape lurched around the corner and threw itself upon them.

A wing slammed into the gnome's face, almost knocking him senseless. He fell back. The draconian leapt at Zorlen. Something clattered to the mine floor among the rocks and dirt. Zorlen cried out in pain, lashed out with both feet, and caught the draconian in the chest. It flapped its wings and came on a second time, claws out and jaws wide.

"Light!" cried Zorlen, stabbing at the darkness. "I need light!"

Gilbenstock scrambled away and tried to get to his feet. His fingers found a hard metallic thing on the ground. He snatched it up. It was a wrench, the one Zorlen had brought—a huge twenty-pounder normally used on the driver wheels.

Draconian and human battled on the mine floor, the human on the bottom. Gilbenstock saw the draconian's powerful arms strike down at the human time and again, wings whirling and pumping. Zorlen's agonized screams echoed wildly through the mine tunnel.

Without thinking, the gnome swung the wrench and ran forward.

The blow landed solidly on the draconian's lower back. The sharp crack of bones breaking was audible even over Zorlen's shrieks. The creature fell forward, catching itself on its clawed hands. Curious wheezing sounds came from its jaws, as if it couldn't breathe. It tried to turn around.

Gilbenstock charged forward, too frightened to do anything but attack. He ducked under a wing and swung the wrench again, up and over. It smashed into the draconian's muzzle just in front of its eyes. A scaled arm lashed out and struck the gnome in the face, throwing him flat on his back. He banged his head as he fell.

The world exploded in a shower of stars and sparks. Gilbenstock marveled at it all. It was an impressive display. For some reason, though, he knew he was not going to like it when the stars went away.

The stars soon left, replaced by the onset of a skull-pounding, vision-throbbing, record-breaking headache. All was darkness.

"Help me," Zorlen moaned. "It's clawed me. Help me."

Dizzy and aching, the gnome rolled over, then got unsteadily to his hands and knees and crawled toward the human. Zorlen lay on his back, hands grasping his left thigh. He was bleeding from a dozen places. A few feet away from him lay another body, a knife sticking up from its motionless chest.

The dead body was Zorlen.

"Help me," Zorlen gasped. "I think it broke my leg."

The gnome hesitated, remembering earlier conversations. It was hard to think when his head hurt so much. "Are you really Zorlen?" he asked. "You could be the draconian, couldn't you? I mean, you could have taken Zorlen's shape when you killed him, and you could be waiting for me to—"

"You rotten little midget," hissed Zorlen weakly. "I'm

not the damn draconian. My leg's broken." He lapsed into a string of curses that amazed Gilbenstock with their creativity and pithiness.

Head thundering, Gilbenstock managed to get to a wall and pull himself to his feet. He carefully made his way to Zorlen's side. The human had fallen silent again, except for his moaning.

"You must be Zorlen, then," the gnome said. "As someone once told me, draconians are good actors, but they're not that good."

"Gods, just shut up and get me out of here."

"You're going to have to stand up and put your arm around me," said the gnome.

Zorlen levered himself up, one hand still grasping his left thigh. His face twisted with pain. "You're too damn short," he muttered. "I can't do it."

Gilbenstock groaned. He sighed and looked around in the darkness. "Well, I suppose I could make up some kind of splint for your leg with the wrench, and maybe I could even improvise some sort of tourniquet, since I think I remember a lecture about that given by the Guild of Anatomy, Physiology, and Meat-Packing, and I'm fairly certain I can avoid the lecturer's mistakes and not have the same thing happen to you as happened to the tourniquet volunteer, which was quite a pity considering that—"

Zorlen gritted his teeth and reached out blindly. "Forget it. I can make it," he said. "Help me up before the other draconian gets here."

"It wouldn't take but a moment to assemble the materials for—"

"Up! Up! Where the Abyss are you?"

With terrible slowness on the gnome's part and endless curses on the human's, Gilbenstock managed to get Zorlen to his feet. After some experimenting, they were able to devise a sort of three-legged walk; Zorlen gripped the top of the gnome's head with both hands and hopped slowly through the tunnel behind his shorter companion. The pressure made Gilbenstock's neck ache, which aggravated his headache. Nonetheless, the system seemed to work.

Time became meaningless as they plodded along. There was only their slow footsteps, the night of the tunnel, and pain. Neither spoke. Years came and went.

Then light appeared ahead. They were almost at the Iron Dragon.

Zorlen sagged suddenly. Gilbenstock fell, mashing his nose into the debris-strewn floor. The human collapsed on top of him. It took a few moments for the gnome to pull himself free and check Zorlen for life. The man was alive but unconscious. He had lost too much blood.

"Rat poop," muttered Gilbenstock, using the strongest profanity he knew. He clutched his aching head and staggered toward the Iron Dragon.

Cross-eyed Squib was pulling debris from the vehicle's wheel assemblies. He wore his earmuffs and was so totally focused on his job that he missed the gnome's approach, just as he had missed seeing Zorlen earlier. When Gilbenstock poked his friend in the side, the gully dwarf jumped a foot and dropped his pick. "Brave Squib," Gilbenstock gasped when the trembling gully dwarf had removed his earmuffs. "We must flee! We must take the Iron Dragon back to Palanthas at once. We are in the gravest danger!" He glanced back. "Oh, and we'll have a passenger. Let's hurry."

Gilbenstock started up the iron ladder for his cabin, almost falling twice. His headache made the world seem distant and unreal, like a bad dream.

Zorlen's overturned crate half blocked the door. Dust still covered everything. Gilbenstock pushed the crate out the door, then turned to the controls and activated them for a rapid start-up. If the last draconian showed up, it would get an unpleasant taste of a triple-headed rock drill. The thought kept Gilbenstock amused as he flipped switches and twisted knobs. Nearing the end of the start-up sequence, he automatically reached for a lever mounted in the floor and tugged.

Nothing happened.

The gnome tried again, then stopped everything else he was doing and threw all of his weight into moving the lever.

It didn't budge.

Gilbenstock's hands began to sweat. Zorlen must have accidentally shoved the crate against the lever, jamming the mechanism. The lever was the Iron Dragon's Tertiary Back-up Emergency Brake—it locked the driver bars.

Gilbenstock released the lever and stepped back. His heart stopped. Even his headache stopped. The Iron Dragon could not move an inch with the brake jammed. Major repairs were called for; cables would have to be cut and iron pins sheared off.

But there was nothing he could do about it here. Not a thing.

The Iron Dragon was finished.

The gnome looked around the cabin as if seeing it for the first time. He knew every bolt, every gear, every blot of paint. He thought of the sore thumbs and pinched fingers he had suffered, the endless rolls of bandages he'd used. All of it for this, his only child, and now it was stuck in a long-abandoned mine and could not move.

The last draconian would be coming. It'd have no trouble finishing off a gnome, a gully dwarf, and an unconscious human. Then it would free the dragon, and then . . .

A blast of steam blew out from one of the side valves on the great machine. The boiler pressure had built up inside the Iron Dragon over its long idle. Gilbenstock reached up automatically for a control that would widen the valve and let off the steam.

His hand gripped the wheel valve, then he hesitated. The gnome stood unmoving, his eyes looking at the valve but seeing beyond it. He bit his lip, and a tic caused his left eye to twitch.

I must be a dragon inside. I must be a dragon, too.

A precious minute passed. Then the gnome's hand gripped the valve tightly and began to turn, but not in the direction he had originally meant to turn it. The steam blast was shut off by degrees until it was gone.

Gilbenstock felt the floor creak. He reached up and turned another valve, closing it as well. He turned three more, moving more quickly now, then turned the boiler up to full power with a set of backup controls. He left the cabin quickly. He thought he was going to cry, but no tears came. He did not even look back.

At the bottom of the ladder, Gilbenstock found the gully dwarf hunched over Zorlen's semiconscious form. Squib again had a cup of warm, meaty broth and was feeding it to the human in sips, holding Zorlen's head in one dirty hand.

"We'll have time for that later!" the gnome said quickly. "We must abandon the Iron Dragon! Let's drag him with us and get out!"

Squib stared in astonishment at his friend, then looked up at the towering bulk of the black engine. The Iron Dragon was starting to rumble slightly and made loud knocking sounds as its pipes and boiler walls began to expand.

"Run for it! Flee! Escape! Evacuate! Abandon ship!" shouted Gilbenstock, waving his arms in Squib's face. "A draconian is coming up the tunnel! The driver brake's jammed! Let's go!"

Squib drew back, bug-eyed and openmouthed. He dropped his cup of broth on Zorlen's head in astonishment. The human sputtered and groaned. Gilbenstock and Squib grabbed Zorlen's clothing at the shoulders and heaved. The human weighed a ton, but he could be moved, head lolling back, hair just brushing the rocky ground.

Grunting with effort, the gnome and gully dwarf made for the dimming light at the tunnel's mouth. It was almost nightfall. Coughing on the dust they stirred up, they stumbled over wheel ruts and nearly fell on loose gravel. The entrance grew nearer. Thirty feet. Twenty feet. Ten.

Behind them, a pipe burst in a wheel housing. Metallic debris ricocheted off metal and rock. A pressure-warning whistle went off, the shriek washing through the tunnel like a dying animal's scream. They reached the entrance.

Gilbenstock paused, looked back. The Iron Dragon blazed in his infravision like the sun. Even at this distance, he could feel the heat from the boiler through his clothing. Warping metal cried out. Small seams burst and steam roared out.

"Good-bye," Gilbenstock said without breath, so his words were silent. "Good-bye."

They pulled Zorlen from the mine into fading daylight and dragged him about fifty feet away from the entrance to one side, behind a large boulder. The wind was cool, the evening sky almost free of clouds. Overhead were the planets and the first stars of night.

"Gods, my leg hurts," Zorlen mumbled as they sat together, exhausted. It was the first thing he'd said in many minutes. Bleeding and pale, he looked for all the world as if he were already dead.

"Yes, I recall your mentioning that," said Gilbenstock. He got on hands and knees and crept around the rock to take a last look at the mine entrance. He was half tempted to go back and see his creation once more. Maybe it wouldn't explode after all, in which case he could—

Gilbenstock froze.

The last draconian was at the mine entrance.

It was holding Zorlen's hunting knife, now clotted with dark blood. As its eyes roved the scenery, the draconian spotted the motionless gnome. Its eyes widened slightly, and a slow, thick smile played over its features.

"Gilbenstock," it called, its voice like rocks grinding together. "I've been looking for you. You haven't finished your job for us yet. Your Iron Dragon is overheated but unharmed. Don't leave now." The smile grew. "We have a use for your friend Zorlen, too. I know he's there. You tried to trick us, I think, and that won't go over well. You weren't supposed to tell anyone about this, but you did."

The tip of the long knife rose slightly.

"We'll sit down and talk about things after you finish this last job for us," the draconian said. Its teeth came together, shining and white. "Business first. You're a businessman, so you know that. Then, when the business is done—"

The ground jumped.

In the blink of an eye, the draconian was gone. A monstrous jet of flame, smoke, and rock exploded from the mine entrance. The blast leapt up at the sky and mountaintops, carrying away a part of the mountain with it.

The gnome threw himself flat and covered his head with his short arms. Shards of rock tore at his hands and neck. The mountains across the great valley rang over and over, repeating the Iron Dragon's last great roar.

And then, all was silent.

Minutes went by as things calmed down. When it seemed safe, Gilbenstock raised his head and blinked away dust. The mine entrance was gone. A mound of fallen rock buried it to a depth of hundreds of feet. There was no sign of the draconian. Not even scales.

Gilbenstock remembered to breathe. He filled his lungs with the cool night air.

"Well," he said. "That should do it." He got unsteadily to his feet and wiped at his eyes. Turning around, he saw Zorlen and Squib staring at him in amazement.

Gilbenstock straightened up, brushing himself off with a more professional air. "You understand, of course," he said, "that catastrophic events are not uncommon where advanced technology is concerned. You can't help but burn down the kitchen at least once in making a waffle."

"The mine—" began Zorlen.

"Is no longer," finished Gilbenstock. "No dragon, no draconians. That's the good news, as they say. The bad news is that we shall have to walk home. Rather, Squib and I will walk home, but we can rig up some sort of litter for dragging you along with us." He paused. Dalamar had said . . .

"On the other hand," the gnome added, "walking is known to be invigorating for the circulation, so perhaps that's not such bad news after all."

As Gilbenstock and Squib scouted the area later for materials to use in making the litter, the gnome found himself thinking about the Iron Dragon. His thoughts at first were sad, but after a few minutes he remembered that he still had quite a lot of money left from the draconians' advance payment, and he did still have the plans for that new drilling machine, the one that made the triangular holes. He was still a young gnome, only in his forties. An Iron Dragon II was not out of the realm of possibility.

After all, one never knew what the next trend would be in tunnel boring.

Dragon Breath

Nick O'Donohoe

The building was lopsided, leaning in the dark as though it had drunk too much. A badly carved sign proclaimed that this was the End of the Road. For those who couldn't read, there was a signboard featuring a sleepy-eyed man with one arm around a sleepy-eyed horse, both waving ale steins. Strangely, for an inn, there were no horses nearby, no visitors entering or leaving. The moon shone on an empty road all the way into the town of Graveside.

The door was barred and the ragged curtains pulled shut. It was testing night, when the newest batches were checked.

Traditionally, testing was done quietly, with cautious sips in near darkness, so as not to be distracted by the company or by the spirits' appearance. On this occasion, however, firelight flickered on a copper tank topped with copper coils, dripping liquid into a huge open vat. In the glow of the flames, a fat, middle-aged man named Graym laughed until tears leaked from his eyes as the Wolf brothers, leaning greasy shoulders against each other for support, pounded the table, chanting, "Drink! Drink! Drink!"

Darll, a grizzled ex-mercenary, manipulated a lit splinter with exaggerated care and touched it to a tiny glass of brownish liquid. Flames shot up from the liquid. With a flourish, Darll snatched up the glass, opened his mouth, and threw the burning concoction in the general direction of his throat.

Unfortunately, this was his fifth taste-test. He missed his mouth and hit his beard, setting it on fire. Graym laughed so hard he fell off his wooden bench onto the floor.

Darll's eyes went wide as he tried to blow out his own beard with quick puffs. He gestured frantically to the Wolf brothers, who were still pounding the table; they hadn't

147

noticed that he was on fire. Jarek, the gawky youth next to him, laughed and gestured back.

In desperation, Darll grabbed a full ale stein and dumped it over his own head. The ale running down his face put out the fire.

Graym, struggling up to table level, burst out laughing again and collapsed to his knees. He struggled back onto the bench and leaned on the table, pushing the open bucket of test liquid fondly with his finger. "We have *got* to find a name for this stuff."

Darll, fingering his singed and still warm chin, came out with one.

Graym shook his head. "Inventive, sir, but no, and anyway, I'm not so sure that dead trolls *do* that."

"What *can* we name it?" Jarek—the gawky youth—asked. "There's never been anything like it."

"Came from a still, didn't it, Fan?" Fenris said to his brother.

"Right you are, Fen." The other Wolf brother jerked his head toward the copper tubing and vat contraption over the fire pit, nearly toppling them both backward.

"Well, there you are." Fenris thumped the table. "Still-waters."

"Rundeep," Fanris suggested, and they exploded into gales of laughter even though it wasn't that funny.

Darll coughed—only partly from smoke—and pointed an unsteady and accusing finger at Graym. "You're a damn wizard."

"No, sir." Graym shook his head, which spun obligingly, so he stopped. "Nothing but a good honest cooper with a head for business—"

"No magic?" Darll said it hoarsely, two or three times. "Then how'd you learn to make this stuff?"

"From a recipe Laurin gave me, with directions." He reached forward and picked up the test glass. "Here's to Laurin."

"To Laurin!" the others shouted. At this point, they'd have drunk as readily to crop blight.

Graym dutifully passed the glass around, making sure

the Wolf brothers got it last, then took it back and washed it carefully using a pitcher of water which, so far tonight, had been used for nothing else.

"Where'd she get the recipe?" Darll wanted to know.

"Her late husband found it in the ruins of Krinneor. There's a whole world waiting to be relearned out there, found knowledge to be applied by entre-pergnoirs . . . now that the Cart-Collision's over."

"Cataclysm," Darll corrected automatically. He'd been correcting Graym's mangling of the word for as long as the two had known each other.

Jarek, behind the others, finally pointed at Darll's sopping, half-burned beard and laughed. Darll dipped the tiny glass in the bucket and passed it to him. "Think it's funny, boy? You try."

Graym fondly hugged the small vallenwood aging barrel from which he'd poured the test bucket. Part of him was aware that the taste-testing had gotten out of hand. The rest of him, glowing with visions of success and hazy with test drinks, didn't much care.

The Wolf brothers pounded the table, chanting, "Drink! Drink!"

Jarek pulled a wood splinter from the fire pit under the distillery, lit the drink glass in three tries, and promptly tossed it into his own long hair, which blazed up nicely. Darll laughed as Jarek swung his burning hair this way and that in panic.

His eyes shut tight, Jarek groped for the ale stein. His hands wrapped around the bucket of test drink instead. He lifted it over his own head and began to pour.

Darll knocked the bucket from his hands just in time, upending the ale stein over Jarek's hair. The bucket of flammable taste-test flew across the table and hit the floor. The liquid spilled out in a long, straight stream.

Time seemed to slow. All of them watched in fascination as the streaming liquid ran over the floor stones, past the open vat, down the sunken hearth, and into the fire pit around the still and the holding tank. A finger of liquid touched the blaze. A track of flame moved back toward the open vat. The vat, now full, was trickling liquid down the side. The flame lit the trickle and leapt up it to the vat. . . .

* * * * *

Graveside, the village down the rebuilt road, slept. The mist in the western hills shone in the setting three-quarter moon, and outside the End of the Road Inn, all was quiet.

The roof lifted almost straight off the inn, flaming at the edges. Four men dove and rolled out the ground floor windows. Two of them looked incredibly charred but were merely filthy. One was a grizzled, muscled man dragging a skinny, dazed youth clutching a small, empty glass. Last came a fat, middle-aged man who, with some effort and incredible determination, carried a vallenwood cask with him. They all turned to watch the fire, which was now quite spectacular.

After a moment's stunned silence, Graym turned to the others. "Still and all," he said cheerfully, "except for this last bit, it was a fine party, wasn't it?"

Jarek was near tears. "I didn't mean to do anything except what Darll had done, and when I caught fire, I thought, why not put it out the same way. . . ."

Graym smiled at him, amused and completely free of rancor. "A good idea, boy. A bit muddled in the execution, but a good idea." He put an arm around Jarek's shoulders. They stood in silence, watching the beams blaze.

Darll, who had carried Jarek out the window, stood up painfully. Even former mercenaries get a little old for this sort of thing. "Do you know what can happen when you pour a bucket of that stuff on a flame near your head?"

Jarek stared at him blankly. "No. What?"

Darll let go of him and stood with his face in his hands. After a while, Jarek shrugged and turned back to the fire.

* * * * *

In the first gray morning light, it could be seen that the End of the Road was little more than ashes and more ashes.

The inn's signpost, lying on the ground, was still smoldering. The second-story floorboards were charred and dangling. The steaming barrels were charcoal on the outside, ale-soaked wood in. All of them were sprung, the heat having warped the metal hoops and popped the nails holding them in place. The distillery was buckled from the heat, but Graym thought it might be serviceable, if they could clean it.

Jarek, gawky and vacant, stood peering mournfully through a door frame where no outside wall existed.

Fenris and Fanris, the Wolf brothers, poked through the ruins with interest. Truth be told, they felt right at home around wreckage and garbage.

Darll, unable to shake old habits, patrolled the perimeter, as though the fire had been part of an attack.

Also walking around the edge of the smoking and steaming wreckage was a determinedly cheerful, overweight, middle-aged man with a drooping mustache which had already been singed once in the search for anything of value.

"Here's something." Graym stooped painfully, feeling even fatter and older than he was, and picked up a smoke-blackened rintle, the tiny thumb-guard that coopers use. He tossed it from palm to palm. "There's always salvage, if you know where to look."

He passed it to Jarek, who slid it on his thumb, yelped, and jerked it off. It fell into the rubble, where it vanished.

Graym sighed. "Well, it wasn't much anyway."

Fenris came forward with the glass Jarek had saved, now refilled from the small keg that Graym had carried out. Graym took it and sipped gratefully.

Darll glared at him. "How can you?"

Graym smiled at him placidly. "Well, surely a man ought to be allowed to enjoy a drink at his own fireside."

Darll snorted in disgust.

A few moments later the Wolf brothers chuckled.

Quite a while later, Jarek said suddenly, "Oh, *I* get it!" and laughed until Darll told him sharply to be quiet.

But none of them laughed for long. The ruins of their beds and their business lay in front of them, gray and smoldering.

"So much for the ale batch we had aging," Darll said. Sword in hand—even in a town as peaceful as Graveside, he had refused to give up his sword—the mercenary prodded one of the split, charred kegs. "Now *that's* a loss."

Jarek looked miserable again. Graym waved a hand in dismissal. "Not so great a loss, sir. Remember, the market for Skull-Splitter Premium was dropping off. We needed to attract new customers." He considered. "More, we needed to cut costs somehow."

The others looked at Graym hopefully as he pondered the ruins. "When you think about it, we've cut overhead something considerable. No roof repairs, no keg maintenance—" He looked around at the others earnestly. "It's our chance to start over."

"With the new stuff?" Fenris asked curiously.

His brother added, "The stuff with no name?"

"We'll never have a better time to start it." Graym put his hands on his hips, facing them. "Every eye in Graveside will be watching us. The story of the fire will travel up and down the road, too. As advertising—it'll do wonders."

Darll rolled his eyes.

Graym finished, inevitably, by pumping Jarek's hand. "Best thing that could happen, really. Once again, on the cutting edge of downsizing. Boldly done, sir."

Jarek looked happier.

"Still . . ." Graym eyed the others. "We'll all feel the lack of the old life, while we start back up. After all, living indoors is habit-forming. We'll miss bathing." He glanced at the Wolf brothers and amended, "*Some* of us will miss bathing."

"And the customers." Darll rubbed his jaw, which had a large, slow-fading bruise.

"It was a good inn," Graym said reflectively. "Fights, thievery, crooked gambling . . . venture investment at its best." He sighed. "I'll miss it."

"We'll miss the money," Darll rumbled. "It wasn't much, but it was good enough."

Graym stared into the embers, sighing again. "I was going to use the money to marry Laurin."

"Ahhh."

Laurin had lost her husband of twenty years to a Cataclysm avalanche. She had hair that was partly gray and mostly red; she wore shawls and robes to hide her weight, and she was pretty enough that it worked. Laurin, as Graym had observed once, "curls around your heart like a cat and makes you happy." Even Darll, who had never felt the need to marry, conceded that Laurin, with her sharp tongue and soft heart, made a place feel like home just by walking in.

"And she won't marry you without the money?" he said dubiously.

"She would," Graym replied shortly. "I wouldn't ask her. And there's . . . complications." He didn't elaborate.

"You just lost the woman you love. You don't have to be so damn cheerful."

"I do." Graym looked at Darll earnestly. "It keeps us going. Only think, sir, when none of us is cheerful, of the first hard times that hit us."

Darll, in chains, had been dragged to Graveside by Graym, who called the Cataclysm "a business opportunity." They saved Graveside—mostly through luck at that— from a threatened invasion of men who turned out to be dead. Graym pardoned Darll, made him a military advisor to Graym, 'Graveside's Protector.'

"One of us always needs to be cheerful," Darll admitted grudgingly. "Probably, it'll be you."

He peered up the road toward the town of Graveside. By now, the townspeople could see the smoke. Several of them were trotting toward the inn, gaping at the damage. "Here they come. Frightened, from the look of them."

Graym thought they looked uncommonly fearful. "Nice of them to be worried for us."

"Or for the inn." Darll glanced at him shrewdly. "Are they upset over losing the place or losing their money?" He paused. "Gods, Graym, you did pay them back, didn't you?"

Graym's calm smile wavered. "Actually, we still owe a

little to the city." As a reward for defending the town, Graveside had loaned them money to start the inn and the brewery. Graym had paid some back whenever the city reminded him how far past due he was.

"How little?" Darll growled.

"Some."

"All of it?"

Graym sighed. "Almost."

Darll closed his eyes and said bitterly, "I don't think ashes are viable local trade goods." A thought struck him for the first time: "I wonder why they didn't come out last night? What are they afraid of?"

The good citizens of Graveside hung back, pointing with awe at the smoking ruins. They whispered together, not out of politeness for Graym and the others, but fearfully. A number of them, after inspecting the ruins, ducked hurriedly under trees and watched the sky in apprehension.

A well-rounded, red-haired woman, with a shock of gray above her forehead, bustled through the crowd. "You're all right, then?" She was looking only at Graym.

"All of us are." Graym smiled into her green eyes, feeling suddenly better about everything. "Good to see you, Ma'am."

"I thought you'd be needing breakfast after such a night." Laurin raised the wicker basket on her arm; it was steaming slightly. The Wolf brothers looked sick; Jarek, staring at the basket, was green.

She chuckled and went straight to Jarek. "And for you, young man, dry toast." She pulled out a fresh-baked, lightly toasted bun. "Something in your stomach will make you feel better, no matter what last night was like." She forced it into his hands. "Go on, then, let me see you eat your breakfast. Most important meal of the day."

"The wisdom of the ages," Graym murmured fervently, taking a roll for himself. "Was there ever such a woman?"

"You love me 'cause I feed you," Laurin said, laughing. She handed rolls to the Wolf brothers as well. "There never was a crisis so bad that food didn't make a body feel better."

Graym was watching her and smiling. He heard a discreet cough near his elbow. Jayem, one of the Elders of Graveside, stood by Graym's side.

Elder Jayem spoke in a fussy, solemn voice. "These ashes cry out for revenge, do they not?"

Though he had no idea what the elder was talking about, Graym patted the smaller man's shoulder. "I always try to live and let live, sir. 'Specially with those who don't want to let *me* live."

"Let live?" Jayem cried loudly, and a few nervous townspeople jumped. "I have not heard that dragons are willing to *let live*." He pointed an accusing finger at the ruins. "Can you deny that this is the work of a dragon?"

Jarek stared nervously at the sky.

Graym hesitated. "Haven't thought about it, sir, and what if it were?" he said. "What could we do about it?"

Elder Jayem's voice rang out, clear and echoing with conviction. "What could you do? Go, as Graveside's Protector, and slay the dragon in combat!"

Several townspeople murmured approvingly. The Wolf brothers, who also had been staring at the sky, suddenly appeared very upset.

Jayem folded his arms. "There have been rumbling noises in the night, and sightings of winged monsters in the sky. There have been rumors of damage to cottages and farm buildings." He pointed to the charred ruin of the ale house. "Is there any more sensible explanation for that?"

After a strangled cough, Graym said, " 'More sensible.' Ah. There you've got us." He looked at Darll and winked.

"Exactly." Elder Jayem pointed. "Before, we only had rumors and reports of a dragon in the mountains there— to the west; now we can be sure. We have proof. Something must be done immediately."

Elder Jayem now stood at the center of a hopeful crowd of townspeople. Darll fingered his sword, then moved his hand away. His long combat career had taught him that it is impolitic to reach for weapons in front of someone to whom you owe money.

Graym said skeptically, "So you think we should fight

this dragon?"

"Fight and kill it," Jayem said. The Gravesiders kicked in with a few ragged cheers.

"Kill it?" Darll ventured. "Maybe we should just bruise it. After all, no dragons have been seen in generations."

The crowd ignored him completely.

Elder Jayem was solemn. "There will be danger."

The Wolf brothers edged back.

"There will be horrors unimaginable."

Jarek leaned forward interestedly. Darll pushed him back. One and all were shaking their heads.

Jayem coughed discreetly. "There will be a reward."

The head-shaking froze. Graym brightened, saying heartily, "Always a pleasure when business discussions get down to particulars."

"Fifty steel pieces, raised by the village."

For once Graym couldn't think of a thing to say.

"Just for killing the dragon?" Darll demanded.

"Killing, driving off. Either requires proof or witnesses."

"Naturally." Darll fingered his sword.

Elder Jayem nodded. "So you will kill the dragon for us," he said, as though it were settled. "Promptly." He frowned at Darll's singed beard. "And do something about your personal appearance." He walked away.

Graym caught Darll's arm as the mercenary aimed a blow at Jayem's back. "Now, now. Weren't you taught as a child to respect your Elders?"

Darll growled, "The pompous little twit! He knows we need the money."

Graym shrugged. "He even knows *why* we need it. It's a small town, sir." He turned away from the ruin and stared into the mountains to the west.

Darll rubbed his hands together, suddenly aware how much he had been missing combat. "So. We go to the town armory, get the weapons, and give 'em a good show. . . ." He looked at Graym's face and stopped. The two of them edged out of Laurin's earshot, and Darll said, "Well?"

"I sold 'em," Graym said shortly.

Darll could not have been more shocked if Graym had confessed to selling Elder Jayem's breeches. "You're the town's Protector, and you sold their weapons?"

"Well, look at it." Graym waved an arm at Graveside, which was surrounded by farm fields and spring flowers. "It's completely peaceful. We've hardly had a problem." He smiled around the village. "Lovely place to live."

Darll poked Graym in the chest. "And you're its Protector."

Graym winced, not entirely from the poke. "Well, to be truthful, *you* are, sir."

It was true. When thievery happened, Darll investigated. When fights broke out, Darll stopped them. When rough strangers came down the road, Darll went out and spoke to them—often they retreated, sometimes with bandages.

Darll scratched his bearded chin, thinking. "But still, you're the one with the official sword of office." He glanced around. "Come to think of it, I haven't seen— Graym, you didn't. . . ."

"First to go, sir. A collector's item. High resale value, even in hard times."

Darll bit his lip. "Still, you had some spears—"

"Sold as a single lot." Graym frowned thoughtfully. "I should have got more for them, but some sales are for goodwill and word of mouth."

"Is there anything left?"

"Oh, of course." Graym spread his hands, implying a wealth of weaponry, then gradually brought them in. "Actually, most of what's left has mainly—sentimental value."

Darll nodded tiredly. "Meaning, it wouldn't sell." He shook his head. "All I can say is, it's a damn good thing there's not a real dragon."

"Oh, but there is one!" a voice cried.

They turned to look. Rhael, youngest of the Elders, stood before Graym.

Even now, Graym was happy to see her. Rhael, Elder of Fearlessness, had been Graym's first friend in Graveside. She was also Laurin's favorite niece.

"Please, you're not really going to try to kill the dragon, are you?" Rhael demanded.

"Don't you worry about us," Jarek said. He parried with an imaginary sword, since Graym wouldn't let him carry a real one this close to town.

Rhael said flatly, "I'm not. I'm worried about the dragon."

"There is no—" Graym began.

Darll stepped on his foot, hard.

Rhael went on without noticing, "Dragons are wise, graceful, beautiful beasts, and they haven't been seen for ages before this. You can't kill one, just when they're coming back. You mustn't!"

"Why not?" Graym was frankly puzzled. "We're heroes, such as we are; they're dragons. If we kill them instead of them killing us, that's good-deed-doing."

Laurin stepped forward, handed Rhael a biscuit to eat. "Child, he's the Protector. It's his job."

Rhael shook her head vigorously. Stray ashes from the fire drifted out of her hair and onto her nose. "But a dragon isn't a villain." Her eyes shone. "Dragons are the noblest, wisest, most graceful and beautiful—"

Graym held up a hand, thinking about the money Elder Jayem had offered. "Commitment to beauty's all right," he said dubiously, "but you can't let it interfere with good-deed-doing." He gestured to the men with him. "We've survived the Cat-Collusion—"

"Cataclysm," Darll corrected tiredly.

"Of course, you did," Rhael said quickly. "But you're heroes and warriors—"

"And as such," Graym said solemnly, "we have our work." He glanced at the Wolf brothers and at Jarek, who was practicing swordplay with the heat-bowed poker from the inn's fireplace. "Some would say we have our work cut out for us." He finished solemnly, "Could you respect us, if we turned away from this? Could you see me marrying your Auntie Laurin?" Laurin came closer, put a hand on his arm.

Rhael shook her head firmly. "I can't see my favorite

aunt marrying someone who would kill a dragon. I'm sorry, but I can't."

Laurin said quickly, "Now, lovey, you're just upset by the fire and all. I'm sure if you think about—"

"No." Rhael faced her aunt firmly. "My Uncle Otto wasn't the sort of man who ran around killing dragons."

"There weren't any."

"And I can't let you marry someone who would." Rhael tossed her head and walked off.

Laurin said, "I'll talk to her, love. Don't you be troubled." She handed Graym a muffin, which he ate, then she lifted her heavy skirt and hurried after Rhael.

Darll rumbled, "Let's go see what weapons you couldn't pawn off on anyone."

By midmorning they had a pitted sword, a battered broadaxe called Galeanor, the Axe of the Just, and one real find—a twice-mended lance. According to town legend, it was one of the original dragonlances. Unfortunately, the pole had been shattered. It was now a short and clumsy-looking spear.

They also had splitting headaches—remnants of the new product. Jarek whimpered and said a hundred times that he was sorry the fire had happened.

Graym thought, but did not say, that he was sorry, too.

* * * * *

The whole town saw them off. There was no time to make banners, and Jayem, the Elder of Promptness, wouldn't let anyone make long speeches.

Werlow, the Elder of Caution, stepped forward carefully. "Safe journey. Be watchful."

Warissa, the Elder of Justice, strode out and faced them. "Strike where you must," she said clearly and calmly. "Wrong no one. Safe journey."

They nodded back to her politely. Given their pasts, the Elder of Justice made them most uncomfortable.

Sernaya, the Elder of Thrift, came forward and barely nodded. "Mind your expenses. Take a lunch. Sleep outdoors, not at inns. Don't forget to bring proof of a kill, or of driving it away." She patted the keg of test liquid, set on a small cart to take with them, and said reprovingly, "Don't drink too much of this on the way out of town." She stepped back and added as an afterthought, "Safe journey."

The other Elders came up to them one by one, wishing them luck and giving them advice.

Finally, Rhael, looking troubled, stepped forward and said succinctly, "Safe journey." She turned away.

Laurin walked out of the crowd. She put a cloth-wrapped bag in Graym's hands. "Sernaya always says, 'Take a lunch.' I packed you each one."

"Wouldn't you just," Graym said reverently. It smelled like pork baked into bread, and it was steaming through the cloth. "How many women are there like you?"

She said severely, "Don't you go looking for them." She kissed him on the lips. "Safe journey, and a safe journey back."

Graym's heart swelled. As a young man, he'd been too busy to marry. Later, a poor cooper in a rich town, he'd been too disreputable. He bowed, puffing at the effort to bend his considerable waist. "Did you talk to your niece?" he whispered.

"Some." She glanced sideways at Rhael, who was frowning.

Laurin blushed, scowled defensively, and hurried back into the crowd.

Graym cleared his throat. "Yes, well. Good send-off. You're nice people. We'd best be going now." He grabbed the cart carrying the test liquid and lurched forward. The others followed him.

Laurin pulled out a napkin and waved sadly to him. Rhael glared at her and Laurin stopped. Graym shrugged resignedly.

Two tattered, disheveled creatures detached themselves from the crowd and leapt onto Fenris and Fanris, all but wrestling them to the ground.

Darll drew his sword. Graym, with a gesture, stopped him. They both stared.

Apparently, the creatures were female. More astonishingly, they were kissing the Wolf brothers. The watching Gravesiders smiled tolerantly, though some of them looked queasy.

"The Rulg Sisters," Fenris said rapturously.

"They're new in town," Fanris added.

"I'm sure," Darll said, scowling.

Graym asked, "Where are they from?"

"Some other town," Fenris said.

"They had to leave," Fanris said. "Real quick."

"Don't know why," Fenris said moodily and sighed.

"Well, some things are hard to explain," Graym murmured, then slapped the two on the back. "But well done, and boldly, the both of you. You've met the loves of your lives, and I know you'll be happy."

They were already happy. "They're going to marry us—"

"But we need to have money." Fenris sagged despondently.

"They said they wouldn't marry us without money." Fanris looked to Graym for reassurance.

Graym floundered for a moment, then came out with, "Yes, well, it's nice that you've both met women with standards."

Darll snorted and began walking. The others, pulling the cart, struggled to keep up.

Fanris burbled, "Have you ever seen a woman—"

"—like either of them?" Fenris finished.

They were at the edge of Graveside, passing a stone-walled pigsty. Graym looked at it thoughtfully. "Not a woman, no."

They walked a while, thinking to themselves—all except Jarek, who was happily throwing stones at other stones.

Finally Darll said, "The way I see it, if there were a dragon, and there isn't, we'd be in big trouble. If we somehow managed to kill it, and we can't because there isn't one, you'll lose the chance to marry Laurin. If we try to drive it off, and we can't because there isn't one, it wouldn't go without a fight. If we don't find one, and we won't because there isn't one, we're still going to be broke and none of us will get to marry, including you." He added because he was getting hungry, "Plus we'll probably starve to death."

Graym considered, then squinted upward into the fog. "Anyway, it's a nice day for a walk."

* * * * *

Jayem had directed them toward the mountains to the west. Unfortunately, the road west didn't diverge from the main road until it had passed through the Valley of Death, a huge abandoned cemetery from the ruins of a larger city. The earthquakes and rock slides of the Cataclysm, as well as recent vandalism, had left a great many skeletons exposed. Their bleached, unceasing grins did little for the Wolf brothers' moods.

"Are dragons big?" Fenris asked Graym.

The fat man pursed his lips. "Hard to say. By report, some of them are the size of houses."

"Are they fierce?" quavered Fenris.

"Ahh. Now, there you have me, sir. They say, and again this is only by report, that some of them are fierce enough to fight whole armies." Graym smiled at the two of them. "But likely the legend has grown over the years."

They walked on, the road winding upward. Fenris and Fanris seemed unusually pensive.

Finally Darll snapped, "Would you two stop looking like you're thinking? It's unnatural."

They stopped.

Graym said patiently, "What's on your minds?"

"The dragon," they said in unison.

"We could pretend to kill it," Fanris offered.

"And go home," Fenris added.

"Right now," Fanris finished.

Jarek objected. "What about when the dragon shows up and burns another building?"

Darll rubbed his eyes and said with barely sustained patience, "The dragon didn't burn the first building, now, did he, Jarek?"

Jarek blinked. "Oh, right, right."

Graym puffed his lips out, considering. "Pretending to kill the dragon is an attractive idea—reassures people, brings us home unharmed, even promotes trade. . . . No, no, I forgot. Jayem said we need proof that we've killed it, or we can't get the money."

"I'll say I *saw* it," Fenris offered.

"And I'll say I saw him see it," Fanris added.

"The general worth of your testimony aside, I think they want a witness who isn't getting paid for the death of the dragon," Graym said solemnly.

"Dragons!" Darll couldn't contain himself any longer. "Who believes in them anymore, outside of Graveside and a few farmers? What is it with this town? Something in the water, that keeps folk simple?"

"I like Graveside," Jarek said stubbornly.

"I like it, too," Graym echoed quietly. "I'd like nothing better than to go back to it and rebuild the inn, and mar— and market ale." He glared around. "So we'd all better hope that there's a dragon, and that we kill it. Eh?" He turned to continue pulling the cart on the upward, winding road.

* * * * *

The road narrowed into two ruts. Darll grew more alert, the farther up the ruts they traveled. The Wolf brothers grew more nervous. Graym put them in charge of the keg and cart, but pulling it didn't tire them out enough to calm them down.

The five heroes passed a dismal-looking farm. Graym politely knocked at the door and bowed to the wiry, incredibly gap-toothed woman who opened it.

"Your pardon, ma'am. We're warriors, of a sort—"

The old woman was staring over his shoulder at Jarek; Graym decided not to specify what sort. . . .

"And we couldn't help wondering what happened to your house."

She leaned out, her long white hair waving in the

breeze, and hissed, "The dragon did it."

Fenris made a small, sick noise. Fanris echoed it.

The old woman cocked her head and grinned. "With one claw, he did it, dears, one claw the size of a man. He spun down in the moon and the mist and spit fire over me house, and kicked the corner clean off it." She laughed, an awful cackle that died away slowly.

Graym had never seen a crone, but he was fairly sure this was one. He said politely, "And what is your name, ma'am?"

"Ranissa." She rolled her eyes, stuck a clawlike hand out to him, and finished, "Ranissa the Mad, they call me. What d'you think of that?"

Graym, ever polite, said, "I can see where your manner of speaking might startle quiet folk. . . . Maybe I'd have named you Ranissa-the-not-likely-to-be-asked-for-dinner-twice, but—"

"And the dragon returned," Ranissa wailed, striking her forehead. "Diving from the mist, like a thing of death, straight for me own home and farm." She glared at Darll, who looked dubious. "And he tore at me farm and the hill above it, and he belched fire and swooped to and fro, like a thing gone mad." Ranissa waved her arms and swooped back and forth in front of the cottage, bobbing her scrawny neck and glaring fiercely.

The Wolf brothers grabbed hold of each other and shrieked in terror. Delighted at the effect of the only good story that seventy years of farm life had given her, Ranissa swooped at them twice more, nearly sending them into hysteria.

Darll put a halt to it, saying with more manners than he wanted, "Where did this exceptional dragon go, ma'am?"

Ranissa pointed a skinny finger up the road they had been climbing. "Up into the mist, and there he waits for whoever comes, in the clouds we've always called Dragon Breath."

* * * * *

They climbed the steep road that grew ever steeper behind Ranissa's cottage, unable to help glancing from time to time at the layer of mist hanging above them:

Dragon Breath.

Passing a point on the hillside where the earth was scored with a single gigantic track, Darll bent and examined it.

"See how the front is deeper? Something pushed hard here, maybe leaping."

"Leaping." Fenris wrapped his tattered cloak tighter.

"At farms." Fanris huddled against him, and they looked longingly at the tiny cart, wishing it were large enough to hide under.

All glanced back at the damaged roof of Ranissa's farm-house.

"Something kicked it," Fenris said firmly.

"Something with big feet," Fanris agreed.

"Flying big feet," Darll pointed out. Up until now, he hadn't believed in dragons. But something had kicked that house in. The Wolf brothers couldn't help but notice that he had unsheathed his battered sword and carried it at the ready, in true mercenary fashion.

Graym, in the lead, protested cheerily.

"Didn't kick it in, now. Just knocked it about. In play, like."

Darll muttered to Graym. "You know, I find it hard to believe we might really meet a dragon up here."

"That's your trouble," Graym said. "Not an optimist like me." When Darll stared at him, he added, "And when we do find him, we'll kill him. We need the money."

"Plus it's our duty to the town," Darll said stiffly.

"A wonderful man for duty, you are now, sir. So we'll meet the beastie, and give him our best—" Graym glanced back at Jarek, who was jabbing the air with the mended lance, and at the Wolf brothers, who were flinching away every time Jarek jabbed. "With luck, he'll be asleep. . . ."

* * * * *

They edged upward. Shortly they were surrounded by blinding, bright fog.

A raven cried, somewhere in the mists. The Wolf brothers cowered. Jarek snatched up a sword and peered alertly in the wrong direction. The raven flew off behind them.

"I *heard* something!" Fanris wailed.

"From there!" Fenris cried.

Darll, scowling, kicked viciously at a rock.

A small lizard dashed out from under. The lizard stopped in front of the Wolf brothers, puffed itself up, and hissed.

They screamed in unison. "Dragon!"

Jarek flailed about in the fog, stabbing, the lance narrowly avoiding puncturing the keg. "Where?"

But the Wolf brothers, fleeing back down the road, had no answer.

They had barely rounded the first curve when a robed, cowled figure appeared out of the mist, halted their flight. It turned, raised a slender arm, and pointed at them.

The Wolf brothers, spinning to run the other way, screeched, "Wizard!"

The figure pulled back its hood. "Don't be scared, loves; it's only me." Laurin smiled reassuringly, though she looked worried. "Fenris, Fanris, are you all right?"

They were as close to pale as their unwashed skin could get.

She circled around them, a small crusty loaf in each hand. "Poor dears. Here, eat something."

"We saw it," Fenris wailed, ignoring the bread.

"It's huge." Fanris extended his arms wide.

Graym, catching up with them, puffed and said genially, "It wasn't *that* big."

"Of course not, to you." Laurin looked at him admiringly. "You're not afraid of anything."

"Nor are you. You followed me—us," Graym said, giving her a kiss on the cheek.

Laurin blushed and glanced shyly at Jarek. "Love, not in front of the child."

Darll, limping up to them, snorted.

Fenris quavered, "Did you see Ranissa?"

Fanris echoed, "The Mad?"

"That I did. She screamed in my face about dragon fire, disembowelment, and death. Cheery soul." Laurin laughed.

"And what did you do?" Jarek asked, awed.

"Fed her a berry-jam tart and told her to get more sleep. By the by, have you killed it yet?" Laurin looked around at them complacently.

Jarek blinked. "Killed what?"

"The dragon, child, the dragon!"

Jarek kicked a small stone and said gloomily, "We haven't even seen it."

"That's good, then. I'm not too late." Laurin sat heavily on a boulder by the road. She quickly handed everybody more tarts from her knapsack. "Eat these and relax. Graym and Darll and I need to talk a bit." She eyed them. "I know the truth."

Graym blushed. Jarek groaned.

Darll shrugged. "Not much to talk about then, is there? If there's no real dragon, we can't kill it or chase it out, and we therefore don't get paid. We're finished. If there *is* a dragon, and we don't kill it, we've let the town down. If there's a dragon, and we do kill it, your niece won't let you and Graym get married."

"Right." Laurin beamed at him and handed him a meat pie. "So there has to be a dragon, and you have to drive him away. Good thinking, dear. Proud of you, I am."

A hissing noise came from far off in the mist. The Wolf brothers gulped and clutched at each other.

Graym ignored them. "The problem being, ma'am, no one's seen a real, live dragon for a long time now."

A drawn-out creak, dim and mournful, sounded in the fog above them. The Wolf brothers edged closer to Darll.

Laurin smiled. "Let's say it was a dragon as destroyed your inn."

Jarek dug his toe in the dirt and muttered. Laurin patted his elbow, inserting a cream roll in the crook of his arm. "Be frank with yourself, child. *Couldn't* it have been a dragon?"

"I'd like to think so," Darll rumbled. "Nobody likes careless idiots, but it seems as though everyone wants a dragon."

A grating screech echoed from the hillside. The Wolf

brothers, wide-eyed, stared from side to side. Jarek scratched his head absently with the lance. Darll's hand drifted down to his sword. Graym glanced at him and fingered the axe.

"Has your niece the youngest Elder softened her heart toward progress and dragon-slaying at all?" Graym asked, clearing his throat of an unexpected huskiness.

Laurin threw up her hands. "Oh, you know her when she's full of herself and how magical life is. All she says is, 'Dragons are wise, graceful, beautiful beasts.' "

A loud bellow from above cut her off. Jarek, his mouth hanging open, pointed at the sky.

A huge, bat-winged form careened through the mist, diving straight at them.

All of them ducked . . . except Jarek. At the last minute, Darll dove for him, struck him with an exasperated grunt, and knocked him out of harm's way. The dark figure swooped within a few feet of the road, one wing scraping the dirt. A burst of flame belched from its front; the dark wings overshadowed the entire company. Then, with a loud grating screech, it pulled up and disappeared into the mist.

Darll, checking his bones as he got up, muttered, "Graceful, you said."

They heard a loud thump; the dragon struck a rock somewhere above them on the mountain face.

"Here it comes again!" Graym cried.

They dove for the ground as the dragon spun overhead, losing altitude rapidly and belching fire. The fire smelled like a badly run smithy.

"And wise," Darll concluded. He crouched, waiting for the next flyover.

Laurin shook her head sadly, stared into the fog. "Doesn't seem graceful and wise, does it? Well, we all have our off days. Poor thing; maybe it's hungry."

Fenris and Fanris whimpered in unison.

A full-throated scream sounded like two pieces of metal dragged across each other. A shadow descended from the mist. It wobbled, then flapped its wings listlessly, and finally poured out hot steamy breath as it drifted beyond them. One wing, flapping all the way down to the trail, cut a divot beside Jarek. Laurin pulled him out of the way just before a second wing spur dragged a ragged gouge in the road. The dragon vanished in the mist, flapping up the mountain.

The small party collected in the middle of the road, mouths agape. Even Graym was momentarily speechless. He took the lance from Jarek and poked Darll with it. "Sir, would you mind forming a scouting party with me? And bring the supply barrel."

Darll struggled to his feet. Graym handed him the lance and barrel of taste-test, then dragged him off into the mist.

When they were far enough away from the others, Darll said sarcastically, "Fine idea bringing the brew along. Those Wolf layabouts might drink this while we're out of sight."

Graym shook his head, "You're a fine one for strategy, sir, but you do me too much credit. I was thinking something else entirely." He added thoughtfully, "You know, I'm beginning to wonder if maybe the dragon didn't burn the inn after all. "

Darll stared at him as if he had gone mad.

"Now, now. You're a man of the world, sir, and you've seen folk lumber about gracelessly the way that poor flying beastie is moving. Does that movement remind you of anything?"

Darll opened his mouth, shut it, and stared first at the liquor keg, and then at Graym.

"I'm thinking we weren't the only ones partying that night," Graym continued, "and maybe we have a dragon as needs a morning pick-me-up; a little hair of the troll. Mmm?"

Darll, completely baffled, muttered, "A real dragon, after all these ages?"

"Well, sir," Graym said reasonably, "what else could it be?" He called back to Laurin and the others, "Darll and I are going scouting. Be ready to take cover."

Laurin answered, "Hurry back, then, love," as calmly as if he had said they were going to the farmer's market.

Jarek announced, "I'm ready to fight," at which there

was a loud thud and a yelp in the mist.

Graym said steadily, "That's why I've left you to guard the main body, boy. If anything happens to us, you're in charge."

Darll said aloud, "That's true, boy," and whispered to Graym, "In all my years, I've never heard anything before to make me shiver. That just did it." He climbed uphill beside Graym.

They went a surprising distance before being attacked once again. Graym was puffing, and even Darll was tired, when they heard a strange whine overhead, growing louder every second. Graym raised the axe, straining to see in the fog.

Darll pushed the fat man down. "He's diving."

The dragon skidded overhead, upside down, within a few feet of them. Smoke and steam puffed at them; soot rained down on them. Graym tightly gripped the battered axe, Galeanor, and readied for a direct assault.

Lying almost prone on the road, Darll heaved the lance as the dragon passed over. His throw was perfect. The spear point entered the back of the dragon. The creature reeled upright, and they saw the lance protruding from its belly.

"Amazing shot, sir," Graym said.

Darll, staring after it, protested, "I'm not that strong!"

They heard a hiss and a sigh. The dragon's wings slowed visibly.

"It's wounded!" Graym shouted and ran uphill, his belly bouncing up and down as he charged forward with the axe.

"Careful," Darll warned. Drawing a short sword, he followed more slowly.

With a hiss, a roar, more grating screeches, and a terrible scrape, the dragon slid onto the hill above them.

Darll caught up with Graym within arm's reach of the dragon. Darll was about to hiss a warning when he was distracted by the sight of something peculiar about the left wing.

A broken cable trailed from it. Darll stared harder. The cable ran across a pulley to the wing's outer tip.

The dragon perched on runners, skis, rockers, and a huge, strange, single boot attached to a crouched leg near the tail.

Graym approached, touched the beast's scaly side tentatively. It was covered with rubbery shingles.

A cast-iron ratchet wheel dropped out and landed squarely on Darll's foot. His eyes watered, and he whispered something fervent about wizards and poor hygiene.

Graym clutched the axe tightly. " 'Ware. It's moving."

Darll leapt back and raised his sword. The construct rocked from side to side, seeming terribly flimsy. It settled back in place as a small, bearded figure, waving both arms, jumped to the ground. It shouted what seemed one long, polysyllabic, extremely grateful word.

Darll dropped his sword. "A gnome."

The gnome grabbed his hand, pumped it up and down fervently while expressing his thanks.

He went on for some time. Finally Darll said desperately, "Please! Shut up."

The gnome stopped.

Darll said, "Now—*briefly*—what were you saying?"

"Thank you for providing the steering lever." The gnome made a conscious effort to talk slowly. "How did you know I needed one?"

"Needed one for what, sir?" Bewildered, Graym examined the machine collapsed on the hillside.

"Why, for the Supra-Terrestrial, Unconnected, Aleonic Over-Transport." The gnome gestured. "Surely you can see that it got left out."

Graym looked over the dragon's bulky canvas and wood body, its huge fuel tank, its boiler, its chain drive and spring leaves, its ball screw cylinder with a governor mechanism over it, and its leaking hydraulics. "Frankly, sir, it's hard to imagine your having left anything out of this."

The gnome nodded gravely, accepting the compliment. "Exactly. Unfortunately, my original steering lever, while well designed, was perhaps too aerodynamically sound, and the Back-up Flight Failure Power Unit to which it was connected—"

"Fell out, did it?" Darll snorted.

"Not exactly," the gnome answered reflectively. "It flew on ahead, and I couldn't catch up with it."

"Could you build another, sir?" Graym asked. He was poking interestedly at the boot.

The gnome said hastily, "I don't think I'd touch the Bootapult, if I were you, because it recocks itself automatically on landing, which is very handy in the event of need for a quick launch, but the latch isn't terribly reliable, and it's strong enough to kick the entire machine into the air—"

He stopped. By now Graym was well away from the machine. The gnome finished lamely, "Of course, I'd like to build a better steering lever, but to do that I have to fly back to my workshop—"

"Which is where?" Darll broke in.

"It is called Mount Nevermind by humans," the gnome said with dignity. "Home of the greatest gnome technology imaginable—machines that would make human technicians weep—"

"I believe you."

The gnome frowned at Darll's tone.

Graym said quickly, "By the way, sir, what's your name?" Darll, who knew something of gnomes, said quickly, "Your *human* name."

The gnome had to reflect—or perhaps translate. "I was renamed for the consideration by which I undertook to test the Over-Transport only under cover of darkness, so that chance observation would frighten people less—"

Graym thought of Ranissa and said, "Less than what?"

The gnome opened his mouth, and Graym said hastily, "I withdraw the question, sir. What did you say your name was?"

The gnome gave up trying to explain. "Fly-By-Night."

"A good name," Graym said solemnly, "all things considered. Well, sir, if you need the haven of your workshop, what's keeping you here?"

The gnome sighed. "Apparently, the Over-Transport Steam Propulsion System has a design weakness. I keep taking off for home, but without sufficient fuel I tend to glide more than fly, and this mountain doesn't give me an adequate starting altitude to find an updraft before I land. . . ."

He went on happily about tail winds, thermals, lift ratios, and other strange terms.

Eventually, Graym caught the gist and said, "Hold on a minute, sir. Are you saying that if you could only find sufficient fuel, you'd leave here?"

"Exactly. Ideally I should have a liquid fuel, but in its absence I've tried wood, and I've tried making charcoal, though I had to construct an Ultra-Pressure Charcoal Compactor, and I've even tried inventing a dirt burner." Fly-by-Night regarded them earnestly. "It hasn't worked, so far, but can you imagine a more efficient fuel source?"

Graym exchanged a glance with Darll. He patted the keg beside him in affectionate farewell. "As it happens, sir," he said heavily, "I can."

* * * * *

Under Fly-By-Night's long-winded directions, Graym and Darll crawled over and under the dragon, hooking up cables, pounding on bolts with the axe head, and rethreading fuel pipes. Both of them were slightly burned, Graym on the forehead. Twice Darll was whacked on the head by badly fastened parts; once Graym narrowly avoided being struck by a descending wing. As they clambered about, the gigantic spring that was compressed above the Bootapult creaked and twisted. Both of them stayed as far away from it as possible, tiptoeing whenever they were working on the tail section.

They poured the contents of the keg into the fuel tank at the last minute, figuring (at Darll's suggestion) that something could go wrong if they poured it in too early. Each of them debated taking a farewell sip, but nobly decided the gnome's need outweighed their pleasure and resolved not to have any. Then they went back on their resolve for a final toast.

At last Fly-By-Night climbed into a trap near the front,

where an array of levers, wheels, cranks, buttons, and dials implied at least some measure of control. He shouted long but fairly clear orders to them. With Graym flapping one wing up and down, and Darll flapping the other, the gnome pulled levers and cranked gears until the entire contraption was flapping on its own.

Suddenly Fly-By-Night jerked the spear-lever back and cried, "Stand clear because you never know quite what will happen in the event that the boiler stays under pressure, the heat remains constant, wing lift is sufficient, and the Bootapult mechanism engages without my needing to climb down and kick it free—"

Fortunately, they had already leapt aside. The Bootapult released prematurely and, with a thunderous kick, launched the whole shivering mechanism twelve feet in the air. The Bootapult, shoving off, left a mark in the earth exactly like the giant dragon tracks they had seen on the hillside.

A second later, with a spark and a whoosh, the boiler ignited. Fly-By-Night strapped on a bizarre leather-and-metal helmet with binoculars over the eyes and shouted down at them, "Which way to Mount Nevermind?"

Darll pointed vaguely to the southwest. The gnome, nodding and waving, pulled back on the stick.

With a series of loud creaks and hisses, the dragon flew bumpily around while it built up steam. Graym and Darll ran after it, keeping up easily despite Graym's being out of shape. After two circuits, the gnome waved a final time—again—pulled the lever—again—and let off a magnificent screech from the fully powered steam whistle. The entire puffing assembly flapped purposefully off to the northeast.

Graym and Darll, also puffing, watched it fade into the mist. A faint screech of strained metal echoed across the valley. It sounded like a cry of triumph.

"There's nothing," Graym panted, "like a good deed well done, even if you're not sure what you did."

A few minutes later, Laurin came running up to them, Jarek close behind, tripping every third step.

"Such awful noises! Are you all right, love?" She

touched Graym's forehead. "It hurt you!"

"I'm fine." He patted her shoulder.

Jarek drew himself up and brandished a stout branch. "Where is this wicked dragon? We'll have words, I'll tell you that."

Darll, grinning hugely, opened his mouth to say something.

Laurin cut him off calmly. "But I saw you chase the dragon. I saw him fly off. I witnessed the whole thing."

Graym, thinking faster than he had in his entire life, stepped on Darll's bruised right foot. Darll's mouth snapped shut with an audible click as Graym said with a catch in his throat, "And what did you witness, love?"

"Well, first I saw Darll heave a spear at him—not that it hurt him, of course," Laurin added hastily, "which we'll be sure to tell Rhael. Then I saw the both of you crawl right under his wings and thump him with the butt of your axe, giving him due notice—but not hurting him, of course."

"So," she finished, handing them each a snack. "May I say to my niece that the dragon's been banished from these parts, very much alive?"

Graym pondered and finally said, "Well, he's certainly not dead." Which was true.

"Good enough." Laurin winked.

Darll's eyebrows were pulled together in thought. He opened his mouth again.

"The beastie was lost, and not feeling his best," Graym said easily. "We talked to him, and showed him the way home."

"And that's what I'll testify."

A hoot, perhaps a steam whistle, sounded in the distance.

Laurin looked adoringly at Graym. "A little hint here and there, and it's wonderful what you can make of an opportunity."

Darll shut his mouth again, swallowing hard.

Graym sighed happily. "That's that, then. We can go home."

"Home?" Fenris and Fanris, cringing behind Jarek, said in unison for once.

"Back to Graveside, anyhow." Graym was grinning at Darll's thoughtful expression. The mercenary was struggling between a love for the truth and a love for reward money. "We'll need to rebuild."

"I'll help you," Laurin said firmly. "Me and the whole town. You've earned it." She added hesitantly, "Maybe you could pay back the town with the reward—"

"I was just thinking that very thing," Graym said, so sincerely that even Darll wondered if he hadn't been. "And I need some to set up house, if I should become mar—if I should be not single. . . ." He hesitated until Laurin nodded vigorously, smiling, then he sighed. "Well, then. And Fenris and Fanris will need some money for their own bride-price."

Laurin looked at them in astonishment. "We can have one wedding," Fenris said happily.

"One *big* wedding," Fanris added, scratching.

Laurin put an arm around Graym and squeezed. They fell in step, heading home, though Laurin stared wistfully over her shoulder in the direction the dragon had disappeared.

"I never saw it close up. Was it beautiful?"

"I've never seen its like," Graym said gravely.

"You *didn't* hurt it, did you?"

Graym patted her shoulder. "You know I most likely won't hurt anything, even when I set out to."

Darll hobbled behind them, favoring his sore foot. "I wouldn't go that far." Jarek and the Wolf brothers chuckled.

Later, when Laurin scurried ahead to spread the good news, Graym dropped back beside Darll. "How's your foot?"

"Bad, but better than your head." Darll added grudgingly, "She's a smart woman. Now we get the money, you don't have to kill a dragon, and you can still marry." He added, "And the Wolf brothers marry—gods help the next generation—and Jarek had a good time. Everybody got something but me."

"I wouldn't say that, sir" Graym said slowly. "I've been thinking. . . . As a married man, I can't afford to take the risks a Protector has to. Then, too, I'll need to watch the inn more, make it a going concern."

Darll stopped in his tracks and stared, afraid even to hope.

Graym finished, "All in all, sir, I'd be more than grateful if you'd be Protector instead of me."

When Darll could speak, he sounded almost as gawky as Jarek. "I'll be good at it, Graym. I promise. I've had lots of experience with law enforcement."

Graym clapped him on the shoulder. "There you are, sir. I was never any good at arrests, where you know all the protocol and nuances. You'll be a natural, I predict."

Jarek lunged, empty-handed, and saluted an imaginary foe. Darll had sensibly taken his weapons away before they got to town. "It's good to be heroes again. Think how famous we'll be."

"We've got notoriety, good word-of-mouth, and an established business," Graym said solemnly.

"The business," Darll reminded him, "is burned to the ground."

"Now, now. I've told you many times that you need a positive outlook." Graym thought. "If only we had something new to sell people—"

"How about the new drink?" Fenris said, edging up to Graym.

"If you can make it again," Fanris added, beside him.

Graym stared at them in surprise. "Good thinking. Don't worry; Laurin would never trust me with the only copy of the recipe. We'll market it by the barrelful, and maybe even darken it with charcoal. Paladine knows we've got enough charcoal." His eyes glowed. "And we'll call it—"

Fenris, beside him, belched.

Graym's eyes watered, then flew open wide. "Pure Dragon Breath."

Fenris looked insulted only for a minute.

Fool's Gold

Jeff Grubb

"Of all the Dragonkind, the worst by far are the Golden Wyrms. The rainbow-hued monsters of evil will just want to eat you, but the Golds, they won't be happy until you learn something. Given the choice, I'd rather be eaten."

—Flint Fireforge (attributed)

"This is a gnome story!" bellowed the bard, fully expecting every eye in the room to turn his way. Indeed, every eye did turn his way, as well as every hand—hands filled with pottery mugs, wooden platters, stained cutlery, and the odd food item. A hailstorm of produce and kitchenware pelted the storyteller, and he made for the nearest exit, both expectations and clothes spoiled.

On his way out, the bard collided, ever so briefly, with a towering gentleman who momentarily filled the doorway at the same time the bard was seeking egress. The man-mountain was not very movable, and would not have moved in normal circumstances, and the bard would have rebounded back into the common room of the Wolf's Head Inn. But the newcomer hardly expected fleeing skalds to greet him, so he stepped back under the assault of the terror-stricken talespinner. The bard did not miss a step as he escaped from both the inn and the remainder of this tale.

As the huge man turned, revealing the scabbard slung across his back, he glowered at the retreating form of the bard. He stood poised in the doorway, until a low *ruff* shook him from his thoughts. The huge newcomer entered the inn, a large hound padding along at his side.

The newcomer had that haggard, well-traveled look of an adventurer. A merchant would by nature scan the room, sizing up the market. A thief, or even a former warrior in the dragonarmies would slouch in, hoping to avoid recognition. This one simply did not care. He had the look, it would be said later, of one made wise against his will. His dog was lean and long-faced, but otherwise filled all the basic requirements of dogness.

The man made for the bar, while the dog sauntered through the debris left by the ill-fated bard, stopping only briefly to nose a mostly chewed mutton bone. The dog snorted a rejection, padded on toward the hearth. There he turned thrice around in front of the fire and lay down, curled toward the flames, golden-furred belly up, head upside down and resting on the floor. It was as if the creature were a regular visitor, and this was also later mentioned as curious by those relating the story.

The newcomer held up two fingers to the barkeep. The tavernmaster in turn pulled two mugs, one in each fist, and raised an eyebrow, a silent inquiry. The newcomer spoke for the first time. "One for my companion," he explained, motioning to the animal stretched out by the fire. The barkeep nodded, smothered a grin into a tight, businesslike smile, and drew two ales.

The stranger's canine companion had already attracted an admirer in the form of one of the barmaids, a pretty young woman dressed in a simple white skirt and dark blue blouse, the entire ensemble covered by a many-pocketed apron of azure. Her hair was pulled back from her face, and ran in an ornate braid reaching the small of her back. She was petting the dog's blond belly fur, and the beast made no motion to dissuade her.

The dog only reacted when the newcomer set a foaming mug by his muzzle. And then the dog looked at the mug and the young lady and attempted to choose between them. At length, the ale won out, and the beast licked his chops and raised his head to slightly above the mug's level, lapping the beer with a long, slender tongue. Spurned, the young lady sighed and returned to her task of gathering empty mugs and bottles—"dead soldiers" in the local parlance of a town that had escaped most of the war's worst effects. She brought them back to the bar, taking a less than direct route that swung her well away from an older, well-dressed patron who had been eyeing her throughout the episode.

Said route took her back past the newcomer, who stopped her in her tracks with a motion of his hand. "Bring a second round when he finishes the first, and a third when he finishes the second, and so again until he cares to stop." The woman (a stitchery of light blue thread on her apron identified her as Melissa) made as if to comment, then nodded and returned to the bar. The remainder of the patrons—farmers talking about the upcoming harvest, carpenters and bricklayers driven indoors by the darkness, a bespectacled scribe writing a letter for a middle-aged woman in the corner—had all returned to activities previously interrupted.

All except for the older, well-dressed patron, who looked directly at the newcomer with the sureness of either a wizard or a petty lord. His finery was faded but still serviceable, though his gut stretched the buttons of his vest. The man had a slender wand of worn ivory or bone hanging from his belt, but it was unclear at first glance if this was an enchanted item, a symbol of power, or an affectation.

"That is an interesting animal," said the local noble at length.

"More so than you know," came the reply, flat and automatic.

"I have never seen a dog take to ale."

"He drinks only to embarrass me," said the newcomer with a sigh. "No one ever asks him to clear the check."

"Is he for sale?"

"He is not mine to sell. The dog accompanies me of his own free will. There were times I tried to sell him, drive him off, abandon him, but he always returns, bringing trouble when he does."

At this the dog pulled his muzzle from the now empty mug and yawned, baring a full set of clean, sharp teeth, only slightly yellowed by age. He cocked his head at his human companion.

"You know it's true," added the newcomer, addressing the dog. Then he muttered, "As if it could be anything *but* the truth." And with that, he motioned for the second round.

The conversation died in the flickering of the fire as the older man (petty lord definitely, the eyes were sharp and feral, but not bright enough to indicate wizardry) realized he had been cut out of the dialogue between the man and the dog. He tried again. "You find our village pleasant?"

"I found your village by accident. I was traveling down the coast from Trentwood."

"Business or pleasure?"

"I have no business and very little pleasure."

"Are you a warrior?" His eyes traveled to the sword and sparkled for a moment with awareness. "I—*we*—have need of a warrior, here."

"I . . ." said the newcomer, taking a long draw on his mug, "am a fool. But you can call me Jengar."

"At least you're truthful about it," said the old baron, the chuckle dying in his throat as he realized that Jengar did not share his amusement.

Jengar transfixed the petty lord with a harsh glare, then relaxed, but only a touch. "I do not have a choice in the matter. It is my curse, to tell the truth. Are you interested in the story?"

"Of course, of course," said the petty lord. "It doesn't feature . . . ah, gnomes, does it?"

"Not yet, " growled the man. "But gnomes could only serve to make matters worse. . . ."

* * * * *

The room quieted slowly as Jengar began his tale. He did so without prologue or call for quiet, merely setting in to a recitation of the facts. His quiet demeanor caught many by surprise, so that half the room missed his beginning, yet after the first minute, the entire room went silent. Conversations ended in midsentence, ale went unordered and undelivered, and even the scratch of the scribe's pen was stilled. The only sound was the dog lapping noisily at his mug, and even that fell off as the tale proceeded.

"Let it be known that my name is Jengar. The dog's

name is Fool's Gold, named such for reasons that will become clear. Back during the war I tacked on a nickname for myself typical for warriors—Trollkiller or Flamedeath or something equally stupid. Why I've let such sobriquets perish will also become clear.

"I served well in the last war and fought hard. At Two Wars and Armada and at the Siege of Castle Dire, I was no hero leading the charge, mind you, but was part and parcel of the battle. And if I have previously inflated my own contribution to such victories, well, that is to be expected from a battle-worn veteran. My flaw, like that of many of my companions, was to retell my victories in the most glowing terms possible many times, until at last I believed them myself.

"When the last of the dragonlords were driven from this part of the world, I thought, like many soldiers, that I could just put my sword away and go back to farming, or cobbling, or in my case, smithing. And, like many, I found I could not. My attention was not on my craft, which before the war had been the center and total of my life. The land and the forge just didn't seem to hold the same appeal after I had battled the minions of the Abyss and their fell Queen.

"There were four of us, of similar intent and background. We hatched a scheme that could only be hatched in a dimly lit tavern similar to the one where we now sit. Word was floating about that a dragon that survived the war had made its lair in the mountains to the south. A bard brought both the tale, which he gave up willingly, and a supposedly accurate map, which he parted with at no small cost.

"We intended to beat other fortune hunters to that dragon and to its riches. Four mere men against a dragon! Yet we were full of ourselves and the stories of others who had beaten such fell wyrms, and so we pawned our meager belongings for supplies to make the journey and the chance to strike it rich.

"We traveled four, no, five days into the mountains. Our talk was merry, more of how we were to spend the dragon's hoard than how we would defeat the monster. We made no move to conceal ourselves from our prey, and would have sent it an engraved warning of our approach if we had stopped to think of it. Yes, we were full of ourselves, and our tales of bravado.

"The evening of the fifth day, we were bedding down when there was a commotion in the brush. The mighty dragon hunters, including myself, scrambled for our weapons, sure that creatures from the pits would descend on us at any moment. Instead, the bushes rustled, parted, and out limped . . . this."

He motioned at the dog, who nosed over an empty mug and gave the room a cockeyed glance of expectation. Melissa, the serving girl, brought a fresh mug for the dog. Jengar sat quietly until Fool's Gold was lapping up another ale, ignoring the attention suddenly foisted on him. Jengar sighed and continued.

"We were hard men, tough men. We were prepared for battle and then confronted by this ridiculous, miserable-looking creature. Burrs and nettles covered his body, and he looked mangier than he looks now. After laughing at our own foolishness (and making the mental note to post watches), we debated what to do with him. We did not pack a lot in the way of provisions, and one of the party suggested, half in jest, that we roast him for the evening meal.

"Our supplies weren't really that strained. I volunteered part of my own supplies to feed him, and the beast took to them readily. Even then he was a mooch. He tagged along beside me for the next day, as we discussed how we were going to spend our portions of the treasure. Quick Eddie, the one who had offered to cook our new pet, planned to set himself up as a local lord. A couple others talked about wine and women and status in the community. Me, I wanted to travel for a while in style, then settle down once I had seen everything I needed to."

Jengar gave a sly chuckle, and a faraway look came into his eyes. A man made wise against his will, the people would say.

"The first warning we got about what was to happen

was when the dog disappeared. He's got that ability to vanish at a moment's notice in the face of danger, but at the time I was still learning about his habits, so when I looked down, I was surprised to find he had evaporated. I opened my mouth to call out for him, but Quick Eddie's more frantic shout drowned my cry.

"We had expected the typical dragon's cave such as the bards describe—a huge mouth gouged into the side of a mountain, custom-made for large lizardlike creatures to claim as home. Instead, we saw a wide clearing, the type deer make when they settle for the night. The brush and smaller trees were pushed to the side, and in the center, a forgotten donation to a now dead god, was a huge pile of treasure. Just like the old legends said!

"There were gems of amber and ruby, and platters of what looked like burnished steel, shaped like rounded dwarven shields. Jewelry of gold and other semiprecious metals were gathered solely for our enjoyment. Discarded ivory tusks were planted in a line along one edge of the pile. And the entire assembly was displayed on a bed of golden coins, worthless now as real money, of course, but good enough for trade with craftsmen for good, dependable steel.

"Quick Eddie gave a cry of greedy joy, and we all stood there like fools, smiling at our good fortune. This was excellent! We had found the dragon's treasure while the dragon itself wasn't even home! As one man, we leapt forward, dropping our weapons and pulling satchels, bags, and packs out to scoop up the ancient coinage.

"Then the pile of gold sneezed.

"It was a huge, ancient, windy sneeze of bellows that were antique before we were born. A golden serpentine head rose up from the pile, and great wings unfolded, glittering in the westering sun. What we had thought were steel platters were the belly-plates of the creature, the ivory tusks its teeth, and what we swore were pieces of finely worked jewelry were well-formed muscles roiling beneath its shining scales. Its eyes were the color of glowing rubies, and its whiskers resembled gold spun into fine, soft wire.

"You see, we had forgotten, in our greed and our dreams, to inquire as to the dragon's color.

"Our greedy charge now became a full-fledged retreat to where we had dumped our weapons. Two of my battle-hardened compatriots abandoned everything and kept going, fleeing like children into the woods, and if anyone has ever seen them again, I cannot say. Quick Eddie stopped only briefly to grab for his discarded sword. He was rewarded for his attempt with a short gout of flame, which set his trousers alight and sent him, burning and shouting, deeper into the woods. If he was ever seen again, I cannot say.

"I alone grabbed my weapon and stood my ground. Not out of bravery or heroism or even greed. I was rooted to the spot by my own cowardice, petrified with fear. It is one thing to describe a dragon—the huge leathery wings, the fire, the golden scales shining like newly cleaned gilt-work. It is one thing to see a drawing of one or even a stuffed creation or model. But to be confronted with the genuine article, its maw thirty feet above you and bristling with teeth that glow like hot coals, that was quite another matter. I had thought myself a brave man, serving with other brave men against the dragonarmies, I had boasted myself a hero, but at that moment, alone with the creature, I was shown my true face.

"You have heard the bards speak of the mighty warrior bringing a dragon to heel with a single blow of his sword. Such a blow, carefully aimed with great power, would be of such strength that the force would convince the dragon to retreat.

"You have heard such tales, and so had I. I closed my eyes, placed my faith in the true gods, and swung forcefully, if a bit wildly. I was rewarded for my faith with a hard jolt that began at the flat of my blade and traveled up my arms, the shock almost dislocating them from my shoulders.

"I kept my eyes shut, waiting for either the thunder of the beast crashing to the ground, or the fire-baked exhalation that would be the last thing I ever heard. I heard neither, and after a long moment, popped open one eye.

"The scene was unchanged. The dragon still towered over me, golden whiskers jutting from beneath its ivory teeth, eyes glowing like rubies that had captured firelight. My sword was short a foot, and ended now with a jagged, broken edge. The tip, snapped off by the force of the blow, was lying around somewhere, but I had no use for it. The dragon opened its mouth, showing rows of smaller, sharper teeth.

" 'Are you *quite* finished?' " It spoke, its voice rumbling the ground around me and shaking me to my bones.

"It was a polite if awesomely powerful beast, considering the situation. It asked me my name and business. I had enough presence of mind (I thought at the time) to lie my fool head off. Robbers? Nay, we were mere travelers who happened upon its sleeping form. Killers? Nay, we were going for our weapons for self-protection. Warriors? Well yes, I was a powerful warrior, but only if riled. I remember not quite knowing what I would say next, my mind madly scrambling just to keep the conversation going, since that was all that appeared to be standing between me and extinction.

"The imperial beast would have none of my chicanery. It knew, in the way that all dragons know things—the fullness of the moon, the weight of the human heart, sciences undreamed of, and magics to take the attributes of the lesser mortals and beasts. It knew that I was lying, and that knowledge seemed to both anger and sadden it.

"Yet, the monster did not slay me, nor lay a claw on me. Sometimes I wish it had. Instead it laid upon me a great *geas*, to travel (as had been my wish) and when traveling, to always speak the truth.

"The great wyrm set me free with this heady curse, and then I, too, fled into the forest and far from my home, for I did not want to tell friends of my folly in believing I could best a dragon. The dog caught up with me that evening, and remains by my side. I named him Fool's Gold, for he is the only treasure I received for my foolishness. As I said, I have tried to get rid of him, to trade him, or to sell him, but bad things used to happen when I tried, so I no longer do so. I have also tried to lie, to test the curse, but again, bad things happen, so again I no longer do so. It is my fate, my curse, and my lesson to be an honest wanderer.

"If I say your ale is flat and your beds fit only for fleas, it is the truth, and many do not care to hear that type of slander. So I came to your village and will stay, for a day or two until my manners become unseemly, then I will depart. I am a living example of the foolishness of lying, and the folly of self-deception and greed. And, of course, of the lessons of a dragon."

* * * * *

Jengar finished his tale to a quiet room, the townspeople considering his words. Then there was a sudden explosion as Melissa the serving girl wheeled and struck the petty lord fully across the face, then stormed, red-faced and teary-eyed, into the tavern's back storeroom.

The old baron looked astounded and muttered, loud enough for those in the room to hear, "What got into her?"

Jengar looked at the old baron solemnly. "You had placed your hand in a most ungentlemanly location during my tale. Once it had finished, she realized both its location and your intent."

Now it was the old baron's turn to grow red-faced. "Now, see here . . ."

Jengar interrupted. "I *do* see, here, and speak, here, and speak the truth, here, for that is my curse. Did you think my tale a mere toothless fable? It is true, and that is why I cannot remain long." And with that he took his own empty mug and the dog's to the bar. The audience took this as the official end of the presentation and returned to their own affairs. The serving girl did not reappear.

Jengar signaled for two more, and noticed the barkeep's scowl directed past him, back toward the fireplace and the petty lord.

"You do not like the gentleman?" asked Jengar, and the barkeep returned his attention to him with a start.

"The old baron? I never said . . ." he began, then

shrugged.

"You do not need to. I take it he has eyes for the young woman?"

"It's not his eyes that bother me," said the tavern-keeper. "It's his hands. And the rest of him. He's been pushing for my permission to take her into his service."

"And she does not care for this?"

"Not in the least. She's threatened to run off if I agree. Meanwhile, he makes it more difficult for me to work. He raises tariffs, invokes petty laws, and harasses me with minor matters that will no doubt fade away when I agree to his demands."

"And you will agree eventually."

"It's a hard world," muttered the barkeep, suddenly becoming interested in a spot a few feet away.

Jengar returned to the hearth. The old baron was trying to make friends with Fool's Gold, but was having as much success with him as he'd had earlier with the maiden. The dog recoiled, physically shrinking away from the man's touch, crouching at last against the chair. The dog was grateful for the mug and turned his attention to the ale. The old baron appraised Jengar dubiously.

"Are you still the brave warrior you describe in your tale?" he said, his eyes glinting in the flames. Jengar could almost see the wheels spinning behind them.

Jengar shrugged. "Brave, but within my own limits. My tale should have proven those limits. I know I cannot ever face a dragon again."

The old baron waved a hand dismissively. "I have a problem," he began, then stopped and thought for half a beat. "The *community* has a problem. There is a gnome living nearby."

Jengar shrugged again. "That explained the hostile reaction to the bard, at least. *Caveat lector*. Know your audience. What matter is it to me?"

"I am concerned that this small gnome can present a great danger to my—er, our—community. Explosions. Volcanoes. Sea serpents. Runaway juggernauts and all that."

"I am inexperienced in gnome removals," Jengar said flatly.

"Yes, but you are honest," said the old baron, reaching out to pat the warrior on the knee in a friendly manner. Jengar flinched at his touch and understood at once Fool's Gold's reaction to the man. "I've sent other so-called 'brave warriors' out to the creature's lair to investigate, but they never returned. Cowards all. I want you to drive the creature out, or at least return to me and tell me why the others have failed."

"And if I tell you that you are a repellent little man?" said Jengar plainly. "One unworthy of a warrior's time?"

"I take that as a mark of your honesty," replied the old baron with a mild, theatrical chuckle. "I can make you wealthy for your small effort, and perhaps give you a haven where your . . . indiscretions would go forgiven."

"What do you think?" questioned Jengar, and the old baron was going to continue the conversation until he realized that this time the warrior was addressing the dog.

Fool's Gold, now lying on his side, let out a healthy belch, which seemed to settle the matter.

* * * * *

In the end, the old baron agreed to put up room and board for man and dog ("I have influence with the innkeep," he said with an oily wink) in exchange for Jengar approaching the gnome and discovering what had happened to the previous warriors. Jengar promised to return the next day with the intelligence.

The gnome's tower was a half-day's walk down the coast, a lonely, flat spur of land jutting out into the sea, framed by a smooth beach of golden sand. A second peninsula farther south helped cradle the water in a placid bay, protected from the sea's fury by a broken jaw-line of black-rocked shoals. A low tower of mud-daubed stone dominated the flat landscape, forty feet high and almost that great around at the base. The tower ended in a flat, truncated top cradling a great iron bowl, and the structure looked as though it had served in the past as a lighthouse.

The beach leading to the tower was dotted with pits, as was to be expected with gnomish land, and sprinkled with strange structures. The structures were universally of weathered wood, with tattered banners of canvas hanging from all sides. They were cast about on the sand above the high-tide line, like toys abandoned by some godling.

Jengar was not caught unaware by the machine as it swooped in on him, if only because the noise preceding it was incredibly loud. It was the sound of a bag of bees attacking a sawmill, and it issued from out to sea. Man and dog instinctively looked up, but the culprit was closer to the horizon, on the surface of the bay itself.

It was skittering sideways along the smooth waters, canted at what Jengar assumed was an angle to its intended orientation. A large, silvery crescent, mounted on what would normally be called the "top" dug firmly into the bay, trailing a large plume of salty spray that resembled a rooster's tail. Black smoke issued from a cast-iron stove and spiraled behind it in long, lazy loops. The entire assemblage was heading, very quickly and sideways, toward the beach.

A small figure fought for control of the craft, but in the end abandoned both his course of action and the vehicle. The figure dived into the shallow water, while the craft sped forward another few hundred feet to dry land. Its speed was such that the craft plowed up through the wet sand to the beach, then collapsed on itself, joining the other freestanding sculptures of wood and tattered canvas.

Jengar ran up to the figure, who was already pulling himself from the surf and wringing water from his tunic. Jengar had expected the gnome, but this was a young man, slender and just getting the first fuzz of a beard. The young man was swearing in a manner familiar to veterans of the War of the Lance, but rarely heard from one so young.

"You all right?" wondered Jengar.

The young man noticed Jengar for the first time, then nodded, first at the man, then at the wreck. "Damn. We almost had it."

"Had what?" asked the warrior.

"A windless sailboat," said the young man, then added, "You must be the old baron's latest bully, here to threaten Tug."

"What?"

"The sword, sir," said the young man, and Jengar for the first time realized that he had pulled his weapon when the craft first appeared. With a grunt, he resheathed it.

A small figure came running up from the direction of the lighthouse, bellowing. His head was wreathed in blond hair, thinning on the top, and he wore a pair of coveralls that clanked and jingled as he moved. "Excellent! We almost had it!"

"This the gnome?" asked Jengar.

"Master Tug," said the young man.

The gnome ran up and stopped, for a moment transfixed between curiosity about the wreck and good manners to the newcomer. Good manners won out, but only barely. He extended a hand.

"Pleased to make your acquaintance," said the small humanoid. "Tugawallop Highseamaster Rolloporvikia . . ."

"Tug," said the young man, and sauntered over to examine the crash. Jengar and the gnome followed, the gnome with hand outstretched, continuing the rendition.

". . . Diamocles Diogenes Thrustwaddle . . ."

"Not a complete loss," said the young man, sifting through the shattered remains of the craft.

". . . Miriland Kiriland Yaweigh Henweigh . . ."

"Boilers intact, and the new coal grid held. No fire this time," continued the young man in his inventory.

". . . Jomalia Greatstroke Cannontip Kennelworth . . ."

"Propeller's shot," said the young man. "Upper sail made it. Lower pontoons a total loss."

". . . Breeding Bromwork Haloisius Homebody . . ."

The young man sighed. "Compared to the other tests, this is a bona fide success."

". . . Moridotes Mugglewump Flinders Jones Atyerservice."

Jengar was aware the gnome finally had finished his introduction. He absentmindedly stuck out his hand, his eyes still sweeping the wreckage. "Jengar." There was a low, halfhearted *woof*. "And Fool's Gold," he added offhandedly.

"Call me Tug," said the gnome. "Damage report, Lexi?"

"Have to wait for the boiler to cool, but it looks good."

"How did the metal upper wing surface do?"

"Unbroken, but I still think it was too heavy."

"We need a bigger boiler, then," said the gnome, nodding.

"More weight," replied the young man with a shake of his head. "You'll sink her."

"But also more steam, which rises, and therefore makes it weigh less," countered the gnome. "You have to think these things through."

"Excuse me," said Jengar. "This . . . thing . . . it is supposed to . . . what?"

"Powered, nonmagical sea travel," said the gnome with a grin. "I'm sorry, where are my manners? You probably want to threaten me. Can we do it over tea? It'll take a while for the boiler to cool to the touch, and then we could use some help lugging it back to the shop."

The gnome set off toward the lighthouse without waiting for a reply, the young man named Lexi in tow.

Jengar and Fool's Gold exchanged a glance, as if both wondered what they had gotten into, and trudged after them.

*   *   *   *   *

"This happens regularly?" asked Jengar, helping himself to thirds of the sweet-butter biscuits. Fool's Gold wuffed and automatically Jengar dropped his hand, putting the honey-coated treat within canine striking distance.

"The old baron sending some sword-bravo to inform me that my presence is unwelcome? About once every few weeks for the past three months, since spring broke. Can't figure what's gotten into him of late. He used to be, well, if not pleasant, at least tolerable."

The four of them (warrior, young man, dog, and gnome) were on a small landing overlooking the open main floor of the lighthouse. A huge central clear space had until recently been the home of the wreckage outside. The walls were littered with tool racks and corkboards, and breached by a large set of double doors (currently open). A large blackboard was crowded with the calculations of skipping a stone across a lake. The high ceiling was hung with all manner of models of (presumably) seacraft— ships with the wings of bats and fins of dolphins and horizontal sails, sea dragons and dolphins, wicker bodies covered with paper, folded cranes and origami songbirds. Some were made of metal and clanged against each other musically in the slight breeze. Light flowed in through the open doorway and from a series of openings in the lighthouse high above them.

"But now he wants you gone," said Jengar, without inflection.

"And the question is why? Reorx knows I've had larger, louder experiments. Why doesn't the old baron want me to perfect my powered nonmagical sea travel?"

"What will it do?" asked Jengar

The gnome looked at the warrior, brought up short. "Why, sail *quickly*, of course."

Jengar shifted uncomfortably, "Well, in any port I can buy passage on a large, though admittedly slower wind-powered craft. And at the Towers of High Sorcery, there are said to be rings to be had that allow movement through the air, and others that allow similar movement beneath the sea. Add to that all manner of mounts that allow movement above and below the sea—sea horses, sea lions, dragons, and whatnot. Will it be quicker than these?"

The gnome shrugged, trying to wrap his mind around the question. It was Lexi, his apprentice, who broke in. "There are those who do not have dragons for allies, or can't rely on magic. Regular folk, like you and me."

"You, perhaps," said Jengar with a small smile, snagging another roll. Fool's Gold wuffed and Jengar fed that one to him as well.

The gnome was distraught. "I can't understand the baron's hostility. This project is *much* less hazardous than my automatic harrower . . ."

"Which drove itself off a cliff," said Lexi softly.

". . . or my fire-juggling wood golem . . ."

"Which burned on its first test run," added Lexi.

". . . or my invisible volcano detector . . ."

"Which hasn't been seen since we switched it on," said Lexi.

"I just don't understand," said the gnome. "Why pick *now* to try to run me out of town?

"Do you know, "said Jengar, reaching for another biscuit, "why none of the others have returned?" Fool's Gold wuffed, and Jengar absentmindedly fed him the roll. "The other . . . 'threateners.' "

The gnome shook himself from his thoughts, "Hmm? The other warriors? Well, they come out here, see what I'm up to, and then leave. Some hang around long enough to help with the heavy lifting. The more hard-hearted are tempted, but decide that the old baron might not live up to his end of the promise and leave soon enough for greener pastures. He carries a magical wand, you know."

"I've seen it on his belt, and wondered if it were threat or ornamentation."

"A few of the bravos intended to return to the old baron, but I never saw them again. Either they changed their minds, or . . ."

"The old baron lied about no one returning," finished Jengar.

"The old baron has a *bit* of a temper," said the gnome.

"The old baron is a money-grubbing old pus-ball," growled Lexi.

"Lexi, respect your elders," said Tug sharply, and looked at Jengar, "even if you *are* correct." He chuckled.

The conversation quieted, and Lexi cleared the tea tray. The fish-shaped wind chimes clanked softly, and the late afternoon sun etched bright squares against the far wall.

"So, are you going to threaten me now?" Tug asked

cheerily.

"I can see why the other . . . bravos failed. You are the most disarming threat I've ever encountered." Jengar smiled.

"I'm told I have a winsome way," said the gnome. "But I intend to see that Lexi learns to handle a sword and a sling. Sometime, sooner or later, the old baron is going to find someone who is willing to do his dirty work, and then"—he sighed—"we may have to defend ourselves as best we can."

Jengar sighed in sympathy. "There are too many bravos out there in the years since the war."

"The best thing for you would be to continue your journey."

Jengar picked up another biscuit, examined it, and fed it to the dog automatically. "I cannot. I promised to return to the old baron with news."

"You stand to get more deeply involved than you wish."

"I am afraid I cannot avoid my responsibility."

"You can always remain here for a short while. Help out with the rebuilding."

"Perhaps later. I gave my word to return."

"And you cannot break it, eh?" said the gnome. "Or cook up some good excuse, like I am the only thing preventing an incursion of sea drakes?"

"I am forced to be truthful."

The gnome gave out a long, low sigh that seemed to say "humans," then said, "I'll send Lexi along with you. He needs to pick up some supplies anyway."

At this Lexi brightened. "Give me five minutes to clean up!" he shouted and barreled down the stars. Soon there was the sound of the pump drawing water and a vigorous splashing.

"I cannot convince you to change your mind?"

"It is not up to me. If I promise something, I cannot go back on my word."

"Then may the true gods watch your steps. Another biscuit?"

Jengar reached for the almost empty bowl, then waved it away. "I'll have to pass, even though I must commend your cooking. These rolls are hardly filling, and seem lighter than air."

* * * * *

Lexi was voluble and friendly on the road back to town. Master Tug had taken him on as an apprentice years ago, and the two had talked of a partnership. While he lacked the grand imagination of the gnome, Lexi had a practicality that balanced the gnome's good intentions and kept the damage to a minimum. If anything, Tug seemed *less* dangerous than the average gnome. Which made the old baron's hostility even more puzzling.

Lexi skirted the issue when Jengar brought it up, instead engaging in a rousing game of toss-the-stick with Fool's Gold. Jengar noted that the young man had scrubbed himself to within an inch of his life, odd but not exceptional behavior for a simple trip into town.

Lexi escorted Jengar to the baron's manor and offered halfheartedly to wait for him. Jengar declined. With a pat to Fool's Gold, the likable young man was gone, down into the center of the village.

A brutish-looking guard ushered Jengar into the old baron's presence. The tight, dark little office was lit by a small brazier behind the old baron's seat. The effect was supposed to give the baron the illusion of a halo, but in reality it looked as if the back of his head were on fire.

The old baron half rose and waved Jengar to a seat. "You have taken care of the matter?"

"I have checked things out, as you have requested. I said I would either remove the gnome or find why the others failed. I have done the latter."

This was not the news the old baron had hoped for. He frowned, sat in silence for a moment, then began tapping his wand in one hand. At length, he said, "And?"

"The gnome, Master Tug, is every bit typical of his race, but poses no threat to you or the village. In fact, he is quite the congenial fellow. The other warriors you've sent out seem to have realized this and just kept on going." Another silence, as the old baron tapped.

"But you returned."

"I said that I would. I am cursed to tell the truth."

"So you have said. Anticipating this, I sent a messenger last night to Trentwood, and he brought back proof of your honesty. It seems that the local mayor there is displeased with your truth-telling."

"He took issue with my review of his accommodations."

"Yes, this 'honesty' you keep talking about. It led to breaking up those accommodations."

"A fight broke out, yes. I regret that, but the mayor's sons did attack first."

"The mayor of Trentwood has asked if I would hold you for charges. I am inclined to oblige, since you seem to treat your honesty as an excuse to insult your hosts wherever you go. However, I ought to be fair about this. . . ."

"Meaning?" Jengar shifted uncomfortably. As soon as one side uses the word "fair," he had learned in life, things quickly became less than fair.

"Go back and finish the job. Get rid of the gnome. I'll send word back to Trentwood that you pushed on. The mayor there is an old fool and will soon be whining about other matters."

"I would rather not," said Jengar.

"Your rathers do not count," said the old baron waving the wand absentmindedly at Fool's Gold. "We will hold your possessions as a sign of good faith."

"Possessions?"

"Your ale-swilling hound," said the old baron with a tight, paper-dry smile.

"Were I half the warrior you think I am, I could slay you now."

"Perhaps. And at the cost of your own life, perhaps. Or that of your companion." He motioned again toward the dog. Fool's Gold growled as Jengar reached down a hand to shush him. But Jengar wasn't quick enough, and the creature leapt toward the petty lord.

"Observe and learn," said the old baron, pointing his wand at the hound and muttering something under his breath. Fool's Gold never completed his leap. The dog froze, midway between the warrior and the dais, and hung there, trapped within a sphere of softly scintillating color.

"Pretty, no?" said the old baron with a smile. "This toy was found long ago in what is now the gnome's lighthouse. Watch further." Another mutter, another wave of the wand, and the sphere began to contract from all sides. Fool's Gold shrank as well, diminishing until he was half his original size. The dog gave a whine that was half surprise, half fear.

The old baron leaned forward. "Do I have your promise you will rid the village of this gnomish threat?"

Jengar frowned. "I cannot promise," he said with annoyance verging on anger.

The old baron chuckled. "Yes, you can. That's what makes you ideal for this task. Others I sent, cowards and wastrels all, were bought off with high ideals and a little tea. You can promise, and you must keep your promise."

"Those that disappointed you in the past were shrunk to nothingness," surmised Jengar.

"You said that, not I, and you always speak the truth." A third mutter, and Fool's Gold and the glowing globe floated to the base of the dais, the frightened dog spinning within, looking for an outlet. "The bodily functions are slowed within the globe, but starvation and suffocation do occur eventually," said the old baron in an offhand manner, then added in a half whisper, "One bravo lasted two full weeks, a record.

"I want the gnome and his little industry gone from my barony," the old baron continued, his voice rising with surprising strength. "If you do not so promise, I fear for both you *and* your pet."

Jengar was silent.

"If you need to think about it," said the old baron sweetly, "take a walk around the village. I'll be here. So will the dog."

Jengar knelt and looked at the dog in the sphere. Fool's Gold had calmed and now was seated, tongue lolling out, looking as though he were waiting for dinner. "It's all right boy, I'll get you out." Looking at the old baron, Jengar added, "Give me time to think."

"Take your time but return before nightfall. I retire early, and I would hate to see something happen to your prize possession while you dithered." The old baron chuckled as the door slammed behind Jengar.

The old baron reached down and hefted the magical sphere, admiring his prize. "I should have thought of this earlier—threaten a man, and he resists. Threaten his dog, well, that's another matter, isn't it? Oh, you *are* misnamed, Fool's Gold, because you are *very* valuable to me."

The dog snarled and tried to bite his way through the globe, which caused the old baron to laugh all the harder.

* * * * *

Jengar wandered into the village. The evening wind was already up, blowing inland, and the sun was westering. He had half a mind to leave Fool's Gold behind, but no doubt another warrior would come along who would be merciless enough to do the old baron's bidding and foolish enough to take him at his word.

The warrior made for the Wolf's Head Inn. At least his credit with the old baron was good, and an ale or five would help wear down his resistance to the idea. He could drive the gnome out, he supposed, but it seemed such an unnecessary act. Why would the petty lord tolerate previous gnomish inventions, then suddenly bridle at a powered boat?

So lost in thought was he that he was almost upon them before he saw them. They were seated by the well in front of the inn, the young man, Lexi, and the serving girl, Melissa. They paid him no mind, and would not have noticed if he had approached juggling weapons and singing at the top of his lungs. They were only concerned with each other, face-to-face, foreheads pressed against each other. They spoke too low for Jengar to hear, but then, he did not need to.

After a short while, Melissa rose, kissed Lexi on the forehead, and returned to the inn. Lexi rose and watched her retreating form, and only became aware of Jengar (and the rest of the world) after she had disappeared.

"Have you been watching long?"

"Long enough," said Jengar with a shrug. "How long have you two been meeting like this?"

Lexi blushed hotly, his face even redder in the setting sun. "It's no crime. She's only three years older than I am. And I don't intend to propose until I become a master inventor."

It had the sound of a statement repeated to one's self a hundred times, until it sounded reasonable. Perhaps it was. And such would explain his obsessive devotion to the gnome, thought Jengar. "And how does the innkeep feel about this?"

"He likes me, but thinks I'm too young. I'm afraid he's going to give in to the old baron and pressure her into marrying the old pus-ball."

Lexi's voice quieted as Jengar sat down beside him, waving him silent. After a while the warrior said, "That seems a distinct possibility."

"Is that story you told Melissa and the others true?" asked the young man. "About you being cursed to tell the truth?"

"All too true, such that now I am in greater difficulties than before." He related his earlier meeting with the old baron, and the fact that Fool's Gold was being held as a hostage to force his cooperation. Lexi was outraged but less than helpful, punctuating his thoughts with invectives like "pus-ball" and "money-grubber."

"Be that as it may, now I am faced with this dilemma: To rescue Fool's Gold, I have to agree to get rid of your master, Tug."

"I know! Maybe we can go to Tug and explain the situation to him, and maybe he'll move away just long enough for the old baron to calm down from whatever's bothering him."

Jengar looked at the youth with a long, slow gaze, and said, "But you'd have to go with him."

"Well, I guess I would."

"Exactly. And that does not solve anyone's problems, except maybe the old baron's." He gave Lexi a meaningful look, whose meaning went unnoticed.

"I wish there was some way we could get rid of the old wart. Maybe he can disappear in the middle of the night. You're skilled with swords, can't you . . . ?"

Jengar shook his head. "Some warriors reach for their swords every time they perceive an injustice or an opportunity, then they are surprised when the entire world closes in on them, and everyone is made miserable. I've learned that lesson from the dragon, at least."

A silence fell between them while the shadows lengthened. At last Jengar spoke. "Only one thing to do," he said. "Lexi, go back to your master and tell him I'll take up his offer to work with him." He started to walk back toward the manor.

"Where are you going?" shouted Lexi.

"I have to make a promise to the baron," came the response. "And then I have to talk to my dog."

* * * * *

Jengar showed up at the lighthouse the next morning, just as Lexi and Tug were salvaging the great crescent-shaped sail and the steam boiler.

Jengar told Tug the truth (he could do no less). Jengar was under a great deal of pressure and had agreed to "rid the land of the gnomish threat."

"Those were my exact words," he sighed.

Just as Lexi predicted, Tug volunteered to move and even started sketching some plans to put the lighthouse on two legs to walk it inland. Jengar snatched the plans out of his hands and instead replaced them with another set, drawn up the previous evening at the inn. Tug let out a low whistle and frowned. "It will never float," said Tug, a biting condemnation coming from a gnome.

"Yes, it will," insisted Jengar.

The gnome sniffed. "How can you be so certain?"

"Because I said it will, and I always tell the truth."

The gnome considered the logic of the argument and had to agree.

The rest of the week consisted of rebuilding the craft along the lines of the new plans. Lexi, Jengar, and Tug cut timbers, rebuilt the hull and pontoons, and covered the frame with resin-covered gauze. Lexi proved quite knowledgeable, more so than Tug gave him credit for. Often Lexi would make a suggestion and have it overruled by his master, who was then argued into that very decision by Jengar. By the fourth day, Lexi was making his recommendations directly to the warrior (when Tug was elsewhere, in order to avoid hurting his master's feelings).

What little spare time they had, evenings, Lexi spent with Melissa (under the innkeep's watchful eye), while Jengar went to visit his imprisoned friend. He would bring with him the latest blueprints and calculation books from the day's work, but only pull them out when he and the dog were left alone.

The baron had his men eavesdrop, and they reported back that Jengar spent much of his time telling the dog the events of the day and about the nonesuch device the gnome was currently building. Occasionally Jengar would ask a question and the dog would *wuff* or *ruff* in response. And Jengar also told the dog to be patient. He said that a lot.

Once, the guards reported, when they poked their heads around the corner they saw the warrior kneel over the globe, his arms wrapped about it. At first they thought he was trying to pirate off the entire sphere, but he wasn't lifting the globe, only hugging it and speaking in a soft, low voice. They did not catch any of the words, but the dog had his face pressed against the globe, against the warrior's face. The warrior's voice seemed to falter and catch, and the guards, not wanting to be spotted, retreated.

The old baron shook his head. Perhaps this warrior was

less than he seemed and not capable of the nasty business of taking care of the pest Tug and his mewling assistant. Were it up to him, he would have lopped off the little weasel's head already and banished Lexi, but ah, appearances must be maintained. It is easier to make strangers disappear than long-standing citizens—fewer questions that way.

Still, his spies told him that Jengar and Lexi dined at the inn, every evening, on his account. The warrior's comradeship with the gnome and his assistant made the old baron uneasy. He pressed the point one evening, as Jengar was leaving the manor after visiting his dog.

Jengar was stiff, polite, watching every word.

"You said you were going to get rid of the gnome!" The petty lord exploded in Jengar's face.

"I said I would remove the gnomish threat, and that in seven days' time. It has only been five days."

"Time when you have run up my tab with the innkeep and fortified his idiot helper."

"I will remove the gnomish threat," said Jengar.

"You said that five days ago."

"And I mean it now, just as I meant it then," replied Jengar calmly. "I am helping Master Tug solve a few problems, then all will be ready for the decisive act. I am aware I must hasten in this matter."

"What can I do to hurry you?" the old baron demanded to know.

"Well," said Jengar, smiling grimly as if he had just thought of it, "you can put together a going-away party."

Jengar did not linger for the response of the old baron, whose grumbling and curses followed the warrior out the door.

* * * * *

Two days passed, and all was in readiness. Lexi sent word through the village and posted a hand-lettered sign by the inn, announcing that Master Tugwaddle had solved one of the great mysteries of the age and would

203

demonstrate his latest device at noon. Word quickly spread to the neighboring towns, and by a quarter to twelve the entire populace of the village, plus those of neighboring villages, was gathered expectantly out by the lighthouse. Even Trentwood sent a representative, one of the mayor's unwounded sons, a stuffy, pompous sort who immediately got into a snit over Jengar's continued presence in the area.

The old baron was beside himself. He had, on Jengar's suggestion, offered a picnic to those who showed up, but the raw numbers grew and stretched the larders of the inn. Now he stalked up and down the beach among the assembled guests, watching them eat and drink and be merry at his expense. Of Jengar, Lexi, and the gnome there was no sign yet, and both the innkeep and Melissa were busy cooking.

Ah, well, he thought, once the lad was gone there would be time for more leisurely pursuits. The old baron snarled for another ale, though the heat of the day and the exercise of walking to the lighthouse had already left his face unpleasantly flushed.

At noon there was a flourish of trumpets (slightly off-key, the legacy of a previous gnomish invention), and the doors to the lighthouse flew open. Straining, Jengar, Tug, and Lexi pulled forth a large, wheeled conveyance hidden beneath a tarp. All three were dressed in black shorts and open-necked white shirts, with red bandannas adorning their heads. Jengar looked like a pirate, Lexi like a youth who was playing pirate. Tug looked like a gnome in a red kerchief.

They inched their contraption forward onto the beach, and after about ten yards several villagers came forward to help wheel it toward the crowd. Tug went from pulling to directing, and at last the great craft was in place. Tug waved the crowd to silence.

"Ladies, gentlemen, villagers, worthy nobles, and visitors," Tug said in one breath, the crowd leaning forward to catch his reedy voice. Tug paused, and for a moment Jengar thought the gnome would continue on with his elaborate greeting, but instead the small being caught himself and got (for once) to the heart of the matter. "As you know, I have been undertaking a new direction in my research, to allow man—by which I mean all sentient and good creatures . . . er, without fins and gills and similar adaptions—to sail the seas without aid of wind, monster, or magic. To that end I have been aided by the traveler Jengar, and of course my erstwhile assistant Lexi." There was polite applause, and both Jengar and Lexi took deep, theatrical bows.

"Therefore, without further ado," said the gnome, "I give you the fruits of my labor—the *Sea Dragon!*"

Lexi and Jengar peeled back the tarp to reveal their work. It resembled a canvas-covered saucer on small wheels, the saucer carrying the boiler and winglike sail. A small charcoal burner smoked in the stern, which heated a brass kettle-boiler, and was attached by gears and chains to a propeller facing the rear. A set of outriggers ending in balloon-shaped pontoons jutted out to either side to provide balance. A single seat was positioned where the driving board was located, in front of a webwork of wires and strings leading back to the sail, and a large lever, like a brake to one side, was attached to a rudder hanging at the stern. Two other seats were positioned directly behind the driving board.

The entire thingamajig was painted vivid shades of red. The canvas saucer was dyed a bright crimson, and the wood of the rudder, outriggers, and pontoons was tinted with magenta. Even the brass of the boiler had a reddish sheen to it. The sail had been burnished with a red-brown ochre and gleamed in the sun.

The crowd applauded politely at the appearance of the vehicle. The old baron froze, the ale raised halfway to his lips, as if stunned by some hidden beauty in the design. Then he noticed Melissa, newly arrived with a batch of ale and edibles, gazing dreamily at her hero, Lexi, and his headache returned.

Tug held up his hands for silence.

"To demonstrate this new device, my companions and I will take to the ocean, unaided by magic or conventional wind. Should this work (and I have been assured it will), free rides will be offered to those brave enough to venture into the bay. These will continue for the rest of the day or until the charcoal runs out."

Lexi and Jengar were already manhandling the craft into the water. It failed to sink immediately, which all took as an excellent sign. Once afloat, the wheels easily detached. Both men, young and old, held the craft steady as the gnome waded out to the vehicle. They helped him aboard, then boarded themselves. With due ceremony, they belted and tied themselves securely in their places.

With a great flourish, Tug mounted the driving board and eased the large brake lever. Slowly, the steam valves closed and the propeller engaged, beating the air in wide, smooth strokes. For a moment, all was hushed stillness save for the hiss of steam and the leisurely beat of the propeller through the air. Then, very slowly, the craft began to ease forward.

The drift was imperceptible at first, and more than a few of the observers thought it a mere illusion, their own sense of hope causing the craft to *appear* to move. But no, as the propeller chopped the air, the strange ship began to glide forward of its own volition. Scattered applause was followed by cheers as the gnome's triumph became clear.

As the craft moved forward, it began to rise with greater speed, leaving less and less of the saucer in contact with the water. When it was at the far side of the bay, near the black shoals that blocked the harbor, Tug pulled madly on wires and string, and the ship wheeled obediently back toward the lighthouse.

The first pass barreled directly at the heart of the crowd on shore, breaking to the right only at the last moment. Many of the onlookers instinctively hurled themselves to the golden sand, eminently aware that this *was* a gnome invention, and if something were to go wrong, it would go wrong at the absolutely worst moment. The wind of the boat's passing sent skirts fluttering and hats rolling across the beach.

The second pass was a little faster and a little closer to the shore. Everyone applauded furiously. On the third pass, Lexi pulled out a satchel and swung the contents over his head like a sling. He bombarded the crowd with small bits of wrapped candy, made the day before by the innkeeper's wife. The crowd went wild.

One last pass, this time a leisurely sail past the lighthouse itself as the craft threaded its way through the large, lone rocks at the building's base. Jengar looked across and saw Lexi smiling, waving at the crowd. Jengar noted his own hands were still tightly gripping the sides of his seat.

The *Sea Dragon* came in from the sea, touching ground just about where it had taken off, powering onto the beach itself. The saucer crunched and whitened the damp sand beneath it and came to rest not ten feet from the assembled villagers. All three new sailors dismounted and bowed deeply as the crowd applauded, hooted, and hollered.

"All right," shouted Tug with a smile, "who's first?"

A lid of silence clamped down on the crowd. Then one man waded unsteadily forward. "That would be me!" cried the old baron.

Lexi and Jengar looked at each other.

"I'm going out," said the old baron, towering over the gnome like an unsteady tree in a high wind. He looked around to see Melissa's reaction, but he had lost sight of her in the crowd of happy revelers.

"Of course, sir," said Tug. "Let me check the lines and I'll . . ."

"Not you," he spat. "*I'll* take her out."

"Milord," said Jengar, choosing his words carefully, "Tug is a better pilot for this marvelous device than I. You would be safer with him."

The old baron waved his hands and shouted,"You! You're the one who said you'd take care of the gnome and his assistant. Made them bloody heroes, thank you very much. I *don't* want to hear anything from *you*. It's *my* turn to be the hero."

"I think what Jengar means," Tug responded, "is that this is a tricky operation, such that its subtleties may elude even one as puissant as—"

The old baron bellowed him down. "You mean to say that a failed sell-sword, a gnome, and a callow young man can sail, and not I? I bet even the damned dog knows how to run this rig. I've been paying for this damn party. Let me at it."

Lexi and Tug looked at each other and shrugged. Jengar remained silent and solemn, his eyes focused to the right and slightly behind the old baron.

"Think of it this way," snarled the petty lord. "If this is as successful a creation as it seems, maybe I'll decide to keep it and let you have your flea-bitten companion. Chew on that!"

Jengar sighed as Tug checked the controls. Everything was put into readiness while the old baron tied himself securely to the driving board as he had seen the others do.

Jengar, standing in water to his knees, tapped the various controls. "Throttle. Steam feed. Rudder. I do not recommend you do this, baron, and I cannot in honesty tell you to proceed."

The old baron howled. "Honesty! That means little to you, curse or no curse. You said that you would get rid of the gnomish threat."

Jengar looked down, almost ashamed. "Yes, and that could mean more than one thing. A gnome that does not threaten you is not a threat. And there is also a difference between the threat of a gnome and a threat to . . ."

The old baron shouted him down with a hearty "Stand clear!" and threw the steam feed full open.

The *Sea Dragon* bolted forward as if newly released from captivity. The boat took a mighty lurch and pitched to the left. The old baron labored at the controls, his face an even deeper shade of red.

Although started with a good head of steam, the *Sea Dragon* got even faster by the moment, as if propelled by the anger and resentment of the old baron. It made a first pass close to the shore, the second even closer. In both cases, the passing kicked up sharp sprays of surf that caught the closest of the revelers. The saucer seemed to barely touch the surface as it sped by, the old baron tightly gripping the controls.

Then the craft turned toward the inlet and its black-toothed shoals. The craft bore down on them with a relentless purpose. Jengar could see the old baron's small figure, trying to manhandle the controls onto a safe course.

Tug was shouting now. "I knew it! He's going to wreck it! He's going too fast! Turn, blast you! Turn!" And with that he threw himself on the sand, unable to bear watching. This made him the only member of the group who missed the greatest measure of the gnome's success.

Because that was when the *Sea Dragon* lifted itself completely from the surface of the bay. Not by a great deal, not enough to give the old baron a true sense of flight, but more than enough to allow it to clear the sharp rocks guarding the bay's entrance. The *Sea Dragon* dropped, then rose again and dropped again, a third and fourth time like a flat rock thrown by a skilled stone-skipper. The red saucer of the craft caught the sunlight and glowed like heated blood. The more sharp-eyed observers would later say that the local nobility was still pulling on the controls as the craft become a small dot, then at last was lost to sight.

* * * * *

After the excitement was done and all the ale drunk, the revelers staggered off to their homes. At last the only ones remaining on the beach were Tug, Jengar, Lexi, Melissa (standing very close), and a scribe, the last trying to put his observations down as quickly as possible, chronicling the unexpected tragedy. They all sat at the base of the lighthouse, facing the dying sun, as if at any moment the rush of wind and hiss of steam would signal the *Sea Dragon*'s return.

"It is my fault, I'm afraid," said the gnome sorrowfully.

"No, it is not," said Jengar softly, "least of all, yours.

"I should have realized our plans did the job too well. The lift and support were so perfect that only sufficient weight kept it from flying off on its own volition. The old baron had insufficient weight for the device."

Lexi made a face. "Who is going to trust a device that carries off the local ruling class?"

"Some might think that an advantage in and of itself," said Melissa quietly, but not so quietly that anyone missed it.

About this time, Fool's Gold romped up, lankier for his week of privation but apparently none the worse for all his suffering. Whether he had been released by the returning baron's men, or the magic finally elapsed to allow an escape was unclear, but he seemed to be a dog extremely pleased with himself. He carried a small whitish stick in his jaws.

"With each experiment, we learn something new," said the gnome. "We can make a powered boat, but we need to solve this skipping problem. Anchors. I think I'd better do more work in anchors. One that doesn't weigh anything until you need it would be ideal." Master Tugwaddle began sketching something in the dirt, making his plans.

"We can say," said Jengar, "that a great and terrible beast took your lord from you. A great dragon of the sea. That would be the truth, if not entirely honest. I don't think your baron knew the difference between the two. He may yet live out there somewhere, perhaps on an island far removed from us. At least I hope so," he said, stressing the word *hope* as he patted Fool's Gold on the head.

The dog yawned and dropped the stick. Lexi picked it up, held it aloft. "It's the old baron's wand. Must have fallen into the bay when the *Sea Dragon* took that big leap, then washed up on shore."

"Only reasonable explanation," muttered Jengar truthfully, if not with complete honesty.

Jengar flung the wand back across the beach, and the golden-haired dog went leaping after it. Lexi and Melissa held hands, Tug scratched out his musings in the dying light, and the scribe caught the last moments of the day for future tales.

And Fool's Gold laughed as he caught the bone wand in the air, rolling over and over in the dying sunlight until his fur resembled ripe wheat bending before a summer breeze, or gold spun into fine, soft wire.

Scourge of the Wicked Kendragon

Janet Pack

"But I was only . . . aaahhhh!"

Propelled by the shopkeeper's arm, the kender Mapshaker Wanderfuss became a bird, sailing through the door and thudding into the middle of Daltigoth's main street. Dust clouded around the kender. Indignant and coughing, he levered himself to a sitting position.

"I was just looking at that silver box," Mapshaker defended himself. No one listened. "The shopkeeper said my pouch was open, but I'm sure it wasn't. He must have bad eyesight." The kender brushed at the earth dulling his blue shirt and coughed again. Everyone's temper seemed short, perhaps because of draconians recently spotted in the area.

" 'Way! Out of the way!" The metal-banded wheel of a large handcart loaded with barrels aimed straight for Mapshaker's nose. The kender scrambled to safety on the far side of the road as it lumbered past, driving right over the place he'd been sitting.

A guard dog's huge jaws snapped inches from his shoulder. Mapshaker made himself into a ball and rolled out of reach. Jumping up, he pointed a shaking finger at the bristling dog.

"Good thing you're leashed. I can't imagine who would leave such an unfriendly animal so close to passersby!" He shook himself, shedding dust and rearranging his pouches, then took a closer look at the building. Only one door, no windows. It might be a warehouse. The kender grinned. Guarded by such a fierce dog, there had to be treasure inside!

He was determining the best way to weasel into the building when the sound of pounding from the blacksmith's shop across the street intrigued him.

"I didn't steal that pastry, you know." Mapshaker wandered into the forge area and continued his explanation. "I only tasted it. After all, one corner was hanging over the edge of the table."

"I'm busy. Go away," the smith said roughly, pumping the bellows until the roaring fire made conversation impossible.

A merchant's messenger scurried by with a handful of accounts. Running to keep up, Mapshaker attached himself to the tall young woman. "Then I was thrown out of that shop for just *looking* at a silver box. Now my shoulder hurts—"

"Out of my way!" The messenger brushed past and disappeared down a side street. The edge of her cloak caught around Mapshaker's body, then snapped away, twirling the kender like a top.

He staggered a couple steps, dizzy, then leaned against the blacksmith's wall, his spirits lower than street dust. Everyone was too busy to talk. If he were human or an elf instead, even a dwarf, surely then no one would overlook him!

Two men hefted a heavy object, covered by a blanket, out of the blacksmith's shop and onto a cart. The cloth slipped, revealing a long metal spear with a peculiar appendage sticking out of the underside of the shaft, obviously meant to fasten onto something, perhaps a saddle. But what would be large enough to carry such a spear, Mapshaker wondered, except maybe a dragon?

"What is that thing?" the kender asked. "What does it do? How does it work? What do you put it on?"

"This is not kender business!" The men hurried to cover the weapon and roll the cart out of sight. Mapshaker trailed them down a dark, narrow side street. Suddenly his way was blocked by the largest human he'd ever seen.

"Uh, hello," gulped the kender, staring up into the man's cold eyes. "Is this your alley?"

"Go," the big man grated, pointing in the direction from which Mapshaker had come.

"But I just wanted to see—"

"Seen enough," the man snarled. Huge fists reached out, clamped on Mapshaker's clothing. Flipping him around, the human giant pitched the kender back toward the main street.

"Uff!" Mapshaker dusted himself off once again. "At least that landing wasn't as hard as the first one." Aiming himself toward the outskirts of the city, he began walking.

A raindrop splattered against his shoulder, then another. In seconds, stinging rain had soaked the kender and turned the road into sticky mud. Suddenly he found a house with a porch deep enough to provide shelter. He ran toward it, though stubborn mud sucking at his boots made that difficult. Winded, he finally reached the house with the porch and scooted into its shadows, sagging with his back against the front door.

"Wish I . . . still had my . . . warm red cape," he muttered to himself, inhaling and exhaling in great gusts. While catching his breath, Mapshaker contemplated the silvery downpour, totally unaware that his right hand was creeping toward the door lock. His nimble fingers began working at the mechanism. The kender leaned harder against the faded wood. Leaving the lock, his hand dove into a brown leather pouch, then returned to work with a small piece of metal.

The snick of the releasing latch was obliterated by the sound of the pounding rain. Surprised, Mapshaker fell backward through the opening, landing with a sodden *whump* in a large entryway. To his right, a wooden stairway with delicate wrought iron railings floated upward to the second story. A brace of mullioned windows above it allowed in rain-filtered light. To his left and ahead were three doors, one shadowed by the staircase. That one drew the kender like a lodestone draws iron.

Mapshaker's left hand manipulated this lock. It yielded almost instantly and the door swung inward, creaking. "Shhh!" the kender cautioned it. "Someone might hear!" Curious and alert, he stepped into a mage's workroom.

Shelves filled with red leather books lined the walls from floor to ceiling. Vessels and vials sat in tidy rows on every flat surface. A huge armillary sphere glinted in the far corner. But by far the most interesting thing in the room was the small casket sitting on a marble pedestal to the left of the door.

Its intricate embroidery glowed even in the dim light. Mapshaker held his breath as he lifted the catch, expecting resistance. There was none. Inside, settled on individual cushions of white silk, rested three carved figures. One was a cat in amethyst with an amber necklet. The second was a fish of transparent rock crystal with eyes of pale green and yellow stones. And the third was a dragon of dark golden metal. It was seated with tail curled around its legs and its wings furled as if testing the wind.

Enthralled, the kender gently lifted the dragon from its elegant nest.

"Ow!" Mapshaker nearly dropped the dragon at the sudden sting. A bead of blood welled on his thumb. "It bit me!"

Wiping the blood on his rust-colored pants, the kender quickly forgot about his wound. He carried the dragon—carefully this time—into the hall for closer inspection. The elegant spiral horns and perfect tiny scales suggested dwarven work. Two dark red stones, set as its eyes, winked at him. Delighted with his treasure, Mapshaker dug a leather thong from a pouch, wound it securely about the little dragon's body, and suspended it around his neck. He then confronted the next door.

"It's sooooo terribly hot in here," he muttered. Mapshaker broke out in sweat and tingled suddenly from the roots of his long hair to the ends of his toes. Something clenched his windpipe. He coughed. "Caught cold from the rain faster than I thought." The kender's voice grew rougher, deeper with each word. Fire burned in his belly and flashed to his head. Heat and pain skewed his vision and disrupted his balance. His nose, his feet, his hands seemed to grow and distort.

"I'm . . . I'm . . . aaahhhhhhhhhhhhh!" Mapshaker's voice dropped two octaves. His phrase finished in a booming, roaring howl. Flapping his arms in an effort to relieve the heat, he soared through the roof with a resounding crash and disappeared into the rain.

* * * * *

The falling of broken slates and splintered rafters added more noise to the downpour drumming in the entryway. Nothing else moved in the house for long moments.

Then a door slammed somewhere in the second story. "Kharian! What in the name of Krynn is going on?"

A red-robed mage appeared at the top of the beautiful stairway, thick gray hair sweeping over his shoulders like a cape. "Kharian, where are you? Answer me!" he shouted irritably. He wrapped the balustrade with clawlike fingers, their beauty sacrificed during his Test at the Tower of High Sorcery. He looked about. The rain and debris on the floor below caught his attention. His intense pale eyes jerked upward to view the skeleton of the ceiling.

"By the three moons!" he swore. "Who or what dares destroy a mage's roof?" He quickly descended the stairs, his long braided mustache quivering. "What could have caused such a huge hole . . . ?" At the bottom of the flight he turned toward his workroom. The open portal revealed much. Striding across the wet floor to the doorway, he looked inside to his left. The embroidered casket gaped, only two inhabitants remaining.

"Some thief has the dragon!" he shouted.

"Master Myrthin?" A dripping young female assistant, arms piled with foodstuffs, skidded through the main aperture. "I heard—"

The mage whirled on her. "Didn't I renew the spell on this door? You were supposed to keep track of that sort of thing since my illness!"

He stepped carefully through the foyer, examining shattered roofing for clues as he spoke.

She cowered at his criticism.

"Don't stand there like a fool. Look for anything he, she, or *it* dropped."

Piling her parcels in a dry space, the assistant joined Myrthin, eyes searching the wooden floor.

The mage finally grunted in satisfaction and straightened, a tiny scale from the brass dragon balanced on the tip of one crooked finger. "Get someone to patch the roof well enough so the rest of the house won't flood while I'm gone. Clean up this mess. Then pack everything we'll need for a journey."

"But, Master, you're still not well."

"What choice do I have? Imagine someone evil, now a dragon—the destruction he or she could cause would be devastating. The blame is entirely mine." He turned toward his workroom, the precious dragon scale imprisoned between gnarled thumb and forefinger. "Get to work, Kharian. Now."

* * * * *

Mapshaker's eyes were closed. He felt much cooler than he had a few minutes ago. Wind tickled his ears and soothed the fire streaking throughout his body. He relaxed. An overwhelming impression of falling made his eyes pop open.

He *was* falling . . . through diaphanous clouds, toward green fields divided by fences of piled rocks. There was nothing to catch him except grass and stone outcroppings far below.

"Uh-ohhhh!" His scream emerged as a full-throated roar. Panic blotted his mind. And then something flapped, leveling him off. He peered behind him. "Wings!" he shouted. Delight and curiosity replaced panic as he soared upward.

"I'm really flying," he crowed. "Wonder how that happened."

Thin clouds condensed against his nose, tickling. Mapshaker drew up his right arm to scratch it. His hand appeared huge, roped by thick muscles under brass-colored scales and tipped with enormous onyx claws.

"Claws?" the kender bellowed. "Scales?" He ducked

his head for a survey, his new long neck making that easy. Brass plated his middle. His pouches, tiny against his bulk, hung by their strings from scales. Only tatters of his leather belt were left, and no sign remained of the rest of his clothing. A long sinuous tail whipped behind. He could feel the dragon statuette bumping him high under his neck, still supported by its leather thong.

Mapshaker's head snapped forward again; his mind roiled with disbelief. Joy overcame him and he chortled, a very nondragon sound. "I'm a dragon! No wonder I can fly! Maybe I'll go back to Daltigoth and singe the south end of town. Teach those people to be unfriendly, they won't know what hit them! I—uh . . ."

Far below he spied a scenic pond. All of a sudden he was very, very thirsty. Forgetting all about his revenge on Daltigoth, Mapshaker pointed his head down and pulled his wings partway in. The maneuver sent the kender into an unexpectedly steep dive. Wind screamed past his ears; the ground sprang to meet him. Panicked herds of cows, sheep, pigs, and goats ran bawling and squealing in all directions.

At the last moment the kender tried pushing out his wings a little. The additional sail sent him upward with enough momentum to complete a tight upside-down roll. Mapshaker was so excited over this new talent he repeated it several times. The pond was left far behind.

Hours later, he was still thirsty—but also exceedingly tired. A large hay field covered thickly with short green grass and dotted with long golden ricks seemed a perfect landing site. Except he still didn't know how to land.

He came in much too fast, back claws outstretched. His intention was to grab earth with them, slow down, then dig in with his front claws and stop. It didn't work. Instead Mapshaker got four feet full of mud. He somersaulted into a hayrick, exploded that section of it, and plowed into a second, where he finally stopped.

A horse whinnied in terror and thundered away. Something struggled beneath Mapshaker's tail. He pushed giddily to his feet and shook, sending hay all directions. Then he peeked behind him. His unwitting prisoner thrashed, mumbling, facedown in mud. Mapshaker moved his appendage.

". . . repose and have a dragon descend!" Dark eyes flashing, muddy mustache trembling with irritation, the tall armored knight levered himself to his feet and drew the biggest sword the kender had ever seen. "And you affrighted my steed—he is doubtless in full flight back to Solamnia. Who are you? For by the Oath and the Measure, I, Sir Aric von Kathmann, Knight of the Rose, demand satisfaction for this most cowardly deed!"

Mapshaker scooted for the nearest intact haystack, hoping to hide behind it. It wasn't large enough. His head and tail protruded from either side, allowing the knight to follow every movement he made.

"But I didn't know you were there!" Mapshaker protested as Sir Aric stalked toward him. The knight dripped gouts of mud and hay.

"I'm a ken—" Not anymore he wasn't. Almost too late Mapshaker realized his mistake and snapped his jaw shut. "Dragon," he finished lamely.

"A kendragon?" The knight lowered his sword an inch. "I have never heard of such. You appear as a brass dragon, though much north of your normal clime. But your clan and domicile have no bearing on my honor, nor do they excuse your action." He raised his sword into position again. "Defend yourself, maleficent kendragon!"

Mapshaker beat his wings furiously and rose into the air. His action tore the haystack to bits and sent the pieces soaring. The gust knocked the knight flat on his back, then buried him under a large pile of golden hay.

"I'd better go," Mapshaker called from above. "Goodbye!"

"I will locate you, kendragon!" Throwing off the dried grass, the knight struggled to his feet. "I will search Ergoth diligently until we are met again and my honor can be assuaged!"

Happy to escape without being impaled, Mapshaker soared and spiraled above forest, meadow, and the foothills of Ergoth. He found new energy and flew happily again. He had just discovered an interesting thermal when something sharp like a tiny sword poked him.

"Robber! Thief!" it shrieked. "Nest defiler!"

"What? Wait!" The kendragon craned his head upward to see his attacker, ducking as the beak stabbed at his eye. "I haven't been in any nests—"

"Egg cracker! Fledgling eater! Get out! Help, help! Danger!" Attacking him was an awas, a medium-sized brown and white bird (completely unrelated to goat-sucker birds) whose long pointed beak was normally used to dig insects from trees. These creatures are very territorial, assaulting anything unlucky enough to wander too close to their nests. This particular awas flew above Mapshaker's head, spearing at any vulnerable-looking spot and screaming continuously.

"I haven't done anything," the kendragon protested. "I'm just passing through—"

"Worse, a traveler! Harm, desecration! Get out, get out!"

Deciding that prudence was the better part of valor, Mapshaker increased his speed. Though outdistanced, the awas chased him for some time, yelling incessantly, until it finally veered off to attack another trespasser.

Happy that incident was over, the kendragon flew blithely on, right into a cloud of buzzing insects. They landed on his wings and head, attaching themselves with tiny barbed feet.

"We're hungry," they hummed. "Here's a meal large enough to feed all of us!" When they bit his tender parts, Mapshaker felt as if he'd been punctured by thousands of tiny needles.

"Ow!" he protested. "That hurts!"

The insects, each awaiting its turn to drink his blood, closed around him, obscuring his view. "I can't see!" yelled Mapshaker. He blew at them, puffing hundreds away at a time. Unfortunately, others rushed to replace them. The kendragon lost altitude, his legs and belly occasionally slapping the tops of trees. "Good thing those aren't rocks!" he bellowed.

Suddenly he figured out exactly what he needed to do to get rid of the pests. Exhaling at the insects regularly allowed him to check his position as he painfully winged east. Over the sea, several dragon-lengths from the beach, he plunged into the water.

And sank. Mapshaker struggled to flap again, this time endeavoring to propel himself upward through surging salt water. It was more difficult than he'd imagined, especially when the liquid around him became crowded with fish feeding on the insect swarm. Unfortunately, some of the fish decided to nibble the kendragon also.

Exhausted, Mapshaker finally dragged himself into the shallows and from there to the shore. His wings, his eyelids, the insides of his ear canals, and his lower nasal passages were swollen from bites.

"What a day!" He sighed, easing into the warm sand, his wounds stinging from salt water. "I didn't know birds and insects were such a nuisance to dragons. I also didn't know dragons can't swim." He yawned hugely. "At least I got a big drink out of it." He yawned again, pulling a face. "Ugh! Salt water!" Folding his wings and laying his head alongside his claws, Mapshaker fell asleep.

The next morning he awakened as dozens of small crabs tried to carry him off in as many different directions. Fascinated and amused, the kendragon watched as the little creatures attempted diligently but unsuccessfully to hoist parts of him and skitter away.

He finally spread one wing and tucked the other, rolling onto his side and from there to his back. Pulling both wings closer to his body he twisted, scrubbing all thirty-three feet of his back in the coarse sand.

The entire beach was sinuously patterned by his efforts. Feeling only a little soreness from the previous day's bird pecks, insect bites, and fish nibbles, Mapshaker winged upward.

He soon learned how to sideslip into wide, graceful turns. Tight turns demanded muscle control while pulling in one wing or the other and holding it in position. After much practice, he learned those, too. Updrafts were fascinating, but he tired quickly from holding his wings in almost the same pose for extended periods. Arrowing out of the sky straight at herd animals was by far the most fun because of the mad way they bawled and scattered. During his third day of dragonhood, one befuddled cow slammed full speed into a boulder and didn't get up. Mapshaker felt guilty about causing the beast's demise, yet licked his chops in anticipation of the hot, juicy meal.

"Raw cow?" He circled, peering down at the dead animal. "It might be good. I guess I could try it." Then the kender in him became nauseated at the thought of eating uncooked meat. "No, I don't think so. I don't think I can." Fighting his demanding stomach, Mapshaker flew off in search of another dragon to get some tips on landing.

* * * * *

Myrthin strode along the dirt road, trailed by Kharian with their pack. The mage kept one eye open for treacherous potholes, the other on the black box in his twisted hand. His tracer, with the brass dragon scale imprisoned within, bubbled and blurped, putting out no more than a tiny questing pinna of odorous earth-colored fog.

"Thing made me travel in circles yesterday," Myrthin muttered, thumping it none too gently with a warped finger. He scrutinized the sky hoping for sight of the dragon. The box emitted another tendril of stinking smoke that drifted first southeast, then curled back on itself and pointed northwest. The stuff made Kharian gag. "A gnome might have built this for all the good it's doing."

He walked on, sighing, when suddenly the plume from the tracer thickened and definitely indicated northwest. Hurrying, Myrthin followed it.

Around an abrupt curve in the road, the two came upon a farmer, who stood staring at his barn. Part of it had collapsed under a load of steaming dung. Next to the farmer fidgeted a horse hitched to a cart. At an abrupt signal from the mage, Kharian scurried forward.

"Excuse me, my good man, but did a dragon cause that damage?"

"Yah, rot get to 'is wings. Whoa there, horse. Nothin' left but its smell. Happened half an hour gone. Gotta get to Maygarth now fer nails." The farmer scratched his beard. "Dragon did more'n this, too. Neighbor came by last night telling 'bout it chased his cows. Kilt one, but didn't et it. Strange, that. Jus' left it lyin' there. Been flyin' round Maygarth, spookin' villagers, well as stock."

"The tracer's working again!" called Myrthin imperiously to his assistant. "Come on!"

"Momentarily, Master." Kharian turned back to the farmer. "Thanks for your information. Good luck rebuilding."

The farmer squinted at Myrthin nearsightedly as the mage started ahead of Kharian along the track.

"There be another man lookin' fer it, too," the farmer called after them. "Big one, armored. Says it smirched his honor. 'E's out to kill it, iffen 'e can git it to set still that long."

"A Solamnic Knight?" asked Kharian, surprised.

The farmer shook his head. "Dunno."

Kharian worked the pack onto her shoulder and caught up with her master. "He said—"

"I have excellent hearing," Myrthin snapped. The mage almost ran, following the trace from the dragon finder. The little box poured brown smoke with golden glints. It smelled even more vile than before. "I must reach that dragon before the knight does or chance losing the statuette!"

* * * * *

Clang!

Metal slamming metal awakened Mapshaker the next morning. "Oh, good! A war!" The kendragon popped up his head to see, forgetting the stone overhang of his shelter. "W-owwww!" Mapshaker impacted the roof hard enough to go all wobbly and shower himself with gravel.

Unsteadily, he backed out and tried to focus his eyes toward the din coming from the nearby meadow.

His vision finally cleared after he stared at the combatants for a full minute. A huge ogre wielding a large mace was battling a single knight on horseback. The armor-clad knight fought desperately with long sword and shield. He barely held his own.

The kendragon's anger flared. "I *hate* ogres!" An ogre had kicked apart everything in Mapshaker's hometown. Fanning his wings, he rose into the air. "I'll save you from that ogre, Sir Aric!"

Mapshaker climbed high, then reversed to a steep dive. "Eeeyowww!" He thundered his new war cry . . . which became a frightened "Aaahhhh!" as he flashed past the warriors, flew too near the ground, and had to try every trick he knew to keep from crashing.

The backwash from Mapshaker's passing had little effect on the massive ogre, other than tangling its greasy hair. But Sir Aric's charger staggered in the gale, almost unseating the knight.

Grinning, the ogre lifted its huge mace for a killing blow, while Sir Aric and his mount struggled to recover.

Now well past the scene of the fight, the kendragon labored into a tight turn in preparation for another, hopefully more effective, pass.

"I'll get you, you ugly beast!" panted Mapshaker, flapping full speed toward his enemy. Words—magical words—he didn't know he knew blazed suddenly in his mind; a strange gurgle came from the region near his stomach. He opened his mouth and hiccoughed.

Desert heat seared the ogre's back. The ogre checked its swing, bellowing in pain and surprise as the dragon swooped close by. Sir Aric's charger plunged in an attempt to get away from the singeing blast, and the knight gasped as the sudden increase in temperature made his metal armor truly uncomfortable.

"I do not need help of this sort!" Sir Aric shouted, mastering his horse and forcing it to face the enemy again. "Kendragon, desist!"

But his cry came too late. Mapshaker had flapped again, calling more magic words to mind. This time he belched, spreading a milky opaque cloud that encased first the knight and his charger, then the ogre. Unfortunately, the mist drifted upward. Try as he might, the kendragon couldn't fly fast enough to avoid it as he passed the fighters and banked.

The ogre lifted its weapon again, but whether the blow was meant for Sir Aric or the kendragon, Mapshaker couldn't tell. At the fullest extent of its swing, the enormous mace dropped from the beast's nerveless fingers. The ogre thudded backward into the grass like a felled tree, unconscious.

Sir Aric slumped over his mount's neck, letting go of his own sword as the horse staggered. The knight's grip on the saddle loosened, and he crashed, helmet-first, to the ground. The charger whuffled mournfully, sat on its haunches, then slowly rolled sideways and collapsed.

Mapshaker himself felt strangely sleepy. He yawned, then saw the approaching tree line. It was too close. Backwinging madly, the kendragon slowed, stalled, and tumbled into some saplings, already snoring, a victim of his own sleep breath.

* * * * *

"Wake, Kendragon."

Mapshaker, startled from dreaming, had no idea where his imagination ended and reality started. Surely that familiar prodding voice spoke only in his dream.

"Wake, Kendragon. The hour of our battle draws nigh."

Popping one eye open, Mapshaker found Sir Aric planted before his snout, leaning on his scabbarded sword. The knight favored his right leg, standing with more weight on his left. His helmet was mashed down on his head, with the visor thoroughly askew. Behind him, the knight's gray charger stood unsteadily, head dangling between forelegs.

Sighing, finding himself still a little woozy from the

sleep gas, Mapshaker closed his eye.

"Do not endeavor to deceive me," Sir Aric bellowed. "I ken you are roused. Despite my infirmity, despite no longer being able to see well from under my helmet, I shall dispatch you with the greatest satisfaction. You will never vex my battles or my repose again."

Both of Mapshaker's eyes blinked open. "But I was helping! That ogre would have bashed you with its mace—"

"You staggered my steed with your first uncontrolled passage, nearly unhorsing me. That delivered battle advantage to the ogre, who was not the least discommoded by your current. Piling one indignity upon another, you then employed your desert-heat breath weapon, thoroughly scorching all but yourself. And, eclipsing all else, you further used your sleep breath weapon to render my enemy, my horse, and myself unconscious until deep into this afternoon. I could not complete my duty until I awoke. Only excellent good fortune allowed me to rouse before the ogre. His head is now divided from his trunk. Therefore, prepare yourself. By the Oath and the Measure, my honor will now be assuaged by your blood!"

"But—"

"Excuse me, Sir Knight," came a new voice.

Red-faced with exertion, panting, it was Kharian who appeared at Sir Aric's elbow. "My master, Myrthin the Red Mage, urgently requests words with you before you confront this dragon. The matter directly relates to your honor."

The mage could be seen standing at a slight distance down the road, still clasping the black box in his talonlike fingers and staring at the kendragon. Out of the tracer poured stinking brown smoke, dancing with brassy glints.

Sir Aric lowered his weapon. "By my grandfather's sword, will I never find the moment to dispatch this beast?"

"He's no beast, but a thief with two legs," Myrthin called as he approached the trio, his hard-edged voice chilling the sunlight. "He is my responsibility. I will now return him to what he was."

The knight straightened, staring down at the mage. "And I have sworn by the Oath and the Measure that he shall atone for my sullied honor with his life." His dark eyes glared steadily into those of ice. "I will not be forsworn."

Tension sizzled between the two like lightning. Mapshaker looked from one to the other, horror mingling with pride as he realized a fight was inevitable. A fight over him! The mage's lips started moving; the knight's sword began to rise. The kendragon took in breath to protest, and sneezed.

The tornadic wind whipped Myrthin into Sir Aric, then tumbled both into Kharian, who'd been standing in front of the knight's horse. Tangled, three humans and the charger skidded through the meadow grass almost to the road.

The kendragon blew himself backward. A rock outcropping a goodly distance away halted his momentum painfully. Air *oof*ed out of Mapshaker's lungs and he sagged against the monolith's base. The others sorted themselves out and began looking for him.

"There!" Kharian cried pointing, eyes trailing along the plume of smoke from the tracer. She struggled to follow Myrthin as the mage extricated himself from the knot of bodies and raced toward the kendragon.

The knight, tugging his battered helmet around to where he could see, slowly rose, urged his charger to its feet, then pulled himself into the saddle. The confused horse balked, champed his bit, and finally broke into a reluctant walk toward Mapshaker.

The magic-user reached the dragon first, followed by his assistant. Hunched miserably against stone, the exhausted Mapshaker was wheezing and coughing behind a veil of ocher haze.

"I've got you now, thief!" Myrthin pointed to the statuette bumping against Mapshaker's neck. "That's my property. Give it back, then I'll return you to your natural form."

"Could you turn off that nasty smoke first?" the kendragon asked plaintively, choking.

The mage muttered a few words at the black box. After a final gush, the tracer became quiescent.

"And what kind of being were you before?" Kharian prodded gently.

"A kender." Mapshaker hacked.

"I might have known!" exclaimed Myrthin. "All this effort—only for a kender!" He raised his gnarled hands. "Now prepare yourself—"

"Be not hasty," thundered Sir Aric, propitiously riding up and dismounting. "My honor has not yet been satisfied."

Myrthin faced him, eyes forbidding. "Would you, a Solamnic Knight, fight a kender?"

"Here is no kender," protested the knight. "This be a brass kendragon, although somewhat beyond its accustomed clime."

"That's how he currently appears," snapped the mage. "He stole a bespelled object from me, which turned him into a brass dragon. Now he must return to being a kender." He held out one ugly hand to Mapshaker. "Give the statuette back."

"I only borrowed it," Mapshaker defended himself, untangling the leather strip from his scales with a clumsy claw. Reluctantly he handed the statuette to Myrthin, who popped it into a pouch and began securing the ties to his belt.

"If you remain dragon, it behooves me to fight you," said Sir Aric. "Therefore I shall strike now." Eyes like obsidian, the knight stepped forward suddenly, lifting his sword. "Succumb and make an end."

Mapshaker snatched his left front leg out of the way of the weapon just as the sword whistled by.

"I am smaller, therefore I tire less easily than you," Sir Aric advised the kendragon. He aimed a tremendous blow at Mapshaker, intending to rip him open from high side to low side.

"Su margath naga nulis!" howled Myrthin, pointing at the kendragon.

The knight's blade bit dirt instead of flesh, falling only a hand-width away from the small body. Mapshaker was a kender once more. He sat, breathless and trembling, brown eyes huge in his pale face, while Sir Aric towered above him. Sir Aric raised his mighty sword again and stopped.

"Bah!" The knight snorted in disgust. " 'Tis a kender, in truth."

Wiping his sword carefully with an oiled cloth from a pouch on his saddle, he sheathed it and mounted his horse. "Remember this," the Solamnic Knight declaimed in a dire voice. "If ever you turn kendragon again, your life is mine!"

"Farewell, Sir Knight," said Kharian softly as the knight rode away.

"Kender, I hope you learned a valuable lesson from all this!" snapped Myrthin. "You've caused many people no end of trouble."

"I learned lots," Mapshaker responded, rising, looking mournfully at his pouches scattered about in the grass. He began gathering up his things. "I learned that dragons need landing lessons, and that I can't eat a raw cow." He peered inquisitively toward Kharian's pack. "You wouldn't have any pastries in there, would you? I haven't eaten anything for days. No? Oh, well."

The red mage glowered down at Mapshaker. "Did you learn that things are often not as they appear, and that very seldom does reality approximate what you imagine?"

The kender gulped. "Of course. Isn't that what I said?"

"He's hopeless!" Myrthin turned away in disgust. "I don't know why I bothered transforming him. He'll just 'borrow' something else and begin the whole process all over again." He had a sudden idea. "Perhaps I should shrink him, put him in a jar on my worktable. That might keep him out of trouble."

Mapshaker shivered. "Uh, no thanks, I um . . . I learned

my lesson, I really, *really* did!" He darted away from Myrthin. "Think I'll head for Maygarth. Maybe they have a bakery." He waved, his hands full of pouches, and sprinted up the road. No one noticed there was one more small bag than he had started with. "Good-bye!"

Mapshaker's spirit soared as his feet hit the road. He had a new adventure to tell, one he was certain no other kender could duplicate. His might even be better than some of his Aunt Narylock's stories! And as soon as he found something to eat in Maygarth and a new belt for his pouches, he planned to head for Goodlund.

A splatter of rain hit his shoulder, then another landed on his nose. He looked into the lowering clouds. "Not again. And I still don't have a good cape!" The downpour was sudden. Mapshaker ran, seeking shelter.

He found it at the outskirts of Maygarth. The house sat well back from the road. It was not large, yet the doorway appeared deep enough to protect a kender from the worst of the rain.

"Look at this carving!" Mapshaker crowed delightedly as he stepped onto the porch. "It's as if I'm standing in the mouth of some monster! The door even has eyes painted above it. Wonder what it's supposed to be? Kinda reminds me of that ogre."

The face appeared decidedly unfriendly, but Mapshaker didn't mind. He faced the rain, leaning back against the door, reliving his memories as a dragon. Even encumbered with pouches, one hand fiddled with the lock.

The latch snicked open. Mapshaker fell backward onto a wooden floor, then heaved a gusty sigh. "People have just got to fix these broken locks. I'll have to tell somebody . . . after I investigate. . . ."

* * * * *

Editor's Note: The author thanks Tracy Hickman for his "notes" on awas birds, and for Myrthin's spell.

And Baby Makes Three

Amy Stout

CROESUS SAYS I THINK TOO MUCH, THAT I SHOULD remember my virtue is in my sword arm. Prob'ly so. The two of us always flew together, swung claw and blade when the cause or the money was right, then rode the next updraft. The dragon's back had room for more, but we would have joined the navy if we'd wanted tight quarters.

Till Jax.

When I first met Jakster, the blood on my sword had actually dried and my fist was itchin' for a good fight. As it happens, I also had un'voidable business about to rain all over the dragon's neck. I was beginnin' to think I wasn't goin' to last till we reached one of our reg'lar waterin' holes. I pointed to a rocky plateau barely long enough to keep his tail from hanging over the edge. "That one. One of our old favorites."

The Old Grouch—I never spoke the nickname aloud, though I'd lay odds he knew I thought it—snorted in contempt.

I opened my mouth, not sure what words'd be comin' out, then slapped it shut. Sittin' atop a dragon for days'll stiffen up the most hardened of mercenaries—which I surely became long ago after I stopped countin' battles or bodies. Right then, I needed to stand straight on my own two legs and walk 'em around until they remembered how to do it themselves without help. I kept quiet. Nothin' worse than an argument with a dragon.

Croesus took a sudden dive and brought us to ground. He knew this one cave where he could comfortably settle his great copper bulk. He also knew that a while back I'd spent time here with a certain woman. A *long* while back. We hadn't parted all that friendly, and I swore to avoid crossin' her path again. That gal had talents, the thought of which was enough to give me an itch at the base of my

230

spine.

Croesus's back rippled—from above it'd look somethin' like a belly dancer's stomach just when the audience cheers the loudest—and dropped me none too gently to the ground.

"I smell fresh meat." His mouth opened in a smile. "Unless I'm mistaken, there's a wisp of a fire going somewhere. Maybe we've got friends who know how my tastes run."

That was it then. I might as well head upwind. Croesus would be gassin' some poor stray creature soon. He was always very careful, but I didn't want there ever to be a first time for me to fall under that spell.

I found a spot as far away from the cave mouth as I could. The hand- and footholds weren't the best, but 'least I could let the fluids flow.

I'd just finished my business, when the dragon roared out a great challenge and I scrambled back down. I drew my sword and waited at the mouth in the unlikely possibility that he wanted my help. Sometimes food protested, but I'd never seen the Old Grouch lose—especially when he was hungry.

A high-pitched voice said, "Stop that! I warn you, stop that!"

Croesus thumped his tail against the wall hard enough to crack it.

The high-pitched meal just said, "No! Bad dragon! Get back!"

The dragon hissed.

I was getting curious. I put my sword away and sidled inside to see what was givin' Croesus pause and to get a better view of things. Well, I immediately saw the problem. Lunch turned out to be a kid—what, five, maybe six. Not that it ought to make any difference to Croesus.

But this kid was putting on quite a show, wavin' a small wooden sword at Croesus. He should've been cowering against the wall. Grown men had blacked out from nearly a mile off. These two were close enough to shake hands, yet this kid seemed completely unafraid of a thirty-six-foot copper dragon. It was impossible!

The dragon turned and gave me a don't-that-beat-all look. In between his shoutin' at us, the kid was pokin' at a small fire a few steps back from Croesus. He had talent to keep the fire going with our bulk blocking most of the fresh air, I had to give him that.

"This one bears study." Croesus dipped his head in what passed for a nod in humans. I scratched absently at my backside and waited a beat. We had long ago agreed on a few things. We gave one another room to fight and didn't press too hard about personal pleasures, like a dragon's sweet tooth or a mercenary's . . . well, never mind.

One time I caught Croesus munchin' on some kind of meat after a nasty battle. Lots of flesh everywhere, and not all of it was tough-muscled men. I wasn't payin' much attention till he turned away and bent over as though maybe he was hidin' somethin' from me, which got me curious. Thought maybe he'd found a trinket he was considerin' he might not want t' share.

Turned out Croesus had a soft spot, as it were, for young flesh. Didn't matter what species. He thought just about all of 'em tasted pretty good—'cept maybe the kapaks. He could usually wait till they died on their own (preferably by fire, medium rare), but was outright abashed to admit he sometimes helped 'long the likelier tidbits. It was as much a part of his nature as casual greed was born into his race.

I didn't mind. We all got testy places *closed* to discussion. I figured this wasn't any worse—well, not much anyway—than some of the stuff I'd done when it came to kids or their mams.

Which made it all the more peculiar that the Old Grouch looked stumped by the young'un with the wooden sword. "What about his folks?" the dragon growled. "He's gotta be here with someone. Too small to travel alone." The dragon gave me a piercing look as though maybe *I* ought to have a theory on the subject.

Now that I was forced to give it some thought, there

was somethin' plain odd about the boy. Just bein' near him made my skin pucker. I noticed he carried a small pack slung across his back. I figured it might yield some clues which, if nothing else, would provide interesting after-dinner conversation, so I grabbed for it and him. He was a slippery cuss, but I hooked his arm and tightened my grip—and got a flash of a village in flames.

You see strange things in my line of work—burning towns, distressed damsels, tykes who conjure visions. Few've slowed me down but suddenly I found m'self starin' out at the slice of sky as I told Croesus, "I get the distinct feelin' the bugger's an orphan."

"Then that's settled," he said, matter-of-fact.

I shrugged. The dragon was right. On reflection I thought it best to keep the cave tidy and dragged the kickin', jumpin', swingin', screamin', danglin'-from-my-arm-kid outside. Croesus followed hungrily.

"Stop that! I warn you, stop that!"

The boy's face was the picture of brattiness. As if he thought I'd obey *him*. I couldn't help wonderin' what kind of fool he had for a father. Maybe the kid'd never seen a dragon, so he didn't grasp pure threat when it was vergin' on his throat.

"I'm warning you for the last time!"

"Okay," I muttered, and waited for 'nother phantasm.

And got jabbed in the gut.

I'd forgot about his puny sword. Little bugger knew just where to hit. I dropped him with a loud "uh" and doubled over.

Croesus got a good guffaw out of it, thank you.

Wouldn't be the last time the kid'd catch me by surprise, or even the most painful, but it was the one that woke me quick as a bucket of cold water over my head. I revised my 'pinion of his father . . . and developed some respect for the whelp on account of bein' showed up by someone a tenth my weight. (And a sim'lar portion of my age, but we won't mention that.)

He was a good little fighter with darned sharp survival instincts, and I almost felt a twinge of regret that he was about to become a dragon *hors d'oeuvre*. When I could stand and breathe at the same time, I took a look around. The li'l bastard had scooted on me. He had taken advantage of Croesus's laughin' spell to cut a wide arc around him, all the while keepin' out of my reach, and was dartin' back toward the mouth of the cave. I tell you this kid was impressive.

The boy'd been so quick that I was gapin' at him like a rube who'd just seen the finale of the Dance of the Fifteen Veils. (But, oh, that fifteenth veil!)

The Old Grouch had got his chucklin' under control, and cleared his throat. "Got your breath back?" he asked sarcastically.

Even with the kid's lead on me, I caught up with him before he got far into the cave. I grabbed him by an ankle and dragged him outside again. I dangled the kid in front of the dragon at arm's length (he was swingin' that sword around like a maniac). "Here's your dinner. Plenty of baby fat on those legs."

The Old Grouch's eyes glazed just a second as if maybe his resolve were slippin' 'long with my patience—this kid was more work than a town of thieves—then he said, "No, there's something about this child I would like to explore further. We will have to restrain him, though, don't you think?"

The kid swung up and nicked my hand. It stung worse than an angry vixen, but I was ready this time. I tightened my grip on his ankle, dangled him closer to the Old Grouch (whose breath could be rather intimidatin'), and shook hard. "Do that again, and I'll eat you m'self."

The kid went limp, then turned to study me from his unten'ble position. The set of his jaw stopped me cold. Reminded me of that woman I used to see . . . nah. I shrugged it off. "Behave yourself, and I won't truss you like a pig, 'kay?"

Still upside down, he nodded seriously.

I let go his foot, and he tumbled to the ground. "Okay," he said, comin' up with his hand held out. I took it—and again got the vision of a burnin' village.

This kid sure had an interestin' bag of tricks. I grabbed my hand back and motioned him over toward a rock. Croesus offered no guidance. He had closed his eyes as if the proceedin's no longer interested him, though I knew he was listenin' and would probably eat the boy anyway when the mood struck.

I let the boy seat himself, then put on my best formal voice. "I am Stoic John. My *companion*"—a quiet snort from same—"is Croesus. We have no reason in the slightest to tolerate you. *You* have trespassed on our private sanctuary"—here I was stretchin' the truth just a bit—"and disturbed our peace of mind." (Which he had, 'specially *my* peace of mind. But he'd also been a mostly amusin' diversion, up till now.) "Most disturbances *die*," I continued, givin' that a chance to soak in. "What do you have to say for yourself?"

He looked at me with big eyes, calculatin'. "I'm Jakster," he said proudly, as if that explained what he was doin' in a cave high up in the mountains.

I waited. He repeated. I waited some more. The dragon allowed a quiet, manufactured snore to escape.

I admit I half expected the kid to launch into some outrageous lie, speakin' in perfect elven. I was a little disappointed when he went for sympathy instead. There were large tears, which he bravely wiped away. "My mommy left me."

No doubt. Who could blame her? I showed not a trace of compassion (I had plenty of practice in that department). At last he made a show of sittin' stiffer and straighter and lettin' the tears dry up.

"Okay, Jakster . . ." His name lingered in my mouth.

"Jax," the dragon rumbled, and was still. The Old Grouch liked t' keep names simple. One of his quirks.

"We'll call you Jax," I continued.

The kid gave a friendly shrug and said, "Okay."

"Your show," I told the dragon.

Croesus opened his eyes. They shone brightly. "We've wasted enough time. Why don't you head back upwind?"

Good idea, if I didn't say so myself. I took one last

glance at the kid. He was diggin' in his pack. He didn't pay any attention to the dragon. Either he was fearless, as I said—or stupid. I turned away.

"Uh, Mr. Stoic?"

I froze in surprise. Mr. Stoic?

Before I could respond, he went on, "My mommy said to give you this." I tensed as his hand came out of the pack, but he was only holdin' a note.

It was her handwritin' all right. Raslyn. Just touchin' that bit of parchment felt the same as puttin' my hand in a wasp nest. I jammed the paper into my pocket. I didn't need to look at it. All of a sudden realization hit me, and I knew what it'd probably say. Then I was standin' there, facin' down the dragon and the boy, not quite sure how I got into this mess.

"Anything I should know?" Croesus mocked, waitin' for my departure.

"You already know all about Raslyn," I snapped back.

The Old Grouch gave a good imitation of a shrug. "Yes. And what I didn't know I *guessed*," he said pointedly, rollin' his eyes toward Jax. "But it doesn't matter, does it? He's mine to do with as I will?" Oh, so polite, for one as powerful as he.

"Always has been," I replied, my face red. "And I sure don't screen your food for you. What am I, a taste tester?" I muttered curses, embarrassed at myself for hesitatin' over this no-'count child, and stomped off toward an upper ledge.

Croesus waited till he saw that I was uncomfortably settled, then exhaled in the kid's direction.

To my surprise, Jax didn't seem to react, while I found myself thinkin' of that burnin' village again. I was beginnin' to catch on this time. The vision got deeper, richer, more detailed on the edges. I could hear the villagers screamin', feel the heat of the flames. Odd thing was—no one seemed hurt.

And where were the cutthroats who'd started the blaze? Stealin' loot? What could a poor place like this village have worth takin'?

From my lookout, I could see Croesus circle Jax. The dragon looked behind the kid's little ears, under his pudgy arms, inside his mouth full of gapped teeth. (He'd lost a couple in front.) The kid had a lopsided smile. He had sheathed his toy sword and seemed to be enjoyin' himself as the dragon poked at him.

Suddenly I felt as though I'd stepped into an anthill and sunk up to my neck. The itchin' I'd felt when we'd first landed just set my body afire.

I considered the kid. Nah, no way he could've been trained to that level yet. It took years. Those visions s'gested Jax had a hefty dose of the gift, but it wasn't the kid makin' me itch. No. I finally had to admit, it was much worse than magic.

I hadn't seen or touched Raslyn in six or seven years. We used to dally in this cave right here. Other times we went to her hut 'midst clatterin' and crashin' of magical stuff crowdin' every surface. Raslyn was the most wonderful flesh I'd ever set hands on then or since. Had a nice smile, too. I sure could've got used to wakin' up with her around . . . if she wasn't so, well, contrary. Argumentative.

I left her in the darkest hour of the darkest night, tried to leave without fuss or clues. But her mage breed isn't easily fooled. 'Sides, I was clumsier then. Without openin' those gorgeous all-knowing eyes, she whispered in her conjurin' voice, "You will meet your fate one day. Should you be tempted to escape when Fate calls, know that I have marked you." She opened her eyes then, though her face still held the restful calm of untroubled sleep. "It will not be denied."

Whenever I thought back to that night, I tried to tell m'self I'd left just in time. But the lady taught lessons. She always spoke true, and she had the will to wait even if it took years. I couldn't think of a one who crossed her who didn't 'ventually get a reminder.

Ever since, I guess, I knew my time was comin'. At first, ev'ry peculiar pain or strange itch, I'd been sure was my end. Still, any mercenary has to live with such, and I got used to odd symptoms after a while.

I rubbed at a bruise on my tailbone. Days on a dragon's back, I told myself.

I watched the dragon keep pokin' at Jax as I reluctantly unfolded the note. It said, "Fate. She's yours. Honor her."

Fate—that fickle female. She sure was mine.

I looked up to see the Old Grouch licking the kid's face. You might've thought he was just bein' puppy-dog friendly, but you'd 've been wrong. Jax knew it too. The dragon held Jax out as if to get a better view, then lowered the kid toward his open mouth.

"Stop that!" Jax and I yelled as one.

"Interesting," Croesus responded. He paused, but held the kid dangerously close to those jaws.

Raslyn's magic was powerful. The itchy feelin' got unbearable. Suddenly I had to stop Croesus. I jumped up and slipped on loose rock. "Don't do that!" I shouted as I fell.

The dragon turned to face me, then moved to bring us at eye level. I was half on my back. His bulgin' eyes, his flared nostrils, his huge form blocked all else from my sight. We both knew who was master here and had been from the first.

In a voice he used only when he thought his smarter enemies might yet have the sense to run away, the dragon said, "I've decided to eat the child. What concern is it of yours?"

I shook myself. My face itched. I turned it into an embarrassed smile. "Don't know what got into me. Must've been those fumes you're puttin' out. I spoke hastily," I said, hopin' to loosen him some.

Croesus lowered his face closer to mine. "You know it was nothing of the kind," he said through gritted teeth.

We hadn't been this tight face-to-face for a long time. Probably ever, come to think about it. Croesus wasn't patient with disagreements. He didn't bother to work with fate. He *was* fate. Judgments were instant and final. I'd always liked that about the Old Grouch . . . till now.

"The kid," I reminded him.

"Will keep," he said. "This requires a strong . . . stomach, shall we say."

S'gestin' I'd lost my nerve was a grave insult. Jokin' about it meant I was one step closer to becomin' dragon chow. Either way, no one was laughin'. My skin seemed wild with crawlin' insects. I could hardly keep from brushin' 'em away. In the back of my mind, I sat next to a small child and watched a village burn.

A harsh wind blew. Loose rocks clattered behind us. Croesus waited. I scratched my back and neck with the scrap of parchment amazingly still in my hand.

"Croesus, I'm, uh . . ." I faltered. "I have to *keep* the kid. You *can't* eat him!" I spat it out quick in one breath—then tensed for the worst.

"What will you do with her?" he exploded. "You have no use for this one. Do you think you owe her something?" Croesus was steamin'. We'd never fought like this even when he almost ate me—once.

"I owe her nothin'!" I shouted back, glad for an excuse to blow and plenty angry myself. "I left her, fair and reasonable, as you well know—"

"Not the *mother*, you incompetent human! Jax!"

"Jax! But Jax isn't a her. He's a he . . . isn't he?"

The dragon's face said otherwise, and he backed off enough to let me get the message. I studied the sky. The world spread out before me. The winds were suddenly calm. It made a twisted sense. Fate was surely female. She and my lady mage knew how to teach a mercenary a lesson. I almost laughed as I said, "Girl or boy, doesn't matter. I have to keep . . . *her*."

I said it almost as though I believed it. (A girl, oh sweet dancin' sisters, the blasted woman left me a *girl!*) I handed the Old Grouch Raslyn's note, which he snatched furiously with one claw. "This means nothing," he said, readin' it. "Dragons are not bound by fate."

"But I am," I told him with surprisin'ly little regret (and maybe even a little relief at finally havin' Fate slap me in the rump). Croesus was back to talkin' to me, and the crawlin' ants were retreatin', so I knew I had a chance. "I got no idea what we're goin' to do with an untrained, girl-child magician, but she's the debt I owe." I paused, waitin' for a sign he agreed.

The dragon sniffed, half in contempt but a little sorrowfully too, I thought. "I agree this child will cause us indigestion," he said with a sigh.

The note, impaled on one of the dragon's claws, was stirred by a stray gust of wind, which also brought with it a delicious, unexpected scent.

"Is that smoke?"

"Where did the child disappear to, anyway?"

And then I smiled wider'n at a harem full of dancin' girls. (No, not that. Much, *much* wider—I'm not much for harems. The girls tend to be a little young. Prefer mine with experience.) It finally dawned on me what that smell was comin' from the back of the cave, and how I could put things right with the Old Grouch.

I moved to the cave mouth to eyeball the kid and check out my theory. Croesus was right behind me. Inside, Jax was hummin' a high-pitched tune as she merrily fed a growing fire 'neath a roastin' hunk of venison.

See, I should have realized the village in my visions looked mighty familiar. Besides havin' a penchant for magic, Jakster was a little firebug. *She* had set her village, Raslyn's village, ablaze. Her neighbors prob'ly put out her flames plenty of times before. This time was the last straw. I learned the gory details later, from Jax herself. She was understandably proud.

With his impeccable timin', Croesus tapped me on the shoulder and handed me Raslyn's note. On the back of the parchment, in a messy scrawl—maybe the angry hordes were closing in—it said: "P.S. Jax is a pretty fair cook—but watch the fire." And in a messier scrawl still, "Tell the dragon it will ease his conscience to eat someone else's cooking for a change."

"Well, huh," I grunted t' m'self. I looked over at the kid, but Jax seemed to be altogether caught up in preparations for dinner.

Croesus was still hoverin', lookin' none too pleased at developments. "We could use a cook," I said weakly.

His tail slapped the ground hard enough to add cracks to the ledge and loosen a few rocks somewhere below.

" 'Sides, she don't weigh much, and there's plenty of room." I tried to sound ingratiatin', but I didn't even convince myself.

The dragon slapped his tail harder, making the entire cliff shake.

"Awright, awright. I'm coming!" said a high-pitched voice. And Jax came hurryin' out of the cave carryin' a mounded platter of ready-to-eat venison. "Medium rare!" Jax announced, settin' the meat before the dragon. Like the note said, Jax was a pretty fair cook. Croesus said so himself, shortly after he tore into a good-sized hunk.

Things were settled. Fate well met. I cast a softhearted glance over my shoulder as Jax went back into the cave to prepare another platter, then heard a crack behind me. The dragon, interruptin' his feast, held a branch snapped in two—an olive branch, as it were. My relief didn't escape his notice as he handed the wood to me. He knew full well where I'd take it, provin' he really isn't a bad sort once you get past that tough hide.

Back in the cave, I said, "Jakster, I found some more kindlin' for you."

Jax looked solemn as she took it from me and placed it ceremonially on the fire. "Thank you," was all she said.

I scratched a tiny itch in the small of my back and wondered about the trouble we'd get into. "You are indeed welcome," I told her, barely catchin' the rumble of a snore from a middle-aged dragon settlin' down for a nap.

The First Dragonarmy Bridging Company

Don Perrin

The rain was just ending. The sound of the water splashing in puddles had slowly subsided to light splats. Figures began to emerge from whatever shelter they'd been able to find, cursing the wet, searching in vain for wood dry enough to burn. Someone else was searching the camp, too.

"Kang? Bridge Master Kang? Get yer scaly lard ass out here before I have to hunt you down like a dog! Kang! Kang!"

Unable to believe that someone was actually looking for him, a large Bozak draconian emerged slowly from the barracks tent. He was slightly hunched and wore tooled leather armor. The standard curve-bladed sword worn by most draconian warriors was absent from his belt. In its place hung a small dagger and a coiled rope.

"I am Kang," he growled. "What is it you want, human?"

"Rajak, to you, Bridge Master. Second Aide to Dragon Highlord Ariakas. You will accompany me to the command tent. You will receive your orders for the upcoming operation there."

Kang stared in astonishment. Before the draconian could ask questions, the officer had turned and begun trudging up a muddy track. Sputtering campfires were dimly reflected in the man's plate cuirass. Shrugging, Kang slogged respectfully after him. The draconian was easily twice the weight and a good six inches taller than the human, but there was no thought of anything but obedience—the lifeblood of the draconian. His very existence, from hatchling on, was dedicated to serving the Dragon Highlord, following his orders.

Orders . . .

Kang's long, lizardlike tongue flicked from his mouth in anticipation. At last, after all this time, orders . . .

As Bridge Master, it was Kang's job to train, maintain, and lead a squadron of draconian bridge builders. They had trained for three months now and had practiced building every conceivable type of bridge. They had, however, never used their craft in combat, never gained the praise and respect Kang knew were due them. His squadron had not been through its baptism of fire.

Not that there hadn't been bridges built. The continent of Ansalon was laced with rivers and streams, dotted with lakes. Bridges were needed to aid in the advance of ground troops, to bring up supplies and siege equipment so vital to the continued success of a fighting force. Until a year ago, it had been standard operating procedure to call in the draconian combat engineers.

All this had changed, however, when the Black Robe Golmitack and his small band of wizards and druids had won the favor of Ariakas, Dragon Highlord. Golmitack argued that it was far more efficient to allow the druids to calm the waters and solidify the approaches, and have the mages craft the structures from magical sources. Ariakas—a wielder of magic himself—had been impressed by Golmitack and his flashy methods. The draconian engineers were relegated to rear area security, standing guard, doing kitchen and latrine duty.

Latrine duty.

Kang snorted. He was damn sick and tired of latrine duty.

His was the only bridging squadron left in the entire Red Dragonarmy. His command was made up of the biggest Sivak draconians around, led by himself, a Bozak. His troops were able and ready. They'd been able and ready for months now. And they were able and ready to do something other than dig those everlasting slit trenches. . . .

Kang was pleased that he was being summoned to an orders conference, but he couldn't help but wonder why. It made no sense. The Red Dragonarmy's advance had stalled on a hastily built set of defenses thrown up by human and dwarven warriors across the only fordable section of the river. The might of the human forces was threatening the right flank of the dragonarmy, and there were rumors of silver dragons supporting the humans.

Kang assumed that the Black Robe Golmitack would either devise a method to defeat the defenses or build a bridge over the river. Or perhaps Wing Leader Bartlett would lead the Dragon Highlord's red dragons in a raid bent on destroying the pestering defenders. All in all, the plans added up to more latrine digging for the draconian engineers, and Kang didn't need a division commander or a Highlord to tell him that.

Second Aide Rajak came to a halt in front of the large headquarters tent. "Wait out here, Bridge Master, until you are called for."

Kang grunted in acknowledgment. Rajak entered the tent. As the flap opened, Kang could hear the sounds of heated debate inside. He stood, puzzled. What was the problem?

Apparently, he was about to find out. Rajak reappeared.

"Bridge Master Kang, you are summoned. When you enter, you will turn to your left, march forward to the area in front of the battle map, salute, and face the Highlord. Questions? No? Good. Carry on."

The rank of Bridge Master was officially an officer rank. Kang was not used to being treated like an officer, however. Latrine and kitchen duty tended to wear the shine off his metal clasps. He twitched his armor into place, gave his harness buckles a quick swipe with his tongue. Entering the tent, he performed as instructed, saluted the Dragon Highlord.

"Bridge Master Kang as requested, Highlord."

Ariakas was large for a human. The Dragonlord's cold, expressionless face marked him as cruel, proud, ambitious. Kang, who had only seen his commander from a distance, was considerably impressed.

"Bridge Master." Lord Ariakas's voice rumbled through the tent, silencing all conversation. "How would you rate the operational effectiveness of your bridging squadron in night bridging operations?"

Kang was stunned. How by the Queen would he know? His squadron had not been in combat for over a year! There was no way. . . .

Receiving no answer to his question, Lord Ariakas had begun to frown. "Bridge Master?"

Kang took a deep breath, made the only response he could.

"Highlord, we are fighting fit and ready for combat. It is our honor to serve one such as you. . . ."

Ariakas waved his hand impatiently. "Yes, yes. Fine. Enough with the pleasantries and bravado. I need straight answers, and I need a plan in the next half hour. As you know, bridging has formerly been the domain of the mages and druids. But yesterday, a patrol of elves, aided by powerful magics, ambushed and killed our two druids and seriously wounded the wizard Golmitack."

Kang attempted to assume an expression of deepest sympathy, all the while trying to keep his scales from clicking together in joy.

Ariakas went on. "We have to get round those cursed dwarven fortifications. The army must cross the river, flank the fortifications, and crush the defense. Otherwise, we'll be squashed like bugs with the humans pouring in from our right and no way to cross this damned river."

The Highlord strode over to the large battle map spread out across a crude wooden table. Markers of various types delineated enemy and friendly troop units, fortifications, and terrain. One—the symbol of a silver dragon, on the side of the enemy—immediately caught the draconian's attention. Silver dragons? Could it be true?

Draconian blood normally runs cold, but Kang's ran colder than usual. He had difficulty, for a moment, following Ariakas's words. Then a single phrase jolted the draconian to attention.

"Bridge Master," said Ariakas, "I need a bridge. Where would you put it?"

Kang lost his fear and his awe. His scaly skin literally twitched with anticipation. Lord Ariakas was asking

Kang to commit to his baptism of fire—his first opportunity since becoming commander. Kang studied the map intently. The answer was, to him, obvious.

"Here, Highlord. I would build a single-lane floating foot bridge. Here."

Kang pointed at one of the widest, deepest portions of the river downstream from the enemy defenses.

Lord Ariakas grunted in disgust.

"There? Bridge Master, even for a draconian, you are an idiot. . . ."

The Dragon Highlord paused. His hand rubbed his chin, dark with several day's growth of beard. A slow smile began to slide across the Dragon Highlord's face. The smile broadened to a chuckle. "I see your plan."

Kang began to breathe again. "If I may be allowed to elaborate, Highlord. I would build the bridge downstream in the wide and deep part of the river, first to make the crossing easier due to the calmer waters, and second because no one in his right mind would put a bridge there, thus ensuring our security and secrecy. Once the might of our infantry is across, we will widen the bridge to accommodate siege engines and wagon trains."

Ariakas nodded. "What of bridging materials?"

The scales on the draconian's back tightened and clicked into place, each one aligning itself with its neighbor—a natural reaction to tension and nervousness for dragonspawn.

"Highlord, this forested area here will serve to both cover our construction and provide the materials. We can use the large trees as dugout pontoons and the smaller ones to create a corduroy planking. Long, thin trees will be used to provide girders to link the pontoons together. It will take the squadron three days to have the materials ready to build a floating bridge, Lord."

Ariakas smiled. "You have until tomorrow night, Bridge Master. That bridge will be up before the rise of the sun the next day."

Kang's scales clicked more loudly. "Then I will need more manpower, Highlord. . . ."

"Impossible. I cannot spare any men to aid you in your construction. The loss of troops from the earthworks would alert the enemy to our . . . *my* plan." Ariakas turned away. "Wing Leader Bartlett, you will ground your dragon wing until after the bridge is up, except to fly intercept missions. I want no chance of enemy silver dragon riders observing the bridge construction. Understood?"

Kang had been so awed and nervous, he'd never actually realized other officers were present. Now that he looked, he recognized three division commanders, each with his staff, several of the Highlord's aides, specialists, and guards. The place stank of senior officer.

Ariakas continued to issue orders. Kang stood as silent and unmoving as a bronze-scaled post.

"Bridge Master, you are dismissed. Begin your work at once. Oh, and Bridge Master, you will sit in on my planning conferences from now on."

"Glory to our Dark Queen, Highlord!" Kang said, saluting.

"To the Queen," Ariakas said absently, with a wave of his hand.

Kang almost flew down the mud track to his squadron's barracks tent. He hesitated at the tent flap, savoring the moment. Two words would start his first real combat command. For this, he'd been hatched.

He entered the tent quietly and nodded politely to the sentry. Putting his hands on his leather belt, he drew in a huge breath of air.

"*Staaaaand tooooooooo!*"

He was in his element now, for the first time in his existence. This was his hatch-right!

"Get outta bed, you idle gits! Get moving! Stand to, you lazy bastards! Form ranks on the road in three minutes, combat braces and helmets. Full construction gear. We're going to work! *Move it!*"

This last order caused a sensation among the draconians. Full construction gear? That was only needed for building bridges—real bridges. This was certainly no time for a practice exercise.

The squadron formed up in columns with twenty seconds

to spare. They were going to war. They were back in the business of fighting. . . .

Kang looked everyone over. "Right. Listen up. Troop commanders report to me in twenty minutes. The rest of you, unpack all bridging tools and plans. Reconnaissance Commander, report to me now. The rest of you—dismissed!"

Comos, leader of Reconnaissance Troop, stumped over.

Kang drew him to one side. "Recce Commander, I want you and your troop to check out a good site downstream, where the river gets wide and calm. Yeah, you know the place. The squadron will arrive in three hours. I want trees marked for planking, pontoons, and girders. I want a bivouac site marked, and I want a smokeless fire well hidden from the opposite shore going and at least one large rodent roasting when I get there. Clear? Good. Go."

The area exploded in a flurry of activity. Every single member of the bridging squadron knew the significance of the endeavor. Each one of them jumped at the chance to prove himself in the eyes of the Bridge Master.

The bridging squadron was organized into groups of twenty Sivaks and one Bozak. The Sivaks provided the brawn need for bridging operations. The Bozak acted as the troop commander and the senior Sivak as his subcommander. Their main tasks were the construction of parts and then assembly of those parts into a bridge.

Support Troop, consisting of roughly the same mix of draconians, constructed tools and specialized in digging the approaches for the bridge. Recce, or Reconnaissance Troop, was responsible for picking the exact bridge site, marking the trees needed for the construction of the bridge, and the defense of the site during construction. Several Baaz draconians were mixed in, as there was no need to waste higher quality draconians on sentry or cooking duties. As the saying went, if there was a mundane job to do, let a Baaz do it.

Recce Troop also had the not so enviable task of holding the far bank of the river during bridge assembly. That was, according to the learned scrolls, usually referred to as a suicide mission.

Kang held his own orders conference with his tro
commanders inside the barracks tent. There had never
been so much excitement or such high spirits in the
squadron. No one needed Kang to emphasize the significance of this operation. If they succeeded, not only would
they be covered with glory, but Lord Ariakas might see fit
to dispense with those sneaky Black Robes and the tree-
hugging druids.

After the orders were given, the troop commanders
returned to their preparations. Kang dragged his subcommander, a huge Sivak draconian, off to the side.

"Slith, this is it. We're going to build a godsforsaken
bridge and save the whole bloody day. Now I want you,
as second-in-command, to be the disciplinarian. Keep
those toads in line. Here's how we work it. I want the
troops to look over at us and say 'that Slith, he's a mean
bastard of a dragonspawn, but Bridge Master Kang, he's
okay.' Get my drift? When there's praise or encourage-
ment to be given, that's my job. When there's whips to be
cracked—or perhaps a few heads—you'll do the cracking.
How's that with you?"

Slith had been subcommander for only one month
under Kang, but it had been a good month. Slith had
shown himself to be brighter than most Sivaks and ruth-
less when it came to applying the law. He would likely
never earn a command of his own, but he certainly was
good at subcommanding.

Slith's taut cartilage lips peeled back from rows of
razor-sharp teeth.

"I am looking forward to this, Bridge Master. My only
request"—squinty eyes narrowed as he gauged the effect
of his next few words on his commander—"is that I command the far-side holding section."

Kang was pleased at the request. Slith was eager to
prove himself. He was asking for the most dangerous
position—guarding the side of the river that was in
enemy hands.

Kang clapped the Sivak on his bony shoulder. "I don't
have to remind you that you may never come back across

that bridge."

Slith's toothy smile widened.

Kang nodded. "The honor is yours."

Just as the sun rose above the green hills surrounding the valley, the bridging squadron arrived in force at their destination. They moved with all due caution and stealth through the underbrush. They were outside the defensive perimeter of the dragonarmy, meaning they were in enemy territory. But it was the sun that worried Kang more than elves or even silver dragons at the moment. Within the tree line it was still dark, but already it was obvious to Kang that the day was going to be a hot one.

Spawned from dragons, draconians are cold-blooded and can adjust their body temperature to suit the climate. This spring had been unusually hot, however, and beneath the trees, hot was very hot. Some draconians could not adjust completely. You could always tell a draconian who was exhausted or overheated—he grinned without knowing it. As the scales on his back spread to allow the air to circulate, the skin of his face pulled taut, his mouth opened to allow greater cooling.

Kang was afraid that his troops would not be able to handle the hard labor in the heat, and he had no flexibility in his timetable for a delay. It occurred to him, however, that every draconian in this unit was as excited about the coming battle as he was. He was probably worrying needlessly.

By early afternoon, the thwacking of axes and the pounding of wooden mallets on end posts were sweet music to Kang. He almost started to hum along, caught himself just in time. What if Lord Ariakas happened by, discovered his Bridge Master singing? Kang's scales clicked at the thought.

Rounding up Slith, Kang decided to survey the work.

The first troop was deep in the forest cutting tall, straight pine trees. Those that were to be cut were marked by a double blazing mark on the trunk, made by the members of Reconnaissance Troop when they had first arrived. The trees were felled and then stripped, leaving only the

long trunk. These were to be used as the rails of the brid
and connect the pontoons.

Kang was watching his men work when . . .

Thunk!

Kang rolled for cover. The tree to his right had virtually
exploded with the impact of . . . of what?

All work in the area immediately ceased. The leather-
armored draconians were nearly invisible in the dense
brush. No one made a sound.

Kang rolled to his side to look up at the tree. It had split
dead center six feet from the ground. Kang's gaze moved
first up the tree, and then down, finally examining the
base. Here he found his answer. A small piece of dowel
with silver leaf shards lay broken near the trunk. You
could almost smell the magic coming from the shaft. An
elven arrow. Which meant . . .

"Slith, look at this!" Kang hissed. "There's a damned elf
pansy-assing around out there. Do you see him?"

Slith was moving slowly, snakelike, in the direction of
the shot. He made no sound and gave no reply. But the
Sivak had given Kang all the answers he needed.

Rolling to his left, Kang rose to a crouch and loped off
in a slow arc through the woods.

"There's no way under the Abyss I'll let some pointy-
eared woodsy ruin my first combat command," Kang
muttered.

Rounding a large deciduous tree, he spotted movement. He drew his dagger, then, cursing, returned it to the
scabbard. What was he going to do with a dagger when
he faced a well-armed elf warrior?

With relief, Kang realized that the movement had been
made by Slith. The subcommander, seeing Kang, motioned
to a bush on a knoll. The cursed elf must be hiding there.
Slith was silently asking Kang to draw the elf out, so that the
Sivak could ambush their enemy from behind.

Kang nodded. Although he was a magic-user, he'd only
had time to memorize one spell before being interrupted
for the orders conference. Now it was time to put the spell
to use.

Kang rose to his full height, crashed through the brush. The elf spotted him easily. Another *thwack* sent the draconian sprawling. An arrow embedded itself in the thick trunk of a nearby tree.

Rounding a small rock, Kang sighted the elf. The creature was wearing a green jerkin and trousers over leather boots, with a chain cuirass covering its torso. At its side, it wore a short sword, and in its hand was an ornately crafted elven longbow. The elf loaded its bow and began to aim, all in one fluid motion.

Kang loosed his spell. The forest lit up like a bonfire at one of the death god Chemosh's festivals. The elf appeared to be momentarily confused, but quickly regained its composure and prepared to send the draconian to his Queen.

Slith rose up behind the elf, struck.

A shocked expression contorted the elf's face. It slowly released tension on the bow and, with a grunt, sat down.

Kang started to congratulate Slith, but Slith was no longer there. Standing behind the dead elf was a second elf, exactly the same as the first in every detail, but holding a draconian dagger, dripping with blood.

"I've always wanted to do that!" exclaimed Slith—the elf.

It had been so long since they'd been in combat, Kang had forgotten that Sivak draconians had the power to take the shape of the creature they'd just killed. All draconians were endowed with certain special gifts from their Queen. Even in death, a draconian could inflict serious harm on the enemy. Kang was particularly proud to know that, when it came time to return to his Queen, his bones would explode, doing considerable damage to his killer. A Sivak's corpse took on the appearance of the one who murdered him, while a victorious Sivak could shape-change to look like his victim—unnerving any of the enemy who stumbled across what appeared to be a friend they'd thought dead. Even the lowly Baaz could turn to stone, encasing an enemy's weapon in their bodies, seriously hampering his ability to continue to fight.

Kang let out an undignified sigh of relief. He walked up to his friend, grabbed him by the shoulder.

"Good work, Slith. I thought I was headed for the Abyss there for a second. Damn, but you gave me half a fright looking like that cursed elf."

Slith grinned at the praise. "Sir, there may be more than one elf in this party, and I'm the prancing ninny to find them. After all, don't I look just like one of them twits?"

Kang began to laugh—a laugh that bubbled up from deep in the belly. "Yes, yes, go and hunt them down. When you're done with your fun, I'll see you in your *normal* form back at the camp. If you're not back by sundown, I'll send Comos across with Recce Troop to take the far side."

Slith—the "elf"—wiped his bloody dagger on the back of the dead elf and tiptoed daintily into the woods.

Kang hurried back to the engineering troop. They had resumed work, but he noticed that his draconians were uneasy. The bastards kept stopping to peer nervously around. At this rate, it'd take them six months to build the damn bridge!

Assuming a dour expression, Kang strode purposely up to the troop commander.

"Where in the Abyss are your sentries, Gloth?"

Gloth, the officer in charge, jumped nervously. His eyes darted back and forth across the Bridge Master's massive form, his gaze about level with Kang's shoulders. The slight clicking sound of his scales aligning was all that Kang needed to hear.

"Don't tell me you're scared of a single pointy-ear! You sniveling whelp! Get a grip on your slack and idle body. I've seen braver-looking hatchlings! For the love of the Queen, you better get some ice back in those veins, or I'll have you guarding kender prisoners back at base camp! Now where the devil are your bloody sentries?"

Gloth's eyes were wild, snapping this way and that. "Sir, it's only that you told me I had fourteen hours to complete a three-day job! There's no way I can spare engineers for sentry duty!"

Kang, now that he had taken the officer apart, had to rebuild Gloth in the Bridge Master's own image. His voice softened. He drew the draconian to one side, hand on his quivering shoulder.

"Listen, Gloth, I know that it's tough out here—tougher than it's ever been for us, but this is *our* battle, *our* bridge. You've got to do miracles, and the troop looks to you for those miracles. Give them your heart and your fighting spirit and the miracles will come. I know you've got it in you. Remember our pugil stick fight?"

Gloth drew a breath, probably for the first time since the arrow had hit the tree. During that pugil stick match, Gloth had attacked Kang with such ferocity that Kang was sure Gloth would be in line for leadership someday. The draconian had it in him, and it was starting to show again.

"Yes, sir," Gloth said, straightening. "This won't happen again, and, sir, we'll be ready for bridge assembly this evening. We'll also be ready for any elves that show their ugly faces in this woods again." He wasn't bright, but he had drive enough for two draconians.

Saluting, Gloth moved back to his troop.

Kang had been forced to play both bad draco and good draco in that confrontation, but it needed doing. He'd better check on the other troops. Gloth had reminded him of that damn deadline.

Kang was starting to worry.

* * * * *

In the woods, Slith moved about jauntily. He kept deliberately out in the open so he could be seen, and hopefully spot his elven "comrades." He had rounded a bend in the trail when a strong hand grabbed hold of his arm, jerked him off the path, and threw him to the ground.

He looked up. Standing over him stood two elves, both dressed similar to himself.

"Hey, careful, fellows! I'm a delicate elf. I might bruise, you know. Be nice," said Slith, speaking the Common language and trying to sound and look elflike. He reached out a hand. "C'mon. Help me up. I think you made me twist my ankle."

"Glthgbhe bheee thghdedd bllah?"

The two elves just stood and stared, one of them jabbering at him in that birdbrained tongue of theirs.

Stupid, stuck-up twits. Why couldn't they talk a sensible language like everyone else in the world? Slith had no idea what the pointy-eared doofus was saying.

"Oh, yes, yes, of course!" he answered, again in Common.

The elf eyed Slith warily, but helped him to his feet.

As he reached a standing position, Slith drove his dagger into the stomach of the elf, heaved the blade up into its ribs. Blood gushed, and the second elf stared in amazement.

Almost immediately, Slith had mutated into the form of the dying elf, and turned on the second, living one.

Dropping its bow, the elf reached for a short sword.

Slith drove his fist into the elf's face, at the same time transforming back into his draconian body.

The look of disbelief on the elf's face was laughable, so Slith laughed and double-fisted the elf's neck, breaking it and driving the lifeless body to the ground.

Again Slith mutated, this time into the form of the second elf, who turned out to be a female. Slith was elated. Things were going exceedingly well. If he kept this up, he'd have all the elves in this end of the world dead by sundown.

That gave him an idea. He'd swim across the river in this form and clear the far side of the enemy! It was perfect. He'd be in the right position to retake command of the defense party when he'd finished. Brilliant!

* * * * *

Sundown that night was one of the most eerie and beautiful sights Kang had ever seen. At the horizon, the sky turned the color of blood. All of the draconians stopped their backbreaking work and reveled in the sight. It was an omen of the battle to come.

But just when Kang was feeling really, really good, he saw something fly across the horizon. It was too far away to identify by sight, but the draconian knew, by the terrible stirring of the blood—a stirring that clenched his gut and shriveled his bowels—what it was. A silver dragon.

Draconians had been "born" of the eggs of silver, gold, and other dragons who served the wimp god of sniveling good and righteousness, Paladine. Black magic and dark prayers had altered the dragon eggs, changing weak dragon hatchlings into strong, powerful fighters like Kang.

Kang hated and feared silver dragons. And the draconian knew the feeling was mutual.

He broke the awed silence with a bellowed order. "Troop commanders, report to me in fifteen minutes!"

Work continued. The river was over one hundred feet wide at this point. Ferrying Recce Troop across was going to be a problem. The distance was too great to have the Baaz fly across, and the current was strong, making swimming a problem. Kang didn't want half his command floating off downstream.

The troop commanders arrived at the command tent one by one, ahead of the fifteen-minute deadline. They marked their maps from the master map Kang had nailed to a large slewmuc tree, adding any changes that may have been made. That was the ritual in the dragonarmy. You arrived for orders ahead of time, marked your map, grabbed a mug of steaming gruel from the bivouac area, and waited for the meeting to be called to order.

The troop commanders talked among themselves, discussing their progress and working out details. Kang cleared his throat. All rose to their feet when the Bridge Master took his place at the front of the tent. Normally, the subcommander would call the meeting to attention, but Slith had not yet returned.

"Relax. This is going to be short. I've visited all of the troops, and I'm pleased with the progress. I want all bridge sections assembled by two hours past midnight here in the clearing. Recce Troop will cross at midnight. Comos, what do you think is the best way to cross?"

Comos considered for a moment. "Sir, why don't we fire a ballista bolt with a small-gauge rope attached across the river? If it sticks, we'll swim, using the rope as a guide. If it doesn't, we'll swim and hope for the best."

"Good. I like it. Set up the ballista twenty minutes before you go. Call me then. I'm going to rest and memorize spells. Get at it, and the Queen's wrath to any of you who're late."

The tent emptied. Kang was left alone. A single torch lit the interior. Pulling a worn leather thong from a pouch in his belt, Kang rhythmically wrapped and unwrapped his hand with the thong. He allowed himself to fall into a trance, murmuring the ancient words asking the Queen of Darkness for her blessing and the granting of spells.

Memorization of spells was actually a misnomer, coming from the human habit of reading and memorizing spells from a book. In fact, with the draconians, the use of magic was more similar to that practiced by the ancient clerics, who were granted spells by the grace of their gods. To an outsider, the magic used by the Bozak draconians appeared to be an innate ability. The Bozak knew that his magic was a gift from the Queen herself.

A knock on the tent post startled Kang into wakefulness. "What is it?"

The reply was from his sentry. "Sir, it is just coming up to midnight, and you ordered we should wake you."

"Midnight? Already?"

Kang was obviously more tired than he'd thought. He did, however, have a complete complement of spells. The Queen had sensed his need and granted him all that he had asked.

Exiting the tent, he turned to the sentry.

"Any word from Subcommander Slith?"

"No word, sir. No one has seen him since early this afternoon."

Kang walked over to the clearing. The darkness possessed no major problems for him. All draconians, with their specialized heat-sensing vision, could see fairly well in the night. Three officers descended upon the Bridge Master as soon as he was in sight. Two of them were draconians of the bridging squadron, and the other was a human.

"Good evening, Second Aide Rajak. I trust all is well with the Highlord?"

"All is well, Bridge Master Kang. Lord Ariakas asks for a progress report."

"The bridge will be ready for use just before the first breaking of light, according to his orders. Also, an elven scout was killed. I have sent my subcommander to dispatch the rest of the party. I assume, therefore, that no word of us has made it back to the enemy. Reconnaissance Troop will deploy to the opposite bank in minutes. The assembly of the bridge will begin in two hours. During assembly, I would ask the Highlord to redeploy some of his shock infantry to this area. I won't be able to spare engineers for sentry duty once we begin. The noise will undoubtedly make this a hot spot."

Rajak nodded. "I will report this to the Dragon Highlord. You will notice the troops assembling on the track behind this clearing in an hour or so. When the bridge is open, I will lead our forces to the other side."

The second aide departed. Kang turned to the other two officers, Gloth and Comos.

"Comos, is the ballista ready?"

"Yes, sir, but there is no way to accurately aim in the dark." Not even draconians could see across the vast river.

"Do the best you can."

Kang motioned his officers to follow and walked to the ballista. In slow, methodical tones, the Bridge Master intoned the spell for silent flight, and placed his hands upon the bowstring of the ballista. When he had finished, he picked up the ballista bolt with the rope tied to the end and repeated the process. Then he handed the bolt to Gloth.

"Fire it quickly. The silence spell does not last long."

The bolt flew across the river and landed on the other side, somewhere in the brush, all in unnatural, deadly silence. The only sound was the wood of the ballista creaking, and that was minor. Kang's spell had worked.

He peered into the darkness, thought he saw movement on the far bank. To his astonishment, the rope was inexplicably drawn another ten feet across before it stopped.

Slith! It had to be Slith!

He hoped to the Queen it was Slith. . . .

Recce Commander Comos pulled on his end of the rope, found the other end secure. He ordered his troop across. Ten minutes later, after the last of his command had entered the water, Comos started the journey himself.

The crossing was easy. Each draconian hung on to the rope, pulled himself along, claw over claw. Arriving on the other bank, Comos clambered out of the water, then stopped dead in his tracks.

He reached for his dagger. Facing him was an elf officer in gold plate mail armor. Comos's men had the elf surrounded. One of the Sivaks had a knife to the elf's throat.

"By the Queen, what have we got here?" Comos laughed. "A haughty prisoner caught in a draconian spiderweb, eh?"

The elf cursed—in draconian. "Comos, you dolt. Shut up and take command of this gaggle of yours!"

The Sivak holding the dagger on the elf threw down his weapon in disgust. "If that isn't Subcommander Slith, I'm a faerie princess! All this trouble for nothing!"

Comos stared, narrow-eyed. "Sir, *is* that you?"

"Of course it's me, frog-brain. Who in the Abyss did you think secured your rope on this side? The Queen herself? Now, listen to me. I'll retain this elf form for another hour or two. I'm going to scout around. If something goes wrong, you'll hear my battle cry. And if you run across an elf wearing a helm or a hat, kill it. I'll take my helm off and wave it, so you'll know it's me."

With that, Slith turned and disappeared into the woods. The other draconians spread out in a semicircle and started to work. Using huge mallets, the draconians began to pound large wooden spikes into the ground to form the bridge anchor.

The noise was sure to draw attention on this side, assuming anyone was within hearing distance. Comos prepared for trouble.

Just as the last spike was being pounded, he heard a large splash on the opposite side of the river—Kang's side. The bridge was starting to be assembled. Now, the race was on.

"To the Abyss with giving ourselves away," Comos shouted, grinning to himself. "Let the enemy try to stop us!"

Officers yelled orders. The heaving and pounding of iron spikes into the wood pontoons made a cacophony in the night. Every twenty minutes or so, another splash sounded, another pontoon was pushed into the river. The pounding and yelling renewed.

Tension was rising on Comos's side, however. Slith hadn't returned, and the sentries were quiet—too quiet. Comos was about to go check on things himself when he heard a rustling in the trees.

An elf waving his helm stalked out of the shadows. Entering the clear area at the bank, the elf changed into a Sivak draconian—Slith.

The subcommander was not pleased. He strode up to Comos, grabbed hold of him by the collar of his leather armor, and shook him like a dog shakes a rat.

"You idiot! Never never *never* put a Baaz on sentry duty! You're a fool, Comos. I've known scrambled eggs with more brains! Tell me, what do you think happens when a Baaz is garroted? He just stands there quiet as stone! *As stone*, lizard-breath! All your damn sentries out there have been killed, and they've turned to stone! And you didn't hear a damn thing!"

"But, sir—" Comos tried to explain.

Slith glowered. "At least if a Bozak buys it on sentry duty, he'd have exploded, and we'd have had some warning! Lucky for you I was nearby. The murdering elven scout party is now fertilizing daisies not fifty feet from here. I'm assuming command. You'll act as my aide. Clear?"

"Yes, s-s-sir!" stammered the unhappy Comos, through rattling teeth.

Slith glanced around, noticed the rest of Recce Troop

standing around, doing nothing, watching the two officers.

"Just what in the Abyss do you think you're looking at?" Slith shouted at them. "No one told you to stop working! Form a defensive perimeter! *Move!*"

Recce Troop began to slog off in the direction of the tree line. Suddenly one draconian groaned and sagged to the ground. Another fell, clutching an arrow in his midriff. More arrows whined through the trees, sounding like evil wasps.

"Get going, you maggots!" Slith hollered. "*Enemy to your front!*"

Across the river, Kang stood on a tree stump at the water's edge and surveyed the work. All of the pontoons were constructed, and crossbeams were being nailed into place. As a section was readied, it was pushed into the water, moving the entire floating bridge closer to the opposite bank. The end of the bridge was secured to the rope that Recce Troop had shot across, ensuring that the bridge was not swept downriver.

Sivak draconians, balancing on the beams, nailed half-logs into place, creating a walkway. Several held short bows, their attention on the air and the land, keeping watch.

Kang was more worried now than ever. The bridge was nearing completion, and not one problem had occurred. Surely it can't be this easy, he thought.

He was right. From across the far side of the river, he heard what sounded like Slith's rumbling voice, the words: "Enemy to the front."

"Damn!" Kang peered across the water, trying desperately to see. He could hear the clash of blades, more shouts. And then a huge black shape drifted overhead in the darkness, blacker than black. It was flying above the river, and it could only be one thing.

Kang jumped down from his perch. He raced over to accost the human, standing on the river's edge. "Second Aide, I take it that is one of our dragons?"

Rajak shook his head. "No, couldn't be one of ours, Bridge Master. Our dragons are grounded except to intercept enemy . . ." The human's voice trailed off.

"Holy Mother Takhisis!" Kang swore.

Rajak turned and sprinted to the rear, heading back to Lord Ariakas's command tent.

Kang jumped onto the partially completed bridge, made his way to the center. Pounding his feet, he urged the engineers on.

"Faster! Move it! We've got the enemy on our . . . Blessed Abyss! Incoming!"

The darkness suddenly coalesced into the form of a huge silver dragon.

So that's how it disguised itself. Magical darkness spell! Kang realized.

The dragon now shone bright silver. It swept forward. Its outstretched hind talons raked across the bridge. The damage the dragon did was light, but it carried off two Bozaks in its claws. Kang recognized Comos, screaming curses as the dragon's talons dug into his scaly flesh.

The Bridge Commander swore. The dragon had captured prisoners alive. Torture couldn't make a draconian talk, but give that wretch Comos a couple of drams of elven wine and . . .

Kang was blinded by a flash, then deafened by an explosion, followed quickly by another. It took him a moment to realize what had happened. The two Bozaks had blown apart in midair! The force of the blast ripped the underbelly of the silver dragon wide open. It screamed, rolled over onto its back, and plunged into the river.

"Not bad shooting, eh, Bridge Master?"

Subcommander Slith, holding an elven bow, was grinning at Kang.

The Bridge Master stared at him in wordless astonishment.

Slith shrugged. "Couldn't have that lizard-livered Comos and that other officer blabbing about our bridge, could we, sir? So I shot them. These arrows are from an elven officer, and I guess they don't miss. I remembered that with you Bozaks, your bones explode when you're dead—begging your pardon, sir. Nothing personal. It's just that I figured if those two went up, they'd take the dragon with 'em."

Kang found his voice. "Slith! Where in the Queen's name did you come from? How in the Abyss did you get over here?"

"The bridge has reached the opposite shore. Recce Troop is securing the other side as we speak. We're being overrun by elves over there. That's what I sent Comos to tell you."

Kang hadn't realized they'd made this much progress. He peered across the river, could see his troops all over the opposite bank. He could also see the flash of metal, hear those nerve-grating songs those cursed elves sang when they went into battle. He looked back at the near bank. The first engineering troop was just finishing the planking. Good for Gloth. He had not permitted his men to stop work, even when the dragon attacked.

Kang was suddenly, deeply, righteously angry.

Sprinting onto the bridge, he rallied his forces. "Keep First Troop working!" he yelled at Gloth. "The rest of you, come with me! We're not going to let any Queen-cursed, pointy-eared, sing-songy, gimpy-legged elves take *our* bridge! Are we?"

The draconians answered with one resounding voice. "No, sir!"

The engineers working on the bridge did not go armed; swords would only get in their way. Now they grabbed anything that could be used to kill: hammers, mallets, axes, spikes. Wielding their crude weapons, the draconians swarmed across the bridge—*their* bridge. Elven arrows picked off more than a few, but the draconians surged on.

By all the gods in the dark pantheon, their bridge would stand.

The force of the draconian onslaught smashed the elven line. Soon, the far bank was awash with elven and draconian blood.

Kang, hacking the head off an elf warrior, heard the elven trumpets sound retreat. The elves left alive—and there weren't many—made a dash for the safety of the woods. Kang was forced to stop his battle-mad troops from pursuing.

Their job was the bridge. Let Rajak and his army finish off the elves.

Weary but triumphant, Kang slogged back across the bridge in company with Slith. The draconian was licking elf blood from his dagger.

"You know what I heard one of them ninnies say to another, right before I slit their throats? 'What's got into these devil-spawn? Usually they're pushovers.' "

"Obviously, they've never fought the engineers before," Kang said, grinning. Once he reached the other side, he looked over the bridge, rubbed his claws together in satisfaction. "Good, it's ready to cross."

"Speaking of crossing, where's the army, sir? Shouldn't they be here by now?"

"You're right," Kang muttered. "I hope nothing's gone wrong. . . . Ah, here comes Rajak! He's leading the crossing."

"Yeah? Well, he's in no hurry, is he, sir?" Slith observed.

Through the darkness, the draconians could make out a warmly glowing body—a human—strolling at a leisurely pace along the riverbank.

"Couldn't he hear we were under attack?" Kang swore. "What's he lollygagging around for?"

Kang dashed up to meet Rajak. Despite the fact that most of Recce Troop had paid for this bridge with their lives—or maybe because of that fact—this was Kang's proudest moment.

"Second Aide Rajak"—Kang saluted smartly—"you may report to Highlord Ariakas that, as Bridge Master, I hereby declare this bridge open. Your army can cross immediately!"

Rajak barely spared the bridge a glance. "Good work, Bridge Master," he said absently. His gaze shifted back to Kang. "But we won't be needing it."

Kang's mouth fell open. His lizard tongue unrolled, dropped down nearly to his waist. Realizing he looked undignified, he hastily sucked his tongue back in. "If you'll excuse my asking, sir . . . did you say the army *won't* be crossing?"

Rajak swatted irritably at a mosquito. "Correct, Bridge Master. We will not be needing this bridge."

"Uh, begging your pardon, sir, but could I ask why?"

"We won't be crossing the river. Not here, at any rate. That damn Golden General and her silver-plated knights are a hundred miles north of here. Stole a march on us.

"This"—Rajak waved a hand at the opposite bank—"was all a diversion. Intelligence fell for it. Intelligence!" The soldier snorted. "Now *there's* a misnomer. Damn spooks couldn't find Paladine if he fell out of the sky and landed right on top of 'em!"

"I . . . I don't suppose Lord Ariakas would like to come take a look at the bridge we built?" Kang asked wistfully.

"Lord Ariakas has seen a bridge before, you know," Rajak said sarcastically. Then he sighed. "Besides, you wouldn't want to be around him just now, Kang. My lord is not, shall we say, in the best of moods."

The human massaged his jaw. Kang noticed a large and swelling bruise starting to develop on the left side of Rajak's face. Apparently it didn't pay to be near Ariakas when he received bad news.

"Well, Bridge Master, I should be heading back to camp. Taking my time, of course."

Second Aide Rajak added, as an afterthought, "You'll be receiving new orders."

"Going to be needing a lot of latrines where we're going, eh, sir?" Kang grunted.

Rajak laughed appreciatively, slapped the draconian on his scaly shoulder, and moved off. Kang stood staring after him disconsolately. Slith, who had been watching, but keeping out of earshot, sidled up.

"What's the word? Where in the Abyss is everyone?"

"They're not coming," Kang said. "They're not crossing."

"Not crossing?" Slith gaped. "After all— Well, I'll be a skinny-assed elf!" He flung the dagger into the mud in disgust.

Kang didn't respond. He was looking at the bridge— his bridge. Undulating gently on the surface of the flowing water, it stretched across the dark river the way a ribbon of the finest silk might lie across his Dark Queen's bosom. He made his decision.

"By the gods, someone *will* cross our bridge," he

announced.

Slith stared at his commander as if he'd just newly cracked out of his shell.

"Form ranks," Kang ordered. "Have the troops fall in. Let's go."

The First Dragonarmy Bridging Company laid down their tools. They formed a double line behind their officers. Kang took his place in front.

"Quick march!"

With claw-footed precision, the draconians marched across their bridge.

Once on the other side, they formed ranks.

"First Troop, fall out," Kang ordered. "Bury the dead. According to custom," he added, trying to keep his voice from shaking.

They buried the remains of Recce Troop near the foot of the bridge, their bridge. The rest looked on solemnly, the ranks as rigid as if they'd all been turned to stone. Not a word or a sound, other than the digging. When the job was done, Kang ordered the troop to fall in. He marched forward and embedded an iron mallet into the top of the mound. Anyone who saw it would know that engineers were buried here.

Kang saluted the dead, then returned to the squadron.

In silence, the First Dragonarmy Bridging Company marched back across their bridge.

"Move 'em into camp," Kang ordered Gloth. "Make sure every worker's got his shovel."

Gloth, a bit dim-witted, didn't understand the sarcasm. He blinked, slurped his tongue, and did as he was told.

Bridge Master Kang and Subcommander Slith fell out of the procession and stopped, standing alone on the riverbank. The bridge bobbed gently in the water. An entire squadron of draconians had marched back and forth across it and not one plank had given way, not one log slipped its moorings. The bridge was a masterpiece, a miracle.

"What do we do now?" Slith asked solemnly. It seemed a solemn moment.

Kang drew his dagger. "Cut 'er loose."

The Middle of Nowhere

Dan Harnden

It was a very small but ordinary village, the kind city dwellers often think of as idyllic, offering a simple, more peaceful way of life. At the town's center were just a few stores. If the villagers' needs could not be satisfied by these local merchants, then a long wait for delivered goods or an even longer journey to some distant location were their only other alternatives. But this was rarely necessary. The town was self-sufficient and, in fact, had little or no contact with the outside world. All very quaint.

Although some residents lived at a distance from the village proper, others chose to build their houses right in town and rather close to one another. The dwellings and other structures were simply designed. Almost all the homes were sheathed with bark in the manner that was popular among country folk. The main street, which wasn't long, was paved with dirt and crushed rock and lined with lush old trees that partially hid many of the houses from view. But the main street did not pass all the way through the village as one might expect. Instead, it widened and ended in a circle with a village green in the center. If one were flying above the town—as say a dragon might—the street would look something like a keyhole. Really quite charming.

Not all the structures were made of bark. The ones at the circumference of the circle were built of weathered gray stone. This was the business district, which included a blacksmith's shop, a combination feed and general store, a tavern, and a large building that served as the archives. The village's only source of negotiable income came from the preserving, copying, replicating, and subsequent selling of ancient manuscripts. Very meticulous work. Of the four buildings, the tavern was by far the most popular.

As it was too early this day for any decent citizen to be

imbibing, the tavern was without patronage. This was not out of the ordinary. But the lack of activity at the feed store and blacksmith's shop was far from normal, as were the shouts of anger that rose from the archives, which doubled as the town's meeting place in times of crisis. Fists crashed down on tables and accusations flew. Fear was in the air, and the serenity of this mostly sleepy hamlet had been shattered.

* * * * *

The sighting of a dragon had prompted the emergency session at the archives. Without exception, all the residents had turned out for the meeting and were in good voice.

"What kind of dragon was it?" someone shouted.

"What kind do you think, idiot?" snapped Glykor, who directed the work of the archives.

"How can we be sure it was on a reconnaissance mission? Why would the dragon attack us?" another villager inquired.

"Shut up! You know why," replied Smorg, the town's forge smith.

A loud, extended session of incoherent shouting ensued. Moin Rankel had long ago learned to ignore the outbursts of his constituency and was confident he had found the solution to their dilemma. He was just waiting for the whooping to die down.

This was by far the worst situation Moin Rankel's administration had ever faced, and there existed the real danger that panic among the people would threaten everything they had worked so hard to achieve. But Moin Rankel was a resourceful leader—some thought him a bit pompous—and when he rose to his feet, the townspeople gradually began to fix their attention upon him. The room grew silent. Moin Rankel, an imposing figure, let the silence hang in the air for an extended moment before speaking. The consummate politician.

"And what, pray tell, is *your* suggestion?" he asked, fixing his gaze on Smorg. "Swords and arrows from your forge against a dragon?"

Smorg could find no reply.

"And what about you?" Moin Rankel shifted his attention to Glykor. "Perhaps you could write the dragon a letter. Maybe your eloquent way with words will convince the beast to seek out another town to destroy."

Silence.

Moin Rankel turned to the assembly. He adopted a more conciliatory tone. "These are indeed troubled times. The truth is there is no acceptable solution to our dilemma, and thus we must choose from the unacceptable options. I'm certain, when you each have had time to consider the realities of our situation, you will agree that my plan is our only rational course of action."

He went on to detail his plan, then sat down with a weariness that suggested his own acceptance of the inevitable. A master manipulator at work. But make no mistake about it, like the rest of the community, the sweat pouring from his brow was quite genuine.

Many hours later, shortly before sunrise, Moin Rankel's strategy was finally accepted. Of course, if his plan should fail, the fault would be solely his. Only Moin Rankel realized there would be no such recriminations if his plan did not succeed. No one would be left alive to recriminate. As he left the meeting, he found himself wondering why the gods had seen fit to give him such a town of imbeciles to govern.

Why me? he thought as he headed into the forest on his way to what was the most important and terrifying meeting of his life.

* * * * *

He worked his way along the seldom-traveled path; the forest grew darker and more foreboding with every step. Leadership is a double-edged sword, Moin Rankel realized; this was his idea and therefore his responsibility. Still, he wished there were some other way. But it was clear that any conventional defense against a dragon would be useless, which left only one alternative: magic.

And for better or worse, that meant Lozlan.

There were plenty of reasons why nobody wanted anything to do with Lozlan. His manner and appearance were terrifying. Lozlan's eyes were glowing red slits. His face was exceedingly wrinkled, with none of the lines characteristic of one who has any occasion to smile. He was the kind of man impossible to imagine having ever been a child. It was rumored, in fact, that he was born old, complete with a beard. Whatever the truth, it was clear he was an individual whose childhood was far, far behind him, and although he was not in league with the dark gods, neither did he side with the light. You never really knew where you stood with the man.

The only prospect more frightening than a dragon and Lozlan was a dragon and no Lozlan. So Moin Rankel pressed on toward the mage's lair. As he came to the top of a rise, he became suddenly aware of an all-encompassing presence. He stopped dead in his tracks. From the corner of his eye, he saw something shift behind a tree.

Nothing there.

He turned at another movement, but again saw nothing. Whatever it was managed to stay in the corner of his eye, always one step ahead of him. It was maddening. And then, all at once, a crow cried out loudly, causing Moin Rankel to whirl around and, catching his foot in the protruding root of a tree, fall to the ground.

"Damn! Be damned!" Moin Rankel cried out. Angry, he staggered to his feet, brushing the dirt from his legs.

Lozlan was standing directly in front of him.

Moin Rankel gasped. The mage smiled sadistically.

"Well, if it isn't the great leader himself," Lozlan hissed. "Come," he commanded.

And the great leader followed.

Lozlan's abode was as peculiar as the man. A perpetual mist clouded the structure, hiding it from view. Once inside, the same mist gave the viewer the unnerving impression that the world outside no longer existed. And perhaps, in some way, it did not.

Lozlan offered Moin Rankel a cup of tea, and the teapot

began to walk down the table toward them. Lozlan was amused by his guest's nervous reaction. That was his style.

Moin Rankel fought to keep his wits about him. When the teacup asked him if he wanted milk or sugar, he couldn't help himself, he began to stammer.

"I'm s-s-sorry to bother you, Lozlan, but I have c-c-come because—"

"I know why you have come," interrupted the mage. "And it will cost you."

"How much?" Moin Rankel asked fearfully.

"Not *quite* everything."

This was the kind of response Moin Rankel had expected. And yet, what option did they have?

"You will protect us from the dragon?"

"I don't know. Dragons are dangerous," Lozlan said coyly.

Moin Rankel sensed the mage was toying with him. "Then, you think we should abandon the village?"

"Not necessarily. I, too, am dangerous, and if the price is right, I might defeat the dragon . . . conceivably."

"Then you think you can save us?" Moin Rankel persisted.

"I can't hide the town, at least not indefinitely," Lozlan mused. "And it is unlikely I can dissuade the beast from attacking."

"Then what can be done?"

"Why, we will have to trick the dragon, naturally."

"We?" Moin Rankel had a sinking feeling.

"Yes. You, me, and the morons you so ineptly govern."

"I don't understand."

"Then I'll explain."

For the first time, Moin Rankel saw something almost suggestive of a smile cross the old man's face.

Lozlan's idea was to have the villagers collect all their gold, silver, jewels, coins, pendants, and anything else of value they owned and heap it in a conspicuous pile on the village green. Dragon bait, he called it. The sight of the treasure, he conjectured, would be an irresistible distraction to the winged creature. Enough so that it would spare the town immediate destruction and move in for a closer look. As it approached, the dragon would (hopefully) not notice Lozlan's magical sphere forming around it. By the time the winged serpent sensed what was afoot, it would be too late. Its lethal breath of fire would not be able to escape Lozlan's invisible globe, and the dragon would incinerate itself rather than the village. As for the residents, their part was to go about their business in plain sight, acting as though it were an ordinary day and not arouse the dragon's suspicions.

"Clever, don't you agree?" asked the mage.

Typical, thought Moin Rankel. Not only does he ask an unthinkable price, but he also makes us risk our lives to provide amusement for him.

"The treasure will most likely be destroyed by the heat. But whatever portion of it that should survive, we will consider part of my fee," Lozlan added.

After several hours, the negotiations finally came to an end. They went even worse than Moin Rankel had expected, with Lozlan demanding a huge yearly percentage of the town's meager earnings in return for his magical services. For his part, the mage agreed to protect the village from this and any future dragon attacks for as long as he lived. Moin Rankel insisted on the last part.

"You drive a hard bargain," Lozlan said.

"When do we put your trap into operation?" asked Moin Rankel, ignoring the sarcastic comment.

Lozlan looked out his window into the opaque gray mist. Apparently the mage was able to see into it or through it, for when he finally turned back to Moin Rankel, he had the answer. "In the morning, three days hence."

"Three days! That isn't much time!" Moin Rankel gasped.

"Well, then you best be hurrying off to your little enclave and tell those morons to start collecting their valuables or packing their bags. Now, I've got important matters to deal with."

Lozlan turned away. Moin Rankel's chair pushed him to a standing position, and the door swung open. The meeting was over.

Moin Rankel paused in the doorway, about to ask a final question of the mage. But as he did, the door swung shut, struck him on the nose, and propelled him backward onto the ground.

"Damn! Be damned!" was the best Moin Rankel could muster. Wiping blood from his nose, he began the long walk back to town.

* * * * *

"The price is too high!" insisted Smorg.

"Sixty percent! He's mad," piped up Glykor.

"Yes, he is," fired back the beleaguered Moin Rankel. "And the deal, quite frankly, offends the nostrils. But remember this, Lozlan is very old and can't possibly live many more years." The truth was, he had no idea how old Lozlan was, but he *looked* old and one must not forget, Moin Rankel was a politician.

"I don't like it," grumbled Smorg.

"Neither do I. But what is our choice? Abandon our homes, our beloved archives? I know this is not the best of deals, but I tell you, it is the only chance we have. Our only chance."

"But *all* of our valuables?" One of the senior scribes spoke up.

"Yes, in a pile on the village green," Moin Rankel responded. He explained Lozlan's plan in detail to the agitated crowd and produced a bag of black crystals. "Lozlan said we each must carry one of these on our person and be standing around the circumference of the green when the dragon arrives. He is adamant that every one of us, without exception, be present at the crucial moment, or else the magic will not succeed. The crystals will activate spontaneously at just the right time."

"You ask us to put our faith in these worthless pieces of coal?" Glykor demanded.

"No. I ask you to put your faith in me!" was Moin Rankel's response.

Faith not coming easy to this bunch, the debate went on for hours and hours. But early that morning, the decision was finally made. With the help of Lozlan, the gods, and some weird-looking black rocks, they would attempt to smite the dragon.

* * * * *

Preparations were begun at once. The normal daily business of the community was suspended while Moin Rankel scoured the village, collecting the people's valuables. It was not easy forcing a group of people as tightfisted as these to hand over their treasures, even when their lives were at stake. It took prodding and, at times, outright threats to get many of the citizens to do their civic duty. Moin Rankel felt certain most of the residents were holding back.

Still, it was remarkable just how much wealth a community as seemingly humble as this was able to keep hidden from itself all these years. Everyone marveled at the size of the pile of treasure as it grew on the village green. The small mountain of opulence was a thing of pride—while at the same time serving to confirm the suspicions these villagers had long harbored of each other.

When the fateful day arrived, the people milled about the street at the edge of the village green, not really knowing what to do with themselves, nervously checking for the black crystals in their pockets.

It is hard to say exactly when the drinking began. Fear and the tavern's close proximity combined to lure the nervous residents inside. As the morning dragged on, the brew flowed at an increasingly generous rate. Even Smorg and Glykor fell under the spell of the bubbly intoxicant. Moin Rankel himself was somewhat surprised when he looked down to discover an overflowing mug clenched tightly in his own hand.

It was soon generally agreed that, under different circumstances, the event could have been a rather pleasant experience. Many found their long-lost courage in the cold mead; some even displayed a sort of cockiness Moin Rankel found totally inappropriate. In general, though, he did not object to the drinking, for it might help the people hold their courage when the crucial moment was at hand. He knew it was helping him.

After a while, the ordeal actually began to transform itself into a festival. There was dancing and singing and laughter. Even the most dour members of the community got caught up in the celebration. It was the most fun they'd had since the village's founding. If this is to be our last day, then why not make it our best? became the motto. The brew flowed and flowed.

"It doesn't get any better than this!" It was hard to believe such words came from the mouth of Glykor.

"You've really outdone yourself this time!" a woman yelled at Moin Rankel, as she and her partner whirled past in a frenzied dance. By afternoon, the dragon was long forgotten.

The first sign that the party was about to come to an abrupt end was a subtle something in the air, something indefinable. Smorg, Glykor, and Moin Rankel were the first to notice it. Soon everyone felt it and stiffened, as they remembered what they were really there for. Moin Rankel urged them to get into position and not look up. At this point, the dragon was merely a speck on the horizon, but it was clear the creature was rapidly closing in.

The people became more frightened with each passing second. Moin Rankel prayed they would not break and run. "Maintain!" he screamed.

For whatever reason, they did as they were told. Like himself, they were probably petrified. When he heard the sound of the wind rushing beneath the creature's enormous wings, he took a last gulp of brew and looked up.

Moin Rankel stood there frozen in horror as he stared into the face of a dragon now close enough to breathe infernal death upon them all. But the dragon did not immediately attack. Transfixed by the sight of the treasure, it was hovering just above them.

Lozlan had been correct so far, but why, Moin Rankel wondered desperately, hadn't the black crystals activated? Suddenly the dragon looked directly at the residents, and at that instant it became clear the beast realized this was a trap. It was then, while unspeakable terror filled the souls of every villager, that Moin Rankel felt something stir in his pocket. Looking around him, he could see an eerie glow radiating from the pockets of all who were present. He now knew what it was that triggered the crystals at precisely the right instant. It was the level of fear. He was cursing Lozlan when an ungodly force hurled him and the rest of the villagers against the stone walls of the buildings behind them. Multicolored beams of pure energy emanated from the pockets of every person. The rays formed a huge translucent sphere that now surrounded the heinous creature just above the center of the green. The dragon opened its mouth, and there was no doubt in Moin Rankel's mind what was going to happen next. He closed his eyes.

Several seconds later Moin Rankel found himself still alive. He dared to slowly open his eyes. Before him was a sight he would never forget. Lozlan's sphere was undulating, holding within it a wildly writhing dragon, trapped in a fire of its own creation. Moin Rankel could clearly see the beast shrieking in pain, yet not a sound of any kind escaped the diabolical sphere. It was many minutes before the dragon finally stopped struggling.

And then, at once, the sphere began to disintegrate. As the crystals became dormant, Moin Rankel and the others slid down the walls to the ground. The dragon's charred flesh began to fall from the sky, landing in a smoldering mass no more than ten feet from Moin Rankel. Sparks singed his clothes and arms. His breathing came hard and fast.

It was done. The miracle had occurred, and the dragon lay dead in the center of the village green next to the pile of treasure that had survived unharmed. The residents ran to reclaim their loot, but as they did, the treasure disappeared. Moin Rankel now understood that this had been Lozlan's plan from the start. He could almost hear the mage laughing.

Stunned, the villagers stood staring at the huge smoking carcass and at one another. Eventually someone handed someone a mug of brew, and within minutes several of the townspeople had begun to plunge their swords into the lifeless mass. Others joined in until it became a frenzy. By sunset, tales of individual courage had begun to circulate. All lauded their great leader, Moin Rankel, saying he had led them to victory.

That's how it began, the yearly festival on the village green. An uninhibited time of decadence and overindulging, the festival had been held every year for seventeen years. Most of the original participants were still alive and now, on this day, were gathering for their moment of glory, becoming drunk with something even more potent than brew—imagined memories of bravery. It was self-deception that really kept alive the town of Lozlania, now its name, by Lozlan's final demand.

All very quaint.

* * * * *

The sun darted in and out of the clouds throughout the morning. The weather could go either way. It didn't matter much to Moin Rankel, who stood at his back door. This day was to be one of rest and relaxation, weather be damned. If it rained, he would stay beneath his nearly leak-free roof. If not, his hammock would do nicely. The important thing—for a man of his years—was to get sufficient rest. It was only two days before the festival.

The last seventeen years had not been particularly kind to the Lozlanian leader. His once burly, intimidating form had rounded quite a bit, and he was certainly less agile. His mind was still sharp though. He had managed to hold on to power all this time, in spite of ever-increasing threats from ever-increasing detractors. The ungrateful fools. How was he to guess that Lozlan would live this long?

The unpredictable sun broke through the clouds, revealing a very promising patch of blue sky. Moin Rankel thought the hammock appropriate for the day's repose. He gazed upward at the rustling leaves high above his head. It was an auspicious day, well suited to the deep thoughts of a man of his potential. And there was much to think about.

A meeting at the archives was scheduled for that evening, and Moin Rankel was sure to come under heavy criticism. He always did at this time of year, when Lozlan's annual payment came due. The overtaxed villagers had long ago stopped being grateful for their deliverance and now bitterly blamed Moin Rankel for their dire financial straits. The sixty percent yearly cut to Lozlan put too great a burden on the small community. Many now believed Moin Rankel should have driven a harder bargain back when.

What is needed, the Lozlanian leader thought to himself as he awkwardly rolled over, trying to get comfortable on the hammock, is some new demonstration of my leadership to impress the townspeople. That would require some thought. Soon Moin Rankel was asleep.

Several hours later, he opened his eyes. The leaves were still dancing above his head. The sun had beaten back the clouds, causing Moin Rankel to squint as he lay there without moving. The sounds of wind, birds, insects, and small creatures stirring in the brush blended into a soothing lullaby. The leader was drifting back into sleep when something shook his barely conscious mind to attention.

An unlikely sound.

His eyes now wide open, he listened intently. Yes, there it was again. It blended so well with the sounds of the forest, one could have easily missed it. It was strange music.

Sitting up, Moin Rankel grabbed his sword and marched into the surrounding forest. He intended to find the source.

Moin Rankel stopped in a clearing. The oddly stirring music was coming from just over a small rise, somewhere behind the thick foliage straight ahead. Not known for the lightness of his tread, Moin Rankel tried to soften his steps as he neared. He could now discern that the melodic intruder was playing some sort of stringed instrument, and quite skillfully at that. When he was only a few feet away, the music suddenly stopped and so did Moin Rankel. He stood frozen, not quite knowing what to do, feeling somewhat foolish. He held his breath for several long seconds, until another tune began—and this one had words.

It had been many years since he had heard such vocal proficiency. The voice had a pleasing timbre, was mellow and skilled. The lyrics, subtle and oddly compelling, seemed to speak directly to Moin Rankel.

"When to yield and when to be stern, when to lift the sword and when a spell to learn."

How appropriate, thought Moin Rankel. He listened, careful not to stir the leaves at his feet. Yes, the song truly went to the heart of his problems. He listened, transfixed and mesmerized. It was the most beautiful music he had ever heard. But who would choose these particular woods to serenade, and why? When the song finished, it was time to find out. Fighting an urge to applaud, Moin Rankel brandished his sword and charged through the underbrush.

The singer was a young man in his teens, lithe, with blond hair falling to his shoulders. His amber eyes flashed in fear as he jumped to his feet, knocking his instrument to the ground.

"Who are you? What do you want? I have no money," the young man said, trembling.

"Who am I? Why, I'm a man with a sword who has discovered a stranger in the woods near his home. Now, who are you and what are you doing here?" Moin Rankel narrowed his brow, imitating what he considered one of Lozlan's most unnerving mannerisms.

"Visiting."

"Visiting whom?"

The minstrel hesitated. "I'm visiting the land." Seeing this was inadequate, he quickly added, "Passing through."

"On your way to where?" the leader of Lozlania pressed.

"To work in the great northern cities. Times are lean where I come from. Few can afford my services," he said, pointing to his instrument. His tone changed to one a shade more haughty. "You need not point your sword at me. As you can see, I'm unarmed."

There was a touch of defiance in this young fellow that reminded Moin Rankel of himself at a similar age. He suspected the stranger's story was not altogether true. But the minstrel's music was surely a gift from the gods, the likes of which had never been heard in this small, isolated community. Having discovered a talent such as this in the middle of nowhere would surely be a feather in the leader's hat. He made his decision.

"Perhaps I have misjudged you," he said as he sheathed his sword. "What is your name?"

"I am called Aureal," the young man replied.

"If it is work you seek," Moin Rankel continued, "I may have some for you. Your music is most remarkable. Totally enchanting."

"So they say, Your Grace," the minstrel responded, bowing slightly.

"Well, I know of an audience that would truly appreciate a bit of culture after having lived without it for a long time. It would not be a large crowd, mind you, but a grateful one nonetheless."

"I would consider the opportunity a stroke of good fortune."

"Well, grab your instrument and follow me. No doubt you are hungry."

"You cannot imagine how much so," Aureal replied, as he gathered up his musical device and began to follow his new employer.

"What do you call that thing you play?" asked Moin Rankel as they worked their way through the underbrush.

"I call it a slither. It is of my own creation."

It was as curious and complex an instrument as Moin Rankel had ever seen. The slither had double fingerboards and two sets of sympathetic strings. Music was produced by playing both ends against the middle. The more he looked at it, the more Moin Rankel was amazed that anyone could master such an intricate device.

"And tell me, Your Grace, does your village have a name?" Aureal inquired, as the two men walked along.

"We call it Lozlania." And maybe someday, Rankelia, added Moin Rankel to himself.

"What a pleasant sounding name," commented Aureal.

* * * * *

They ate in silence, the minstrel devouring his meal.

"You are in good spirits, Your Grace," Aureal said as he watched Moin Rankel wash down his supper with several large gulps of brew.

"Yes, it is a happy time for the Lozlanians. In two days the village will hold its yearly festival to commemorate our miraculous deliverance—thanks to me—from certain destruction." He chewed his way through a particularly tough piece of meat. "My idea is you will perform at this festival."

"I look forward to it, Your Grace."

"I predict, Aureal, that you will prove the best entertainment in these parts for many a year," Moin Rankel said, refilling their mugs and taking another generous swallow. "And you will probably be the last."

"What do you mean?" asked the youth.

"Our village is one of several settled deep in these forests, far from civilization, far from one another. We did this to ensure our isolation in order that we not be distracted by things that might slow the progress of our important work. Two of the settlements were destroyed by an unmentionable horror." Moin Rankel paused to wet his gullet again. "Thanks to me, *we* are doing quite well. Soon we will have achieved our goal, and the people will most certainly disperse and spread our wares throughout Ansalon. Then this middle-of-nowhere will, once again, be the middle of nowhere. What do you think of that, minstrel?"

"It is a strange melody," came the response.

"Have you one to match it?" laughed Moin Rankel, now slightly inebriated.

"Always, Your Grace," Aureal said. He reached for his instrument.

Once again the melody seemed to speak to Moin Rankel, touching some inner part of him. The young minstrel wove his voice into the intricate tapestry of sound. He sang of people and places far away, though he could well have been singing of Lozlania. Apparently, all small hamlets have similar people in similar situations. Of course, as the shrewd leader knew and the young lad could not possibly know, there were certain things about Lozlania that were unique.

When the song finally came to an end, several lines from the refrain lingered in Moin Rankel's mind:

It was long agreed, tight lips to heed, lest we succeed, it was long agreed.

It seemed to augur something to Moin Rankel. He was now certain that Aureal's performance would be exactly what the village needed to hear.

"So what exactly do the people of Lozlania *do*?" Aureal added, picking up the conversation where it left off.

"We do what we must," Moin Rankel returned cunningly.

"As do we all, Your Grace. I meant no intrusion."

Moin Rankel rose to his feet and smiled. "You must forgive the suspicious nature of an old man. We have had so few visitors. Basically, we are a village of translators and scribes."

"What are you transcribing?"

"Ancient books of little interest to most people."

"And one day soon the task will be completed, Your Grace?"

"I hope to see that day."

"What are these books about? Who wrote them?" Aureal's voice was soothing. Like his music, it put one at ease.

"It has been a long day, and I have business early in the morning. It is time to retire," replied the wily politician as he walked away. Moin Rankel was not a man readily put at ease.

* * * * *

Moin Rankel stopped outside the entrance to the archives. He knew what awaited him inside. This was the day that Lozlan's percentage of the village's profits came due. The town's elders were always on hand as the leather sacks were handed to Moin Rankel, who in turn carried them to the mage. Over the years, the elders had gradually relinquished all responsibility for their collective decision of seventeen years past, proportionally increasing the amount of abuse they heaped on the one all blamed for the unbearable financial burden. Moin Rankel sucked in a deep breath of crisp air and pushed open the large wooden door.

"Ah, there he is," one of them muttered.

"Come to bring his wizard our blood money," came

another comment.

"You would be a pile of ashes had it not been for this blood money," Moin Rankel said, defending himself as usual.

"Maybe a man would be better off ashes than to spend his life toiling for a fraction of his worth!" Smorg returned.

"Then, perhaps, you would like to go in my stead today and explain to Lozlan that you've decided not pay him anymore."

It was now Glykor's turn to twist the knife. "The people have lost confidence in your leadership, Moin Rankel. After the festival, we will ask the people if they still choose you as the one to guide us into the future."

For the first time any of those present could remember, Moin Rankel was at a loss for words. He knew, with the situation as it was, he would never survive a vote of confidence. Everybody in the room knew this as well. Moin Rankel hoisted the leather sacks over his shoulder, looked his detractors in the eye.

"We'll see," he said, and turned and headed for the door.

"Moin Rankel!" Glykor snapped. "You brought this on yourself."

"Yes, the price of saving ungrateful fools," Moin Rankel retorted. He walked out of the building angry and shaken, made his way down the well-worn path into the woods. He had no idea how he was going to turn this situation around. His grip on power seemed to be loosening by the hour. There must be some way out. He walked along, quite thoughtful, heading for his dwelling.

* * * * *

Not far from Moin Rankel's house, a bubbling stream wound its way through the forest in search of the sea. Moin Rankel found Aureal sitting by the stream. Holding his instrument, he was staring into the gentle turbulence at his feet. As the troubled Lozlanian leader drew closer, the minstrel began to play a most enchanting melody.

"Power will recede, if you dare not the deed, these words you

283

must heed, lest we succeed."

And suddenly many things seemed clear to Moin Rankel. He knew what course of action he must take.

"Beautiful, absolutely beautiful," Moin Rankel spoke up.

"I, myself, prefer the sound of the stream," said Aureal.

"Yes, I suppose it is much like music."

"But unlike music, which only gives, a stream also takes away," came the minstrel's strange reply.

Moin Rankel—not one for philosophy—turned to the matter at hand. "I have a proposition for you. The fact is, our town has been suffering an unbearable situation for years. A greedy old mage has unfairly forced a tax upon the villagers. If you will help me deal with this mad wizard, I will make you rich beyond your wildest dreams."

"If that is your wish, Your Grace," responded the gracious youth.

"It is," said Moin Rankel, "and you will most certainly want to bring your instrument. I'll explain as we walk."

The young man did as he was told, slinging the unique instrument over his shoulder and following Moin Rankel onto the seldom traveled path that led north toward Lozlan's place.

* * * * *

After Moin Rankel explained his plan, they progressed in silence. Somehow, this unlikely duo had developed an understanding that went beyond words. A kind of peace seemed to surround Aureal. This peace extended to Moin Rankel and provided a much needed break from the pressure and worries of these past years.

How fortuitous it is, thought Moin Rankel, that this remarkable young man has come into my life.

They entered the clearing outside of Lozlan's dwelling. The old mage's abode was no longer shrouded in fog, but weakly accented by wisps of vaporous mist. The two were almost to the door when it suddenly opened, and there stood Lozlan.

If seventeen years had been less than kind to Moin

Rankel, age had been outright cruel to the old mage. His wrinkles twisted his facial features into something that was only partially human. He stood hunched over, leaning on a stick, trembling, and generally appearing quite frail. Lozlan's eyes now appeared pink in tint and shone without their previous intensity. Moin Rankel had often wondered, over the years, just how much magic this bedeviled sorcerer had exhausted, and how much he still had left in him.

"I have brought someone for you to meet, Lozlan," Moin Rankel began. He knew the usual courtesies were of no interest to the mage, who had already shifted his gaze toward Aureal.

"Why?" Lozlan's feeble voice still had all the charm of a coiled snake.

"Because he has a talent that is unique and pleasurable. I thought you might take some interest in him."

Lozlan stared at the minstrel for a long time, then shifted his gaze to the leather sacks that hung across Moin Rankel's shoulder. No one knew what the wrinkled wizard did with his treasure. Moin Rankel suspected the mage found sufficient pleasure in merely collecting it from the villagers.

"Very well, come in," Lozlan said ungraciously.

Aureal seated himself across the small room opposite Lozlan and Moin Rankel. The chair the minstrel chose, much like the other sparse furnishings, had seen better days.

"I have lost interest in the primitive trappings of this world," Lozlan said, "and now devote almost all my attention to matters you could never hope to appreciate or fathom."

Moin Rankel always found Lozlan's ability to read his thoughts unnerving. He changed the subject. "I think you will soon agree that our young visitor has much to offer."

Moin Rankel nodded at the minstrel, who was already adjusting his instrument, preparing to play.

"The tree has no more fruit to bear. It was then and you were there. Unbalanced nature unaware. Do you care? Do you care?"

The song, Aureal's most captivating yet, went on and on, building to an intensity that filled the room. Moin Rankel could see that Lozlan was deeply affected. The mage was rocking slowly, rhythmically, side to side. The music continued.

"So heed the words of one so young. Doubt not the truth of this fair tongue. To those for whom the bell has rung, I come to sing the song I've sung."

Lozlan rose to his feet, as if to applaud, but the expression on his face was not one of pleasure. Instead, his mouth was gaping as he looked down to find Moin Rankel's sword protruding from his chest. He tried to speak, but no words came out. The mage staggered and turned toward Moin Rankel, fighting to maintain his balance. He appeared ready to unleash a deadly spell upon his killer. Once again he tried to say something to Moin Rankel but failed. Then he fell to the floor.

Lozlan stopped struggling; a strange calm came over him. And then, unexpectedly, he looked up at Moin Rankel and smiled. He spoke one word, then his eyes flickered several times and finally went dark.

Moin Rankel remained motionless. It was several moments before he dared to breathe again. He was amazed at how easy it all had been. He had faced a hopeless situation and triumphed.

He felt even better about things when he discovered the treasure and all the money the town had paid over seventeen years hidden under the floor.

Aureal, who had been promised a good portion of the find, proved helpful in carrying as much of it as they could handle back to Moin Rankel's place. Lozlan's last word came back to Moin Rankel's mind.

"Fool."

Moin Rankel only laughed.

* * * * *

The breeze carried the smell of incense, roasting meat, and strong brew far into the woods. Moin Rankel could hear the sound of shouts and laughter. The festival was obviously well under way. Moin Rankel was eager to report Lozlan's death and receive the acclamation he was due. He picked up his pace.

* * * * *

Smorg handed an overflowing mug to the man whose job it was to furnish the parchment essential to their holy project. Several feet away, a group of women were laughing over someone else's misfortune. Glykor approached the blacksmith and his companion. Setting his mug between the other two, without greeting or invitation, the master of the archives launched into his first complaint of the day. It wouldn't be his last.

"This beverage is not properly brewed. It never is."

"I'm damned sick and tired of this place," Smorg added.

"Who isn't?" Glykor agreed sullenly.

"It's this endless poverty we've been forced to endure," muttered another.

"Well, it's certainly not *my* fault we're in this dreadful situation," Glykor said.

Smorg stretched his huge shoulders. "I don't see why we just don't abandon the village. We have already translated and copied more than enough material to saturate all Ansalon."

"We've been through all this," Glykor snarled, really angry now. "Leave the thinking to those with brains, Smorg. We were ordered to copy and spread all the Dark Queen's teachings, and we will do nothing less! We will stay until all are inscribed!"

"Some would disagree! Some would say we have already fulfilled our commitments."

The infighting for control had already begun, in anticipation of their current leader's demise. Glykor, knowing it was useless to argue, stood and walked toward a small group of men who were discussing a particular section of manuscript that had recently been copied and preserved.

They, like Glykor, were dressed in black. All the Lozlanians always dressed in black.

* * * * *

Moin Rankel's happiness was apparent in his step. He briskly bounded down the path that led to the village. He would give his detractors ample opportunity to ridicule him. Then he would call forth Aureal. After the minstrel's performance, Moin Rankel would tell the people of Lozlan's fate and of the recovery of *some* of the treasure; he was still deciding how much. Once again, he would be in charge. In addition, he would be exceedingly wealthy. Not a bad day's work.

As he approached the village, Moin Rankel reached in his pocket to feel for the black crystal. Although a dragon attack was the last thing anyone expected, it was customary for Lozlanians to carry their crystals this one day of the year.

The town looked exactly as it had those seventeen years ago. Same people, same everything. About the only thing that had changed was the grass on the village green. It grew lush and beautiful over the place where they had buried the golden dragon's remains.

Moin Rankel was greeted with boos and hisses. He returned the salutations indifferently and pushed his mug into the free-flowing stream of the blessed beverage.

It was a typical festival. Old stories, forgotten dances, inflated egos, uninspired poetry, and absolutely terrible singing combined to create another hallowed anniversary of the slaying of the dragon.

The brew isn't bad this year, thought Moin Rankel as he silently watched the arm-wrestling contest. Smorg won it. He won it every year. Not much of a show.

It wasn't long before most of the residents grew bored with the proceedings and drank increasing amounts of brew to cope with the tedium. Moin Rankel did not blame his neighbors. They were sick and tired of one another. He was sick and tired of them.

Still, they had no choice but to go on.

"And do you think our great leader cares?" Smorg shouted drunkenly. "He probably has some private deal with Lozlan."

"That's a lie!" said Moin Rankel.

Many heads turned toward the old politician—the source of all their troubles. Within minutes, Moin Rankel was defending himself against an angry mob.

"He has betrayed us!" Smorg continued, encouraging the unruly crowd.

"He should be removed!" added Glykor. "Maybe even killed."

The crowd surged forward. Moin Rankel, knowing well the mind of such a group, made his move. He, too, surged forward. The villagers hesitated, fell back.

"Now, you drunken half-wits, listen to me. First, you'd all be dead if you'd listened to these two seventeen years ago." Moin Rankel pointed at Glykor and Smorg. "Remember that! Second, later this very day, I will make a dramatic announcement that will improve our lives. But before I do, I feel it is appropriate to mark this occasion with a special event. So as a gift to you, my neighbors, allow me to present my good friend, the great minstrel, Aureal."

He turned around, waved at nothing but air. Aureal was nowhere to be seen.

Glykor laughed unpleasantly. "If this is some trick to try to hold on to power, it's not going to work."

Moin Rankel looked into the faces of his constituency. He shared his neighbors' loyalty to the dark gods, but now, he realized, that evil was all they had in common. After several minutes, the crowd again grew restless.

Where was Aureal?

"Year after year we suffer because we let a fool negotiate our future away," Smorg said.

Still no Aureal.

"He should pay!" shouted Glykor, and the crowd edged in.

Aureal, where are you? Moin Rankel wondered desperately.

"Wait! You must listen," he cried out.

"We've had enough of your worthless gibbering! Take him!" Smorg grabbed hold of Moin Rankel.

Screaming, faces twisted in hatred, the people in the crowd started to drag their leader to the village green. They stopped dead in their tracks. There, standing on top of a table, was Aureal. His blond hair blowing in the wind, he held his instrument close to his body, his eyes fixed on the villagers. The startled crowd released Moin Rankel. He collapsed to the ground.

The Lozlanians—such proud citizens—moved closer to the minstrel, like a dark cloud descending upon the sun. As the first strains of music reached their ears, they slowed their steps.

"Listen well to the song of she, the song of me I sing to thee."

Into the villagers' minds came the same moving image—that of an infant, alone in a forest, close to a village not unlike their own. Even the most evil Lozlanians could not help but to be swept away by the minstrel's tale.

"Can you imagine, losing your mother a day after being born," one villager was heard to mutter. Another wept.

"Drifting in a stream of light. Dreaming till the time was right."

When the child was old enough, he began to spy on the village, being particularly careful to avoid discovery by the local mage. In time, the boy came to know all the town's secrets.

"Child of forest possessed of the sight. Denizens of darkness in the Village of Night."

Aureal could well have been singing of Lozlania. He sang of things no outsider could possibly know. It was wonderful and strange.

"Time grew nigh in the heart of fear. But how to pierce the sorcerous sphere?"

Aureal's voice grew louder and deeper in timber.

Smorg shot a questioning glance at Moin Rankel who was basking in his moment of triumph and did not notice. The blacksmith managed to catch the eye of Glykor. Something was very wrong.

"All shall descend, as the dark must fall. I hear the music, I

heed the call."

Moin Rankel finally snapped out of his trance long enough to see Smorg and Glykor frantically gesturing him toward a nearby tent. An indefinable sense of terror crept into his soul as Moin Rankel hurried to join his longtime rivals.

"The golden flight once begun, now fallen to the golden son."

Still louder and deeper came the minstrel's voice.

"The deed to you I now confide. The task of finishing what had been tried."

Deeper and louder than any human voice could ever be.

Inside the tent, Smorg screamed at Moin Rankel, "You idiot! Do you have any idea what you have brought upon us?"

The great Lozlanian leader could only gasp and stutter.

"It doesn't matter. We all still have our crystals, and Lozlan swore he would protect us as long as he lived!" Glykor shouted.

Noticing the horrified expression on Moin Rankel's face, Glykor grabbed his leader. "What's the matter with you? Moin Rankel, what have you done?"

From outside came the sound of huge wings flapping, followed by the terrified screams of the dying townspeople. The three men rushed to the opposite end of the tent and tried to escape through an opening in the side.

* * * * *

The returning sun broke free of the clouds, warming the air below. From high above, the dragon could see a stream reflecting light off the rushing water. Small streams go on to become raging rivers in the course of their journeys. It would be interesting to follow this one. A sudden rush of wind swept through the trees. The lush peace of the woodland seemed unbroken and eternal. The charred, keyhole shaped patch was barely visible from above. The dragon could hardly see the slightest sign of it. It was a very large but ordinary forest, the kind city dwellers often think of as idyllic.

The middle of nowhere.

Kaz and the Dragon's
Children

Richard A. Knaak

He had learned to sleep with the battle-axe
clutched in his hands, a trick that had saved his life more
than once. Even now, with the war supposedly over for
more than a month, it was a wise thing to do, for there
were still those who would have seen him dead simply
because of what he was. Three days ago, he had barely
escaped the local militia. They'd wanted to make him pay
for what his kind had done in the service of the Dark Goddess, Takhisis. Small matter that *he* had served with the
Knights of Solamnia and chosen to fight against his old
masters in the waning weeks of the war. Kaz was a monster in the eyes of humans, and to some that made him
forever an evil that needed to be extinguished. Birth alone
had condemned him to that fate.

The savage history of the minotaur's race had not
helped, either.

Kaz's huge hands tensed imperceptibly. He opened his
eyes a crack. He could see little, for the moons were hidden by the clouds, and dawn was still at least an hour
away. What little he did see did not aid him. And so he listened. A sound, a slight sound, had broken the normal
pattern of night noises and stirred the veteran warrior to
waking. It might have been nothing more than an anxious
rabbit, a clumsy bat, or Tempest, his own horse, shifting
position, but Kaz didn't think so. He had not survived this
long jumping at animal noises. This was something more.

If those infernal soldiers have tracked me down again, Kaz
thought in bitterness, then this time I will stand and fight
regardless! In the war against the legions of the Dark Queen,
he had fought beside a lone knight called Huma, a knight
whose honor and skill would earn him the titles of Drag-
onbane and Huma of the Lance. When defeat had appeared

imminent, Huma had brought to the desperate defenders of good the legendary dragonlances, which had turned the tide by bringing down the dragons of doom and despair. Huma himself had died defeating the Dark Goddess.

Honor was the most important force in a minotaur's life, and Kaz had admired Huma for his honor. The knight's unshakable belief in the goodness of the world had changed the minotaur. Kaz had sworn that his weapons would be raised against only those who followed the path of evil. It was his tribute to one he considered the greatest champion of all.

A tribute he was finding very difficult to survive. The soldiers who had almost captured him three days ago had basically been good men trying to clear their land of the stragglers and marauding bands that had sprouted up like weeds after the Goddess's armies had been routed. It had been quite reasonable for them to assume that a minotaur wandering this far south was a part of those scattered forces. Unfortunately, they had not allowed Kaz any time to present proof otherwise. The documents and medallion given to him by the masters of the Solamnic orders were secure in the hidden compartment of his saddlebags. He doubted that his pursuers would believe the proof even if they allowed him the chance to display it. Scared humans had the bad habit of killing first, asking questions later.

Kaz continued to listen, but the night was now silent save for the anxious movements of his horse. The silence in itself was ominous, for even the sounds associated with the dark had ceased. Kaz opened his eyes a bit farther.

Something hissed. His mount, tied to a tree behind him, began to shift in unease. All notion of a human foe vanished. Nothing in Kaz's experience had ever made a sibilant sound quite like that.

He leapt to his feet, axe at the ready. The hiss had come from so close that he was certain that the . . . thing . . . would instantly be upon him.

Nothing. The night was silent again. Kaz, however, did not relax. An unwary warrior was a dead warrior.

"This is what I get for seeking solitude," the minotaur

muttered, snorting.

A piece of the night shifted among the trees. Kaz hefted the axe and snarled but did not take a step toward the nebulous shape. Let whatever was out there come to him.

It did. The minotaur's horse whinnied as the thing materialized.

"Sargas!" Kaz shouted, forgetting—in his astonishment—and calling on the dark god his own people worshiped. Kaz had forsaken Sargas for the just god Paladine, patron of the knighthood, but in times of great excitement, his heritage caught up with him.

The monster was huge. Standing, it would have been at least as tall as Kaz. In the darkness, he could not make out specific details, but the creature had a tail and looked like some sort of bizarre reptile playing at being human. Most important, the thing had long, wicked talons and jaws wide enough to snap a minotaur's head off.

The monster stank. Kaz wrinkled his nose. Fighting back the urge to throw up, Kaz thrust the shaft of the battle-axe into what he hoped was the monster's stomach.

He might have been striking rock, so armored was the beast.

Talons raked at his arms. The minotaur grunted in pain, but fortunately his attack had taken some of the fight out of the horrific creature. Kaz fought down the pain and pushed forward, trying to overpower the beast before it recovered. Once again, though, hitting it was like hitting a wall of stone. Kaz drove back the slashing claws of the thing, but nothing more.

Even this close, Kaz could not see what it was he fought. It was reptilian, yes, but like nothing the minotaur had ever come across in the war. Almost it resembled . . . but that was impossible.

It came for him again.

Twisting the axe around, he brought the flat of the double-edged blade against the snout of his adversary.

The beast hissed in pain but did not back away.

Kaz struck the sensitive snout again and again.

Howling, the reptilian monster stumbled back. Kaz

shifted the axe to drive the deadly blades into the monster's head, but the beast suddenly sprang backward. It stopped, looked around, as if it had heard a call. Then, without warning, the creature turned and leapt for the safety of the woods. The minotaur started to pursue, but the monster's tail struck him in the side like a whip. It was all Kaz could do to maintain his hold on his weapon. Through pain-blurred eyes, he watched the shadowy thing vanish into the safety of the night-shrouded woods.

It was several heartbeats before the pain became bearable. Kaz's wounds continued to sting, but a quick check revealed that he had been fortunate. The jagged wounds were shallow.

"What was that all about?" Kaz muttered. He had been stalked and assaulted, but then his attacker fled before the battle had really been joined. A bloody nose shouldn't have been enough to make that thing run off. . . . What was it after?

The minotaur snorted in annoyance. In the early days, before Huma had taught Kaz patience, he would have sought out something to batter with his heavy fists. Now he could only clench his fists in frustration. He had ridden here in the hopes of finding solitude, sanctuary. He had sought out this forest and the nearby mountains because few creatures of the intelligent races were said to dwell in this region. Kaz was not a hermit, but it was good to be able to rest and reflect now and then, even when one was a warrior born.

The monster had ruined Kaz's peace. Now he would have to spend the next several days pondering its abrupt appearance, while constantly looking over his shoulder.

Snorting, he turned to see to his horse.

The horse was gone, spooked by the monster. Kaz felt around the tree and discovered the tattered remnants of the tether.

"The gods are out to get me!" the minotaur snarled. There was no time to tend his own wounds. He had to begin searching for his horse immediately. Every second meant less chance of recovering the animal, and without Tempest, he would be faced with a long, hard journey.

His campfire had gone out while he slumbered, and there was no swift way of starting a new one. Kaz decided to forego a torch and hope that his night sight and hearing would be up to the task.

As he moved, Kaz made clicking sounds with his mouth. If the horse was near, it would recognize them. Knights of Solamnia often trained their horses to respond to a whistle, but minotaurs' mouths were not designed for creating such sounds.

He was climbing a squat hill in the predawn light, when he heard something on the other side. Kaz cautiously completed the climb and peered down.

Something moved among the trees beyond the hill.

Unable to tell whether or not it was his horse, Kaz readied his battle-axe and started down the slope. His wounds continued to burn, but he ignored them. He had ignored worse ones during the war. As he reached the bottom, Kaz caught another glimpse of something, but it was still too far away and too obscured by foliage to be identifiable.

Picking up his pace, he darted among the trees. At last, Kaz caught a better glimpse. He exhaled in relief. His mount. The animal was glad to see him, seemed to wonder where he'd been.

Putting his annoyance aside, Kaz called out. The horse trotted toward him. Kaz replaced his battle-axe in the harness he wore on his back. He was pleased to note that his packs were secure and that the horse was uninjured. The horse rubbed its nose in Kaz's shoulder and sniffed him. Kaz took the reins, which dangled loosely over the horse's neck, and patted the animal on the side. "Brave warhorse, aren't you now? They told me that you'd face up to just about anything! Ha! Still, I can't blame you for running from that hellish creature, but the least you could've done was take me with you!"

A sense of dread suddenly washed over Kaz. He looked swiftly around, but saw nothing. It was the silence again. The same eerie silence that had fallen when he was attacked by the monster. Still scanning the area, Kaz mounted his horse. He had a great desire to be far away from here.

"I must have monsters on the brain," he muttered. Was this what it was going to be like now that he did not have the war to occupy his every moment? Jumping at every sound—or lack of sound. Imagining foes behind every tree and rock?

"Let's go!" he growled at his horse.

The animal trotted a few steps, then came to a halt.

Kaz prodded the animal again. He *truly* wanted to get away from this place. "What's the matter with you, Tempest? Get moving!"

This time, the animal began to plod along; the pace it set was so slow that Kaz began to wonder if he would make better time carrying Tempest instead of the horse carrying him.

The wind began to pick up, tossing dead leaves about. Clouds were gathering in the sky in what might be the precursor of a storm. "Sargas take you, beast!" Kaz kicked the horse's flanks. "Move, I said!"

Unbelievably, the horse began to slow its pace.

Black clouds swirled. The wind was a howling fiend that tossed leaves and broken foliage around the horse and rider. Kaz shielded his eyes against the stinging dust and began debating the possibility of stopping where he was and seeking shelter.

As if reading his thoughts, Tempest abruptly halted. Kaz tried to urge the beast on again, but it stood fast. Furious, Kaz started to dismount, thinking perhaps he could lead the animal.

The wind buffeted him back onto the saddle.

He tried again to dismount.

Once more, the horrendous wind seemed to hold him fixed in place.

"By Paladine's blade! I'll not be bested by *air*!" The minotaur let go of the reins and tried throwing himself off his mount.

A wall of wind tossed him back.

Then, it was as if a tornado had sprung to mad life. Wildly tumbling leaves and twigs cut visibility to a foot or two beyond the horse's nose. No matter which direction he looked, all Kaz saw were leaves.

No, not all directions. Gazing up, he noted that the air was inexplicably clear a few feet above his head. With the exception of the clouds that had gathered directly overhead, the sky was sunny and bright. All around him the forest was peaceful, yet Kaz himself was caught up in a veritable maelstrom.

Instinctively, he reached for his weapon, though what he would do with it was beyond him. Kaz was a born warrior and understood nothing about the workings of magic, but he knew its malevolent touch when he saw it. He also had the sinking feeling that finding Tempest had not been the good fortune he had assumed, but rather the lure with which the unknown mage had drawn him into a trap.

Paladine, Kaz prayed, if you still watch over me—assuming you ever have—I could use your help about now!

The whirlwind started to close in around the minotaur. Now, only a few inches separated horse and rider from the thickening wall of dead foliage.

A leaf struck the side of the minotaur's snout and stuck there. Kaz reached up to tear the leaf away, but—to his bewilderment—it remained fixed to him. A second leaf caught on his hand, and when the minotaur tried to shake it free, that leaf, too, clung.

Kaz's legs and torso were already dotted with leaves, none of which would shake loose. His horse was nearly half buried under a growing skin of foliage, but, unlike Kaz, Tempest showed no concern. The animal did not move at all, seeming to accept its fate.

Not so the minotaur. Snarling, he tried to shield himself with his leaf-encrusted axe, but the barrage was too great. Leaves blew over, under, and around him, sticking on his face and arms, clinging like blood leeches to his skin.

"Blast you, mage!" he roared, covering his mouth in order to prevent suffocation. "Come and face me! Fight me as a warrior, not a coward who must hide behind cursed tricks!"

No one responded. He had not truly expected anyone

to do so. Mages were, in his opinion, conniving milksops who worked from shadows or anywhere far from danger.

The onslaught continued. Leaves almost completely buried him alive. His snout was already covered, and leaves complete obscured vision in one eye and partially in the other. It was nearly impossible to move. He was forced to breathe through his mouth.

Round and round the wind blew, adding leaf after leaf to the pile. The minotaur was near to suffocating. He struggled desperately to clear the leaves from his nose and mouth, but he couldn't lift his leaf-coated arm more than an inch or two. Kaz began to choke. . . .

"Kiri-Jolith, god of just cause, is this any way for a warrior to die?" Kaz demanded in helpless fury.

If there was an answer, he did not remain conscious long enough to hear it.

* * * * *

"Amazing—the things one finds in one's nets," a voice said in the darkness. "I was expecting to catch a knight, not a minotaur. When I captured the horse, I assumed its rider would be human. Silly of me."

Kaz stirred and slowly noted that while he could neither see nor move, he was most certainly alive.

"Ah. Awake at last. Feeling better?"

The groggy minotaur forced his eyelids open a slight crack. What little he could see was blurry, but at least it was not leaves. He had the vague impression of a robed figure standing almost below him. Nothing else was clear enough to even guess at.

"What are you doing in these parts, so far from your kind, my solitary minotaur? You'd best answer me before I lose my temper and feed you to my other guest."

Feed me to it? Kaz opened his eyes wide.

He was in a magical prison, a clear bubble floating several feet above the floor. Although delicate in appearance, the bubble held firm when he pressed his hands against it. Kaz snorted and gaped. His weapons were gone.

"Really a simple sort of spell, my bovine friend. Nothing so spectacular," said the voice. Yet, there was a touch of pride in the tone.

Kaz glared down at his captor. He wore the familiar ebony garments of the dark mages, or Black Robes as the evil magic-users were called. The mage was tall for a human, almost as tall as the minotaur, but so gangly as to make a scarecrow look fat. His face looked as if someone had wrapped a bandage of skin around the skull. Long, flowing gray hair hung to his waist.

Kaz searched nervously for the "hungry" guest. He was imprisoned in a cavern chamber, one that had apparently been hollowed out by some force other than nature. The walls and ceiling were smooth. A curious blue sphere floating above his gaunt host illuminated the chamber.

Shelves lined the cave walls, shelves filled with scrolls, books, and artifacts that even Kaz, who had no sense of magic, could tell were powerful talismans.

Below his floating cell, a pattern had been etched into the center of the floor. A series of triangles and pentagrams were bound together by an overlapping circle, nearly twice Kaz's height in diameter. Directly below Kaz, a small metal stand with a top resembling a hollowed-out gourd stood in the circle's center.

Kaz breathed easier. No sign at all of the hungry "guest."

The mage had been silent during his captive's inspection, but now he spoke again. "What is your name, minotaur?"

"I am Kaz."

"And I am Master Mage Brenn." The spindly figure bowed sardonically. "You are much too far south and west for one of your kind, my horned friend. I ask again—what are you doing here?"

Kaz thought quickly. Brenn must not have bothered to inspect Kaz's gear closely. He had obviously missed the hidden compartment containing the Solamnic documents and medallion. Good—a Black Robe would not be friendly toward a friend of the Knights of Solamnia.

"I've been on the run since the Lady fell, Master Brenn."

Kaz answered boldly. "The minotaur army was scattered, the forces of Paladine blocked my way back. I killed a knight, stole his horse, and fled south."

"Why did you not fight to the death like a good cow?"

Kaz growled, barely succeeding in keeping his temper in check. Such an insult would have had the mage's head rolling from his shoulders if Kaz and his axe had been free.

"The cause was lost," he said. "The battle was over. I thought it preferable to preserve myself for the day when my skills can be put to better use."

Brenn smiled. "You have a finer head on your shoulders than most of your kind."

The magic-user snapped his fingers. Kaz found himself standing on the rocky floor. He glanced up. His magical prison had vanished. All that remained was the pattern on the floor, the stand, and, of course, the Black Robe.

"As it happens, Kaz the Minotaur, you have come to the right place. I will have need of your skills before long."

"Where is this right place, Master Brenn?" Kaz demanded.

"You are in the mountains near where I found you," Brenn replied. "You are fortunate, my horned friend. Had you been a knight—as I first presumed—you would be dead. I am too close to success to allow my secrets to be discovered."

The gaunt mage paused. "Tell me, minotaur, did you see anything . . . unusual . . . in the forest?"

"What did you have in mind, Master Brenn?"

Brenn frowned, irritated. "You would know what I meant if you had seen it."

Kaz was certain that the Black Robe meant the monster, but he elected not to share the details of his encounter with his host. What Brenn did not know might benefit the minotaur. Did the mage have something to do with the monster? If so, what? And where was it? Kaz was debating the danger of probing for more information when a mournful wail echoed throughout the mage's sanctum. The sound reminded Kaz of a woman sobbing, but at the same time he knew that it was not human. It was unnerving, terrible, and extraordinarily sad.

Brenn, quite calm, nodded at the sound and cryptically said, "She's awake. She should be more *manageable*, by now."

"She?" the minotaur rumbled.

"Come. I will show you." Brenn started toward the cavern's entrance. Abruptly, he turned. He studied the minotaur, then commanded, "Hold out your hands."

Kaz obeyed.

Suddenly he was holding his lost axe.

"You will feel more comfortable with that in your possession. Do try to be careful with it."

The mage turned his back on the minotaur and resumed walking. Kaz hefted the weapon, thinking briefly of parting the mage's long gray hair. Kaz knew better than to attack, however. If Brenn had given the axe back, it could only be because he had no fear of it.

Things were not looking promising.

The glowing sphere flew ahead of them, lighting the way. Kaz followed the gangly magic-user through a maze of tunnels that led from one cavern chamber to another, until they came to one larger than all the rest.

Brenn paused at the entrance, one hand on the rocky wall, and turned to the minotaur. "I think perhaps it would be best if you stayed in the background. She becomes distraught at the slightest thing. I will speak to her in private." His eyes narrowed a bit. "*Don't* wander off."

With that warning, Brenn entered the chamber, the blue light following him. Kaz was more than satisfied to be left behind, but he was also interested in a glimpse of the Black Robe's other "guest." Standing to the side of the entrance, the burly minotaur peered into the cavern.

"There, there, my dear!" Brenn called out. "I think things will look brighter from this point on, would you not agree?"

A huge reptilian head rose from the cavern floor. The gleaming eyes of a silver dragon stared at Brenn. Kaz had never seen such open hatred and revulsion in all his life.

"I want . . . my *children*, you vile . . . vile monster!" the silver dragon cried in a low, anguished voice.

There were no dragons left in Krynn. They had all vanished soon after the defeat in battle of dread Takhisis by the knight Huma. *All* dragons, whether followers of the Dark Lady or servants of shining Paladine—her victorious foe—had departed from the world.

Kaz the minotaur wondered if someone had forgotten to tell this particular dragon that she was not supposed to be here.

The silver dragon was enormous; Kaz had never seen one so large. Brenn was little more than a mouthful to such a grand creature, yet the dragon made no hostile move toward the master mage. Kaz dared to step a bit closer, and saw the dragon in a better light. The dragon was badly injured. Deep, fetid scars scored the massive body. Her wings were torn. One eyelid drooped and the orb that it half-obscured did not focus well. Most of the wounds were old, yet untreated. If not cared for soon, they would almost certainly mean a slow, painful death.

The minotaur's respect for the mage's dark powers grew a hundredfold. Brenn could not have possibly inflicted such damage . . . at least, Kaz *thought* not . . . but even this badly wounded, the silver dragon must be a terrible force to reckon with.

"Your children are safe, as you can plainly see, madam," Brenn said, stretching his right hand to the side to indicate something. Kaz tried to see, but couldn't from his vantage point. Did the mage have a cage full of young dragons as well?

"Monster!" The silver dragon moaned.

Brenn crossed his arms. "You can say that, madam, when I so thoughtfully allow you to gaze upon your precious eggs whenever you desire? I thought it rather a kindness on my part."

"*Kindness?*" The dragon struggled. Like Kaz earlier, she was held in place by invisible magical bonds. After a moment of intense effort, the glittering dragon's head sank to the ground.

Kaz feared she was dying.

"Kindness . . ." the dragon whispered. "Torture . . . is . . . is what you mean, mortal! Placing my eggs where I can see . . . but not . . . touch! Eggs that . . . that you stole from . . . my lair!"

"Well, madam, no one seemed to be taking care of them. I thought to give them a good home." Brenn chuckled. "And you know well, my dear, that I have made a very fine offer to you that would see your children back in your care in perhaps two or three days at most! Just give me what I want, and I promise you that your eggs will be returned to you."

"How . . . how can I believe you?"

The spellcaster shrugged. "Believe what you like, madam, but either accept my offer or . . ."

Brenn must have performed some spell on the hidden eggs, for suddenly the injured dragon renewed her struggle to escape. "No! Don't hurt them!"

"Well?"

"Yes!" She spat, turned a burning gaze on the black robed spellcaster. "You win, fiend! I will do as you wish, but"—the dragon was rocked by spasms of pain—"if you harm my children, I will find some means to destroy you!"

Brenn laughed. "I would make a poor meal, madam, for your kind. All gristle and no meat to speak of."

"You . . . have my word now, *human*. What do you want of me?"

"That you shall learn on the morrow, madam." Brenn bowed. "For now, other things demand my attention. I recommend you try to rest. You will certainly need your strength."

The silver dragon was no longer paying any attention to him. Instead her gaze returned to the area that Kaz could not see, to her eggs. Despite her weakened condition, the gleaming dragon craned in that direction.

Kaz eyed the mage. The minotaur's grip tightened on the axe, yet he forced himself to hold back, fearing Brenn's magic.

"At some point, though, there will come a moment when you let down your guard, Master Brenn," Kaz muttered. He simply had to survive until then.

Returning to the passageway, Brenn sagged, leaned wearily against the outer wall. His imprisonment of the dragon was apparently costing him a great deal of effort. After a breath or two, the mage straightened and proceeded past Kaz.

"Come," Brenn commanded.

They had taken a dozen steps or so before Kaz decided to speak. "You've captured a *dragon*."

"Weak as she was, it was easy. I caught her while her attention was on *other* things. That is all I have to say on the subject." After a moment of silent contemplation, Brenn turned to a new topic. "I will show you where your horse is being stabled. It will serve as your quarters, too. If you are hungry, I will also show you where you may find food. I think I am being quite generous. All I ask in return is your obedience. Fair enough?"

Kaz grimaced. There was nothing he could do but continue playing the grateful prisoner.

The minotaur ate the provisions and cared for his horse. His quarters consisted of a small cave accessible from inside the mountain by means of a tunnel but also open to the outside world. Kaz considered escape, but a trip to the cave's entrance revealed that the edge ended in a sheer cliff several hundred feet high. No escape from this exit.

He was polishing his axe, his thoughts running over the pattern of tunnels he had walked through, when the mage entered. Brenn looked distracted. "Come with me. I have need of your physical prowess. Bring the axe."

Acting the obedient soldier, Kaz followed Brenn back through the maze of underground corridors. As he walked, the minotaur kept careful track of the steps and turns he and his host took. If he was to have any chance of escape, it would be essential to know his way around the sorcerer's domain.

They returned to the cadaverous mage's sanctum. With distaste Kaz eyed the magical pattern on the floor and the metal device that stood on it. He could still recall his bubble prison.

Brenn, too, studied the pattern. His words were more to himself than to the minotaur. "Now that I have her word, I can wait no longer. It has avoided the traps I've set. There's no telling if it still even exists. I will have to use more extreme measures and try to bring it here now." Without looking at his companion, Brenn added, "Stand to the side and do exactly what I tell you to do."

The mage raised his bony hands high.

A bubble—identical in shape to the one that had held Kaz—formed just above the top of the metal device. At first the bubble was no larger than an egg, then it grew to the size of a melon, then larger until its diameter was greater than the length of Kaz's arm. A tingle ran through Kaz, who readied his axe, even though he was not certain what good the weapon would do under the circumstances. The bubble did not cease its expansion. Kaz wondered whether it would eventually fill the entire chamber.

Then Kaz saw something in the center of the bubble. Kaz squinted to see better. Inside the bubble was a *wooden chest*—a simple wooden chest devoid of decoration. As the bubble grew, the chest grew.

When the chest was almost as big as the minotaur, Brenn flicked a finger at the magical bubble. The transparent sphere floated over to him, coming to rest at the mage's feet. As it touched the cavern floor, though, the bottom of the bubble dissolved. The bubble continued to sink, and as it did, it dissolved. Before long, there was only the chest.

Another flick of Brenn's finger opened the lid. Brenn removed several leathery-looking fragments of what might have been pottery from the chest. He eyed each piece carefully, especially the edges, then—every fragment held securely in his arms—the mage stepped away.

The lid closed and the chest began to rise. The bubble formed around it, and the entire process that Kaz had just witnessed repeated itself, only in reverse. The bubble and chest returned to their place above the pattern and the metal device. Then the chest and the bubble gradually shrank until at last both vanished.

Brenn entered the pattern the moment the bubble disappeared, and he began piecing together the fragments in the large bowl at the top of the talisman.

Soon the true form of the object became apparent. It was not pottery, as Kaz had first surmised.

An egg! He was rebuilding a broken egg! An egg so large and so peculiar in appearance that it could only come from . . .

"A dragon!"

Only after he had said the words did Kaz realize that he had spoken out loud. Fortunately, Brenn was too engrossed in his work to notice. The mage put the finishing touches on the egg. He stepped out of the pattern and turned to the minotaur.

"Now your skills may be necessary, my friend. Ready yourself."

Kaz had no time to consider what Brenn was doing with the eggshell of a dragon. Already something was happening in the center. Another bubble—this one reddish in tint—formed around the shell, growing larger and larger until it could have easily contained Kaz and the mage.

Brenn stretched a nearly fleshless arm toward the bubble and muttered something. A fierce look glowed in his eyes. The skin of his face, already taut, pulled so tight Kaz thought it would soon tear away, revealing the skull underneath.

The eggshell wavered.

Brenn stretched forth his other arm. Sweat poured from his forehead; his hollow eyes flared.

"Wherever you are," he shouted, "you *must* come to me! The pull of your birth will *not* be denied!"

In the bubble, the reconstructed shell smoked. Plumes rose above the egg, swirling and forming a cloud.

Kaz blinked. For a moment, he would have sworn he saw an arm in the cloud.

A shape coalesced slowly over the shell, which seemed to be dissolving as the thing above it solidified. The thing was not human; that was obvious after the first few seconds. It was not like any creature that Kaz had ever seen. It had wings and a long, powerful tail. The thing in the bubble was bent over and seemed undecided as to whether it should stand on two legs or four. Standing, it would have been taller than Brenn and possibly even Kaz. It was also likely twice the minotaur's weight. Kaz stared in shock and amazement at the creature.

It was the monster that had attacked him! He recognized it by the bruised and bloodied snout. Yes, this was what he had fought.

But what was it?

The monstrosity inside Brenn's bubble opened its blunted, reptilian maw and let loose with a roar . . . or tried to. No sound escaped the bubble. The creature clawed at the interior of its cell with hands that looked almost human.

It was a dragon . . . yet it was not. Kaz knew of the silver dragon's ability to shapechange, but this thing looked as if it had changed its mind midway through the transformation and had been unable to shift back to its natural state.

Brenn walked to where the monster could see him. Its hatred for the Black Robe was evident. Fortunately for the mage, the bubble was stronger than the monster. "Roar all you like, my dragon-man," Brenn remarked. "Not only will *this* prison hold you better, but your mother will never hear you in there."

Mother? Kaz looked closely at the monster's scaly hide. What he had taken for gray was actually a muted silver!

The thing was one of the silver dragon's children! There could be no other explanation, yet Kaz had never seen a dragon that looked like this one. It was, as Brenn had put it, more of a dragon-man. . . .

What have you done, mage? Kaz wondered. What vile sorcery have you performed?

"Good. The shell holds," Brenn commented. He walked around his creation, studying it as a child might inspect a newly acquired pet. "Some further distortion, but the spell has not completely broken down yet. Another few days, though . . . Yes, I think I was correct after all," Brenn muttered.

Kaz could restrain himself no longer. "*You* are responsible for that creature?"

"It is something of a disappointment, is it not? Interesting, but not quite what I had in mind, and I do hate to leave a thing half done. There is also the problem that my magic refuses to stay bound to it. Given three or four more days, the spell would break down, and we would have neither this creature nor a young hatchling, nothing but a nasty mess. Until *she* gave in, I was ready to let him remain loose until the unraveling of the spell tore him apart. Now that I have her cooperation, I can remedy the situation. I can start on the others."

"So that was one of the dragon's eggs?"

Brenn ceased his inspection of the dragon-man and gazed thoughtfully at the minotaur. "Of course. Almost newly laid, in fact. This was my first attempt. Very strong he is. Tore apart the nice iron cell I had him in and fled to the woods. I was elsewhere at the time."

"*That* is your reason for stealing the eggs? That thing?" Kaz asked.

"The idea was another's—an old companion of mine who had become a cleric of the Dark Queen. He once mentioned to me how delightful it would be if Paladine's greatest servants could be tricked into fighting for Takhisis. What better way to destroy their morale than by turning their children into creatures dedicated to the darkness?" Brenn's expression was almost wistful. "His power was insufficient for the task, however, and he died in the process. . . . The fool."

The mage shook his head. "Clerics! They are too limited by their fanatical devotion. A mage, on the other hand . . . well, you see what I have accomplished!"

"Not what you intended," Kaz growled.

The observation did not seem to bother the magic-user. "No, but unlike Augus, my poor, unlamented friend, I understand my limitations . . . and then devise ways of overcoming them. *She* will provide the added strength I need."

Brenn stepped around the pattern and rejoined Kaz. The mage walked much more slowly than before, a sign that he was exhausted. "We have a busy day ahead of us tomorrow, minotaur. I need to conserve my strength for the spell I plan to cast. The physical exertion must fall to you. Therefore, it would be best if you went to bed now. I shall summon you when the time comes."

The minotaur bowed obediently. "Yes, Master Brenn."

"Since you do not yet know your way around this place, I shall give you this to guide you to your quarters." The skeletal figure flicked a finger at the blue light. The orb shimmered, then split into two identical spheres. One of them fluttered over to the startled warrior. "It will remain in existence so long as you need it to reach your quarters. After that, it will fade away, leaving you in complete darkness."

Warning me not to wander anywhere afterward, Kaz thought, nodding his understanding.

Brenn returned his attention to his monstrous creation. "You may go."

Kaz started to leave, but felt something make the hair on his neck stand on end. He looked back at Brenn. The mage's gaze was still focused on the thing in the magical bubble. The minotaur's brow furrowed, then he chanced to look up at the dragon-man.

It was watching Kaz.

The minotaur stalked quickly toward the passageway, not once looking back. Only when he was several steps down the tunnel and far from the unnerving eyes of the monster did he pause. It had been years since anything had so disturbed him, but the hungry, knowing gaze of the dragon-man had burned into Kaz's very soul. Brenn had created something insidious, something whose inner darkness perhaps even the magicuser did not fully comprehend.

Kaz did not like magic. An axe could not cleave magic. Yet, Kaz knew he could not leave unless he destroyed Brenn's creation first. Kaz added up his chances of succeeding in such a mad quest and snorted in frustration.

Little chance, indeed! He would have to be a suicidal fool to seriously consider doing anything other than escaping at the first opportunity!

"Paladine preserve me!" Kaz muttered under his

breath. Just as he made that decision, he realized there was no decision to make. He could not permit Brenn to continue his unearthly experiments. He had to act.

The gods, Kaz decided there and then, really are out to get me . . . and this time they'll probably succeed!

* * * * *

His memory served him well. Kaz was pleased to discover, some hours later, that despite the utter darkness, he was able to retrace his route. Only once so far had he made a wrong turn, and he had realized that mistake almost at once.

Kaz had been tempted to use a makeshift torch, but the light would have put him at risk. He was fairly certain that the weary Brenn was now asleep, but the minotaur was taking no chances. He was counting on the darkness to hide him.

Kaz had been tempted to attack Brenn in the night. But Kaz knew no mage would go to sleep without *some* protective spell. In Brenn's case, it would be a powerful ward. No, the minotaur's best hope was to remain on the course he had decided.

Only *she* could aid him.

He turned a corner and saw a dim light ahead. At first, he feared that he had miscalculated, that Brenn was still awake. It was a moment before Kaz recognized the dim illumination as coming from the chamber where the silver dragon was imprisoned. With more confidence, he approached the mouth of the cavern and peered inside.

The silver dragon lay still, so still, in fact, that the minotaur feared that she had already died in her sleep. Then, Kaz saw her stir in obvious agony. Understanding to some extent her injuries and wounds, he could not help but admire her determination to live.

The other dragons had all departed, but she stayed behind, unwilling to take the time to heal herself, and all because of her love for her children.

Kaz was outraged at the thought of what Brenn had

done to one of those children. The minotaur *had* to tell the silver dragon the truth . . . providing she would believe anything a minotaur said. The last was the part of the plan he had been unable to resolve to his own satisfaction.

Kaz started toward the dragon . . . and ran into an invisible wall.

Cursing, he slammed his fist against it. "What now?" he muttered.

Frustrated, the minotaur shifted position in an attempt to see if there might be another entrance nearer to the dragon. As he moved, he put a hand against the rock wall of the cavern.

Air currents shifted. A tingle ran through the minotaur's hand. Startled, he pulled his hand from the rock. Kaz recalled something Brenn had done both when entering and departing the dragon's prison. Twice the spellcaster's hand had touched the wall. In fact, Kaz realized, Brenn had gone out of his way to touch the rock.

Kaz tried to touch the invisible wall.

It was gone.

Kaz quickly entered the chamber and, with some hesitation, approached the massive prisoner.

"You come . . . quiet . . . in the night," a soft voice whispered suddenly. "The mage . . . has acquired himself a new servant. You should not be here without your master, minotaur. I should tear you . . . tear you apart."

The head shifted. With her good eye, the silver dragon stared bitterly at the tiny figure to her side.

Being devoured by the very thing he had come to rescue was not part of Kaz's plan. "I am a prisoner here also, Great One. By my ancestors, I swear that what I tell you now is the truth. You have my word of honor."

"Minotaurs are . . . are known to lie now and then. For a prisoner, you have very . . . very long chains."

Kaz snorted. "Like you, Master Brenn made assumptions."

"Why . . . have you truly . . . come to . . . to me?" The dragon might not believe him—not yet—but she evidently knew enough about minotaur honor to at least listen to him.

"To get you out of this." Even as Kaz said it, he realized

how ridiculous he sounded. *He* was trying to rescue a *dragon.* "I need your power to help end this."

"Even if . . . if I believed you, I cannot . . . leave without my *children*, minotaur. I *will not* leave . . . with . . . without them." The silver dragon flinched several times during the course of her reply. She turned her head and indicated the wall before her, the one Kaz had been unable to see from the entrance. "Look there. Just beyond my . . . my reach."

Kaz followed her direction. His eyes widened. There in a nook in the rock wall were six large, leathery eggs identical to the fragmented egg Brenn had pieced together. It seemed strange that the mage would put the eggs here, when he would be forced to move them for his experiments. How did he hope to maintain the dragon's cooperation if she saw them vanishing, one by one?

The dragon swung her head around. "They were only freshly laid a few days before he . . . he . . . *stole* them. Although time has passed, his accursed spell has . . . kept them as they were."

Kaz snorted. "How was it he was able to seize them?"

"A battle forced us to leave them for a time. A terrible battle as you can see. I came back, helped by my mate, to discover them gone!" She grimaced as pain shook her. "My mate and I swore that only death would keep . . . keep us from our children." The dragon paused for breath. "It seems I will be held to . . . to that vow. I am beyond either help or helping. Yet, if you would do me any favor, minotaur, save my children."

Kaz fought down his disappointment at finding the dragon too weak to aid him. He studied the eggs. He could not abandon them to the fate of the other. He could not allow Brenn to create any more such monstrosities . . . even if that meant destroying the eggs.

It was only when he dared reach up to the eggs themselves that he discovered something strange. He couldn't reach the nook. He felt a rough, rocky surface beneath his hand. Had his eyes been closed, he would have been unable to tell where the wall ended and the nook began.

He ran his hands around the edge, trying to find some

mechanical means to open it, like the entrance. Nothing. He contemplated trying his axe on the wall, but the noise would certainly wake the spellcaster and most likely accomplish nothing but damaging the weapon. Defeated, he turned back to the dragon. "Is there nothing that you can do?"

"Would I be here?" She sighed. "My only hope is that he will keep his word and give . . . them back."

"He will do nothing of the kind." Kaz snarled. "He intends to take your eggs and draw on your power to twist your children into abominations obedient to him!"

The dragon lifted her head. "Even he could not do that; he dares not!"

"Haven't you wondered why the eggs aren't all here?" Kaz asked her.

Now she appeared suspicious. "What sort of trick is this? All of my eggs . . . *are* there. I see them."

"What? They can't be!" Kaz was astounded.

"They are." The dragon eyed him. "Whatever you were plotting has failed. Perhaps you should return to your master."

"By Paladine! Listen to——"

Before he could finish, another voice cut through. "Kaz, you know I ordered you *not* to torment our guest! You would do better to learn to obey!"

Brenn stood near the entrance. Kaz cursed silently; he had been a fool not to guess there might be some sort of magical alarm.

Kaz tried to reach for his axe, discovered he couldn't move. The silver dragon regarded the minotaur with much loathing. She would never believe him now.

"You are going to have to be punished for this disobedience, Kaz," Brenn continued.

A bubble formed around Kaz, a floating sphere identical to the one that imprisoned the dragon-man.

He found he could move now, but where could he go? Even as he thought that, there was a sudden, ominous change in the bubble. It began to shrink! Now the top barely cleared his horns, and the sides were so close he could touch them with his fingers.

Being slowly crushed to death in a magical bubble was not an honorable way to die. He tried breaking the bubble with his horns, but realized it was more likely his horns would break before the sphere would burst.

Unable to do anything else, Kaz cursed Brenn in the name of every god he could think of, then began telling the malevolent magic-user what the minotaur would do when he got free. It didn't matter that Brenn probably couldn't hear him; Kaz was quite confident that the mage would understand.

Brenn apparently did. As Kaz took a breath, the mage pointed a finger at him. The air caught in Kaz's throat.

A moment later, he collapsed.

* * * * *

Kaz woke up, looked swiftly around. He was still trapped in Brenn's accursed bubble, but his location had changed. Now he floated in one corner of the Black Robe's inner sanctum, near the huge pattern and the other sphere that still floated above it. Too near. Brenn's dragon-man stared at the minotaur as if nothing else in the world mattered. Now and then, the creature would blink or its forked tongue would dart out, but otherwise the dragon-man did not move.

"Size me up all you like, lizard," Kaz growled, not caring whether or not the beast could hear or even understand him. "You'll find me a meal that bites back!"

The dragon-man took no notice of Kaz's ravings and simply continued to stare at him.

Kaz was not certain how long it was before Brenn entered. An hour, maybe two.

"Ah, both of you are awake!" Brenn remarked. He took some time to inspect the dragon-man, which suddenly recommenced with its snarling and clawing. Brenn turned to Kaz. A flick of the mage's finger brought the minotaur's sphere floating to him.

"You may notice that you can hear me, but nothing

else."

It was true. Despite the many times the dragon-man opened its mouth in what was obviously a roar, the chamber was silent, save whenever the spellcaster spoke.

The cadaverous mage gave Kaz a smile. "In a way, you make this much easier. I admit I would have felt guilty about sacrificing a useful soldier like yourself if you had not revealed yourself to be the traitor you are. Imagine! A minotaur with a *conscience!*"

"You actually know the word?" Kaz snarled.

"Still defiant. Good. It means you will put up a strong fight when the time comes. The battle should be entertaining, even if the outcome is inevitable."

Battle? Kaz did not like the sound of that. "What battle?"

Brenn turned and strolled back to the pattern. As he walked, the minotaur's sphere followed. "When I said your arrival was timely, I meant it. I was trying to devise a way in which to test the strength of my creation—once I recaptured it—and then you fell into my hands. My original intention was to let you become comfortable, put your mind at ease, so that when the time came to fight, you would be at your best. Then, of course—"

"You plan to have me *fight* that thing?" Kaz roared, pointing at the snarling dragon-man.

"I would have thought that was obvious, even to you," the mage commented, looking at Kaz with mild surprise. "I hope your wits are sharper during battle, especially since you will be fighting claw-to-claw."

Kaz reached back. His axe was gone. He scowled at Brenn, who pointed to one of the tables nearby. The battle-axe now lay upon it.

The minotaur looked from Brenn to the dragon-man, then to the spellcaster again. "This is your idea of a fair fight?"

The mage studied his creation, who continued to scrape at the bubble with talons nearly the length of the minotaur's hand. The dragon-man opened wide its jaws, revealing once again its razor-sharp fangs. After some deliberation, Brenn turned to Kaz. "No, but it will satisfy my curiosity."

"Let me loose, and *I* will satisfy your curiosity!"

The mage smiled. "I think it's time we begin."

The bubble containing Kaz retreated several yards. The other sphere also moved away from the pattern. Brenn eyed the magical design and raised a narrow hand.

A bubble appeared, and inside was the huge chest from which Brenn had removed the egg fragments.

Brenn directed the bubble to him. As before, it dissolved when it touched the cavern floor, leaving behind the chest. The spellcaster opened the chest and reached in.

Giving a nod of satisfaction, Brenn pulled out his prize. Kaz could not see what he held at first, but when the tall mage lifted it high, there was no mistaking.

Another silver dragon egg.

"Illusions!" Kaz gasped. "I understand it now! The eggs she longs after are only illusions! No wonder the barrier felt as if it were made of rock!"

Brenn held the egg for Kaz to see. "Of course. I needed a lure, but I was not about to risk my prizes. Dragon eggs are quite difficult to come by."

He lowered his burden. "It is simple, really. Her own obsession feeds the strength of the illusion as her own power feeds the spell that binds her. Why waste my own energy when I can make use of others? Still, after the incomplete success of my first attempt, I decided to stop hiding from her and instead draw her into my domain. You see, if one sort of magic is not enough, then maybe two combined will achieve success. When I began this, I thought to create an army, but with the other dragons gone, I will be satisfied with my little band and the knowledge that I have once more triumphed where others have failed."

"I knew a mage like you once," Kaz growled. "Galen Dracos. He's dead now, Paladine be praised!"

Brenn laughed. Then he replaced the egg in the chest and closed the lid. Reaching into the collar of his robe, he pulled out a bejeweled pendant. Kaz caught the flash of an emerald crystal embedded in the center.

The mage directed his attention to the dragon-man, which had renewed its attack on the imprisoning bubble. Brenn brought the sphere back to its original resting place above the metal device in the center of the pattern. Then, taking a deep breath, he put both hands on the talisman hanging from his neck and closed his eyes.

"The time has come, madam," the mage said softly. "You know what I expect from you!"

Kaz sensed intense power, but Brenn appeared disappointed. He opened his eyes. "Your *children*, madam! Remember our bargain!"

An intense wave of magic overwhelmed Kaz. He shook his head and grunted in pain. Brenn's fleshless face lit up. The emerald crystal gleamed.

Inside the bubble, the dragon-man clutched at its throat in obvious anguish. Its skin began to ripple. Kaz leaned forward until his snout rubbed against the interior of his prison, looking closer. The dragon-man's skin was melting!

Power continued to flow from the dragon to Brenn. Dragons were magical creatures; Brenn had only succeeded in capturing the silver one because of her deadly injuries. To alter a dragon—even one not yet hatched—was to work against the natural magic of the legendary race. A formidable task for any mage, no matter how powerful.

The dragon-man's skin sloughed off in horrid gobbets, yet, instead of becoming smaller, the creature appeared to grow. It reminded Kaz of a young snake shedding its skin. The dragon-man was in horrible pain, so much so that Kaz almost pitied the thing.

His pity faded when he recalled that he would soon be forced to do battle with the monster.

With each shedding, the dragon-man became more humanoid in appearance. Its snout shortened until it was little longer than that of the minotaur. Its forelegs changed into arms and taloned hands. The tail shortened, and the dragon-man's wings became vestigial. Despite the alterations, Kaz did not think his chances of winning any better. Not only was the dragon-man now larger than before, but there was also a look in those reptilian eyes that spoke of true cunning. It was the look of a warrior.

Warrior or monster or both, I'll give you the fight of your life! Kaz promised. He was fairly certain the battle would take place soon. The creature was still in a state of flux, but the changes were becoming more subtle. For the first time, the dragon-man seemed to take note of its own shape. It studied itself carefully, then stared at the one who had made it.

Power continued to flow into the talisman and from there out to the creature in the bubble. Brenn was no longer smiling. Strain showed on his face as he pushed for the completion of his spell. Dragon magic continued to flow to him through the talisman. The force was so overwhelming that even Kaz felt stunned by its intensity. Brenn gasped at one point, but did not falter.

Suddenly, the stream of magical power wavered. Brenn glared into empty space and roared, "Remember your children!"

His warning did not seem to help. The power faltered more and more . . . then dwindled away. With a painful grunt, the mage broke his own connection to the spell. "Damnable lizard!"

Kaz wondered if the dragon's tremendous exertion had finally killed her. The mage twitched, then rubbed his pale face. Kaz yearned to be free of his prison. If there was a time when the spellcaster might be weak enough to be attacked, it was now.

Brenn gazed at his creation. "Wonderful!" the mage breathed. "Complete at last!"

The dragon-man stood erect within the confines of its cell. Its gaze shifted back and forth between Brenn and Kaz. Each time it stared at the minotaur, the dragon-man clenched its taloned fists.

"Perfect!" the Black Robe proclaimed. "Perfect!" He turned to Kaz, the only witness to his magnificence. "Do you see—"

The dragon-man abruptly bent over and howled. The monster's skin began to peel off in large pieces.

"What is wrong?" The mage brought the bubble closer to him. Brenn walked up to the wall of the transparent cell and peered down at the dragon-man, which was now on its knees. "What is the *matter* with you? You *must* be stable now!"

The dragon-man, eyes wide and red, glared up at its creator and, driven by pain, reached for Brenn. The spellcaster flinched but did not move away.

The dragon-man's claws dug into the bubble and tore it open as easily as if it had been formed from thin cloth. The bubble popped, dropped its prisoner to the ground.

Brenn stared at his creation in disbelief.

The dragon-man lifted Brenn by the collar and, in a voice both sibilant and deep, rumbled, "You hurt me!"

"Put me down! I can make it——"

The dragon-man ignored the command. "I will hurt *you!*"

Raising Brenn above him, the dragon-man threw the magic-user across the cavern.

Weakened by his spellcasting, Brenn could not help himself. He crashed into a shelf, crushing artifacts and containers, finally bringing the entire set of shelves down on himself.

Brenn tried to rise, but could not. It was clear that he was badly injured. The dragon-man started toward the mage. Brenn pointed weakly at Kaz, then slumped back, not unconscious, but unable, at the moment, to do anything else to save himself.

The bubble in which the minotaur was imprisoned faded. With a grunt, Kaz struck the hard cavern floor.

The dragon-man turned toward the minotaur, hissing. Talons flashed as it started for Kaz. The dragon-man lunged for Kaz's throat.

Kaz threw himself to the ground and rolled toward the table where his weapon lay. He hoped he could reach his axe before the creature struck again.

The action caught the dragon-man by surprise. For a breath or two, the creature stared down at the spot where its intended victim had been. Then, hissing again, the creature whirled. Locating Kaz, the dragon-man stalked toward the minotaur, talons extended and maw open wide. Kaz realized that he would never make it to the table before the monster was on him.

Then another wave of pain rocked the dragon-man. It fell to one knee. Its form began to shift again, almost as if liquefying.

Making the most of his unexpected opportunity, Kaz dashed over to the table and put his hand on the axe. Behind him, the howl of pain died.

The dragon-man was on its feet again. It lunged at Kaz, moving even more swiftly than before. Raising the axe with one hand, Kaz succeeded in fending off the attack. The creature was agile despite its grotesque appearance. Kaz tried a second swing. The dragon-man grabbed hold of the axe by the upper half of the shaft, nearly wrenched it from the minotaur's grasp. Kaz fought to pull the weapon free. He did not like to think about his chances in hand-to-hand fighting.

Remembering their struggle in the woods, Kaz shifted his weapon and tried to repeat his tactic from that battle, tried to hit the creature on the snout. The monster was much more wary this time, and once more Kaz almost lost his axe.

Intent on avoiding the jaws and talons of his adversary, the minotaur saw the slithering tail too late. It darted toward his leg. Kaz struck the tail with his axe. One well-honed blade caught the tip and severed it.

The dragon-man howled with pain, lashed out without thinking. The blow caught Kaz as he worked the axe free, for the edge had not only cut through the tail but gouged a slit several inches deep in the rock-hard ground. Pain coursed through the minotaur. The axe came free just as the dragon-man attacked again. The wounded minotaur stumbled out of reach. His left arm was covered in blood, pouring from ragged gaps near his shoulder.

A red rage began to overwhelm the minotaur. The creature had wounded him!

"I . . . have . . . had . . . enough!" he snarled.

Kaz brought the axe around and forced his reptilian

adversary back. Each swing sent shivers of pain through the minotaur, but Kaz knew he could not let up. If he stopped even for a moment, the dragon-man would have him.

The upper edge of one of the axe's blades cut a streak of green slime across the dragon-man's chest. It hissed and stumbled, but Kaz could not pursue his advantage soon enough. Recovering, the creature glared at the minotaur, then suddenly leapt straight at him. Had Kaz been uninjured, he would have cut his opponent down then, but the ache in his shoulder slowed him. The axe struck the dragon-man in the upper arm, but the wound was shallow and, even worse, the monster now finally had a good grip on the shaft of the minotaur's weapon.

Kaz tried to hold on, but he was too weak. The dragon-man pulled the axe from the minotaur's grip and tossed it aside.

"Now," it hissed, "you will die!"

Kaz, however, was already moving. Even for a creature as strong as the dragon-man, a full-grown minotaur was a very, very heavy burden. A charging minotaur was even more so. Kaz lowered his head, aimed his horns at the dragon-man.

Wicked talons cut and tore into his body, but Kaz did not stop. The dragon-man grunted in agony as the minotaur's horns caught it near the chest wound. The horns pierced its hard, armored skin.

Propelled backward by the minotaur's attack, the dragon-man stumbled and fell. Kaz almost fell, too, but managed to free his horns just in time.

The wounded monster began to shift again. Less and less it looked like a man and more like . . . like nothing in the minotaur's experience. The dragon-man roared and struggled to its feet. Kaz wondered wearily where the abomination continued to draw its strength. The wounded minotaur was virtually finished. He barely had the power to stand, much less renew the battle.

The dragon-man hissed. Out of the corner of his eye, the minotaur tried to estimate his chances of reaching his battle-axe. Those odds were not what he would have hoped, but if the continual magical transformations had slowed the dragon-man even a little bit . . .

The creature also glanced in the direction of the axe.

Kaz started for the weapon. The dragon-man sought to intercept him. The monster moved with more speed than Kaz could muster. The battle had worn down the minotaur. His legs and arms felt like lumps of iron, and with each step the room seemed to whirl.

Then the dragon-man stumbled again. Not much, but enough to give Kaz two or three precious seconds. Just enough time to grab the axe and barely roll out of reach.

Kaz turned back in time to see a hideous sight. The monster's flesh dribbled off as it moved. The creature continued to howl in fury and in pain.

Summoning what remained of his strength, Kaz swung the battle-axe over his head and brought it down.

The blow caught the monster in the skull. To Kaz's astonishment, the axe went clean through the skull into the body.

Literally cleaved in two, the dragon-man collapsed.

Then it disappeared. Kaz saw only a tiny remnant of Brenn's creation. The minotaur studied the head of his axe, but found little trace there, either. As far as he could gather, the dragon-man had dissolved the moment Kaz had killed it.

A shuffling noise caught Kaz's attention. He whirled, thinking the dragon-man had somehow returned from the dead. He saw the battered form of Brenn instead. The mage had dragged himself to the center of the patterned floor. His face was taut. One leg dragged uselessly. Seeing the minotaur, Brenn managed one of his ghastly smiles.

"My gratitude for . . . for cleaning up that little mess." The mage glanced around anxiously, as if searching for something on the floor. "I shall endeavor to avoid such an occurrence the next time."

Kaz snorted. "*Next* time?" He hefted the axe.

Brenn pointed at Kaz.

The warrior's movements slowed. He was reminded of all those times during the war when he and the others had been forced to wade through hip-deep mud. He moved as if in a dream.

Brenn saw that his spell had only half succeeded. For the first time, the mage's eyes looked a bit frantic.

Kaz suddenly knew what Brenn was seeking. The mage was looking for his crystal talisman. It must have been torn off when the dragon-man tried to grab the gaunt sorcerer by the throat. Both Brenn and Kaz saw the crystal at the same time. Brenn was closer; he would have the talisman before Kaz could reach him.

Fighting against the spell, the minotaur swung the axe to one side. As he did, he saw the mage's hand hovering over the talisman.

Kaz threw the axe, aiming not for the mage but for the metal stand in the center of the room.

The flying axe struck the metal device. Sparks flew.

A bubble formed over the center of the pattern. Unlike the previous bubbles, it did not float off the ground. It was sinking, almost exactly where Brenn was trying to drag himself away.

His injuries slowed him. The bubble touched him. Suddenly Brenn was inside.

The mage struggled, but his efforts only brought him back to the center of the pattern and the bent mechanism from which the bubble had been summoned. Kaz saw frantic fear on Brenn's face as the bubble drifted back to the magical device. The sphere froze as it reached the center.

The bubble began to contract. Brenn screamed, but no sound could be heard. The sphere now gave him little room to move. The mage locked eyes with Kaz and pointed at the talisman. Brenn was pleading.

Kaz grunted, shook his horned head. The bubble shrank, and with it shrank Brenn. All the while, the increasingly tiny figure of the mage silently screamed.

The bubble vanished. Kaz picked up the gem and tossed the talisman among the rest of the wreckage.

"Can't say that I'm sorry, *Master* Brenn."

* * * * *

The dragon was dead.

Kaz had gathered up the remaining eggs and dragged them to her cavern, only to discover the silver dragon was no longer alive. He also noted that the illusionary eggs were gone. Perhaps she had realized that Kaz had been telling the truth: The mage had tricked her and was using her own power to experiment on her children. The shock must have been too much in her injured state.

He tried not to think about that as he made plans for his departure. There were many things to be done. Kaz had his own injuries to deal with, injuries that made dragging around five heavy eggs painful. He had to find a path out of these caves. Locating the dragon's mate would be diffi-cult, but Kaz had some idea of where to look. His time as a dragon-rider had given him insight into where the drag-ons nested. One way or the other, he would locate the male and return the eggs. Kaz had the feeling that—like his mate—the male silver dragon would not leave Krynn until certain the eggs were safe.

Kaz also had to make sure that no one would be able to use Brenn's sanctum again. The minotaur was determined to wipe away all traces of the foul mage.

The death of the black-robed mage, alone, cheered Kaz. Brenn's experiments would be lost to the world. There were enough monsters on Krynn without adding such horrible specimens to the list. Thanks to Kaz, Krynn would never know there had ever been such a thing as a dragon-man.

Kaz envisioned an entire army of the creatures. The image was enough to make even a minotaur blanch.

Kaz snorted. Dream armies were not worth worrying about. Krynn had nothing to fear of dragon-men. Not now.

Not ever.

Into the Light

Linda P. Baker

The screaming trickled into silence, the way a nightmare slips away with daybreak, and stillness settled like snowflakes floating delicately to ground.

A creaking, aberrant wind swept over Torin and disappeared, taking with it the darkness and the terror, leaving behind smells so fiery and terrible his mind did not want to name them. The unnatural fear that held him pinned in the sand dissipated. The iron grip it held on his eyelids lessened, and he opened his eyes to the hot, clear blue of the desert morning. His ears rang with abrupt silence, a quiet that was thick and menacing after the roaring, trumpeting blackness.

The white ball of the sun had not moved from where it was when the darkness overcame him. Could the panic and the smells and the voices raised in pain all be remnants of a dream? A waking nightmare in which his sword lay beside him in the sand, too heavy for his paralyzed muscles to wield?

He wished desperately for the last few moments to have been a nightmare, but his senses were not so easily convinced. Fear still lay in his stomach, knotted and real and shameful. His mouth was full of sand where he had opened it to shout, and his fingers were cramped, clutching the hilt of his sword. He had fallen in the act of drawing it.

He rolled to his feet, passing his fingers down his thigh to the dagger concealed beneath his summer robe. The knife was still in its sheath, and the reassuring balance of the sword in his hand brought sanity as nothing else could. He would have welcomed the weight of his staff across his back, but it was in his tent on the other side of the camp. He would meet the enemy armed with only sword and dagger, and they would have to be enough.

He crawled on his stomach up the little spine of desert rock that marked the northern edge of the oasis. Only his eyes cleared the ridge of stone.

Nothing moved in the summer camp of the Kedasa nomads except for wisps of smoke wafting in the desert breeze. Heat shimmers marked where each sand-colored tent had stood; smoke seeped from blackened, twisted lumps that had once been living beings.

Torin leapt to his feet, sword ready in his hand, and surveyed the camp again. Surely more people of his tribe were hiding in safety just over the dunes, just behind . . .

Behind what? The tents were flattened, the oasis a scorched wasteland. Across the spring, the animal pens were dark squares of ash corralling charred shapes that bore vague resemblance to goats and horses. The palms were burned and blackened spires, rising up out of sand that had been fused and melted like glass.

The scent of burned flesh was strong, and it brought the memory of the attack sounds. Screams, roaring blackness, the camp.

The so silent camp . . .

A sound—a real sound, not one remembered—broke through his sorrow, and he dropped, rolling down the incline. He came to his feet, coiled, sword up and ready, pulse racing, ready for battle. The fear he now felt—unlike the fear during the attack—made him awake and ready to fight. He was glad to be taken away from the recollection of the sinister darkness, if only for a moment. But the sound, a choked intake of breath, had not come from an enemy.

Biar, the mage's apprentice, lay on his stomach, a shadow's length away, staring at the ruined camp. His face was twisted with horror, making him look like a wizened old man, instead of a boy who had seen only thirteen summers.

Torin remembered darkness descending, fear so overwhelming it devoured all light and will.

Even with the heat of the morning sun warming his shoulders, the recollection made him cold. He turned away to hide his shame. What had happened?

I am no fledgling boy like Biar, he thought. I have seen thirty summers. I am a seasoned warrior of many battles, and in none of them have I quailed like a frightened child. What witchcraft left me cowering in the sand while my tribe was massacred?

"Elim!" Biar cried the name of his master.

On the ground in front of his tent, a blackened shape formed an **X**, as if Elim had died with his arms outstretched, calling down a spell on those who murdered him. The boy started to scramble on his hands and knees over the ridge toward the burned tent that had been his home.

"Wait!" Torin leapt and caught the boy's thin arm. "It is not safe. Whoever attacked the camp has surely not abandoned it." He pulled the boy back over the ridge and pushed him down low. "Do not come until I call."

Torin brushed sand from the folds of the jelaya, which had come unwound from his head, then he wrapped the thick cloth back into place, fastening the last long length so that only his coppery brown eyes showed through the slit.

Though Biar was half crazed with shock and disbelief, his fingers mimicked Torin's, pulling his own jelaya around his head and across his face until only his eyes, brimming with tears, showed through.

The Kedasa wore the jelaya not just for protection from the sun, but also to appear more fierce to an enemy. And Torin had no doubt he would face an enemy this day. If he spent his last breath, he would avenge the attack. Someone would pay for the death and destruction. Someone would pay with blood for blood.

He stalked the decimated camp, the curved blade of his sword flashing in the sunlight. At every turn, he expected an enemy warrior, clutching a sword already blooded and hungry for more, to rise up to face him.

Instead, all that greeted him were the dead, all the more horrifying because he recognized them only by their possessions—the red sash Kaya's mother had made him when he passed his warrior's test, the elaborately scrolled sword of Jerim, the handle of the cradle-basket Sadaar had been making for her baby, soon to come.

His anger burned strong and hot, without an outlet. His shame was a thing too heinous to bear. How many of them could I have saved? Warrior of the Kedasa, he snorted to himself. What good have I been?

For the first time in the ten seasons since his wife and parents had been killed in a raid, Torin was glad that no one he loved was alive to witness his shame, to see the ruins of their beloved camp.

Behind him, Biar shouted, his boyish voice shrill with excitement and fear. Torin ran back across the camp to find the boy tearing at a tent, which had been blown off its mooring and lay half in, half out of the spring. Fire had licked at its edges, but the water had saved it. At first, Torin thought the boy mad, but then something moved beneath the heavy, twisted folds of canvas.

Torin shoved Biar aside and raised his sword, just as whoever was inside found the door slit and pushed through. A woman scrambled out. Her robes hung in disarray; her long black hair tumbled about her shoulders. Seeing the sword-wielding man, she whimpered and fell to her knees, one hand raised in supplication. Her eyes were stretched wide, pupils so large and black they seemed bottomless. Her fair skin was bloodless with terror.

For a moment, Torin remained still, sword poised high. Then he turned away in disgust. The woman was Herik's city-born concubine. Torin sheathed his sword savagely. The woman saw the burned-out camp and moaned.

Herik's body lay nearby. A thin piece of blue-edged robe was all that distinguished it from the other mounds of ash. The woman moaned again, a sound as low and mournful as winter wind across a dune. In unison with her whimper, Biar sniffled.

Torin knew, in another moment, they'd both be wailing. "Stop this!" He wheeled so abruptly they both ceased in midsound. "The time for mourning will come when we have avenged this treachery."

Shamefaced, Biar wiped at his eyes. "Who did it, Torin? And why?"

Under the jelaya, Torin's mouth hardened into a grim, straight line, and he needed no face-covering to make his eyes burn with ferocity. "I do not know. But I will find them. And I will bury their heads in these ashes."

"You will not find the ones who did this," said Herik's woman. She struggled to her feet and stumbled clear of the wrecked tent.

Torin frowned, a scathing retort ready, but the words died in his throat. Not a season had passed since the merchant returned from a trip to Tarsis with the woman astride his horse instead of the usual bolt of fine silk or heavy canvas. And each time Torin saw her, he was as surprised, as dazzled by her beauty as he had been the day Herik brought her to the camp.

Though Torin had never seen an elf, he'd heard them described. He knew there must be elven blood mixed in the woman's veins.

Seen from a distance, she appeared small, fragile, and sharp-featured—breakable like all city-made things. Herik had certainly treated her so, keeping her apart from the rest of the camp like some jewel too precious to share. But up close, all those impressions were shattered, blown apart like the petals of a sisc flower in high wind.

She was as tall as Torin, who was tall among the Kedasa, so graceful and poised she seemed more likely to bend than break. The sharpness in her features and the strange tilt to her black eyes blended into a beauty that was disturbingly alien. And strangely soothing.

"Cover your face, woman!" Torin snapped and motioned for Biar to come away. He was vaguely aware that the woman had said something that angered him, and he had to struggle to remember the words—something about not finding his enemies.

The woman blushed and fumbled with the folds of her jelaya, wrapping it until only her exotic black eyes were visible through the slit. "My name is Mali," she told him.

Her voice was lightly accented and surprisingly without reproach for Torin's churlishness.

This, too, was irritating, and Torin turned his back on her. "Search Herik's tent for things I can use," he told Biar. "I must be on the trail before the enemy's footprints have grown cold."

Hesitantly, with a quick glance over his shoulder at the woman, the boy did as he was told, scuffling his boots in the sand to show his reluctance.

Torin caught hold of the woman by the arm. "What you said before. Tell me what you know of this." He waved his free hand to indicate the destroyed camp.

Mali pulled herself up, strong and straight, for a moment so tall she seemed to tower over him. Her eyes were filled with distaste and haughty disdain.

He snorted. A concubine who did not like to be touched! But he released her.

"What did you mean, I 'will not find the ones who did this'?" Torin insisted.

The woman refused to meet his gaze, tried to turn back to Herik's tent. He placed himself in front of her. "I must know what you know!"

"I know nothing."

Torin took a menacing step toward her.

"Dragons," she whispered. "Dragons did this."

Torin was so astonished, he stood openmouthed. "Are you sun-mad?" he asked at last. "There is no such thing." He glared, daring her to repeat the ridiculous statement.

Biar interrupted. "Elim told me he heard rumors that dragons had returned to Krynn."

"What are you talking about?" Torin demanded, turning his glare from the woman to the boy.

Biar glanced at Mali for support, then continued. "It was in the spring, when he journeyed to Tarsis. Elim said he heard strange stories, that the dragons had come back. But"—Biar shrugged apologetically at Mali—"he didn't believe them."

Torin growled in wordless anger. Dragons! Was he expected to believe in myths old even before the plains were formed? But who, or what, had the power of such destruction? Who, or what, had the power to make him so afraid he'd cowered while his people died? A wizard, perhaps?

He surveyed the destroyed camp, and rage knotted the muscles low in his belly. "Only a sorcerer could have done this," Torin said scornfully.

Biar flushed, his small hands balling into fists.

"Only a sorcerer, a very strong one," Torin repeated. He had little use for wizards, with their disdain of the sword and their motives hidden always in shadow. "It took great power."

Mali's eyes narrowed over the rim of her jelaya. "It took the power of a dragon. Look about you! What wizard could burn a man so that not even his bones remain? What wizard could make sand melt into glass like sugar into candy? A dragon's breath did this! A dragon's power made me so afraid I could do nothing but lie in the darkness of my tent and pray for death."

At this, Torin's anger sputtered and died. "What do you mean?"

The woman gazed at him with her extraordinary eyes. "Did you not feel the dragonfear? Did you not cower where you stood?"

Torin frowned. He wanted to deny her charge. He wanted to say he'd stood strong and tall before the enemy. But he could not. "If what you say is true, and we were attacked by a dragon, why did it do this? What did it want here with us?"

"I think I know," Biar said.

Mali grew very pale, lowered her eyes.

The boy patted the pockets hidden among the folds of his robe and withdrew a leather bag worn soft with age and handling. "The Aquara. Just before . . ." He choked, couldn't go on.

Torin made an irritated gesture.

Biar drew a deep breath. "Elim said I could study the crystal. I was sitting at the edge of the oasis, and just as the darkness came, the crystal glowed with heat and colors such as I have never seen. I shouted out to Elim. . . ."

Torin narrowed his eyes, remembering. "I heard you. . . ." And then the black fear had come upon him, so powerfully, so suddenly it had been a physical pain. And the screaming. The Kedasa being massacred while he lay helpless and frightened. "But that proves it. The attack was sorcery."

Biar shrugged, obviously reluctant to agree. "The crystal is silent now." He removed a silk-wrapped object as long as his hand, folded the edges of the cloth back to expose the Aquara of the Kedasa. The jewel gleamed in the sunlight, shimmering with the colors of honey and new grass and fresh water. Light refracted off the strange symbols etched into the facets of the crystal, casting rainbowed crescents onto Biar's face.

Mali made a soft little sound—surprise, appreciation, apprehension. Her hand darted out, reaching for the Aquara, and only at the last moment did she pull back.

Biar grinned, the smile of a child sharing a new toy.

"Watch, Mali." Biar ran his fingertips along one of the faces, touching the etched markings. The crystal twinkled weakly in response, its colors deepening.

The jewel was as old as the Kedasa, a tribe that claimed ancestors from before the Cataclysm. Some said the Aquara was of the ancient gods, the ones who had brought destruction to Krynn. The crystal supposedly had wondrous powers, but no one had seen it do anything other than glimmer when touched. But the mages kept it and studied it, hoping to regain the significance it had once held for their forebears.

Biar held the Aquara out to Mali, silently giving permission for her to touch. Hesitantly, she laid a fingertip on one edge. The crystal responded more strongly to her than it had to the boy, glimmering azure and dark silver in its depths, the colors swirling like clouds before wind. Startled, she pulled her hand away, then looked at her fingers, rubbing the tips together as if she had never seen them before.

The boy gaped at her with awed approval. "Elim said

the Aquara collects the energy of every person in the tribe and saves it for a time when it will be needed."

"And what will it do with the life energy of a city dweller?" Torin asked coldly.

He had touched the Aquara when he was no older than Biar. The crystal had glittered red. He could well remember the sensation, like the cold of winter night, that had snaked all the way to his elbow before he could pull away. But Mali did not seem to be in pain.

She stepped back, putting distance between the Aquara and herself. But she still leaned as if it tugged at her. Torin could remember feeling the same repulsed fascination.

"Elim said the day would come when the jewel would once again be a thing of great power to the Kedasa," Biar said, straightening the edges of the silk wrapping.

"There are so few of the Kedasa left, I would say it matters not," Torin muttered. That knowledge hurt more than he would ever admit. The Kedasa, an ancient people, would travel the Plains of Dust no more. He and the boy were the last.

Torin left the two huddled over the crystal and went in search of the things he had marked as salvageable during his earlier tour of the camp. He gathered them quickly: a waterskin, a steel knife with the handle burned off, half a blanket.

Torin started to pick up Jerim's sword. Like the knife, the sword could be repaired, but Torin found he could not bring himself to part it from the warrior's charred hand. Jerim had died in the manner Torin wished for himself, sword in hand, meeting the enemy. He deserved to remain so for the afterworld that awaited him.

Torin circled the camp once again, passing the rubble of his own tent without a glance. He walked more slowly this time, looking for the one thing he must have to carry out his vengeance—the trail of the enemy. He found nothing he could mark as a path, other than a wide swath of sand that looked more as if it had been swept by the wind than disturbed by feet. Several paces north, at the ridge of a dune, the trail disappeared.

By the time he returned, Biar had sorted the contents of Herik's tent into piles of usable and unusable items: a blanket, waterskins, leather bags. Torin hoped those contained trail food. There were also silk gowns, slashed at the arms, city-style, and a robe so soft and fine it poured through his fingers like sand. Herik had provided well for his concubine. Biar had also found a satin bag, which probably contained Herik's cache of jewels and coins.

Biar had apparently taken the time to sift through the ashes of Elim's tent, also. The boy sat cross-legged on the stone ridge with Elim's spellbook and the bag containing the Aquara clasped between his hands. The forest-green binding of the spellbook with its unfathomable markings was stained gray with ash, but appeared whole.

Herik's woman sat beside the boy, her legs drawn up under her voluminous robes, her cheek resting on her knees, her eyes closed.

Torin dropped his bundle and began to form a travel pack. The knife, a bag of dried meat, a bag of hard, dried cheese, another of unleavened travel bread went into the folds of the blanket. He added the two partially full waterskins from Herik's tent to the one he'd found.

Torin weighed the satin bag in his palm, gauging the clink of coins, then threw it to the feet of the woman. "Spoils of the living. I'm sure you've earned it." He sneered, not bothering to conceal the disdain in his voice.

Mali stirred and straightened, but said nothing. Her eyes, showing through the slit in the jelaya, were both guileless as a child's and wiser than her years. So otherworldly, so emotionless, she betrayed no anger at Torin's words.

Biar, however, looked at Torin with reproach. He picked up the bag and handed it to Mali. "What was Herik's is yours now, just as what was Elim's is mine."

She took the pouch and cupped it in her hands. "It is mine, but not by right of death," she said quietly. "I brought it with me when I came from Tarsis."

Torin could not bear the quiet sadness in her eyes, though the revelation made him respect the woman no more and trust her even less. Why would anyone be a slave when she had the money to buy freedom?

Biar patted a hidden pocket. "Torin, shouldn't we take the Aquara to someone and tell them what has happened? Chire, maybe?"

What the boy suggested was akin to blasphemy. No one outside of the Kedasa had set eyes on the Aquara for several lifetimes. And Chire, though acknowledged a most powerful mage, was of a tribe that had never known kinship with the Kedasa.

But Torin only shrugged. He didn't care what Biar did. Honor demanded that Torin be on his way, stalking, seeking a direction for his anger, vengeance to assuage the spirits of his tribespeople. Not wet-nursing a boy-child on a foolhardy mission.

When he didn't respond, Biar asked in a small voice, "Are you going to leave us here? Alone?"

"There are none left here to harm you, boy."

"But what if the dragons come back for the Aquara?"

Torin shook his head and gathered the waterskins. He was not thoroughly convinced there was such a thing as a dragon, or if there was, that it killed for a piece of antique glass.

Kneeling, he opened one of the leather bags to dip it into the water. The water, normally clean and clear, was murky. He bent closer and sniffed. How had he missed it before? The rank, oily, malignant scent was unmistakable.

"Poisoned," Biar said in a voice dull and flat with horror.

Torin nodded, disgust a thick slime in his throat. Only a madman would do such a thing! Water was as precious as life. Water *was* life. No rival, not even a mage, would do such!

Mali sank gracefully to her knees beside him and stared at her reflection in the tainted pool. The skin around her eyes was bloodless, as white as bone bleached by the desert sun. She reached out, as if to dip her fingers into the water.

Torin grabbed her wrist roughly. "Do not touch it!"

She looked at him calmly, not attempting to extricate herself from his grip as she had before.

Her skin was cool beneath his fingers, soft and smooth and pale. The scent of the woman washed over him, not of perfume, not like the Kedasa, who smelled of sun-warmed skin and desert air. Mali smelled of something dark and shadowy, something . . . cool.

After a moment, she asked, "What will we do now?"

He released her and edged back slightly, putting a space between them, but the scent pursued him, unidentifiable, magical, and rich with a solace he did not want. "Did you expect to stay here? You'll have to follow a route to another camp."

"But, Torin!" Biar clutched his shoulder. "We don't have enough water!"

Torin clenched his fists and stared at the horizon. He couldn't track an enemy while dragging with him a boy-wizard and a desert-ignorant woman. "I cannot take you with me," Torin growled.

Mali hissed with surprise. "You cannot be thinking of going after them?"

"I will avenge the deaths of my people."

The woman shivered at the sound of blood in his voice. "If you *could* find them—which you will not—you would not live to draw your sword." Mali leaned forward urgently, touching him this time, laying her soft, cool fingers on his wrist, wrapping her disturbing scent about him. "It is certain death!"

"Then it is death!" he retorted. "What matter when my honor lies cowering in a sandpit, and I have no home to return to?" He stood and turned so abruptly, so angrily, he almost stepped on her.

They were looking at him, waiting for his decision, making him responsible. All of the Kedasa massacred in their summer homes, and he was burdened with a stripling boy barely out of his mother's tent and a city-raised whore! He could not leave them alone in a tomb of an oasis without water, and the boy was not trail-wise enough to follow a direct route to safety.

A night and a morning, maybe more, before he could be rid of them. The trail of the enemy would be more than cold. It would be gone. Torin kicked the half-empty water-skins.

"Bundle up anything we can use. I will guide you to Gelen Oasis. From there you can go on alone. The summer camp of the Faraezi is south of Tarsis. My mother's people will take you in."

* * * * *

Torin led them along the wadi, which curved up and out of the vast depression encircling the oasis. In midsummer the winding channel was dry, a streambed waiting for the melting snows of winter, a path for the nomads of the plains.

It was a relief to be away from the stench of the oasis, out into the hot, dusty air of the sands. Muscles strained as he climbed the shifting sand. Torin paused at the ridge of a dune and looked out over the sprawling land. The plains spread out before him, silent, changeable as the wind, colors shimmering from deepest bronze to blazing white.

"It is said, 'The gods created the desert to give people a place pleasant to walk.' "

Biar joined him and faced the sun, nodding in agreement. The city woman came up behind and stood in the meager shade cast by her companions, protecting her eyes with the folds of cloth wound around her head. She stood peering fearfully from the corners of her eyes at the sweeping panorama before her.

Torin shook his head in disgust and started down the face of the dune away from the trail.

Biar followed, tripping on his robe in his rush to keep up. "We're not going to follow the caravan route?"

"No. It will add a day and a half for which we do not have water. We'll go straight into the sun. Then follow the stars to Gelen."

The temperature rose steadily as the sun climbed. The

land grew whiter, losing its rainbow shadings of gold, reflecting heat in shimmering waves. Sweat dried before it had time to slip down Torin's skin. The fine sand for which the Plains of Dust had been named rose with each footstep, puffed up around them as they walked, and settled on their clothes and skin until, head to foot, the three were the same dusty color as the desert floor.

They passed midday in the lee of a dune, sheltered under a blanket stretched from slope to ground. It offered scant relief from the blazing sun, keeping back the worst of the heat but also blunting any hint of breeze that might have freshened the oppressive air.

Biar curled up between the two adults and slept immediately, a boneless rest punctuated with the whimpers of disturbing dreams.

Herik's woman sat as she had on the ridge before the decimated camp, long legs drawn up under her robe, her chin resting on her knees. "You said . . ." she paused hesitantly. "You called the Faraezi your mother's people?"

"Yes," Torin answered shortly.

"Was she . . . Was your mother in the camp this morning?"

He worked a strip of leather, making a wrapping for the handle of the knife he'd salvaged. He did not want to share himself with a stranger, not even one who had lived among his tribe. But in a land where the names of family were cherished, to know something of a fellow traveler was a request he could not reasonably refuse. "My wife and parents are dead many years." His voice was so gruff that Biar stirred.

Mali soothed the boy, patting his shoulder and making nonsensical noises. Softly, she said, "I'm sorry."

Torin grunted and poked savagely at the strip of leather, and the knife point sliced through, splitting the material instead of making a hole.

Mali was silent for a moment, then spoke as hesitantly as before. "The Faraezi, did you say their summer camp is near Tarsis?"

"Yes, woman." Without offering more, Torin finished

the intricate wrapping for the knife handle.

"You don't like towns. Or city dwellers."

Torin grunted again, this time with disdain. "Barbarians. Where water is plentiful, people become slaves."

The woman's exotic eyes narrowed over the rim of dusty cloth, but she said no more.

He moved on as soon as the heat followed the sun into the evening sky, pushing the woman and the boy harder than he would have pushed seasoned travelers, the thought of the enemy disappearing into the plains giving him speed and energy. The faster he could get the two to water, the faster he could be rid of them. The faster he could be on the trail.

The sun set, falling below the horizon with a spectacular show of purple and red. With the night came the wind, racing across the sands as if it were chasing the waning sun.

Torin called a rest. He would wait for the light of the rising moon. They sat in the shelter of a crescent dune and shared bread and cheese and precious sips of water. Mali and the boy leaned against each other, almost too tired to eat.

Only red Lunitari rose to shed its light on the desert, limning the rocks and the dunes in a rosy glow. Despite being told all his life that the red moon was the power of the neutral wizards, Torin found its light baleful. The curves and hollows of sand became places of suspicious shadow, bathed with a blood-red glow that made him cold. But it was light nevertheless, and it lit their way east. Perhaps three hours of good traveling time remained when Torin stopped them for another rest. The chill in the night air made him want to keep moving, to warm his muscles with effort. But Biar was no longer walking a straight line, and exhaustion had robbed Mali of her graceful stride.

Torin chafed at the limits they set upon him. Alone, he would have continued well into the morning, then slept away the worst of the coming day's heat, but the woman and the boy did not have his stamina. Biar was nearly asleep on his feet before he could help unroll the blanket. Mali stood nearby, leaning on the sheltering rocks.

"We will rest sooner if I have help," Torin said, glaring up at Mali. He realized the woman was not resting. She was staring up into the night sky, her eyes reflecting red in the light of the moon.

Torin dropped the blanket. "What—?"

Mali made an abrupt cutting motion. The whites of her eyes stood out against her dusty skin as she searched the sky. "They're up there," she whispered. "They're near. I can feel them!"

"What?" Torin repeated, drawing his sword. The blade flashed in the light of the moon, and he slapped it against his thigh to hide the revealing reflection. "Where?" He could see nothing but stars against the blackness of sky.

Behind them, Biar gasped. "The crystal! It's warm!"

"Put it away!" Mali cried. Grabbing the boy, she dragged him back into the thin shadow at the base of the rock.

"But—"

She clapped her hand over Biar's mouth and shoved him to the ground, yanking at Torin as she dove for cover.

Torin resisted the strength in the arm that tugged at him. The sounds were closer this time, clearer without the voices of the dying, and more frightening without the swirling blackness for distraction. Creaking, flapping, stirring the wind from above. What was it that sent the desert sand swirling about his legs, that blotted out the light of Lunitari? He didn't have the courage to look up.

He pressed back into the scant protection of the shadows and waited for the blackness that had come with the sounds, for the debilitating terror. But the unnatural fear didn't come.

He gripped his sword tighter and shifted to a crouch. He would not cower in the dirt this time! He would be stronger than the darkness.

Mali's grip tightened on his arm, silently urging him to stillness. Torin could feel the woman's body shivering against his shoulder, could smell the sweetness of fresh sweat. But Mali was not quaking with fear. She was shaking her head, warning him not to move.

The moment's hesitation was enough for Torin to realize the sounds and the blackness were passing them by, were growing fainter as the sand settled around his feet, as the moonlight and stars returned.

The three stayed silent, huddled together for long minutes after the sky was clear. It was Biar who finally moved, protesting the weight of the woman on top of him.

Torin stood slowly and surveyed the moonlit landscape in all directions. He saw nothing but the scarlet outline of dunes, the pinpoint twinkle of stars. "What was it?" he demanded, angry because he already knew her reply, because belief was more confusing than not knowing the answer.

Mali shook her head and turned away to worry with the blanket.

"How come you know so much of these mythical beasts?" Torin caught the woman's arm and spun her so the moonlight illuminated her face.

Mali extricated herself from Torin's grip. "I was told . . . I heard as Elim did, that the dragons had returned to Krynn."

"In Tarsis? Is this the same city rumor Elim did not believe?"

She hesitated, looking at him silently, eyes pleading above the edge of her jelaya. The cloth drooped across her face, below the line of dust around her eyes, and the clean skin shone pale and bloodless, even in the red light of the waning moon. She took a deep breath and said, "I was told in Silvanesti."

"You're elven?" Biar breathed, his voice awed.

"Yes," Mali admitted, still watching Torin.

He gazed back at her through slitted eyes, surprised. This was no human with exotic blood mixed in her veins. Not if she'd been in Silvanesti. What was a Silvanesti elf doing living among the tribes? He opened his mouth to ask, saw that she flinched before the words even formed on his lips. "What—?"

"What's your elf name?" Biar interrupted.

With a quick glance at Torin, Mali smiled and answered. "Amalie. Amalie Canaradon."

"It sounds like music," Biar said. "I've never met an elf."

Torin snorted, turned his back on them both, and walked a few steps away. The desert floor was inky black nothingness. Above, the matching darkness of the sky was peppered with brilliant stars. In all the darkness, nothing disturbed the silent land, nothing flew, blotting out the pinpoints of diamond light.

Sand slithered against sand, interrupting his reverie, and Biar sidled up beside him. "Torin, why don't you think the dragons are searching for the crystal? If it warns of their presence, they'd want to destroy it."

"Then why didn't they destroy it in the camp, mage?" Torin asked bitterly. "We would not have been much hindrance."

"Perhaps they can't sense it as it senses them."

Mali's voice, coming from just behind him, startled Torin. She had moved so silently he hadn't heard her.

Oblivious to his glare, Mali continued, "Perhaps they couldn't find it."

"Then why are they seeking it now? If they can't find it, how do they know it wasn't destroyed? Why—" Torin stopped. Questions were a waste of time. "There is no time to discuss this now. We must travel while we can."

Torin pushed on, even though he knew the other two were near the limits of their endurance, even after Lunitari had set, and he could guide only by instinct and the dim light of the stars. They walked as far into morning as possible, slept through the heat of the day, then moved on again.

The woman and boy stumbled as they walked, sometimes going to their knees as they trod dunes that seemed to grow in steepness as the sun climbed across the sky. Biar had slipped again, sinking to his knees near the top of a dune, when Torin saw the thing of which he'd dreamed.

Gelen Oasis. Still hours away, but so close he could smell moisture in the air. It shimmered on the horizon, a green slash more beautiful than any jewel, an island of green in a sea of dust.

Revitalized by so simple a thing as a strip of vegetation in the sand, Torin set his own pace, rapidly leaving his fellow travelers behind. When Biar called out for him to wait, Torin ignored the boy. The two could find the oasis without him now, and he could not bear to hold back, to move slowly when he could run.

The promise of water drew him, made the discomfort of thirst a bearable thing. The aches and pains in his legs disappeared, and he could have flown across the hot sands, buoyed by the scent of water.

Gelen Oasis was only a small watering place along the caravan trail, a green spot not large enough to support a seasonal encampment, but it was as pleasing to Torin as a roaring river. He stumbled across the rocky border, fell to his knees with weariness, and stayed there for the pure pleasure of feeling grass beneath his palms. The scent of life was a balm after the memory of scorched land. He sank down beside the pool to drink and to wait for Biar and the woman.

They stumbled into Gelen just as Lunitari cleared the horizon. With a whoop, Biar rushed ahead and threw himself down beside the clear pool. Without bothering to remove his jelaya, he thrust his whole head into the water.

Mali followed more slowly, pausing before she dipped her hands delicately into the pool. "I feared you would not wait," she told Torin. "I thought you might leave us here."

Irritated, he ignored her. He caught Biar by the back of his robe and hauled him bodily out of the water. "Don't drink too much. You'll get sick."

The boy pulled away. "I know that." Then he plunged his face back into the pool and splashed water onto his head and shoulders, splattering Torin.

Mali unwound her jelaya and draped it around her

shoulders. She dipped the end of it in the water and used the dampened cloth to wipe her face and neck, to pat moisture onto her dry lips. The pointed tips of her ears peeked through the heavy, dusty mass of her hair.

Who was this stunning, exotic creature colored of the night, so unlike the women of the plains? She was so very alien in her beauty. So very alien in her serenity. It was not so wondrous after all that Herik had passed up silk for the right to touch her pale skin, to run his fingers through her dark hair. Looking at her made Torin feel alive.

Torin tugged Biar from the pool once more and sent him to fill their waterskins on the other side, away from the cloudy water the boy had stirred up with his thrashings. Biar grumbled his way around the shallow pool, dragging the waterskins in the sand.

When he was out of hearing range, Torin asked, "How do you come to be here?"

His tone made her look up, and something in his gaze made her look away even more quickly. "What do you mean?" she asked.

"Why does a Silvanesti elf live among the Kedasa as a slave?"

When she didn't respond, Torin continued, "I have always been told of the pride of the Silvanesti, of their belief in their superiority. How could you live among us as a . . . as a concubine?" He finished hurriedly, before Mali could realize he'd been thinking of a less kind word.

But she understood anyway. "I was never *harln*." Without blushing, she used an even ruder word than the one Torin had considered, a word that meant "less than slave" or "whore" or both, depending on the context and the user. "Herik was kind to me. He gave me a home when I had none. He protected me in Tarsis when . . ." She stopped suddenly.

"Protected you from what?" Torin persisted.

She shook her head, her mouth a hard, straight line. "I am . . . exiled." She said the last word so softly Torin almost didn't hear it, and she sat with her head bowed, waiting for his reaction.

"I don't understand."

Mali stiffened and winced, fine lines appearing in the flawless skin at the corners of her eyes. She had not replaced her jelaya, but Torin made no comment on it.

"I am in exile." She spoke the words this time with a plea in her voice, as if she feared his reaction.

"So you said." Torin didn't understand.

Mali hung her head, shoulders slumped low. She fumbled with the skirt of her jelaya, trying to fasten it, but her fingers were trembling so badly she couldn't push the cloth into place. "It is difficult to believe . . . I thought you would recoil from me in horror. *My* people would."

She allowed the dusty cloth to fall away from her trembling fingers. "It is . . . I am . . . To my people, I am a thing reviled. I am what they call a dark elf. If I returned to my homeland, my people would kill me.

"That is why, when Herik wanted me, I went with him. I was . . ." She paused and hung her head once more. "I was alone in a land I did not understand, with no hope." She raised her head once more, and her eyes glittered like a pool of clear water in Solinari's light. "I was afraid."

Biar returned, dragging skins now full, saving Torin the need to respond.

Torin took a piece of bread and cheese and wandered away to the edge of the oasis. He settled in a nest of sand, his back against a rock still sun-warm. The more he learned of the woman, the less he understood. Yet when asked the most prying questions, she bared her soul. And her honesty spawned even more questions. Kept apart and protected by Herik, she had been an enigma to the Kedasa, and she remained so. And she would continue to remain so. With first light, he would leave her and the boy to make their way alone.

Torin put aside his speculations to plan his trek across the desert. Instead of taking a straight path back to the ruins of Kedasa, he would cut higher west. Perhaps he could intersect the path of the enemy.

Solinari rose, a mere sliver of silver tinged red by Lunitari, and together the two moons cast their light over the desert, creating a work of art out of heaps of sand, a sculpture in black and white and crimson. A bird ventured out of its hiding place in the rocks and called to its mate, a sound as soft and silver as the night. Then all was silent.

"The land rewards stillness." It was an old Kedasan proverb, and Torin remembered it when he saw something stirring at the edge of his vision. Something was behind the nearby dune, where nothing should be moving. He rose to a crouch, sliding his sword free of the scabbard.

A whisper of sound slithered through the silence—the gurgle of spring runoff in the wadis, of water where none should be.

Not quite hidden behind the slope, a shadow swelled, outlined in moonlight and icy glimmers. He caught a glimpse of hard, glistening scales and upswept wings and gleaming talons.

The shadow shifted, rustling its huge wings, turning its head. In the center of the dark blot that was its head, eyes glowed red-black like the heart of a slow-burning fire.

Torin's breath froze in his lungs; the blood thrummed in his ears. He suddenly perceived, as he never had in battle, the proximity of death. This creature exuded evil the way Mali radiated serenity.

Mali! She and the boy were beside the pool, oblivious to the monster. Torin had to warn them, hide them. Get them away somehow!

He stepped backward to put the dune between himself and the beast. He expected at any moment to be discovered, struck down by darkness and fear, to be incinerated where he stood.

He sheathed his sword, took a step. . . . Sand closed over his boots. He leapt back, and the dune shifted. The ridge at its top crested and broke. Sand roiled down the slope toward him in a growing wave.

Torin shouted a wordless warning, then the rushing sand knocked him off his feet and washed over him. He struggled to regain his footing, but the movement of the sand twisted him, wrenched him to the side. The muscles in his right knee stretched and pulled. Pain shot up his leg.

He screamed and grit poured into his mouth, smothering the sound. The sand ran into his clothes, his eyes, into his ears, moving as water would move. It spilled like liquid through his fingers as he clawed for a handhold, gushed into his throat as he gagged and gasped for air. He thrashed beneath the weight of the granules, frantic that he was going to drown in the depths of a dune.

His hands touched something solid—a hand! He fought to hold on as the sand churned around him, tore at him, threatening to break his tenuous grip. The soft and fragile-feeling hand clasped around his fingers, hauling Torin along. His head broke the surface of the dune. Bobbing in waves of surging dust, Torin threw back his head and greedily sucked in air. Though filled with grit, the breaths were as welcome and sweet as the crisp, clean air from winter's first snow.

Torin blinked enough sand from his eyes to see that he was gripping Mali's arm. The woman guided him toward solid ground. With his good leg, he kicked as if he were swimming in a stream. Mali dragged him, gasping and coughing, until his feet were out of the moving sand.

Torin rolled to his knees, peering through a haze of grit and tears, and watched Mali stumble back to the edge of the roiling pool and disappear into the cloud of dust and sand. Over the roar of the storm, he could hear the elven woman screaming Biar's name.

It seemed an eternity before she reappeared, dragging the boy behind her as she'd dragged Torin. She dumped Biar on firm ground and fell to her knees beside him, clawing at the jelaya wound tightly around his throat. For long seconds, Biar lay still, then he gasped—a long indrawn wheeze—and began to cough.

Mali pounded him on the back with one hand and clawed the skirt of her jelaya from her face with the other. She breathed deeply of the dust-filled air, then sneezed.

Torin crawled the two paces to them.

Biar gazed up at him with eyes so red and shot through

with blood that they made Torin's tear in sympathy.

Mali added another sneeze to Biar's wheezing. To Torin, the sounds were loud and dangerous. He pantomimed for silence, touching his jelaya. His fingers loosened the sand caked in its folds, and he, too, fought a sneeze. "Quiet!" He forced the word out past a throat scrubbed raw by inhaled sand.

Obediently, Mali caught the skirt of her jelaya and held it against her nose and mouth.

Biar rolled onto his side and hid his face against Mali's knee, trying to smother the sounds of his coughing.

Torin shook him to get his attention. "The crystal?"

Wheezing and nodding, the boy clutched at a fold in his robe. "Here. Safe."

Torin climbed to his feet, ignoring the sharp pain in his knee, and drew his sword. The blade grated against the scabbard as it slid free, unnaturally loud in a land suddenly unnaturally quiet. His eyes were so clouded with tears and dirt that only blurred shades of green and tan filled his vision.

Impatiently, he waited for his vision to clear, though he knew he would find nothing. If the creature were still about, he and the others would not be alive.

The view that slowly swam into focus was so changed it was not recognizable as Gelen Oasis. Torin stood on a crescent of yellow-green, all that was left of the sunburned grass. The few palms that Gelen supported were almost buried by the sand. The dune itself was gone, flattened, its mass poured into the bowl that had held the lifeblood of the oasis. There was no water left in the pool, though the sand that filled it still moved sluggishly, lapping the sandy shore as if it were water, as if something stirred its silent depths.

Mali climbed to her feet and turned slowly, searching the sky. Torin also gazed upward, but the night was as clear and empty as the desert.

He limped to the edge of the rocks and gathered his pack, all that was left of their gear. Everything Mali and Biar had been carrying—food, blankets, waterskins—was now beneath an ocean of sand.

Mali joined him. "What do we do now?" she asked quietly.

Torin shrugged to show that he didn't know. He was once again responsible for the two of them. Once again sidetracked. He had already thrown away his best chance to face the enemy.

He expected to be furious, with himself and with them. He *wanted* to be furious. But he wasn't. The lack of anger left an emptiness he wasn't ready to face. Without his fury, without the crying-out of his honor for revenge, what was the purpose in his life?

Mali touched him, and her fingers on his were soft and dry. Her nearness brought a strange, sweet, earthy scent to his nostrils. The ache in his knee receded into the background, forgotten as he breathed in the smell of flowers and tree-shaded glades. Despite the heat of the sun, he shivered.

"You saved us both," he said harshly, to cover his feelings. "I owe a debt even taking you to safety will not repay."

"You owe me nothing," she answered softly.

He turned to face her, so close he could feel her breath on his face, the coolness of her body all along the length of his own. She radiated an energy, a power, that made the hair at the nape of his neck stand up.

"My life is not nothing," he said huskily.

Mali flushed, a lovely high pink that rivaled the sunrise. She stepped back, fumbling to cover her face. "I did what anyone would have done. Without thinking. It was not an act for which I expect payment."

Without the distracting touch of her slim fingers, Torin's tiredness returned, and with it, the need to make decisions. He wished for her hand upon his again. "We have to go north," he said.

Mali froze, her eyes growing large with some emotion Torin couldn't read. Fear . . . or hope.

"Toward Silvanesti?" she whispered. "I cannot go back there. They would kill me."

"Surely you exaggerate."

She shook her head, and a deep sadness clouded her eyes. She turned to walk away from him.

He caught her arm and stopped her. "Perhaps you should tell me more."

"You will not believe me. As my people did not believe me."

He took a small swallow of water from his waterskin. He ached to rinse his mouth of the sand that grated between his teeth, but their water was once again too precious for such comforts. "Perhaps I will."

She looked at him, measuring.

"Perhaps I will," he repeated, more softly. Softly so that she would not be frightened.

She took a deep breath and let it out slowly. "In the depths of the River Thon Thalas, I died."

Torin's surprise was too involuntary to hide. Mali turned her head away. "You see? You do not believe me."

He was so shocked he could think of nothing to say. The words were totally beyond his imagination, but as she had spoken those few words, he had seen more animation in her stark face than in all the days of their journey.

"I will believe, or disbelieve, *after* I have heard your tale," he said sternly.

Taking another deep breath, she continued in a small, faraway voice. "I fell into the water and hit my head." Her fingers went to her skull, touching a place behind her ear in remembered pain. "The water was dark. And heavy. I saw . . . faces of those who had died before me. I heard their voices welcoming me. Then . . . then the light came."

"The light? What light?" Torin's tone communicated his disbelief, and the spell was broken. The luminous life he had seen in Mali's eyes faded.

Torin felt suddenly guilty. "You have to admit it is a fantastic tale," he said, trying to explain. "But . . . go on."

Mali's face hardened, and for just a moment, he saw what he would have expected of an elf—the haughty demeanor, the arrogant scorn in the lines above her silky brows. Then the expression faded, replaced with no expression at all. In a dull, flat voice, she told the rest of her story.

"A voice beautiful beyond imagining. Music . . . like nothing of this world. Sounds . . . The water, which had seemed so heavy, was like floating on clouds. A voice, the beautiful, musical voice of a goddess told me that I must carry her message of healing back to my people. She told me of the return of dragons to Krynn, and of the return of the old gods. She told me I must warn my people of the danger, and spread words of hope. She said I must save my people."

Mali's face was as white as the morning of the attack, as bleak as winter. "The goddess said, 'Bring out the souls that are in darkness.' And I have failed, you see. My people did not believe me. Lorac—the king—called me blasphemous. He sent me away in exile. Now I cannot do the goddess's bidding." Mali sighed deeply. The intake of air seemed to reach to the depths of her soul. "I cannot bring their souls into the light."

"I thought the elves had not turned away from the old gods."

"They have not. But apparently only the elders, or those worthy, may talk to the gods. Who was I—a low-caste woman—that the goddess would talk to *me*? My people believe, but they do not *believe*. And sometimes," she added softly, "I begin to doubt myself."

Torin shrugged, unwilling to admit in the face of such sorrow that his own first instinct was disbelief. But he had seen the dragon, felt the power in Mali's touch.

He touched her cheek, and the caress climbed up, across her face, over the silky brows, into the thickness of her black hair. The heavy strands fell forward, hiding her face, exposing her delicate ears.

As he traced the pointed tip, she covered his fingers with hers.

He closed his eyes, seeing the desert spread out behind his eyelids as clearly as if he'd held a map in his hands. The foothills of the Kharolis would be perhaps a half day closer than one of the oases spawned by the Torath River. The trail would be more difficult, especially with his injured knee. But Mali and Biar would be safe. "I'll take you east. To the foothills of the Kharolis Mountains."

* * * * *

In blazing hot midafternoon light, they entered the foothills of the Kharolis Mountains, home to the dwarves of Thorbardin. They traveled faster than Torin had hoped, Mali and Biar pushing so hard, at times he was the one who had trouble keeping up. When he wavered, when the climbing put too great a strain on his injured knee, Mali had dropped back, offering her shoulder for support.

Even limping, Torin had no trouble keeping pace now, for Biar was wide-eyed and reckless, stopping to touch the lush grass, so unlike the yellowed oasis stubble. He turned his head this way and that, looking everywhere but where he was going.

Mali stood for a long time on the trail, her fingers moving over a tree as a blind man's would. The tree was a pitiful sight, scraggly and stunted, twisted as if caught between stretching to the sky and trying to hide from the unforgiving sun. But she touched it reverently and smiled at Torin as if given a great gift.

Warmed, Torin returned the smile and held his tongue. For himself, he could find nothing enjoyable in the scenery. Already he was cold, his lungs not satisfied with the damp, heavy air of the mountains. His pulse jumped with every crackle in the vegetation, at the things slithering unseen in the underbrush, at the rustle of leaves overhead, at the hard patter of his own footsteps on packed ground. He had never enjoyed the woodland climb to water.

"This is the way into the valley," Torin said. He put one foot on the trail that led down and stood braced. The coolness beneath his boot leeched the warmth from his foot, aggravated the soreness in his knee.

"It'll be just as Mali said. A running stream"—Biar

laughed—"with water rushing past, and great mossy boulders standing in deep patches of shade."

Over his shoulder, Torin saw Mali's dark eyes lift at the corners. Beneath the jelaya, she was smiling.

He smiled back. Torin could hear her melodious voice in Biar's description and wondered when she had painted the scene for him. He tried to catch the boy's enthusiasm. Clean, clear water. More than enough to wash away the grit that still grated between his teeth.

Biar brushed past him, running down the trail at a quick, eager pace.

"Biar!" Torin called and started down the trail, too. His limp hampered him, however.

The boy slowed and waited for them to catch up, almost dancing with impatience and excitement. "I want to see the running water."

"I'll go ahead with him," Mali offered. Biar waited for her to catch up, then they disappeared around a curve in the trail.

Torin switched to a slower, sidling gait that didn't jar his knee with every downward step. He had almost reached the fork in the trail when he heard a scream— Mali's voice, high-pitched and terrified.

Drawing his sword, Torin ran, not sure that he could control his own legs. His knee finally succumbing to the punishment, he stumbled and almost fell. The path forked before him, turning back on itself, continuing downward another twenty paces to the stream. To the left, at a diagonal, the path sloped gently upward, continuing farther into the mountains.

Fear and running had robbed him of breath, and he had to pause, to gulp in air, to steady himself. Would he find them at the end of the path, melted into lumps of charred, unrecognizable flesh? Moving carefully, favoring his knee, he eased down the trail toward the stream.

Biar was there, not burned, but dying just the same.

He lay on his back, half in and half out of the running stream he had so longed to see. A dagger protruded from his chest, and his blood mingled with the clear water.

Torin knelt beside him and felt for a pulse, knowing as he did that the act was useless. The boy's face was uncovered, his jelaya unwound from his curly brown hair. His childish mouth was drawn back in a feral grimace. Tears streamed from his eyes as blood poured from the wound in his chest. The boy clutched the bag that held the Aquara.

"They took Mali," he wheezed.

Torin slid Biar up onto the ground, out of the water, and pressed the boy's jelaya against the wound, trying to stanch the rapid flow of blood.

The boy groaned softly, but whispered, "Don't let them hurt Mali."

The ground was scuffled from a struggle, the water-skins scattered, but there was no sign of her.

"Mali!" Torin hissed, afraid to call too loudly.

The only responses were the alien sounds of the forest: a gurgle of water over stones, the soft rustle of wind in the trees, the anxious warning cry of a bird in the underbrush. Everywhere he looked, he saw darkness and light, hiding places for the enemy.

Torin placed Biar's hand against the jelaya and whispered, "Press hard, here. I'll be back."

Mali could not be far, if she still lived, which Torin doubted. But alive or dead, Torin would find her, and those who had attacked Biar.

He was almost back to the fork when he heard Mali cry out. The sound was strangled, a scream severed abruptly.

A hundred paces up the diagonal trail, Torin found her, kicking and struggling, being dragged along the path by a vision from a nightmare.

The creature was at least four hands taller than Mali, and looked for all the world like a desert lizard grown to huge size. Except no desert lizard walked upright, or had wings, or the twisted face of a man.

One large, clawed hand was clamped over the lower half of Mali's face, the other hooked in the folds of her robe. It hissed as it tried to subdue her.

Mali twisted in its grip and yanked its hand from her

mouth. "Go back, Torin!" she screamed.

Alerted to Torin's presence, the creature gurgled with displeasure. It drew a huge, double-edged sword and continued its flight up the trail, dragging Mali with it.

Torin leapt, jumping so quickly from startled trance to attack that he took the creature by surprise. He slashed at the lizard-man, the sword biting deeply into the leathery neck. Green ichor spurted from the gash.

The creature shrieked and dropped Mali. Planting one heavy foot on her robe to keep her from getting away, the lizard-man swung the huge sword in a high arc toward Torin's head.

Torin ducked below the high swing and slashed quickly with his sword, a mosquito attacking a horse. His curved blade, which had always seemed so strong, barely marked the scaly hide. The vicious cuts had not even scratched its chest, but the ferocity of Torin's attack drove the creature back a step, then another, away from Mali.

Torin pressed, slashing wildly with no hope of doing damage, but gaining enough space to put himself between Mali and the creature.

"Run!" Torin shouted to Mali without looking back. "Run!" He held his sword at ready, waiting for the lizard-man to charge.

It moved toward him, treading heavily, clumsily. Its weighty sword was pointed at his chest, the tip unwavering. But the creature's gaze kept shifting to Mali.

Torin risked a quick glance back. Mali had only gone a few paces down the trail.

"Go!" Torin yelled. "Run!"

He didn't have to glance back to see if the woman had obeyed him. He could tell she hadn't from the way the creature's gaze wavered back and forth between the two of them.

Taking advantage of the lizard-man's distraction, Torin danced in close, struck a quick, slashing blow, and slipped out of range just as the creature swung at him.

The creature struck left, then right, then whipped the sword around in a whistling arc.

Torin dodged the blows, instinctively dropping beneath the last swing as he had before. The power behind the sword was enough to cut him in half, but the creature was swinging high. High enough to allow Torin to move beneath the flashing blade.

He fell back out of range and repeated the attack, slipping in just close enough to sting with his sword, then skipping back from retaliation.

When the lizard-man's high, arcing swing came again, Torin was ready. He rolled, came up beneath the swath of the blade, and stabbed. His curved blade, intended for slashing attacks, slid horizontally into the creature's abdomen, between its scaly chest and the scaly armor, tearing a gaping wound.

The lizard-man gurgled and dropped its weapon. The haft hit the ground, clanging like the bell on a city gate. Green blood splashed across Torin's hands. His sword was snatched from his fingers.

The creature gurgled and toppled backward, Torin's sword still buried in its stomach. It landed with a heavy, dead thud.

Torin wheeled about to find that Mali still stood only a few paces away. "Are there others?" he started to ask, but at that moment, he reached to remove his sword from the monster's body and almost wrenched his arms from their sockets.

The blade was stuck in the wound. The body of the lizard-man seemed to have petrified! It was as solid as stone. Torin's sword was held so tightly, the blade would break before coming free.

He grabbed the dead creature's huge sword instead. Lifting with both hands, he managed to raise the tip off the ground. "Are there others?" he demanded again.

Her face white and bloodless with terror, Mali shook her head, but she was trembling so badly Torin wasn't sure if she meant "no" or "yes."

Torin limped back to where she stood, quaking with fear. He shook her gently. "Are there any others, Mali?"

"Two." Mali shuddered. "There were two."

"Where's the other one?"

Mali shook her head. "I don't know. It didn't—" She gasped, her white face going even whiter.

"What?" Torin cried. Hefting the sword to readiness, he wheeled, expecting to find the other creature. But there was nothing there. Not even the body of the lizard-man he'd just killed. It was gone!

He blinked, blinked again, and swiped at his eyes before he believed what he saw. One moment, the body had been as he had left it. Now his sword lay whole and clean in an irregularly shaped layer of fine dust.

"It disappeared," Mali whispered. "It just . . . disintegrated."

Torin dropped the creature's sword and picked up his own. It had not even a drop of green blood on it.

Beside him, Mali began to sob, her breath coming in quick ragged gasps. "Biar . . . ?"

Torin shook his head.

"No!" Mali screamed. She ran back down the path toward the stream.

Torin followed more slowly. He knew the boy was dead by now.

He found Mali kneeling beside Biar's body, talking to him in short gasping words that made no sense and were raw with pain. She was holding the bloody jelaya Torin had wrapped around the shaft of the knife, pressing on a wound that no longer bled.

The boy's small hands had slipped to the ground, limp and lifeless. The Aquara, the object for which Biar had died, had fallen from his grasp.

Torin retrieved the pouch, clammy and wet with Biar's blood. He could feel the crystal, hard and cold inside.

"It's still here!" Torin said in amazement. He pulled the silk-wrapped crystal from the pouch and flipped the cloth back to expose it. The Aquara glittered in the dappled sunlight, and a tingling sensation wiggled its way up Torin's fingers into his wrist. "That thing killed Biar, and it didn't even bother to take the Aquara." He flung the crystal to the ground. "What was it really after?"

His question quieted Mali's sobs, though large tears continued to roll down her cheeks. She had lost her jelaya in the struggle, and her hair hung in tangled strands around her shoulders. There was blood on her robe, but Torin didn't know if it was hers or the boy's.

Torin limped painfully toward her. "The crystal is still here." He grabbed her and twisted her up and around.

Mali cried out, pushing out at his hands. "No! Don't!"

"That monster wasn't after the Aquara. It left the crystal here, on a dying boy. It took you."

"No!" Mali dropped to her knees beside Biar's body and held out a hand in supplication.

"It was you, from the beginning." Torin said, staring at her, stunned with realization. "They were looking for you when they destroyed the camp. What have you done?" Anger flickered and caught. His people were dead. The boy was dead. And why? For what? Who was this woman who warmed him as the sun, and was as deadly as its heat?

"You don't know that." Mali sobbed, patting at the wadded jelaya on Biar's chest as if she could force the life back into him. "It can't be! It can't be! Not all of this, because of me."

Torin needed answers, but the other creature was probably still nearby. He caught hold of the woman's shoulder. "We have to go. Now!"

"Torin, please . . ."

"Biar's dead. There's nothing you can do."

"No!" Mali cried. She hugged herself, clutching at her own arms and shoulders as if she could hide, as if she could fold in upon herself until there was nothing left. "Not true," she whispered. "Not my fault." She crouched lower, whimpering, her forehead almost touching the ground.

"Mali . . ." Torin glanced around nervously, thinking he heard something. This time he hooked a hand beneath her arm and tugged, not gently.

She lifted her head; her eyes widened. Shrieking a warning, she struck at him, shoving him so hard he stumbled.

A sword whistled through the air where he had been

standing only moments before. Torin wheeled and faced another lizard-man.

The creature struck again, quickly, swinging its sword in a half circle. The deadly blade sliced cleanly through Torin's robe and the flesh beneath.

A streak of fire flashed up Torin's ribs into his shoulder. He felt the warm slickness of blood gush down his right side.

His elbow pressed against the wound, Torin staggered sideways, away from Mali, hoping the thing would pursue him. "Run!" he gasped.

Clumsily, trying to stanch the flow of blood from his side, Torin drew his sword, but there was no chance of striking.

This lizard-man, though as lumbering and clumsy as its brother, was quicker. And a better swordsman. The creature swung its huge sword viciously, side to side, up and down as it advanced on Torin.

Torin shifted his sword to his left hand. He barely dodged the blows. His blade felt unbelievably heavy, and his feet seemed to have lost all feeling.

The creature lunged, thrusting, and the sharp edge of the weapon grazed Torin's hand.

He grunted in pain, barely holding on to his sword, barely holding on to consciousness. So much blood. He could feel it pouring down his leg, dripping onto the ground, his life running out rapidly. The next blow, he knew, would be the last.

The lizard-man raised its sword high for the killing stroke.

Then Torin's vision began to play tricks on him. It seemed that the creature's sword slowed as it began its descent. Mali scrambled, also in slow motion, on hands and knees, not away to safety, but toward Torin, toward the creature.

Torin's scream came from somewhere far away, warped and twisted. He threw himself forward to shield her, and the movement was like swimming through deep sand. Too slow. Too late.

Her hand came up, slowly, slowly, rising up into the air. The Aquara of the Kedasa was clutched in her fist. It shone in the sun like a jewel in firelight, all blue fire and golden rainbow.

The lizard-man's sword crashed into the Aquara, steel clanging against crystal. Metal shrieked and crystal rang with ear-splitting clarity. Blinding lightning erupted.

Moving at normal speed again, the creature yelped and fell backward, its body crackling with a deathly light. Its sword, split asunder, showered down in pieces.

The crystal's blue glow faded, and Mali collapsed into Torin's arms. She was so limp that his breath caught fearfully in his throat. Carefully, he turned her over. A pulse beat strongly beneath the fair skin of her neck, and he groaned with relief.

A moment later, her eyelids fluttered open. She jerked up, her eyes darting wildly, searching for the creature.

Its body lay still, one of its leathery wings crackled into pieces like stone. Pieces of the sword littered the body.

Mali stared at the crystal lying in her palm. It no longer glittered with the rainbow colors of the desert. It gleamed a transparent silver-blue—a mixture of sky and clear water and sisc flower. The symbols etched into the crystal showed clearly now against the background—two teardrop shapes scribed in unending lines.

"I don't understand. What happened?" Mali whispered. Her soft, confused words trailed off as she looked from the crystal to the body of the creature and its shattered sword.

Torin touched the Aquara warily. It felt smooth despite the etched symbols, and his fingers warmed slightly, pleasantly. Gone was the irritating, discomfiting tingle. "You do understand," Torin told her. Without a word, he took Mali's free hand and guided it through the torn edges of his robe to the bleeding wound above his ribs. "You have only to believe."

Mali stared at him, wide-eyed, unsure.

He pressed her hand tighter against his wound, and though his eyelids felt as if they were too heavy to remain open, he tried to meet her gaze with his own unwavering belief. "Believe, Mali. Believe what the goddess told you."

Holding the crystal to her breast, Mali nodded. She closed her eyes and took a deep, deep breath and exhaled slowly.

Torin twitched as the energy poured into him, gushed as if it were spilled, as if the souls of hundreds were flowing into his veins. Energy and heat and spirit, tinged blue, chased away shadow and death. Life flowed, pulsing. He could feel his own blood gliding beneath his skin, the air in his lungs caressing him inside.

Mali gasped and sank backward, withdrawing her touch and the influence of the crystal.

Exhilarated with the spirit coursing through him, Torin pulled apart the cut edges of his robe and peered at the wound. It was closed, no longer bleeding, but it had not healed, not completely. It still throbbed, but it was closed. It was enough for now.

"Torin?" Mali whispered. Her hand cupped his cheek.

Her power flowed into him, the healing touch, the loving warmth. He covered her hand with his, found it sticky with blood but still so warm, so soothing. He kissed her palm, and when she didn't protest, he kissed her full lips, too, lightly, quickly, then pulled back.

"Biar," he said, still holding her hand.

She stiffened. "But how can I? He's dead."

Torin covered the hand holding the crystal. "You have been chosen by the goddess. How can you not?"

Mali shivered. She shook her head in assent, and Torin helped her to her feet. Together they went to Biar's body.

Holding the crystal between her palms, Mali glanced at Torin for reassurance. Then she turned her beautiful face upward, to the canopy of trees and the sky peeking through. "Please, Blessed Mishakal. Help me."

Mali closed her eyes and held the crystal to her heart as she had before. Nothing happened.

She laid the crystal on Biar's chest and cupped her hands around the blade embedded in his chest. The blue within the crystal began to glow, brighter and brighter until it encompassed Biar's body and Mali.

Then Torin, too, was enclosed within the soft, healing light. The remainder of his exhaustion slipped away. He felt the skin across his wound and the muscle beneath ripple and shift as it healed. He knew if he looked now, the skin would be flawless, as unblemished as when he was a child. But the physical comfort was nothing compared to the peace, the joy, in his heart.

The light intensified, became a blue as brilliant as a summer's sky, as sparkling as the surface of a pool. With tears flowing silently down her face, Mali wrapped her fingers around the blade of the knife where it had entered Biar's flesh. The crystalline glow cascaded along her fingers, down onto the body, wrapping bright streamers around the knife. Slowly Mali pulled the blade from the wound.

No flow of blood followed the removal. The wound closed, and a second later, there was not even a scar left. Mali's hands fell away, and she drooped back on her heels.

Torin held his breath as the blue glow dimmed.

Then, with a jerk, Biar's thin chest heaved. He gasped in a lungful of air, and his eyes fluttered open, wide and surprised. He touched his chest where the knife had been. "Mali," he whispered, smiling up at her. "I dreamed the souls of the Kedasa came to save me."

Mali stared at the boy, disbelief and delight mingled on her face. When she turned to Torin, holding up the crystal for him to see, the joy in her eyes burned like fire, brighter than the sun at noon. " 'Bring out the souls that are in darkness,' " she said, musing, awed. "Now King Lorac will have to believe me!"

Torin touched the Aquara. It was blue now, the clean, clear blue of sky and pure water. Instead of the cold, jittering sensation of ants prickling his skin, he felt the pleasure of Mali's power, of Mali's purpose.

And his own.

"If your king does not accept your word, Mali, I will tell him myself."

The Best

Margaret Weis

A story from the ancient times . . .

I KNEW THE FOUR WOULD COME. MY URGENT plea
had brought them. Whatever their motives—and, among
this diverse group, I knew those motives were mixed—
they were here.

The best. The very best.

I stood in the door of the Bitter Ale Inn and, surveying
them, my heart was easier than it had been in many, many
days.

The four did not sit together. Of course, they didn't
know each other, except perhaps by reputation. Each sat
at his or her own table, eating, drinking quietly. Not making a show of themselves. They didn't need to. They were
the best. But though they said nothing with their
mouths—using them for the bitter ale so famous in these
parts—they were putting their eyes to work: sizing each
other up, taking each other's measure. I was thankful to
see that each seemed to like what he or she saw. I wanted
no bad blood between members of this group.

Sitting at the very front of the inn, short in stature, but
large in courage—was Orin. The dwarf was renowned
through these parts for his skill with his axe, but then so
were most dwarves. His blade—Splithair—lay on the table
before him, where he could keep both an eye and a loving
hand on it. Orin's true talent lay beneath a mountain, as the
saying went. He had traversed more dragon caves than any
other dwarf who had ever lived. And he had never once lost
his way, either there or (more important) back out again.
Many a treasure-hunter owed his life—and about a third of
the treasure—to his guide, Orin Dark-seer.

Seated near the dwarf, at the best table the Bitter Ale
had to offer, was a woman of incredible beauty. Her hair

was long and black as a moonless night; her eyes drank in men's souls the way the dwarf drank ale. The tavern's regulars—a sorry lot of ne'er-do-wells—would have been nosing around her, their tongues hanging out, but for the marks on her clothes.

She was well dressed, don't mistake me. The cloth she wore was the finest, most expensive velvet in all the land. Its blue color gleamed in the firelight. It was the silver embroidery on the cuffs of her robes and around the hemline that warned off the cheek-pinchers and kiss-snatchers. Pentagrams and stars and intertwined circles and suchlike. Cabalistic marks. Her beautiful eyes met mine, and I bowed to Ulanda the sorceress, come all the way from her fabled castle hidden in the Blue Mist Forest.

Seated near the door—as near the door as he could get and still remain in the inn—was the one member of the four I knew well. I knew him because I was the one who had turned the key in his prison cell and set him free. He was thin and quick, with a mop of red hair and green roguish eyes that could charm a widow out of her life savings and leave her loving him for it. Those slender fingers of his could slide in and out of a pocket as fast as his knife could cut a purse from a belt. He was good, so good he wasn't often caught. Reynard Deft-hand had made one small mistake. He'd try to lift a purse from me.

Directly across the room from Reynard—dark balancing light in the scales of creation—was a man of noble bearing and stern countenance. The regulars left him alone, too, out of respect for his long and shining sword and the white surcoat he wore, marked with the silver rose. Eric of Truestone, Knight of the Rose, a holy paladin. I was as amazed to see him as I was pleased. I had sent my messengers to the High Clerist's Tower, begging the knights for aid. I knew they would respond—they were honor-bound. But they had responded by sending me their best.

All four the best, the very best. I looked at them and I felt awed, humbled.

"You should be closing down for the night, Marian," I said, turning to the pretty lass who tended bar.

The four dragon-hunters looked at me, and not one of them moved. The regulars, on the other hand, took the hint. They quaffed their ale and left without a murmur. I hadn't been in these parts long—newly come to my job—and, of course, they'd put me to the test. I'd been forced to teach them to respect me. That had been a week ago and one, so I heard, was still laid up. Several of the others winced and rubbed their cracked heads as they hurried past me, all politely wishing me good-night.

"I'll lock the door," I said to Marian.

She, too, left, also wishing me—with a saucy smile—a good night. I knew well she'd like to make my good night a better one, but I had business.

When she was gone, I shut and bolted the door. This clearly made Reynard nervous (he was already looking for another escape route), so I came quickly to the point.

"No need to ask why you're here. You've each come in response to my plea for help. I am Gondar, King Frederick's seneschal. I am the one who sent you the message. I thank you for your quick response, and I welcome you, well, most of you"—I cast a stern glance at Reynard, who grinned—"to Fredericksborough."

Sir Eric rose and made me a courteous bow. Ulanda looked me over with her wonderful eyes. Orin grunted. Reynard was jingling coins in his pocket. The regulars would find themselves without ale money tomorrow, I guessed.

"You all know why I sent for you," I continued. "At least, you know part of the reason. The part I could make public."

"Please be seated, Seneschal," said Ulanda, with a graceful gesture. "And tell us the part you couldn't make public."

The knight joined us, as did the dwarf. Reynard was going to, but Ulanda warned him off with a look. Not the least bit offended, he grinned again and leaned against the bar.

The four waited politely for me to continue.

"I tell you this in absolute confidentiality," I said, lowering my voice. "As you know, our good king, Frederick, has journeyed to the north on invitation from his half brother, the Duke of Norhampton. There were many in the court who advised His Majesty not to go. None of us trust the twisted, covetous duke. But His Majesty was ever a loving sibling and north he went. Now, our worst fears have been realized. The duke is holding the king hostage, demanding in ransom seven coffers filled with gold, nine coffers filled with silver, and twelve coffers filled with precious jewels."

"By the eye of Paladine, we should burn this duke's castle to the ground," said Eric of the Rose. His hand clenched over his sword's hilt.

"We would never see His Majesty alive again." I shook my head.

"This is not why you brought us here," growled Orin. "Not to rescue your king. He may be a good king, for all I know, but . . ." The dwarf shrugged.

"Yes, but you don't care whether a human king lives or dies, do you, Orin?" I said with a smile. "No reason you should. The dwarves have their own king."

"And there are some of us," said Ulanda softly, "who have no king at all."

I wondered if the rumors I'd heard about her were true, that she lured young men to her castle and kept them until she tired of them, then changed them into wolves, forced to guard her dwelling place. At night, it was said, you could hear their howls of anguish. Looking into those lovely eyes, I found myself thinking it might just be worth it!

I wrenched myself back to the business at hand.

"I have not told you the worst," I said. "I collected the ransom. This is a wealthy kingdom. The nobles dipped into their treasuries. Their lady wives sacrificed their jewels. The treasure was loaded into a wagon, ready to be sent north when . . ."

I cleared my throat, wished I had drawn myself a mug of ale. "A huge red dragon swept out of the sky, attacked the treasure caravan. I tried to stand and fight, but"—my face burned in shame—"I've never known such paralyzing fear. The next thing I knew, I was facefirst on the ground, shivering in terror. The guard fled in panic.

"The great dragon settled down on the King's Highway. It leisurely devoured the horses, then, lifting the wagon containing the treasure in its claws, the cursed beast flew away."

"Dragonfear," said Orin, as one long experienced in such things.

"Though it has never happened to me, I've heard the dragonfear can be devastating." Sir Eric rested his hand pityingly on mine. "It was foul magic that unmanned you, Seneschal. No need for shame."

"*Foul* magic," repeated Ulanda, casting the knight a dark look. I could see she was thinking what an excellent wolf he would make.

"I saw the treasure." Reynard heaved a gusty sigh. "It was a beautiful sight. And there must be more, lots more, in that dragon's lair."

"There is," said Orin. "Do you think yours is the only kingdom this dragon has robbed, Seneschal? My people were hauling a shipment of golden nuggets from our mines in the south when a red dragon—pull out my beard if it's not the same one—swooped out of the skies and made off with it!"

"Golden nuggets!" Reynard licked his lips. "How much were they worth, all told?"

Orin cast him a baleful glance. "Never you mind, Light-finger."

"The name is Deft-hand," Reynard said, but the rest ignored him.

"I have received word from my sisters in the east," Ulanda was saying, "that this same dragon is responsible for the theft of several of our coven's most powerful arcane artifacts. I would describe them to you, but they are very secret. And very dangerous, to the inexperienced," she added pointedly, for Reynard's sake.

"We, too, have suffered by this wyrm," said Eric grimly. "Our brethren to the west sent us as a gift a holy relic—a finger bone of Vinus Solamnus. The dragon attacked the escort, slaughtered them to a man, carried away our artifact."

Ulanda laughed, made a face. "I don't believe it! What

would the dragon want with a moldy old finger bone?"

The knight's face hardened. "The finger bone was encased in a diamond, big around as an apple. The diamond was carried in a chalice made of gold, encrusted with rubies and emeralds. The chalice was carried on a platter made of silver, set with a hundred sapphires."

"I thought you holy knights took vows of poverty," Reynard insinuated slyly. "Maybe I should start going to church again."

Eric rose majestically to his feet. Glaring at the thief, the knight drew his sword. Reynard sidled over behind me.

"Hold, Sir Knight," I said, standing. "The route to the dragon's lair leads up a sheer cliff with nary a hand- or foothold in sight."

The knight eyed Reynard's slender fingers and wiry body. Sheathing his sword, the knight sat back down.

"You've discovered the lair!" Reynard cried. He was trembling, so excited, I feared he might hug me.

"Is this true, Seneschal?" Ulanda leaned near me. I could smell musk and spice. Her fingertips were cool on my hand. "Have you found the dragon's lair?"

"I pray to Paladine you have! Gladly would I leave this life, spend eternity in the blessed realm of Paladine, if I could have a chance to fight this wyrm!" Eric vowed. Lifting a sacred medallion he wore around his neck to his lips, he kissed it to seal his holy oath.

"I lost my king's ransom," I said. "I took a vow neither to eat nor sleep until I had tracked the beast to its lair. Many weary days and nights I followed the trail—a shining coin fallen to the ground, a jewel spilled from the wagon. The trail led straight to a peak known as Black Mountain. A day I waited, patient, watching. I was rewarded. I saw the dragon leave its lair. I know how to get inside."

Reynard began to dance around the tavern, singing and snapping his long fingers. Eric of the Rose actually smiled. Orin Dark-seer ran his thumb lovingly over his axe-blade. Ulanda kissed my cheek.

"You must come visit me some night, Seneschal, when this adventure is ended," she whispered.

The four of them and I spent the night in the inn, were up well before dawn to begin our journey.

*　*　*　*　*

The Black Mountain loomed before us, its peak hidden by a perpetual cloud of gray smoke. The mountain is named for its shining black rock, belched up from the very bowels of the world. Sometimes the mountain still rumbles, just to remind us that it is alive, but none living could remember the last time it spewed flame.

We reached it by late afternoon. The sun's rays shone red on the cliff face we would have to climb. By craning my neck, I could see the gaping dark hole that was the entrance to the dragon's lair.

"Not a handhold in sight. By Paladine, you weren't exaggerating, Seneschal," said Eric, frowning as he ran his hand over the smooth black rock.

Reynard laughed. "Bah! I've climbed castle walls that were as smooth as milady's— Well, let's just say they were smooth."

The thief looped a long length of rope over his shoulder. He started to add a bag full of spikes and a hammer, but I stopped him.

"The dragon might have returned. If so, the beast would hear you driving the spikes into the rock." I glanced upward. "The way is not far, just difficult. Once you make it, lower the rope down to us. We can climb it."

Reynard agreed. He studied the cliff face a moment, all seriousness now, no sign of a grin. Then, to the amazement of all of us watching, he attached himself to the rock like a spider and began to climb.

I had known Reynard was good, but I must admit, I had not known how good. I watched him crawl up that sheer cliff face, digging his fingers into minute cracks, his feet scrabbling for purchase, hanging on, sometimes, by effort of will alone. I was impressed. He was the best. No other man living could have made it up that cliff.

"The gods are with us in our holy cause," said Eric reverently, watching Reynard crawl up the black rock like a lizard.

Ulanda stifled a yawn, covered her mouth with a dainty hand. Orin stomped around the foot of the cliff in impatience. I continued to watch Reynard, admiring his work. He had reached the entrance to the cavern, disappeared inside. In a moment, he came back out, indicated with a wave of his hand that all was safe.

Reynard lowered the rope down to us. Unfortunately, the rope he'd brought was far too short. We couldn't reach it. Orin began to curse loudly. Ulanda laughed, snapped her fingers, spoke a word. The rope quivered, and suddenly it was exactly the right length.

Eric eyed the magiced rope dubiously, but it was his only way up. He grabbed hold of it, then—appearing to think of something—he turned to the sorceress.

"My lady, I fear your delicate hands are not meant for climbing ropes, nor are you dressed for scaling mountains. If you will forgive me the liberty, I will carry you up the cliff."

"Carry me!" Ulanda stared at him, then she laughed again.

Eric stiffened; his face went rigid and cold. "Your pardon, my lady—"

"Forgive me, Sir Knight," Ulanda said smoothly. "But I am not a weak and helpless damsel. And it would be best if you remembered that. All of you."

So saying, Ulanda drew a lacy, silken handkerchief from her pocket and spread it upon the ground. Placing her feet upon the handkerchief, she spoke words that were like the sound of tinkling chimes. The handkerchief became hard as steel. It began to rise slowly into the air, bearing the sorceress with it.

Sir Eric's eyes widened. He made the sign against evil.

Ulanda floated calmly up the cliff face. Reynard was on hand to assist her with the landing at the mouth of the cave. The thief's eyes nearly bugged out of his head. He was practically drooling. We could all hear his words.

"What a second-story man you'd make! Lady, I'll give you half—well, a fourth of my treasure for that scrap of cloth."

Ulanda picked up the steel platform, snapped it once in the air. Once again, the handkerchief was silk and lace. She placed it carefully in a pocket of her robes. The thief's eyes followed it all the way.

"It is not for sale," Ulanda said, and she shrugged. "You wouldn't find it of much value anyway. If anyone touches it, other than myself, the handkerchief will wrap itself around the unfortunate person's nose and mouth. It will smother him to death."

She smiled at Reynard sweetly. He eyed her, decided she was telling the truth, gulped, and turned hastily away.

"May Paladine preserve me," Eric said dourly. Laying his hand upon the rope, he started to climb.

He was strong, that knight. Encased in heavy plate armor and chain mail, his sword hanging from his side, he pulled himself up the cliff with ease. The dwarf was quick to follow, running up the rope nimbly. I took my time. It was nearly evening now, but the afternoon sun had warmed the rock. Hauling myself up that rope was hot work. I slipped once, giving myself the scare of a lifetime. But I managed to hang on, heaved a sign of relief when Eric pulled me up over the ledge and into the cool shadows of the cavern.

"Where's the dwarf?" I asked, noticing only three of my companions were around.

"He went ahead to scout the way," said Eric.

I nodded, glad for the chance to rest. Reynard drew up the rope, hid it beneath a rock for use on the way back. I glanced around. All along the sides of the cavern, I could see marks left by the dragon's massive body scraping against the rock. We were examining these when Orin returned, his bearded face split in a wide smile.

"You are right, Seneschal. This is the way to the dragon's lair. And this proves it."

Orin held his find up to the light. It was a golden nugget. Reynard eyed it covetously, and I knew then and there it was going to cause trouble.

"This proves it!" Orin repeated, his eyes shining bright as the gold. "This is the beast's hole. We've got him! Got him now!"

Eric of the Rose, a grim look on his face, drew his sword and started for a huge tunnel leading off the cavern's entrance. Shocked, Orin caught hold of the knight, pulled him back.

"Are you daft, man?" the dwarf demanded. "Will you go walking in the dragon's front door? Why don't you just ring the bell, let him know we're here?"

"What other way is there?" Eric asked, nettled at Orin's superior tone.

"The back way," said the dwarf cunningly. "The secret way. All dragons keep a back exit, just in case. We'll use that."

"You're saying we have to climb round to the other side of this bloody mountain?" Reynard protested. "After all the work it took to get here?"

"Naw, Light-finger!" Orin scoffed. "We'll go *through* the mountain. Safer, easier. Follow me."

He headed for what looked to me like nothing more than a crack in the wall. But, once we had all squeezed inside, we discovered a tunnel that led even deeper into the mountain.

"This place is blacker than the Dark Queen's heart," muttered Eric, as we took our first few tentative steps inside. Although he had spoken in a low voice, his words echoed alarmingly.

"Hush!" the dwarf growled. "What do you mean dark? I can see perfectly."

"But we humans can't! Do we dare risk a light?" I whispered.

"We won't get far without one," Eric grumbled. He'd already nearly brained himself on a low-hanging rock. "What about a torch?"

"Torches smoke. And it's rumored there're other things living in this mountain besides the dragon!" Reynard said ominously.

"Will this do?" asked Ulanda.

Removing a jeweled wand from her belt, she held it up. She spoke no word, but—as if offended by the darkness—

the wand began to shine with a soft white light.

Orin shook his head over the frailty of humans and stumped off down the tunnel. We followed after.

The path led down and around and over and under and into and out of and up and sideways and across . . . a veritable maze. How Orin kept from getting lost or mixed up was beyond me. All of us had doubts (Reynard expressed his loudly), but Orin never wavered.

We soon lost track of time, wandering in the darkness beneath the mountain, but I would guess that we ended up walking most of the night. If we had not found the coin, we still would have guessed the dragon's presence, just by the smell. It wasn't heavy or rank, didn't set us gagging or choking. It was a scent, a breath, a hint of blood and sulphur, gold and iron. It wasn't pervasive, but drifted through the narrow corridors like the dust, teasing, taunting.

Ulanda wrinkled her nose in disgust. She'd just complained breathlessly that she couldn't stand another moment in this "stuffy hole" when Orin brought us to a halt. Grinning slyly, he looked round at us.

"This is it," he said.

"This is what?" Eric asked dubiously, staring at yet another crack in the wall. (We'd seen a lot of cracks!)

"It leads to the dragon's other entrance," said the dwarf.

Squeezing through the crack, we found ourselves in another tunnel, this one far larger than any we'd found yet. We couldn't see daylight, but we could smell fresh air, so we knew the tunnel connected with the outside. Ulanda held her wand up to the wall, and there again were the marks made by the dragon's body. To clinch the matter, a few red scales glittered on the ground.

Orin Dark-seer had done the impossible. He'd taken us clean through the mountain. The dwarf was pretty pleased with himself, but his pleasure was short-lived.

We stopped for a rest, to drink some water and eat a bite of food to keep up our energy. Ulanda was sitting beside me, telling me in a low voice of the wonders of her castle, when suddenly Orin sprang to his feet.

"Thief!" The dwarf howled. He leapt at Reynard. "Give it back!"

I was standing; so was Reynard, who managed to put me in between himself and the enraged dwarf.

"My gold nugget!" Orin shrieked.

"Share and share alike," Reynard said, bobbing this way and that to avoid the dwarf. "Finders keepers."

Orin began swinging that damn axe of his a bit too near my knees for comfort.

"Shut them up, Seneschal!" Eric ordered me, as if I were one of his foot soldiers. "They'll bring the dragon down on us!"

"Fools! I'll put an end to this!" Ulanda reached her hand into a silken pouch she wore on her belt.

I think we may well have lost both thief and guide at that moment, but we suddenly had far greater problems.

"Orin! Behind you!" I shouted.

Seeing by the expression of sheer terror on my face that this was no trick, Orin whirled around.

A knight—or what had once been a knight—was walking toward us. His armor covered bone, not flesh. His helm rattled on a bare and bloodstained skull. He held a sword in his skeletal hand. Behind him, I saw what seemed an army of these horrors, though there were—in reality—only six or seven.

"I've heard tell of this!" Eric said, awed. "These were once living men, who dared attack this dragon. The wyrm killed them and now forces their rotting corpses to serve him!"

"I'll put it out of its misery," Orin cried. Bounding forward, the dwarf struck at the undead warrior with his axe. The blade severed the knight's knees at the joint. The skeleton toppled. The dwarf laughed.

"No need to trouble yourselves over this lot," he told us. "Stand back."

The dwarf went after the second. But at that moment, the first skeleton picked up its bones, began putting itself back together! Within moments, it was whole again. The skeleton brought its sword down on the dwarf's head. Fortunately for Orin, he was wearing a heavy steel helm. The sword did no damage, but the blow sent the dwarf reeling.

Ulanda already had her hand in her pouch. She drew out a noxious powder, tossed it onto the undead warrior nearest her. The skeleton went up in a whoosh of flame that nearly incinerated the thief, who had been attempting to lift a jeweled dagger from the undead warrior's belt. After that, Reynard very wisely took himself out of the way, watched the fight from a corner.

Eric of the Rose drew his sword, but he did not attack. Holding his blade by the hilt, he raised it in front of one of the walking skeletons. "I call on Paladine to free these noble knights of the curse that binds them to this wretched life."

The undead warrior kept coming, its bony hand clutching a rusting sword. Eric held his ground, stood fast, repeating his prayer in sonorous Solamnic. The skeletal warrior raised its sword for the deathblow. Eric gazed at it steadfastly, never wavering in his faith.

I watched with that terrible fascination that freezes a man in his tracks until the end.

"Paladine!" Eric gave a great shout, raised his sword to the heavens.

The skeletal knight dropped down in a pile of dust at the knight's feet.

Orin, who had been exchanging blows with two corpses for some time and was now getting the worst of the battle, beat a strategic retreat. Ulanda with her magic and Eric with his faith took care of the remainder of the skeletal warriors.

I had drawn my sword, but, seeing that my help wasn't needed, I watched in admiration. When the warriors were either reduced to dust or smoldering ash, the two returned. Ulanda's hair wasn't even mussed. Eric hadn't broken into a sweat.

"There are not two in this land who could have done what you did," I said to them, and I meant it.

"I am good at anything I undertake," Ulanda said. She wiped dust from her hands. "Very good," she added with a charming smile and a glance at me from beneath her long eyelashes.

"My god Paladine was with me," Eric said humbly.

The battered dwarf glowered. "Meaning to say my god Reorx wasn't?"

"The good knight means nothing of the sort." I was quick to end the argument. "Without you, Orin Dark-seer, we would be food for the dragon right now. Why do you think the skeleton men attacked us? Because we are drawing too near the dragon's lair, and that is due entirely to your expertise. No one else in this land could have brought us this far safely, and we all know it."

At this, I glanced pointedly at Eric, who took the hint and bowed courteously, if a bit stiffly, to the dwarf. Ulanda rolled her lovely eyes, but muttered something gracious.

I gave Reynard a swift kick in the pants, and the thief reluctantly handed over the golden nugget, which seemed to mean more to the dwarf than our words of praise. Orin thanked us all, of course, but his attention was on the gold. He examined it suspiciously, as if worried that Reynard might have tried to switch the real nugget with a fake. The dwarf bit down it, polished it on his doublet. Finally certain the gold was real, Orin thrust it beneath his leather armor for safekeeping.

So absorbed was the dwarf in his gold that he didn't notice Reynard lifting his purse from behind. I did, but I took care not to mention it.

As I said, we were close to the dragon's lair.

We moved ahead, doubly cautious, keeping sharp watch for any foe. We were deep, deep inside the mountain now. It was silent. Too silent.

"You'd think we'd hear something," Eric whispered to me. "The dragon breathing, if nothing else. A beast that large would sound like a bellows down here."

"Perhaps this means he's not home," Reynard said.

"Or perhaps it means we've come to a dead end," said Ulanda icily.

Rounding a corner of the tunnel, we all stopped and stared. The sorceress was right. Ahead of us, blocking our path, was a solid rock wall.

The darkness grew darker at that moment. All hint of outside air had long since been left behind. The scent of blood and sulphur, now enhanced by a dank, chill, musty smell, was strong. And so was the scent of gold. I could smell it and so, I knew, could my companions. Our imaginations, I suppose, or perhaps wishful thinking. But maybe not. Gold has a smell—its own metal smell and, added to that, the stink of the sweat from all the hands that have touched it and coveted it and grasped it and lost it. That was the smell, and it was sweet perfume to everyone in that cave. Sweet and frustrating, for—seemingly—we had no way to reach it.

Orin's cheeks flushed. He tugged on his beard, cast us all a sidelong glance. "This must be the way," he muttered, kicking disconsolately at the rock.

"We'll have to go back," Eric said grimly. "Paladine is teaching me a lesson. I should have faced the wyrm in honorable battle. None of this skulking about like a—"

"Thief?" Reynard said brightly. "Very well, Sir Knight, you can go back to the front door, if you want. I will sneak in by the window."

With this, Reynard closed his eyes and, flattening himself against the rock wall, he seemed—to all appearances—to be making love to it. His hands crawled over it, his fingers poking and prodding. He even whispered what sounded like cooing and coaxing words. Suddenly, with a triumphant grin, he placed his feet in two indentations in the bottom of the wall, put his hands in two cracks at the top, and pressed.

The rock wall shivered, then it began to slide to one side! A shaft of reddish light beamed out. The thief jumped off the wall, waved his hand at the opening he'd created.

"A secret door," Orin said. "I knew it all along."

"You want to go around to the front now?" Reynard asked the knight slyly.

Eric glared at the thief, but he appeared to be having second thoughts about meeting the dragon face-to-face in an honorable fight. He drew his sword, waited for the wall to open completely so that we could see inside.

The light pouring out from the doorway was extremely bright. All of us blinked and rubbed our eyes, trying to adjust them to the sudden brilliance after the darkness of the tunnels. We waited, listening for the dragon. None of us had a doubt but that we had discovered the beast's dwelling place.

We heard nothing. All was deathly quiet.

"The dragon's not home!" Reynard rubbed his hands. "Hiddukel the Trickster is with me today!" He made a dash for the entrance, but Sir Eric's hand fell, like doom, on his shoulder.

"I will lead," he said. "It is my right."

Sword in hand, a prayer on his lips, the holy paladin walked into the dragon's lair.

Reynard crept right behind him. Orin, moving more cautiously, followed the thief. Ulanda had taken a curious-looking scroll from her belt. Holding it fast, she entered the lair after the dwarf. I drew my dagger. Keeping watch behind me, I entered last.

The door began to rumble shut.

I halted. "We're going to be trapped in here!" I called out as loudly as I dared.

The others paid no attention to me. They had discovered the dragon's treasure room.

The bright light's source was a pit of molten rock bubbling in a corner of the gigantic underground chamber. The floor of the cavern had been worn smooth, probably by the rubbing of the dragon's enormous body. A great, glittering heap, tall as His Majesty's castle, was piled together on the cavern floor.

Gathered here was every beautiful, valuable, and precious object in the kingdom. Gold shone red in the firelight, jewels of every color of the rainbow winked and sparkled. The silver reflected the smiles of the dragonhunters. And, best of all, the cavern was uninhabited.

Sir Eric fell on his knees and began to pray.

Ulanda stared, openmouthed.

Orin was weeping into his beard with joy.

But by now, the secret door had slammed shut.

Not one of them noticed.

"The dragon's not home!" Reynard shrieked, and he made a dive for the treasure pile.

My treasure pile.

The thief began pawing through the gold.

My gold.

I walked up behind him.

"Never jump to conclusions," I said.

With my dagger, I gave him the death a thief deserves. I stabbed him in the back.

"I thought you should at least have a look," I said to him kindly, gesturing to my hoard. "Since you're the best."

Reynard died then—the most astonished looking corpse I'd ever seen. I still don't think he'd quite figured things out.

But Ulanda had. She was smart, that sorceress. She guessed the truth immediately, if a bit late—even before I took off my ring of shapechanging.

Now, at last, after weeks of being cramped into that tiny form, I could stretch out. My body grew, slowly taking on its original, immense shape, almost filling the cavern. I held the ring up in front of her eyes.

"You were right," I told her, the jewel sparkling in what was now a claw. "Your coven did possess many powerful arcane objects. This is just one of them."

Ulanda stared at me in terror. She tried to use her scroll, but the dragonfear was too much for her. The words of magic wouldn't come to her parched, pale lips.

She'd been sweet enough to invite me to spend the night, and so I did her a favor. I let her see, before she died, a demonstration of the magic now in my possession. Appropriately, it was one of my most prized artifacts—a necklace made out of magical wolves' teeth—that encircled her lovely neck and tore out her throat.

All this time, Orin Dark-seer had been hacking at my hind leg with his axe. I let him get in a few licks. The dwarf hadn't been a bad sort, after all, and he'd done me a favor by showing me the weakness in my defenses. When he seemed likely to draw blood, however, I tired of the contest. Picking him up, I tossed him in the pool of molten lava. Eventually, he'd become part of the mountain—a fitting end for a dwarf. I trust he appreciated it.

That left Sir Eric, who had wanted, all along, to meet me in honorable battle. I granted him his wish.

He faced me bravely, calling on Paladine to fight at his side.

Paladine must have busy with something else just then, for he didn't make an appearance.

Eric died in a blaze of glory.

Well, he died in a blaze.

I trust his soul went straight to the Dome of Creation, where it's my guess his god must have had some pretty fancy explaining to do.

They were dead now. All four.

I put out the fire, swept up the knight's ashes. Then I shoved the other two corpses out the secret door. The thief and the sorceress would take the place of the skeletal warriors I'd been forced to sacrifice to keep up appearances.

Crawling back to my treasure pile, I tidied up the gold a bit, where the thief had disturbed it. Then I climbed on top, spread myself out, and burrowed deeply and luxuriously into the gold and silver and jewels. I spread my wings protectively over the treasure, even paused to admire the effect of the firelight shining on my red scales. I wrapped my long tail around the golden nuggets of the dwarves, stretched my body comfortably out over the jewels of the knights, laid my head down on the magical treasure of the sorceress's coven.

I was tired, but satisfied. My plan had worked out wonderfully well. I had rid myself of them.

They'd been the best. The very best.

Sooner or later, separately or together, they would have come after me. And they might have caught me napping.

I settled myself onto the treasure more comfortably, closed my eyes. I'd earned my rest.

And I could sleep peacefully . . . now.

The Hunt

Kevin Stein

Galan rose from his cold bed in the muck. He had fallen asleep some time ago, exhausted from his journey. He felt his legs almost collapse beneath him in the damp darkness as, with an effort of will, he forced himself to stand.

The swamp offered none of the comforts Galan had known before he began his hunt for the black dragon, Borac. He had finally found a spot that the mushrooms had not quite started to devour, the murky waters had not yet embraced. He could not remember how long he had lain sleeping in this place.

With a groan, he straightened, flexing his muscles beneath his armor. He wiped away most of the mud that covered his mail, carefully removing the last traces of swampy filth from the engraved Solamnic roses.

The light from the twin moons trickled slowly through the curtain of mists hanging in the air. Eerie shadows of red and silver danced on the dark leaves, setting Galan on edge more than he would have liked to admit. A breeze that he could barely feel through his plate armor shifted the reeds and rushes. Yet he shivered.

The thought of the black dragon made the knight shiver again, but with fury. That fury had kept him going, moving untold miles during his hunt. He had seen the world change while the hunt continued, but he paid little heed. The War of the Lance might be over, but that did not mean evil had been driven from Krynn. As a Knight of Solamnia, it was Galan's duty to purge the land of vile creatures. He was the spirit of vengeance summoned by the dragon's rampage.

Shaking his head, he muttered through gritted teeth, "Soon, Borac. Soon."

Galan sniffed at the midnight vapors, smelling nothing

but corruption and the too familiar scent of his enemy. He had chased Borac for many seasons, tracking, hunting, and finally, cornering. He would make his last stand in this swamp before the ravages of age took too great a toll on his body.

"Soon, Borac!" he hissed, his anger so bright within his soul that he knew he could travel by its light forever in search of his prey. He smelled the dragon's black acid breath. His dragonlance cut the air in a dazzling series of maneuvers, one-handed, two-handed, thrusting and parrying. "Soon, Borac, I will send you to your grave."

* * * * *

Galan checked his map, not because he was lost, but because he wanted to know the exact place of Borac's death. Nordmaar was far north of the Khalkist Mountains. According to his map, which was slowly disintegrating due to the damp and rot of the swamp, the city of Valkinard was to the west.

The scent of his prey led the knight forward. Galan clenched his jaw tightly. The need for the hunt was the very thing that set him on his course. The hunt was all he had in the world. The hunt sustained him and would continue to do so right through his last, dire encounter.

Galan stopped a moment and lowered his pack onto a spot of soft earth. Lifting his armored leg from the waters, he shook off the leeches that clung hungrily to what flesh they could find. The cold mists from the swamp continued to penetrate the padded armor beneath his mail, and he felt sure he would never be dry again.

Glancing down at the earth, the knight saw something unusual in the way the mud settled against the black waters of the swamp. He stared a moment longer and wondered why the water bubbled with strange regularity. There was no sign of any living thing that might cause undue churning of the silt.

Galan bent his legs and reached down with his hands. The foulness of the bog sickened him, but he forced his hands to probe through the darkness. He felt the contour of the mud change, dipping evenly in several places. At the end of each shallow there was another depression in the shape of a rough triangle.

The knight rose from the water. His lips pulled back in a feral grin. The mark was that of a dragon's claw, heading in the direction Galan was pursuing. He spit, running his hands over his face. The dragon would soon be dead.

Galan held still and listened, brandishing the dragonlance; its barbed tip caught rays of blood and silver.

Something screamed. The fearful sound echoed from the depths of the swamp. Galan's heart beat hard in his chest, blotting out other sounds. With great discipline, he calmed himself.

The air shivered around him, the reeds rustled, and the water continued to bubble. Nothing stirred. Letting go the breath he held, Galan planted the dragonlance in the ground, sinking the end-spike in the deep mud.

An immense weight struck him from behind, pummeled his back, dented his armor. He pitched forward into the water, attempted to struggle up from under the stagnation. He could not throw the attacker off his back. He heard trapped gases bubble as decay burned his eyes. He thrashed in panic as his breath ran out.

Galan brought his legs up from underneath him and rolled forward, using the attacker's weight as a counter. His head burst out of the poisonous waters, and he swallowed air, gasping. The thing on his back slid off him. Galan grabbed the dragonlance and brandished its great length, holding it with both hands, set wide apart near the end-spike. He could see nothing.

There was silence. Galan tried to see through the veil of mists that hung lazily about the swamp, but the light from the moons could no longer penetrate. The dragonlance dripped moisture into the water. The drops sounded too loud in his ears.

Instinct and training blended together in Galan's stance. He firmly planted his right foot forward and swung the lance wide to the left. The haft struck something solid, and the knight turned, backing two steps and lunging. He thrust the spear.

The thing screamed, and it seemed that the mists parted with its cry. Galan let the fury of battle guide him, and he pressed forward, cruelly running the shaft farther through the thing's body. It screamed again, and Galan got a glimpse of its face, deathly pale, with long lanks of ragged hair. The knight stared into the shimmering green orbs that were the thing's eyes, and he saw torture and hatred, the desire to kill, the taint of curses. He saw his own reflection staring out from those dying orbs.

The specter writhed painfully on the tip of the drag-onlance, the weapon of heroes. The knight's lips pulled back in a snarl. He spat as he breathed. He lifted the lance, his enemy clinging to it. Rushing forward as quickly as the clutching mud would allow, Galan pierced the center of a dying tree, pinning his foe.

"Die!" he muttered. "Die and curse this place no longer!"

The specter's skull jerked as the creature attempted to yank the lance head from its body. Galan thrust forward again, cracking the tree with his strength. He cruelly twisted the weapon.

The knight withdrew the speartip with a deft pull and stabbed forward again, taking the creature in the throat. The thing threw its head back with a final, terrifying wail.

Knightly plate armor fell into the water. Galan kicked the mail in fury. Before it sank forever beneath the waters, he caught sight of a sculpted rose.

Galan's face worked with nearly uncontrollable rage. He had dispatched a creature so vile that his soul quavered with revulsion. The knight withdrew his weapon from the tree, slowly gaining control over himself.

Galan dug his lance into the soft mud a second time. The fight with the specter continued to make his limbs shake with battle fury, but he ignored the sensation. He checked his map again and saw that the marsh ended nearly sixty miles to the north. He had less than sixty miles to go before he was avenged.

* * * * *

Galan did not think the sun ever shone on the swamp. He had wandered for many hours since the attack of the specter. All he had to show for it was the mud in his boots and the creak in his limbs.

The swamp's vapors shifted constantly, making travel difficult. He had a vague sense of direction but did not consult his compass. From all the time he had spent on the dragon's trail, he knew that he could trust his instincts, even in the Great Moors.

The knight felt himself begin to tire. The journey through the swamp had been a constant struggle. The mud seemed to take on a malevolent hunger, clinging to his every step; the air still had the taint of the dragon, but it had also turned from foul to rot.

The map showed that the swamp was only sixty miles at its farthest reaches. Galan knew that it might go on forever.

The mists were thick, and Galan did not see the rotted forest until he had stumbled over a dead stump. The water was waist-high, and as he waded through it, he was forced to hold the lance above his head. The light from Solinari and Lunitari finally burst through the mists and illuminated the area, giving the knight a clearer view.

Mushrooms grew everywhere, clinging with poisonous life to the rotting wood. The knight felt more leeches penetrate the cracks in his armor and affix themselves to his flesh. The water itself was brackish and black, despite the silver and red light from the heavens. There was no sound other than his passage through the bog. His breath labored as his legs churned the silt, releasing other tenacious life.

A strange scent suddenly filled the air. He peered through the gloom. Galan had the sudden urge to drink, to give his life something clear and wholesome to which to cling, but he remembered that he had drunk the last of the fresh water some time ago.

The ground rose slightly. Galan's knees cleared the

water. He gradually entered an ancient, dead forest. The knight suddenly realized what the mysterious scent must be: the scent of age and decay of the flesh, decay of the spirit. It was a scent with which he was very familiar from distant battlefields.

Galan struggled to keep his footing as the mud and banks of festering rot rose higher. He used the end of the dragonlance for support and almost toppled over into the dark waters when the end-spike split a large tree in half, releasing myriad venomous insects. He found himself drawn forward by the overpowering scent of decay.

Galan stopped at the top of a ridge. In a circle of deep mud lay sleeping the object of his hatred. Borac's great length was curled around itself, black scales blending with the surrounding death of the forest.

Galan had always been certain of his course of action. He would catch up with the huge dragon and pierce it with his lance, driving the evil from the world forever. Krynn would be freed, and past wrongs would be avenged. But the smell of age, now mixed with sickness, gave him pause.

The knight's hands shook as the weak moment passed. His mouth slowly pulled back into a snarl, and the muscles in his legs tightened, ready for action. With a deafening roar, Galan threw himself from the tall ridge-line down into the pit. The hatred and anger he had contained, that which he now personified, ruled his movements. He raised the weapon high above his head.

Galan charged down the remaining length of the slope, kicking up mud and wet splinters. Borac slowly opened his left eye. The knight was not about to give the evil dragon the chance to cast a cursed spell or use the acid that had destroyed so many young lives. He was upon the monster in a moment, his shining lance casting mixed silver and red reflections into the pit.

Borac closed his eye and dug his head deeper into the decay.

Galan stopped abruptly, though his sinews demanded vengeance and his mouth spat blood. He wanted to quench his lust for vengeance in the blood of his foe. Borac should be on the offensive, not cowering in the mud. This was not the confrontation Galan desired. He wondered if this were some trick and for a moment panicked, raising the dragonlance higher to strike an even deadlier blow.

Borac did not move. "Kill me, Galan. Kill me now and end this struggle."

The knight lowered his weapon, but maintained his guard.

Borac opened his left eye again, lifting his head to get a better view of Galan. "Why do you wait, knight? This is the end of your hunt. You have me. Borac. Borac the Reaver. Borac the Destroyer." Before he had finished the last word, the dragon laid his head down again.

In silence, Galan stared at the beast and could not understand why he did not kill the creature he had hunted so long. He stared at the beast and wondered why it did not kill him. The scent of age was almost overwhelming, but the knight concentrated on those two questions.

"What is happening here?" he asked the heavens rhetorically. He relaxed his guard.

"What does it matter, knight?" Borac answered, his voice weary. The dragon's mouth was filled with teeth, but most of them were broken, and the thing's voice had the rasp of an old man's. "Slay me now and finish this hunt."

Galan's head dropped. There seemed to be nothing left in the world but himself and the dragon. The hunt seemed to have never existed, was nothing more than a creation of his hatred.

"I *will* kill you," the knight muttered.

"It should be easy," Borac replied, shifting his weight. "Look at me, Galan. I am eight-hundred-forty-three ages past. My wings are tattered. I am blind in one eye. Those scales that once kept me safe from harm are now rotted with more disease than the whole of these moors can carry. Slay me now and end my pain."

Galan suddenly lifted his head, his eyes blazing once again. "Your pain? Your pain! What of *my* pain?"

The knight brandished the dragonlance threateningly. He walked around the bulk of the dying dragon. "Why should I grant you your death as a boon?"

Borac laughed. "What did I do to hurt you, Galan? Did I slay your kin? I do not remember slaying your kin. All I remember is the hunt."

Galan's arms shook with fury. The beast wanted to die, but the knight did not want to grant the favor of eternal rest. He had seen this shining moment as triumph, not hesitation.

Galan raised the lance high, aiming for the dragon's throat. Many scales were missing there, and the weapon would easily penetrate the beast's tough hide.

He lowered the lance, his arms losing their strength.

Borac fixed the knight with its single eye. "Who are you, Galan? When did you start this hunt? What are the memories you hold? Those of your wife, your children, your estate?"

The dragon raised its head slightly as it continued. "Tell me something of your life, Galan."

Galan stood, stunned. He tried to remember what had driven him to it, tried to see the past, tried to see the faces of a wife . . . a child . . . friends . . . compatriots. . . . Nothing. He could see nothing but the dragon. He recalled only hatred.

"You are a wraith, Galan. A specter. You rise from the swamps to haunt me. You have been dead as long as I am old. Soon, I will rest. Will you?"

Borac laid his head down again and closed his eye, murmuring, "Put me to the blade, knight. Perhaps my death will free you."

"No," Galan muttered. "No! This cannot be! I live! I am flesh and blood like any other man."

"You are dead, Galan. You cannot even remember when you died."

Galan dropped to his knees. He stared at his gauntleted hands. The blood and silver of the moons ran through his flesh and mail like light through a curtain.

The dragon was right. He hadn't killed the specter. He *was* the specter. The knight he'd killed had been real, alive, hunting him. The armor he had forced beneath the black waters had been solid.

Galan covered his face with his hands. The swamp around him teemed with life.

"I remember only vengeance," Galan disconsolately muttered to himself. "Borac lives. There is only hate."

Galan slumped down against the dragon's hide, clinging to the dragonlance. He looked at its sharp, cruelly barbed tip. The weapon of heroes. The weapon of his curse.

"This will be my grave, fool knight. Where did your kin bury you?" Borac asked.

Galan took a breath, unsure if he truly needed to breathe. The scent of age was strong in the air, but it didn't belong to him. Had he aged? How had he died? He could not answer the dragon's questions.

The great length of the black beast shuddered, and Galan thought he heard a laugh escape from its maw. Galan rose from his place and held the dragonlance aloft in the moons' light. His prey was dead, and he was left behind as testament to its life.

He plunged the weapon into Borac's flesh. He plunged again and again without effect. His anger burned within him, warming his flesh and giving him cursed life. He raised up the lance and continued to attack.